The Amaryllis Ascension

Book One of The Ascension Prophecy Series
A Slow Burn Fantasy Why Choose
Lacey Hall

Book Cover by Amanda McGlynn

Line Edited by Lexy Ray

Proofread by Sage Santiago

First edition 2024

CONTENTS

This book, as silly as it seems, is dedicated to my younger self. I've always wanted to create, to make readers feel something.

To my seven year-old self, thank you for starting.

To my fifteen year-old self, keep holding on. It gets much better.

To my eighteen year-old self, it's okay to be lost. We find ourselves when we need to most.

To me: We did it. Just keep writing.

You got this, kiddo.

CONTENT/TRIGGER WARNINGS

An extensive list of trigger and content warnings is on my website.

http://laceyhallwrites.com

PLAYLIST

Lying on the Hood of Your Car – Andrew McMahon in the Wilderness
EVERGREEN – Arankai
Bad Moon – Hollywood Undead
Satellites – Sleeping with Sirens
Memories – EarlyRise
Alright – Charlotte Sands
East & West – In Her Own Words
Fade With Me – Attack Attack!
Puzzle Pieces – Framing Hanley
Infinitely Falling – Fly by Midnight
She's Quiet – The Home Team
Worst in Me – Bad Omens
Ghost – Parachute
Feint – Linkin Park
Crutch – Set It Off
Fearless – Pink Floyd
February – No Love for the Middle Child
Volcano – Emily Hearn
Chaos – Hollywood Undead
Help – Papa Roach
Voices – Motionless in White
Flying Dreams – Katie Campbell

THE AMARYLLIS ASCENSION

Collide – Dishwalla

Perfect by Design – NateWantsToBattle & AmaLee

Changed by You – Between the Trees

ceilings – Lizzy Alpine

Hollow – Lø Spirit

Safe and Sound – Point North & The Ghost Inside

Mess of Me – Citizen Soldier

Deep End – I Prevail

HELLO LØNELINESS – Ekoh and Lø Spirit

The Blues – Self Deception

PRONUNCIATION GUIDE

Volsifi – Vol-s/i/-fee

Elvafe – ell-vuh-fay

Upir – oo-peer

Syrena – sigh-ree-nuh

Luxnositel – luxe-noss-/i/-tell

Levende – Luh-vend

Kuorir – Koo-wah-reer

CHAPTER 1

LUCIEN

I t is an odd thing, to feel the pounding of your heart inside your skull instead of your chest where it belongs. It seemed profoundly difficult to pay any mind to the voices around me when I could barely manage to keep the bitter dregs of coffee in my rioting stomach. How curious it was that elvafe magic couldn't cure the hangover its very pixie dust created?

"We must do something about Cadence Nocetti." I looked up from my now empty mug at that name. "I've heard whispers among the High Table that her brother is exceptionally powerful already, and they're still months from Ascending. Should I also remind everyone that twins are a sign of change? We might have an impending war on our hands." Arthur Greaves of the Harvest Moon Pack was red faced, spittle flying from his quivering lips. "Lucien, are you even listening?"

My fingertips pressed into my temples, doing nothing to relieve the persistent headache. "As I've already said, we have been watching the girl closely and she's shown no signs of anything unusual for a seventeen-year-old volsifi. My son is with her constantly, and her hybrid status appears to be irrelevant," I snapped, tired of the dancing circles this meeting kept taking.

Arthur leaned toward me, the fire in his eyes amplifying the nausea in my gut. "If things go wrong, Cadence and her twin brother could go nuclear. We all know the stories of the volatile hybrid magic: the species mingle to make ravenous monsters that ruin the delicate balance of the supernatural world. Need I remind you of when the magraunma mated with a colony of elvafe nearby? They were creating volcanic eruptions all over the globe and causing mass hysteria among the humans. We had to bury their island in the ocean and wipe out the entire species of magraunma to get it under control," he seethed, his arms flapping about in manic fury. "We have hidden ourselves from the humans for a millennium since then, and we can't let two abominations destroy what we have built for ourselves!"

The bellowing timbre of his voice caused my left eye to twitch. I was hopeful that the trembling vein in Arthur's forehead might actually burst and kill him on the spot. His eyes were wide and bulging as he looked among us, clearly wanting some support on his side.

"What else would you propose we do, Arthur? Slaughter the child? Make an example of the twins and the tainted blood of their whole family?" Maximus Warrick of the Shadowed Moon Pack spoke up, leaning back in his seat, his fingers steepled over his middle. "You cannot be suggesting that we kill two potentially innocent children," he sneered, his oily tone making me immediately suspicious.

Everyone's attention was on Maximus now, waiting for him to suggest what he was thinking.

Even my misery couldn't stop me from replying. "Do you have a better idea, Maximus? Do enlighten us with your brilliance," I muttered.

"Perhaps we just wait to see what she is, and if she is as powerful as the whispers claim, we can use her. Maybe she will be a goddess among wolves, but she could be just a wolf herself. Do remember that neither her, nor her brother, bore the mark of the elvafe on their backs. If her and her twin are magic incarnate, they could be the weapon we use to bring down the rest of the species and actually make ourselves the mighty predators we all want to be. Of course, the final verdict is up to our *King*," he said, giving me a pointed look.

The heavy silence that followed made the grin on his face even more smug.

"For once you actually had something brilliant to say. All in favor, say aye." I finally straightened and held one hand up.

A chorus of ayes filled the air with the exception of one. I stared Arthur down, waiting for him to offer any motion or dissent. Fortunately for us, he was outnumbered four to one.

A low growl rumbled between us as he finally gave his answer, sealing the fate of our future. "Aye."

Adjusting the sleeves of my suit jacket to just the right length, I became distracted by the silver scars on my hands. My mind flashed back to the moment she died, my gorgeous mate and our bond shattering as she took her last rattling breath as our only child took his first. The shatters blew backwards, slicing my flesh and leaving scars that reminded me of that moment every time I saw them. My gaze lifted to that very child, happily talking with the very abomination we'd made a verdict on that morning.

It was his eighteenth birthday, a day I've been dreading since his birth. Ezra's Ascension was that evening, and the entire pack was gathered to see it. "I hate having the Deltas and Omegas present for this," I muttered, garnering a snort from the pack doctor beside me.

3

Dr. Reginald Barber stood with his arms behind his back, the flaming hair he'd given his children kept short and coifed. "Same. They're tainting the celebration of our Prince and future Alpha."

Reggie's hand brushed against mine and I had to hide my grimace in a cough. I knew what he'd done, and I was foolish for not attempting to hide my flesh from him when he arrived by my side.

"I agree." Reginald regarded my son. "He does look like his mother, doesn't he?" he commented, causing me to barely suppress a wince. He was goading me. "I think that Ezra would do much better with a different mate. We cannot allow some mixed breed monster to become the Luna of our pack. Perhaps I could suggest my own daughter?" he conspired, picking my thoughts from my brain with the ease of a touch. He pointedly glanced to the side of the room where his daughter, Jessica, stood talking with some other teenagers her age. Her fiery red hair was easy to pick out amongst the crowd and I scowled.

"Perhaps. Unfortunately for us both, the Goddess tends to have the most say in these matters," I grumbled irritably, thinking less than fondly of the mate bond that fused two volsifis together. The same bond that shattered and left scars during death.

He chuckled, though it held no amusement. "True, but the Goddess, Levende, cannot force two people to *honor* their bond. You could still . . . persuade him to reject it if the Goddess aligns their lives."

I hazarded a glance his way. "You of all people should know that, Reginald. How many mistresses have you entertained over the years?" He did not look amused to find that I knew of his many affairs.

We both looked to his mate and wife, standing among other Beta wives who held glasses of liquid Crystal, a bubbly alcohol spiked with elvafe magic. It wasn't my preferred drink of Bismuth, but it packed its own punch and was frequently consumed at parties by Beta women. Reggie cleared his throat, drawing my attention back to him.

"I think you'd do kindly to remember that I know the secret of her being . . . tainted. We wouldn't want that information getting out, would we? It would cause fear and mutiny among the lower castes to know that the feared hybrids existed in our very pack. And *twins*, no less. You'd do well to . . . encourage Ezra to court my Jessica, or secrets may very well become public," he threatened, swirling the green liquid in his cup. The smell of licorice burned my nose, and I took a sip from my own glass of Bismuth. Black licorice burned the tongue as much as it did the sinuses.

I didn't take kindly to his blackmail, and he must have known that, since he attempted to step away. I reached out and grabbed his arm, smiling as I dug my elongating claws into his bicep. He turned to look at me, his eyes wide with surprised anger.

"Reginald, you may want to consider being more polite to your Alpha and King. Also, there are better ways to assure your ascent into the Alpha rank than blackmail. You'd do well to remember that."

Releasing him with a slight shove, I gave him a pleasant grin as he fixed his suit and escaped. Adjusting my tie, I garnered everyone's attention by tapping a butter knife against my glass. As all eyes turned to me, I gave a kind smile and gestured around the room.

"Welcome to the Ascension of my son, your Prince and future Alpha, Ezra James Wolfe."

Applause and cheers filled the room, echoing off the stone walls and vaulted wooden ceiling. I let it go on for a beat longer than I wanted to before raising my hand to silence everyone once more.

"It's been a long eighteen years waiting for this moment. I've enjoyed raising my one and only child to his Ascension on this day, November the third."

My eyes finally met his, though I wasn't surprised to find him guarded and wary. I had done nothing to warrant warmth from him, nor did I want any from the murderer of my beloved mate, Giselle. I hadn't loved him from the moment our bond shattered and left these silver scars on my ruined flesh.

"I couldn't be prouder of the man you've become." A lie. "You are my life, the person I love the most." Another lie. "And I will hold on fondly to the next few years until you take your place on the throne," lie, "as Alpha of the Scarlet Moon Pack and King of the Volsifi."

Cheers and applause erupted as I raised my glass along with everyone else. Ezra looked around, nodding to those nearby who slapped him on the back and congratulated him for just existing in the status I had provided him with through loving his mother. After a silent toast, I swallowed the rest of my glass, enjoying the burn of absinthe and magic as it scalded my throat and landed heavily in my stomach.

With that finally out of the way, I lead the pack out into the Gardens of Ascension. This late in the year, the bushes along the paths were mostly naked or on their way to being undressed for the winter. Some of the bushes and trees were evergreens, quite common this far north in the Adirondacks, though there were no vibrant colors in the garden until we reached the Ascension Pedestal.

Ezra passed me, heading toward the pedestal so he could appeal to the God, Kuorir, and the Goddess, Levende, to grant him Ascension into a full volsifi. His golden waves glowed champagne in the moonlight, and I swallowed heavily, those locks reminding me so much of my lost Giselle.

As Ezra stepped onto the dais, I saw that he'd already removed his clothing. Most Ascending volsifi did strip down to nothing to avoid their clothing being destroyed when they shifted into their wolf form. Reaching into the sacred box, carved with ornate moons and stars, I pulled out the Cloak of Ascension. The cloak was blessed with magic from our ancestors. The threads were created from the Datura flower, sacred to the volsifi, and steeped in moonlight before being woven together. The cape was ancient, though it remained white and pristine.

Standing beside him, I made sure to keep enough distance so that we didn't touch, but close enough that I appeared the loving father I pretended to be. The red and black granite inner circle was plenty large enough for two volsifi to stand in, the outer ring of white granite glowing in the light, heavily veined with deep grays. I always thought the choice of granite was appropriate for the Scarlet Moon Pack, fit for the many generations who had Ascended on this very dais.

"Father," he growled, not bothering to look at me, his blue eyes gazing out at the crowd as I took the heavy cape and draped it over his shoulders.

He clasped it himself, pulling the hood over his own head until his eyes were completely hidden beneath the white satin. This close, I could see the embroidered moon and stars glittering silver in the light from the moon as it hung above us, full and beautiful.

I gave a bright smile to the crowd before stepping down from the dais to allow him his time in the spotlight.

I glanced at Cadence as I descended into the crowd. Her black hair gleamed as her gaze shifted to meet mine upon sensing my fervent stare. Even in the darkness I could see those eyes of hers, those black pits broken with a splash of blue. She hadn't been born with the mark of the elvafe, but I still wanted her gone. Dead, preferably, but out of my pack and away from my son would do well enough.

Her cheeks flushed and she turned from me, looking up at her father who had wrapped his arm around her shoulders when he saw me watching. Our gazes clashed, though he didn't shy away from me like his abomination of a daughter. Even knowing that he'd created two monsters, he didn't seem to be ashamed of himself like he should be. I stopped next to Reginald again, who was turning out to be a royal pain in my ass.

"It appears that Eileen didn't bother to show up to see her future Alpha Ascend," he commented, giving me an appraising look.

"No, fortunately, Eileen Nocetti had the decency to not further soil this evening with her unwanted presence. Seems she has more sense than the rest of that wretched family," I muttered, turning to face my worthless son as he stood on the dais with his hands out at his sides.

I could hear the tremor in his voice, causing me another pang of annoyance.

"Mother Goddess Levende, most precious divine Luna, I stand before you as naked as the day you and Kuorir, most divine Alpha, gave me life. I offer to you my body, my soul, my life on this night. Please grant me the gift of Ascension, so that I may shift into the glory of the wolf you have given me and so that I may join my pack as an equal."

There was silence all around as he waited for his plea to be heard. Then, suddenly, cracking echoed around the grounds as Ezra's body began to shift. The only sense of pride I felt was his ability to keep from crying out as his bones shattered and reformed until his wolf stood upon the dais. His eyes were still blue, his wavy fur shaggy and dark blond.

He took a moment to regain his bearings before raising his head to the full moon above and howling, signaling for the rest of the pack to shift and begin the run.

Chapter 2

CADENCE

With a huff, I tried to calm my breathing as I flopped into my usual seat at the dining table, the chair screeching angrily on the brown tiled floor. I tried my best to be casual, picking up my fork and smashing my over easy eggs as my dad lowered his well-loved hardback copy of *The Princess Bride*. I displayed a cheesy grin and shoved a large mouthful of dripping egg into my mouth.

"Running late again, Cady?" he mused aloud, his deep brown eyes glittering with humor as he noted my disheveled appearance.

I blinked at him as I regarded the dust cover that he always left on his hardbacks, noting the title once more. "Reading the same book again, dad?"

His dark eyes, almost identical to mine, stared me down with feigned annoyance. "It's November," he responded simply, one dark, scruffy brow quirked over his glasses before his face disappeared into the book once again, leaving me to gaze at his thick head of black hair peeking over the top.

"I didn't think you were still doing that," I stated casually, knowing he'd sigh in exasperation and put the book down. It was a common ploy of mine so he would actually eat his own breakfast. Watching him do just that, I smiled to myself, happy I could help him eat at least something that day.

"Cady, why would you think I'd stop my tradition now? I've been reading this very copy of this book every November since I was a child." He speared some scrambled eggs and stuffed them into his face. It was like a switch flipped at that first taste and he realized he was starving because he started eating zealously.

I paused for a moment, staring down at my plate as I shuffled my food around, momentarily distracted from my morning rush. "Does it make you feel closer to Grandpa Henry?" I asked, wondering if I'd actually get a clear answer this time. I never had before, but it was always worth a shot.

"Is Ezra coming to get you again this morning?" Dad disregarded my question completely. I took that as a sign to drop it . . . again. I knew it was a memory trigger for him, something he and his father had done when he was a child after my grandmother was killed. Neither he nor grandpa had elaborated further than that.

I glanced down at my phone where it lay unlocked on the table, the app my friends and I used to track each other letting me follow his path to me. "Yeah. He should be here soon."

I hurried, suddenly remembering my time crunch, shoveling the last of my eggs into my mouth and chugging my orange juice.

Dad made a grunting sound in response, picking up his mug of coffee and avoiding eye contact with me as he prepared to embarrass me. His pensive face warned me about the question before it was said, tension hanging in the air between us.

"Is that boy keeping his paws to himself?" he inquired, taking a sip of coffee while feigning innocence.

I cringed. "*Dad*," I whined, throwing my head back in exasperation. This was brought up constantly, and I wasn't sure how many times I could repeat my answer. "It's not like that between us. Ezra is just . . . Ezra. He's my best friend and the future Alpha of our pack. Definitely not interested in being with a Delta like me." Not even his clever play on words in the form of a dad joke could lessen the humiliation of that thought.

The look on his face became enraged for a second before he carefully wiped his features back into a neutral expression. I knew with just that flicker of a look that I was heading into dangerous territory with my father.

"We weren't always Deltas, Cade. We were a Beta family once, and you'd do well to remember that fact. The Council of the Volsifi could have made us Omegas instead . . . Or worse: Rogues."

Another conversation we'd had multiple times, though it always ran around in circles with no resolution to speak of. The downfall of the Nocettis was like this pack's best kept secret. All I was ever told was that it happened when my twin brother and our grandmother disappeared and my grandfather was left murdered in the house. Dad was no longer able to be the pack's doctor, and we were no longer Betas.

"Right. And why are we not in the Beta rank anymore?" I asked, unable to keep the annoyance from tainting my tone.

His dark brown eyes lifted to meet mine, a muscle twitching in his jaw as anger flickered just beneath the surface of his gaze. I knew dad hated when I confronted him like a dramatic teenager, but I never knew why I couldn't get any real answers. It was *my* life after all.

"You know we were cast out of the Beta rank when your brother and grandmother were taken," he bit out in response, echoing my thoughts.

I could sense the thinly veiled warning in his expression. I was treading on shaky ground.

My gaze dropped to the empty plate across the table from me and I chewed on the inside of my cheek nervously before saying the most stupid thing possible.

"Mom not joining us again? Is she still hiding in her room like the resident ghost?"

Dad stood abruptly, his chair toppling to the floor behind him. I'd overstepped by a mile.

"I'm working a twenty-four-hour shift at the hospital again, and tomorrow morning I'm working at the Omega clinic. I'm leaving you some money to order pizza." He turned to walk through the small arch into the kitchen before stopping and turning back to me. "No sleepovers with Ezra Wolfe."

I nodded, standing in a much calmer manner than him and taking my dishes to the sink. I knew I needed to defuse the situation by returning to my well-practiced, chilled-out facade.

"I can make my own food, dad. I know we don't really have the extra money for me to be buying a pizza every time you work overtime."

Dad grunted in response, and it hung in the air between us that dad couldn't afford to buy the groceries it would take for me to make dinner as he dropped cash onto the counter. I let the conversation go and ran into the bathroom to brush my teeth before Ezra arrived. The feeling of fuzz on my teeth was not something I could tolerate the entire day, even if it got both Ezra and myself even further behind schedule.

"One day you're going to make that boy very late and he's going to be quite upset," dad called out, the smile evident in his voice even over the sound of bristles against my teeth. At least his anger with me didn't stick. It never did.

I was just dropping the toothbrush back into the glass holder with a clatter as honking brought a smirk to my lips. Right on time as always, Ezra was quite the punctual being. Why he hung around with me and my perpetual lateness, I would never know.

"Bye, dad!"

I stopped for a moment to peck him on the cheek before rushing to the door, my purple socks sliding against the hardwood of the living room and entryway floor. Jamming my feet into my well-worn leather boots, the slight heel gave me just a bit more height. Being the shortest of my friend group, I could use the extra boost so I didn't feel quite so much like an ant among giants.

Throwing a black hoodie over my purple sweater, I grabbed my backpack and tossed it over my shoulder before going outside into the crisp November air. Squinting, I looked up at the swirling gray sky as a mist of rain landed on my face like dewy freckles. Perhaps I was a rarity, but I always enjoyed the rain just as much as the sun. I always missed the warm summer months, but the chill was peaceful and reminded me of fuzzy socks and warm mugs of hot chamomile tea, curling up with a warm blanket and an excellent book.

Another jarring honk cut through my meandering thoughts, and I realized I was still standing on the creaky, wooden porch steps and staring up at the cloudy sky like an idiot while Ezra watched and waited for me.

With a laugh, my eyes dropped to meet the baby blue ones of my best friend as he stared at me expectantly through the driver's side window of his car.

"Coming!" I shouted as I hurried down the sidewalk and around the black SUV parked in front of my house. Hopping in the passenger side, I gave Ezra a beaming smile and inhaled his scent of teakwood and amber. He met my grin with a well-practiced and quite impatient scowl that made zero dent in the happiness consuming me from being in his presence - not that it was what he wanted anyway.

"Good morning, sunshine." I gave him another charming smile that made his frustrated facade crack just slightly under the pressure. "Don't you look pleasant? Get up on the wrong side of the bed this morning?" I added, biting my lower lip to tame the grin.

His blue eyes dropped to my mouth for a second before meeting my gaze. "Fortunately, no. Not this morning. However, I was hoping to arrive to school a bit earlier than we will be," he replied, reaching between us and picking up a paper cup with a lid. He pressed the cup into my hands, the hot paper warming my chilled fingers.

"Thank you for the tea." Crossing my legs, I relished the warmth of the cup. "You always worry so much, but you're the Alpha's son and eventual Alpha of our pack. You're also, like, a literal *prince*. It's not like anyone will say something to *you*."

I watched the muscles in his jaw clench at the mention of his father. "You know you can talk to me about anything, right?" I asked, hoping that he'd open up to me about it. I always appreciated it when he trusted me enough to talk to me about their . . . difficult relationship.

Without responding verbally, he nodded. Knowing the Alpha, I could hardly blame Ezra for despising him. He was aggressive and an overpowered Alpha who cared very little for those who didn't cater to his demands or reside within the Beta rank. He ruled the pack with an iron fist; most of the pack didn't even shift into their wolves after the Ascended because of the harsh law he'd put in place shortly after he took the throne as king. Ezra's grandfather wasn't much better. The volsifi of our pack were terrified of Alpha Lucien, knowing he wouldn't hesitate to demote or banish anyone who got in his way or caused too many problems. Those of us in the Delta and Omega ranks knew to keep our heads down and keep our wolves locked up. I was dreading ignoring my wolf when I finally got to speak to her.

The way his lips pressed together, exposing the shallow dimple just below the left side of his mouth, told me it was time to change the subject. My fingers found the string that dangled the tea tag against the side of the cup. "Chamomile. You haven't brought me hot tea in months." I put it to my lips and took a cautious sip. "Thank you again. It's perfect."

Ezra's tense expression finally broke, his mouth curving into a pleased smile. "It hasn't been this cold in several months. Besides, I needed to restock my stash of cups. I don't get to go into the city very often," he replied, opening the center console and pulling a book from within to hand it to me. A crimson amaryllis was placed in the center of the book like a beautiful bookmark.

Confused, I looked at the cover and then gasped. *Mrs. Frisby and the Rats of NIMH* was emblazoned across the cover. I examined the book cover, my fingertip running over the letters before touching the red cape the mouse wore over her back. The cover was worn, the spine creased, a well-loved copy of an old book. It was one of the most thoughtful gifts I'd ever received.

"I saw it while I was at Volsifi Council meetings in Georgia last week. It was at a tiny used bookstore. As soon as I read the title, I knew I had to get it for you."

Tears stung my eyes as I flipped through the pages, the yellowed paper carrying the distinct scent of a book read many times. The edges were crinkled and at least one heathen had dog eared a couple pages while reading. I tucked the amaryllis behind my right ear.

"The movie doesn't have the same title," I murmured. "Dad found the VHS tape on his way home from work because I was sick, and mom couldn't get herself out of bed to help me. He said he always related to Mrs. Frisby." As I grew older, that comment became more devastating as its meaning became abundantly clear. Mrs. Frisby was widowed, and her youngest was sick with pneumonia, just like I had been. But dad wasn't widowed. Mom was still alive, though I hadn't seen her in several months. Before that, it was a flash of blonde hair followed by the snick of a door as she disappeared into her bedroom.

Clearing my throat, I glanced at him. His sky-blue gaze watched me closely, his pale brow furrowed with concern as he watched my emotions play out. His full lower lip pushed out slightly in a pout of worry.

"I didn't mean to make you sad. I'm sorry." His voice was quiet in the hushed car.

I blinked at him. "You didn't make me sad. I love it, really. It's just such a huge piece of my childhood being brought into the present, you know? Thank you so much."

Ezra nodded, his expression softening. The concern lingered in the tightness of his mouth. "You're welcome. I'm glad you like it."

Pulling away from the curb, I reached forward and hit play on the stereo. "Laying on the Hood of Your Car" by Andrew McMahon in the Wilderness started playing, picking up where he'd paused it. Ezra decompressed slightly, his thumb tapping to the beat of the music as he drove. I took a moment to admire his face.

His jawline was chiseled and went on for days, his nose was slightly hooked, and his mouth always seemed to have a subtle grin. When he smiled for real, it always made his eyes sparkle with humor. All that handsome face topped with a mop of loose, pale blonde waves that he always had pushed back off his face. He was gorgeous.

After a long moment, those blue eyes shifted to my own face. "What are you looking at, Cadybug?" A sly smirk curved his lips, giving me an unexplainable desire to kiss them. Clearing my throat, I shifted forward and looked out the window beside me, avoiding his watchful eye.

"Ugh, a pest," I teased, breaking into a grin when he laughed aloud. The sound was rich, full, and infectious.

Before I wanted to be, we were pulling into the large student parking lot and Ezra's usual spot by the entrance, and he killed the engine. As we exited the car, the warning bell shrilled over the grounds, echoing off the concrete of the lot. I involuntarily winced against the loud noise, wishing it didn't have to be quite so abrasive. Meeting him in front of the car, Ezra gently placed his hand on my lower back and guided me into the red brick building and through the sea of classmates prepping to go to homeroom. At a divide in the hall, he bid me adieu before taking a left and leaving me to the mercy of Alex.

Alex Pierce spotted me instantly and bolted over; her long, blonde curls bobbing as she approached. She was dressed all in black: from her artfully torn black shirt down to her leather leggings and combat boots. "You will never believe what happened this past weekend!" she gushed immediately. Her scent of salt, rose, and patchouli swept over me and I felt comforted by its familiarity.

I could take a couple guesses, but letting her babble on and spill the whole story was more my style. Alex was beautiful, love crazy, and sharp as a whip. The angelic looking blonde was anything but, and frequently told me stories that made my face flush with embarrassment. I gave my friend a nod and smile of greeting. Alex immediately launched into a story about her weekend, not sparing any of the gritty details. While I did enjoy hearing all about Alex's dirtiest adventures, I had trouble relating to any of them. It wasn't that I was dead, I could spot an attractive person and fawn over them as well, but the idea of having sex myself made me feel vaguely uncomfortable. I figured that I'd be more interested when I found the right person.

"And then, he used his teeth and really bit me. He left a bruise!" Alex's hazel eyes glinted with wicked pleasure as she pulled her low-cut shirt to the side to expose part of her chest. My eyes widened as they took in the deep purple mark that marred most of Alex's modest breast. "Whoever said that small tits aren't a win, I need to speak with them. Who doesn't want a mouthful, right?" Her voice was animated with glee as she spoke. "You know, I really think I'm going to have to invite him over next weekend, too. My parents are going out of town again and I'll have the house to myself. Maybe this guy is worth keeping around for a while."

Completely out of my depth, I just nodded and agreed. "For sure. Maybe he can mark the other side?" I suggested in an attempt to relate to Alex's excitement over pleasurable pain. I could not imagine a galaxy in this universe or the next where I would find any kind of pain pleasurable. However, I honestly couldn't imagine a world where I found sexual intimacy pleasurable at all. Really, the whole idea of two sweaty bodies commingling, *sharing fluids*, and being physically vulnerable was repulsive and left me feeling dirty just thinking about it. I understood my feelings were unusual, and I tried extremely hard not to feel self-conscious about it. So instead of talking about them to anyone, I hid them and pretended to agree with everything Alex said. Life was easier that way. I was already the pack's number one social outcast. I didn't need to add this to the list of reasons people whispered about me.

Alex broke into my thoughts with a question that left me utterly speechless. "So, when are you finally going to actually date Ezra?" She gave me so much side eye that I felt spotlighted. It was like I was the punchline to a joke I didn't know was being told.

Instead of answering, I shoved all my unneeded books and my threadbare backpack into my locker before pulling out the heavy tome I needed for my first class.

Shutting my locker with a little more aggression than necessary, it made a loud clang that echoed down the quickly emptying hall while I continued to feign ignorance. "Why would I date Ezra?" This was not the first time we'd had this conversation, and every time it left me feeling flustered and overwhelmed. I was just grateful that it happened most often without Ezra present.

"Because he's totally into you." Alex flicked her golden hair over her shoulder. "I don't know how you can not see it. He has been eyeing you up for years. Haven't you noticed that he has never dated anyone else?" she asked, her hazel eyes wide as she peered at me. "I'm convinced that you're his mate, you just won't realize it until your birthday when you Ascend," she added, lowering her voice conspiratorially.

I rolled my eyes. "Maybe he's just not interested in dating. You know how hard his dad is on him." I stopped to look directly at her. "His dad expects perfection. Would you worry about dating anyone if your dad wanted you to be this fantastical golden boy?" I was also blatantly ignoring how hard her own father was on her to follow in his footsteps as the Alpha's General.

Alex sighed in exasperation, hiding the hurt that marred her pretty face, and continued walking with me to our first class just as the bell rang. "I sure would. This cat cannot be stopped," she said with a wicked grin. The implication stained my cheeks pink; an embarrassing, hot flush traveled down my neck.

"Ew. Who'd have thought you could get any uglier? When you blush like that, it makes you look like a constipated pig." A voice broke into our conversation, the harsh tone grating on my nerves until they turned into powder.

I turned and glanced at Jessica Barber, cackling at her own joke, the glee obvious in her amber eyes.

Scowling, Alex snapped back, "Ew. Who'd have thought that freckles could actually look like you sprayed your face with cow manure? It takes special talent to make one of the hottest trends look gross."

I didn't dislike freckles. In fact, I thought the small sprinkling across Alex's cheeks were cute. I hated Jessica, though, who made my life hell as often as she possibly could, and part of me enjoyed that Alex went for the jugular.

I beamed, waving my fingers in her direction. Her expression soured and her face heated, causing her pale skin to clash aggressively with her fiery hair. "Don't stare at me with your weird eyes, you creepy freak," she snarled in return before storming away from us in an exaggerated huff.

When she'd rounded the corner and disappeared, I turned back to Alex with wide eyes. Alex's expression immediately conveyed sympathy.

"You're anything but ugly, and I'm very fond of your eyes. That splash of blue in your left iris really emphasizes the black. I think they look epically cool."

She threw her arm over my shoulders and walked me to our first class.

19

CHAPTER 3

CADENCE

Having the latest lunch period made the class before it unbearable, the day dragged unnecessarily as my breakfast wore thin and my stomach growled. I didn't always feel hungry, my brain too preoccupied to realize that my body had functions and needs, but when I was bored with class and needed to pay attention? That's always when my stomach chose to sing the song of its people.

My gaze shifted between Mr. Rutger, droning about sine and cosine, and the clock that I could almost swear was standing still. The second hand kept moving, but it seemed like it was just clicking into the same position. The ticking of the clock drowned out everything around me: Mr. Rutger, the scratching of pens against notebook paper, the rustling of bodies in their desks - all noise became secondary to that incessant ticking. My brain latched onto the sound, and it was suddenly the only thing I could hear. A bomb could go off in the room and all I would hear was the ticking of that wretched clock. Perhaps the chaos of the people around me would pull me away from the metronome; although, when I was so intently focused on something, not even my surroundings could yank me out of my daze.

The sound of the bell did jar me out of my reverie. I knew it was coming, and yet I still physically jumped, dropping the pencil I'd been gripping onto the floor. It rolled under my desk, of course, and I groaned in dramatic misery. Closing my notebook and the thick hardback textbook, I stacked them as I waited for everyone behind me to exit the aisle so I could retrieve my fallen writing utensil. Mr. Rutger had lunchroom duty and vanished from the room quickly and I was alone. Or at least, I thought I was.

Not considering checking behind me after the stampede, I bent down to grab my pencil. My ass stung as a hand slapped and grabbed one of the cheeks. My face immediately flamed as I stood up quickly, slamming the back of my head on the underside of my desk.

At seventeen, this was far from the first time I'd been harassed, but I still couldn't do what I wanted to do. I wanted to whip around and smack what I knew would be a grin off the jerk's face behind me and cuss him out for putting his filthy paws on me.

However, I rarely cursed and what I did do was turn around with my face flaming, my eyes wide like a deer caught in the headlights of an oncoming truck.

Brody Griffin stood there, approximately the size of a truck. A smirk danced on his face, just like I knew there would be. His cronies, the snickering Jason Barber and the frowning Kyle Wilkins, were behind him.

"What's the matter, Delta? Cat got your tongue?" Brody jeered, his dark eyes glinting maliciously. This time I was the 'butt' of the joke, every pun intended. "I'd rather a Beta get your tongue," he added, stepping closer and putting his palm against my cheek. "I couldn't resist that ass, I had to know if it would jiggle as much as I thought it would. I was not disappointed."

His cruel smirk made my face burn hotter; I knew that my cheeks were flaming red.

The worst part about this entire interaction was that I wasn't sure if he was genuinely hitting on me or making fun of me. Regarding my ass jiggling, I assumed that he was making a poor attempt at a fat joke, but the look in his eyes indicated that maybe he was more interested in me than that. I could hear the age-old adage in my head, echoing from the past that boys that are mean are only that way because they liked you. I scoffed externally, answering his question as well as noting how I felt about the toxic lesson we taught young girls.

"Come on, girl. Give me a smooch, huh?" he taunted, his hand sliding through my locks and twisting itself in the hair at the back of my head. Giving it a tug, he pulled my head back to slide his nose up the side of my neck, inhaling deeply as if he were claiming my scent and committing it to memory. His scent of wood smoke and hot cinnamon filled my senses, overwhelming me.

I felt so repulsed I couldn't even move. I was afraid that any action would immediately make me vomit all over this douchebag as my stomach churned with humiliation and revulsion. To say that Brody was the most disgusting creature I'd ever encountered would be an understatement. His frequent attempts at 'wooing' me never did. If he wanted to be on my mind, it was working, but not in the way that he wanted, I was sure.

Brody leaned forward, looking like he was going to put his filthy mouth against mine when something behind me caught his eye. I didn't have to guess who he was looking at; I could feel the Alpha aura pouring off of him and crashing like a wave against my back. His scent of teakwood and warm amber danced around me, pushing out Brody's hot cinnamon aroma. If it were anyone else, I'd be petrified. I'd been in the presence of the current Alpha, and his aura felt very similar; alarming, since Ezra hadn't even taken up his destined position yet. Brody's friends backed off like the cowards they were. Brody squared his shoulders and dropped his hand from the back of my neck, easily staring over my head from his towering height.

"Don't you ever touch her again," Ezra growled. I looked over my shoulder at him, his blue eyes glowing with rage as he jammed a finger into the air toward them.

Brody, foolishly brave or monumentally stupid, puffed out his chest. That was a deadly move, for a Beta to defy an Alpha. It didn't matter that Brody was much taller and outweighed Ezra by at least fifty pounds. I worried that this was a precursor for when we're all adults. Brody's family would claim the title of Alpha if the Wolfe family were to be overthrown.

"It's not like you've claimed her. And she wasn't saying no," he rebutted, his grin making my stomach drop to my gut.

As if he could ever lay a claim on me. I would rather die. The thought of my flesh bearing his mark was one of the most repugnant mental images someone could place into my brain. A shiver rolled down my spine at the thought. I hoped the goddess, Levende, wouldn't mate me with him.

I could feel the rumble of a growl against my back as it rattled in Ezra's chest. "She's mine!" he snarled, practically spitting the words at Brody. "I'm the future Alpha, and as one of my future Beta warriors, you will keep your hands off her."

It took every ounce of strength I had to keep the surprise off my face. I knew Ezra cared for me as his best friend, but publicly claiming me as his future mate was a huge deal that shouldn't be taken lightly or used to keep others off me. I wasn't sure what game he was playing at, and I didn't know if I liked it . . . unless he *had* feelings for me.

However, despite my internal protests to Ezra's verbal claiming, Brody backed down. I didn't miss the hostile gleam in his dark eyes as they met my own. He wasn't done, and I wasn't happy about it. I didn't enjoy fighting, and I certainly didn't want it to be over me. Not even *I* could miss the battle brewing between the two males as I stood right in their sights.

Brody Griffin was the resident bad guy of school and led a gang of future Beta warriors. Brody was Alex's only rival to be the general of the army unless

Brody overthrew Ezra when he went to take his place. Most of the Betas that supported Lucien's politics resented that Ezra didn't show deference to his future position at school and hung out with a Delta like me. Alex was also a Beta and faced backlash for hanging with the traitors of the pack, but it wasn't to the degree that Ezra did. This incident wouldn't help his case in the slightest, and I was sure he was going to pay for it once his father found out – and by the look on Brody's face? That wouldn't take long.

Since the cronies and their leader retreated for the time being, Ezra picked up my books and let me past him so he could follow me out of the room, guarding my flank. Once we were in the hallway and away from Brody, I felt a weight lift off my shoulders. I gripped the problematic pencil in my fingers, twisting the eraser and causing a clicking sound inside the plastic.

"That was a serious claim you made in there," I whispered, knowing he would be able to hear me, even over the din of the hallway. "That will get back to your father and you know it's not even true." I glanced at his face. With his calm gaze locked straight ahead, he didn't seem all that concerned.

"What if it is true?" he countered, his eyes still not meeting mine.

"Why would you think it might be?" I asked again, stopping and grabbing his arm so he'd look at me.

Finally, his gaze met mine, and I almost squirmed under the weight of it. "You haven't Ascended yet." He sounded very self-assured as he nearly repeated me. "Maybe I can tell because I have. Maybe I want it badly enough that I'm manifesting it."

I blinked at him before turning away from him and walking quickly toward the lunchroom. His tenacity was confusing.

He's manifesting? I thought. *Why would he want to be mated to me?*

Thankfully, he let the conversation drop as we entered the cafeteria and made our way through the line. It didn't take long to find Alex at our usual round table in the middle of the lunchroom, picking over her salad with her fork. She looked up and smiled with a flash of white teeth as we sat down with her, our trays clattering against the plastic tabletop.

Alex, always the perceptive one, looked between the two of us with narrowed eyes. "What happened? Something is off." She put down her fork to give us her full attention.

I said nothing and picked up my burger to take a huge bite. I regretted it instantly as the molten cheese burned the roof of my mouth like hellfire. Ezra cast his gaze over me with a look on his face, clearly asking who should tell her. My eyes casually shifted away from him as I stalled for even more time by taking a sip of my water to hopefully extinguish the volcano in my mouth. It didn't help. There was no way I was going to let her make a huge deal out of something that wasn't.

With a sigh, he turned to Alex and gave her a shrug. "Nothing at all happened." He took a large bite of his apple, a blatant attempt to force my hand and make me tell the story. Well played.

"Oh yeah? Because that's not what the rumor mill is saying." Alex gave me a haughty look that made my insides twist uncomfortably. Of course, the gossipers picked it up already. "I heard that Ezra punched him right in the face."

The grapevine always had a way of escalating things that were no big deal. Why not add to the fun and write my own story? "You know what? You're right," I said, putting down my burger and giving her my full attention. "Brody grabbed me, so I reared back and smacked him. But he had no idea what was coming, because Ezra has always followed me around like a creep, and he appeared out of nowhere and just gave him a huge knuckle sandwich right in the throat. While Brody attempts to catch his breath and clutches his throat, Ezra picks me up like the beautiful bride that I am and carries me out of the classroom, but not before he punches a fist into the air like a true Judd Nelson."

Alex's dubious glare morphed as the story progressed, her face lighting up like a beacon of adoration. I let Ezra take the reins as I finished off my burger like a starving animal. Alex looked at him with heart eyes. If we lived in an anime, they would be glittering with stars. "Oh, Ezra . . . Is that true?" she gasped in mock awe, pulling her hands to her chest as she gazed at him as if he were sitting proudly on a horse wearing glittering silver armor. I could tell by her overacting that she knew I was completely full of it.

The amusement on Ezra's face only intensified as the story progressed, his nearly perfect teeth on full display by the time I finished my insanely stupid story. Laughing, he nodded in total agreement. "Yeah, that's definitely what happened. For sure." We all knew that the story was complete malarky, but it was still fun to play pretend sometimes.

Alex dropped the act and smirked at me as she shoved a tomato into her mouth. "I told you, girl. This one is a keeper," she stated around the mouthful, jabbing her fork in Ezra's direction and narrowly missing stabbing him in the cheek. As if I didn't know that he was a great guy. I wasn't dead, blind, or stupid despite her believing that I might be.

Ezra beamed happily at her approval, eyes gleaming smugly. However, Alex didn't seem to think much with her brain, and she had been trying to shove Ezra and me together for ages. I hated to disappoint her, but that was never happening. Ezra was only trying to protect one of his oldest and dearest friends, right? I kept trying to tell Alex that, but she never believed me.

Lunch was over way too soon and the three of us dumped out our trays before ambling into the hallway toward our next classes. Fortunately, we were all in the same English class. The three of us made our way there, and I'd be remiss if I didn't feel relief that we didn't come across Brody or any of his crew. They were offensive at the very least and I was disinterested in any further engagement with them.

The rest of the day passed in a blur, though the chaos was getting to me on a visceral level. Every slam of a locker made my body jerk involuntarily; the loud clang of metal on metal made my brain vibrate inside my skull. I could feel it building, the tension in my gut coiling like a spring and making it harder to breathe. Placing my hand on my chest, I could feel my heart pounding against my palm which only enforced the suffocating feeling. Angry, I quickly twisted the dial on my lock, entering my code with the precision that can only come from years of practice.

Opening the blue door, I stared into my locker, getting lost in the neutral gray interior. I never decorated the inside like a lot of the other students. I found all the extra things to look at overwhelming to my brain. My hand reached down and grabbed the wired earbuds waiting for me in my pocket, knowing what my brain needed. On autopilot, the white buds found their way into my ears and my phone immediately started playing "EVERGREEN" by Arankai, the song I had been humming in my head all day. Relief coursed through my veins as the song blared into my ears and I got what I needed out of my locker. The heavy beat and gravelly voice drowned out the panic that had been assaulting my system.

I could feel his presence beside me, his delicious amber and teakwood scent enveloping me, before I registered the blonde mop in my peripheral. Ezra was there, just like he always was when I needed him. When my attention turned to him, he gave a knowing smile and raised his hands to waist height. His hands formed a fist except his middle and index fingers, which he crossed together. His hands met in the middle and pulled apart, as though opening a set of French doors, signing, *"Ready?"*

When I realized that I could prevent my outbursts by blocking out chaotic noise and instead playing familiar music, Ezra and I started learning PSE or Pidgin Signed English. We knew enough to communicate effectively when I blocked out my hearing, though I would not call us experts on the intricate nuances of American Sign Language.

I gave him a nod as I put my backpack over my shoulder, but he grabbed it from me and threw it over his instead. *Always the gentleman,* I thought as I shut my locker and twisted the dial to secure it again.

"Want my guidance?" He gestured down the hall toward our escape for a second time.

I gave him another nod before he placed his palm flat on the small of my back, steering me toward the exit. Closing my eyes, I tilted my head down toward the floor and fully blocked out the world as his free hand found mine and I placed my palm on his fist. We had a method. That way, he could sign to me that there was a step coming and I wouldn't trip and fall. It was the best way we found to get me safely out of a situation when I was past my point of tolerance for stimulation. I rarely minded his touch, and he knew that, but he still asked every time.

My brain randomly conjured a memory of my twin brother, Callum, and my pulse spiked. We were only five when he was taken, but I still missed him every single day. I always felt like a piece of myself was missing, like a limb that was left to atrophy. I guess it truly was. He was my twin, we shared a womb; then he was gone, stolen from us in a circumstance that no one ever explained to me. *When you're older*, they'd say. Well, I was older, and they still weren't sharing any information.

Using pressure to guide me forward with his hand gripping my hip, Ezra's signal under my palm pulled me out of my brain enough to focus on my steps. Each tick of his fingers let me know I was going down another step. As I made it onto the sidewalk, he flattened his hand beneath my palm to alert me that I would be taking regular steps again and he guided me the rest of the way to the car.

He opened the door for me, and I climbed into the passenger seat, moving to buckle my seatbelt as he shut the door behind me. I opened my eyes as he hopped into the driver's seat and started the car. "Thank you." I tried my best to keep the words quiet, though he jumped, and I realized I'd probably shouted at him. Ezra grinned and nodded in response as he started the car.

Chapter 4

EZRA

Getting into the car, I looked over at Cadence as she shouted her thanks, startling me. I gave her a nod and a smile before starting the engine and driving out of the lot. I was grateful that she let me help her like she did. It took a lot of trust on her part to let me guide her completely. However, I think she knew I would never do anything to hurt her. At least, I certainly hoped that she did.

Pulling up to a stop sign, I took a moment to study her, my gaze slowly drinking in the serene expression on her face as she leaned back in the seat. Her dark lashes fanned out over her high cheekbones, a small smile curving her full lips as she decompressed next to me, the faint beat from her music drifting across the small space. I smiled to myself as I drove off in the direction of her house, getting lost in my thoughts along the way. It was a short drive. Too short for my taste, but c'est la vie.

I pulled into the empty driveway of her house and parked. Her dad always kept his car in the attached garage and her mom didn't drive, so I wasn't sure if he was home yet or not.

I took a moment to gaze up at the small house, its white siding yellowed with age. The black shutters missing a few slats here and there, one of them gone entirely from the right side of the dining room window. Everything looked tired and the grass a bit overgrown. Judgment never occurred to me, since I knew how busy Cadence and David were, trying to help out the Omegas whenever they could spare a moment. All of their extra finances were sunk into charities for the Omegas. It was all according to my father's grand design. A design I couldn't even fathom. The whole thing made me ill.

Reaching over, I gently placed my hand on her shoulder to let her know she was home. Cadence's eyes sprung open as she sat up and removed her earbuds.

"Here already? That was only like, three songs," she muttered, folding the white headphones away into her pocket. "Dad's working a twenty-four-hour shift and he's going straight to the clinic in the morning. Want to stay and hang out?"

The thought of the clinic her dad started to treat the Omegas of our pack made a swirl of rage at my father spiral within me, but I quickly forced it down, refusing to ruin my mood. Giving me a wide smile, she hopped out of the car and hurried into the house. I could never say no to her, so I was right on her heels, closing the front door behind me and twisting the electric deadbolt Alex and I bought them, so it locked. A smile teased my lips, the memory of Alex and I meeting to buy it after Cadence misplaced the house key for the third time in a week. It was quite the Christmas present for the family, but we liked making their lives easier.

As I followed her up the hardwood stairs to her room, her delicate scent washed over me, and I couldn't help but inhale deeply. She smelled of midnight jasmine, berries, and sandalwood, and it made me want to bury my face in her neck and breathe her in forever. It was as intoxicating as her unique black and blue gaze, and I momentarily lost myself in the daydream of snuggling up close to her, of this moment in time, suspending forever. However, the blissful bubble popped as she turned around at the top of the stairs, her bashful gaze letting me know I'd been caught staring. I couldn't blame her. Given our positions, I'd gotten lost in thought while gawking admiringly at her ass.

Wanting to slap myself, I gave her a cheesy smile, though I knew it would do nothing to hide the blush currently creeping up my neck. She huffed and turned away, making her way down the hall to the last door on the left. We dropped our backpacks onto the light gray carpet when we entered her room, the door shutting noiselessly behind us. While most parents would be concerned about leaving their daughter behind a closed door with a male teenager, Cadence's parents never were. Her mother never cared about much of anything, and her dad seemed to trust that she'd beat the shit out of me if I tried anything; not that I ever would.

Cadence wandered over to her bed and plopped down onto her gray and lavender comforter, laying on her back and staring at the ceiling. Her purple socks danced in the air as she kicked her legs, pulling out her phone. "The usual?"

"Of course." My gaze drifted around the familiar room. Despite being here frequently for the past thirteen years, I couldn't stop admiring all the pictures on her lavender walls. They were filled with memories of her, Alex, and me. Smiling down at us were some pictures of her parents from back when they were happy and in love, and even some of Callum. Those ones pulled at my soul, making my heart feel heavy as I stared at the picture of the white-haired boy hugging his twin sister, her dark hair in stark contrast to his. Their cheesy grins stared at me from where they hung on the wall.

I remembered him, having been six when he was taken. We were the three amigos, wreaking havoc daily in the mansion I was raised in while her dad, David, collaborated directly with my father as the pack doctor. David wasn't his direct Beta, Bernard Pierce was, but he was pretty damn close. At least, until the disappearance that shattered this family, ruining the Nocetti reputation and throwing them down the caste system to Delta. It wasn't the lowest. Omega was. Delta was the second rung up, then Betas, then the Alpha family.

They moved here, outside of the Beta's housing. I'd been coming over here ever since, riding my bike across town to get here any chance I could until I got my car for my sixteenth birthday. I could never be far away from Cady. It was like my soul always knew she was my mate. *Our Luna*, a voice whispered to me, the booming tone overpowering my thoughts.

As we'd aged and grew closer, my soul seemed to glow brighter with every intimate moment we shared. It was the way she looked at me with those doe eyes the color of a starless night, black and infinite with a smear of a cloudless blue morning. It was how her cheeks grew pink and hot to the touch when she blushed, which was never as often as I would have preferred.

I was at the point where I could smell her coming down the hall, even above the scents of all the other bodies surrounding us. It was a heady perfume that kept me desperately needing more; even if I inhaled her every day for the rest of my life it would never be enough. It was a delicious concoction that was calming, alluring, and sometimes more than a bit arousing. I couldn't deny that I loved being in a small room or in the car with her, especially with the air on so that her addictive scent could fill my car for days.

Her voice broke me out of my reverie, dragging me back to the present.

"The pizza won't be here for thirty minutes," she whined, tossing her phone to the side and throwing her arm over her eyes as though she were fainting from starvation. "I don't know if I can wait that long." She gave a tormented groan and dramatically threw her arms out to her sides, jostling the mattress beneath her.

I couldn't help the deep chuckle that escaped me as I wandered over to her bed, plopping down next to her. My eyes drifted to the strip of skin exposed beneath her sweater, pearly white lines of stretch marks marbled her perfect stomach, and I wanted nothing more than to drag my fingers over her exposed flesh, wondering if it was as soft as her hands and face.

Realizing suddenly that I was being a complete creep after staring for several minutes, I tore my gaze from her stomach and shifted them to her face, our eyes landing on each other. I knew what she was thinking as soon as she pulled her sweater down to cover herself. A furious blush warmed her face, and she bit down on her lip, something I'd have found very appealing if it wasn't caused by embarrassment.

"You don't have to cover up," I said, hoping to ease some of the tension. "It's not like I mind looking at your skin." I wanted to erase that expression from her face.

"Minding and liking are not the same thing," she huffed, sitting up and wandering over to her closet, leaving me sitting there like a baffled idiot. Maybe I *was* a complete moron, I sure felt like one.

"What?" I balked at her, unable to come up with anything more intelligent to say.

"Listen, I know that no one wants to see this." She gestured to her body before shutting the closet door behind her as she disappeared inside the slatted doors. I heard the rattling of hangers as she looked for something in its dark depths. "I'm sorry." Her voice cracked.

"My name is 'no one,' it's nice to finally meet you," I stated in a stupid attempt at humor, getting up and walking over to the closet. "I want to see your stomach. I want to see all of you." I knocked lightly on the door.

A startled squeal came from inside the door. "Get away from here, Ezra James," she screeched, her voice filled with an outrage I couldn't understand. "Do not start your shit."

Her use of my middle name combined with a curse had me even more amused and interested in seeing more. I wanted to see every square inch of her skin if she'd let me, though I'd never tried. Making her uncomfortable was not something I was interested in doing. "Pulling out the big guns, eh?" I asked, not leaving the other side of the door.

When the door finally opened, she was standing there with an oversized band tee, a concert shirt that we'd gotten together when we went to see A Day to Remember a couple years prior. I was displeased to see that it hung halfway down her thighs over her jeans. I blinked at her in utter confusion as she walked back to the bed to pick up her phone.

"Listen, Cadence –"

She cut me off with a steely glare over her phone.

Frowning, we stared at each other. I could see the hurt expression on her face but had no idea why it was there or what to do about it. "Cady, I don't mind seeing your skin. I know I definitely wouldn't mind seeing more of it." By now, I was desperate to assuage her insecurity.

Cadence flushed so heavily that even her forehead turned red. "Like I said, Ezra, minding and liking are not the same things. I don't *mind* when my dad listens to the Bee Gees, but I don't really *like* the Bee Gees myself. I don't *mind* listening to Pink Floyd with you, but I don't *like* listening to them on my own without the added bonus of experiencing things with you."

I stared at her, baffled beyond all reason. "You don't like Pink Floyd?" Completely baffled, I got stuck wondering why she'd have pretended to enjoy them this whole time.

I was certain that steam was about to explode from her ears as she leveled me with her rage.

"Out of everything I just said, *that* is what you're taking from it?" Her voice was calm, quiet, deadly.

I stared at her for another long moment while my brain computed what she'd said. "But I love your body." Her expression didn't soften. "I want to see more of it. I enjoy seeing you."

She snorted and rolled her eyes. "You have to tell me that as my best friend," she retorted, completely disregarding my confession and undermining it with her insecurity.

Scowling, we gazed at each other before a slow smirk curved my mouth, unbidden. "Show me more. I want to see it."

One of her eyebrows raised at me. "No."

Full stop. I re-evaluated the situation, noting the arched brow, the curve of her mouth as she tried very hard to compress the grin.

"Please?"

She coughed to hide the giggle, but I still heard the waver of it. There was a moment where everything seemed suspended. Her muscles tensed, I could see her legs shift incrementally, her body ready to spring away from me. It was a game we'd played many times since we were kids. A strange form of tag and tackle.

"Cadence Marie. I want to see you. Just a little bit."

She cackled. "Sounds like you're arguing for just the tip."

I snorted a laugh and flushed. "Listen, I wouldn't be opposed, but we have other hurdles to cross before I'd even think to ask for that."

Her eyes widened slightly, the flaring of her thick lashes drawing my gaze. Just when she'd started to relax, thinking I might not actually follow through, I lunged at her.

Another laughing squeal erupted from her, high pitched and shrill as I reached out to grab her. She was too quick for me, leaping out of the way as she clambered farther onto her bed and backed into the corner.

"I always tell you not to get stuck in the corner," I teased, grinning at her.

She stood up defiantly, raising her chin as I knelt at her feet.

"No one puts baby in the corner," she crowed, making me chuckle as my hands slid up her thighs to grip her hips.

"Quoting Dirty Dancing now, are we?" I asked her, gazing up at her as my chin rested on her abdomen.

Smirking, she shrugged. "What can I say? It's a classic."

I nodded, shimmying her shirt up just slightly. She watched me closely, warily.

"Can I?" I asked her, pausing at her unnerved expression and pulling my hands away from her body so her shirt dropped back into place. "I would never pressure you into anything," I assured her, relaxing my hands at my sides and dropping back to sit on my heels.

"I'm not there yet," she answered, leaning back against the corner.

I nodded. "That's totally okay." I looked at her as she gazed at me. "Do you want me to remove myself from your bed?" I inquired, maintaining contact with her bottomless eyes.

She shook her head. "No."

I nodded again, moving out of her way so she could sit down beside me.

"Thank you for respecting my boundaries."

"You don't have to thank me for treating you like a person." My brow furrowed. "But I do like your body. I like seeing peeks every once in a while. You're gorgeous."

I watched the disbelief flicker on her face, and she swallowed the scoff she was about to make. "Thank you."

I nodded, resisting the urge to touch her. The last thing I wanted to do was overstep her stimulation boundaries. "I'm sorry I didn't realize the difference between not minding and liking to. I won't make that mistake again."

She regarded me with uncertainty before nodding and picking up her phone again.

"Oh, the pizza is almost here!" she exclaimed, leaving the room to meet them on the porch before they rang the doorbell and possibly disturbed her mother.

An awoken Eileen Nocetti was a nightmare that I didn't want to experience any more than she did. Given that it was close to five o'clock in the evening, Eileen would be passed out in her room for another couple hours before getting up to eat just enough food to survive and then going back to bed. She hadn't thrived since Callum was taken, and I truly didn't blame her. The rest of us struggled for a long time after, mourning the unsettling loss.

I was relieved when Cadence reappeared in her bedroom nearly fifteen minutes later, the steaming box of pizza in her hands. I decided to leave the awkward moment in the past as she sat down on the bed and I sat next to her, eagerly waiting for a slice. Supreme was always our favorite, and I savored the flavor as I took my first bite. As I was distracted by devouring my pizza, Cady turned on her TV in the corner of the room and put on a random show. We never talked much while we were eating, instead just enjoying each other's company. It was one of my favorite things about us. It was just . . . so easy.

With the pizza pretty much annihilated, Cadence tossed the box onto the floor by her door, and we settled back against her pillows. My head automatically leaned back against the headboard, and I sighed contentedly, my arm around her shoulders. We settled into the silence, only disturbed by the quiet talking from her TV, and I began to doze off in the safety net of her presence.

Mostly asleep, I startled when she spoke abruptly. "How do you feel about me?" She peeled herself away from my side to sit next to me instead; her gaze was unwavering as she examined my face for a reaction.

"What do I feel for you?" I was sure that I looked as confused as I felt at the sudden question. I sat up and leaned forward slightly, elbows on my knees. Her expression showed supreme discomfort and I wasn't sure how to make the crease in her forehead disappear. "Where did this question come from?"

"I've been thinking about it since you mentioned manifesting us being mates." Her unique eyes shifting away from the intensity of my gaze.

I stopped, examining her closely as I'd done millions of times before. "Well, I'm quite fond of you," I answered stupidly, unsure of how much of a confession she was prepared for.

I waited for what felt like a decade before she finally responded, a soft sigh spilling from her lips. "I think I love you, but I also think I'm broken. I don't feel the want or need to have sex with you, and I don't understand why. I see Alex and how she talks all about her escapades, and I just don't have any desire for that. Isn't that part of being in love with someone?"

Blinking, I opened my mouth a couple times as I tried desperately to think of something to say that would appropriately express how I felt. *She's in love with me?* What did I end up doing? Did the great Ezra James Wolfe, next Alpha of the Scarlet Moon Pack, King of the Volsifi, stand up and kiss his mate until both of their heads spun? Did I stand up, proudly announce that we were mates and I'd love to mark her as soon as she Ascended? Did I even reach out to touch her? Of course not. Why would I do something as romantic as that?

"Cadence, I –"

I was flabbergasted by her sudden announcement, struck speechless at the absolute worst time. She was telling me everything I'd ever wanted to hear and yet, here I was, stupidly opening and closing my mouth like a fish trapped on the beach.

The look on her face made my heart crack in half as her jaw dropped and every bit of skin I could see turned an unhealthy shade of red. If I thought dying from embarrassment was possible, I'd have called an ambulance. All because she made me so happy, I couldn't form words.

"Goddess, I knew I shouldn't have said anything. How *mortifying*," she screeched, putting her hands on her cheeks and doing an excellent impersonation of Kevin from Home Alone. "Please just go. Leave me, so I can die alone of humiliation. You don't need to witness it," she muttered, turning her back to me and shifting her hands to hide her entire face.

Cadence looking so forlorn and rejected snapped me out of my stupor and I immediately stood. "Cady, that's not at all what I –"

My words were interrupted as her shoulders shook with silent sobs, and I wanted to punch myself in the face. Hoping I could repair the misunderstanding, I reached out and put my hand on her shoulder.

At first, she jerked away from me with an audible sob, making me want to die a bit inside, but I was persistent. Ignoring her silent 'no' for the first time in our lives was one of the hardest things I'd ever done. I'd always respected her boundaries before, but this time I needed to throw myself past her rejection and explain the truth.

Giving her shoulder a squeeze, I took a deep breath. "Cadence, I've known you were my mate for our entire lives." I moved closer to her as her shuddering slowed to a stop. "I've been in love with you since the first time I saw you when I was four and you were three. Your parents brought you to the estate for one of those stupid Novzima parties my dad always throws, and you were there in your red dress that brought out the playful flush in your cheeks." I barely remembered anything else about that night, but I remembered her. I could still see her clearly: her thick, dark hair hanging in gentle waves around her shoulders, pulled away from her face to proudly display those amazing eyes that pierced right through my soul and stole my breath from my lungs.

Turning around, those same eyes were wide with surprise as she looked up at me. The tears had left tracks in her makeup and smudged some black under her eyes, but she was just as beautiful as ever to me. Without thought, I lifted my hands and wiped the tears from her cheeks before combing my fingers through her thick black hair to cradle her head in my hands. "I'm so in love with you, I can't stand it. I have known since my birthday that you're my mate, our Luna. I will take whatever physical affection you want to give me and never force anything more. If we are never more than we are now, I will still consider myself lucky to be standing at your side." I looked into those eyes that captured my soul over a decade ago.

Moving slowly, I carefully lowered my face to hers, not breaking eye contact until our lips connected. I was hesitant at first, waiting for her to tell me to stop, but she didn't. Instead, her hands bunched my shirt at my sides and pulled me closer. So, I kissed her, greedy and needy, like I had wanted to do for what felt like my entire life.

CHAPTER 5

EZRA

Not long after our kiss, I knew that I had to return home. I hated to leave her, displeased that I couldn't keep looking at her beautiful eyes and her full mouth, swollen with our heated kisses. My lips felt bruised as I gave her one last lingering kiss goodbye before heading downstairs.

Once I reached the bottom, I paused, hesitating as a slow smile crept across my face. I turned, running back up the steps, taking two at a time. Her door was still open and I strode across to the room where she stood at her window, peeking out onto the front lawn and driveway. She whirled as I approached, but I didn't give her a chance to say anything as I grabbed her face and pressed my mouth against hers again. We'd already kissed for nearly twenty minutes, but I hadn't gotten my fill. I'd wanted to kiss her since the moment I met her.

Several minutes later, Cadence finally ushered me out of the house when we heard her mother stirring in her room across the hallway. As I walked across the yard to my car, I felt someone's gaze on me and turned to Cadence's window.

Her silhouette was there, and she waved at me before disappearing into her room. I couldn't stop the wide smile on my face. Nothing could bring me down. I was easily the happiest man in the universe. It would only get better in time, as she got closer to Ascending and closer to our mate bond forming.

Volsifis always Ascended on their eighteenth birthday, taking their place within the pack. There was a huge Ascension Ceremony, and everyone would gather to be there when it happened. It could be overwhelming, but I had the utmost faith that Cadence would be more than okay. I would be there to help her, my responsibility as her mate.

My cheeks hurt as I made my way across town to the Alpha's estate that I, unfortunately, called home. Every volsifi pack had an Alpha, and ours was my father. It was a title he held onto with an iron fist, ruling the Scarlet Moon pack like a tyrant. I was his sorry excuse for a son, the murderous prince who would never, ever amount to his expectations.

We were of royal blood, one of the elites of the volsifi. Every pack had an Alpha, but not every Alpha was a King. It was a title bestowed upon the oldest and most prestigious alpha line. Ours happened to be one of the most prestigious families on the planet and my dad held a seat on the Council for Volsifi as well as a seat at the High Table as the representative of the volsifi. He was one of five, a seat that I, myself, would have someday in the not-so-distant future.

Each species on the planet had royalty, always determined by the oldest families in existence. If the royal family was wiped out, another would step up and take its place. Of the Councils, the King of each species had a seat at the High Table. The High Table was a group of five individuals that looked over all the supernatural beasts on the planet and was comprised of one of each of the races: volsifi the wolf shifters, elvafe the winged magic wielders, upirs the blood drinkers, syrena the water dwellers, and reapers the soul collectors. The reapers were the only ones with two subspecies: wraiths, evil bastards that consumed souls just because they could, and luxnositel. Luxnositels were the good guys, the ones who guided souls to the underworld to face the god Kuorir to see their fate. They had a seat at the High Table, the wraiths did not.

Interbreeding of the species was strictly forbidden, the offspring of those unions creating volatile magic and dangerous creatures. I believed that it was because their powers would be unknown, and the unknown is not something that anyone in the upper ranks wants to deal with. There have been some abominations born in the past, and they were all horrible, evil monsters. At least, that's what we are taught from infancy. I wasn't sure if that was true. I'd never met someone who carried the blood of multiple species.

I pulled into the estate; the large white manor looked as imposing as ever with each of its unlit windows encased in royal blue shutters. The landscaping was immaculate, the shrubs pruned into pristine squares that surrounded the entire driveway until you reached the gravel circle before the front door. The front door itself was huge, royal blue, and surrounded by square windows that matched the square hedges. It was all a mask, appearing welcoming even though the resident was anything but.

I drove my car around the back of the manor, a brief glimmer of hope igniting at the continuing scene of dark, oppressive windows. Then I saw a flickering in one of them and that small flame of hope was flattened and drowned before it could form anything remotely warm and relaxing.

Unsure whether I wanted to go in, I sat in the garage with the car still running. Maybe if I sat here long enough, I would never have to face him again. The thought was fleeting, the smell of exhaust stinging my nose as I turned the engine off and got out of the vehicle.

I could never predict which father was going to be present. As long as he wasn't drinking, I was usually safe. My intuition always knew it was going to be a bad night if he appeared with a crystal glass of amber liquid in his hand. I knew it was going to be even worse if the liquid was green, it was a concoction known as Bismuth, the horrible mix of Absinthe and elvafe magic that never failed to turn him into a mean bastard.

I walked into the house and my father, Lucien, must have heard me coming. He was standing right inside the door. Startling, I did my best to hide it from his keen blue eyes. It was a sign of weakness and that was not something I wanted my father to see in me; it always made the punishments worse. My gaze glanced at his scarred hands, noticing the amber liquid in the glass as my lips pressed together in a firm line. At least it wasn't the shade of poisonous emeralds.

"You're home late," my father muttered quietly, his steely eyes shifting to the grandfather clock in the foyer that proudly displayed the time, midnight. "On a school night." He tried so hard to hide the bite in his tone with fatherly care sprinkled over it. I was not fooled.

"I was at a friend's house." I refused to flinch as he stepped nearer to me to slam the front door shut. The heavy wooden bang echoed through the lifeless house. If I was any younger, I would have cowered at the noise. "I didn't think I had a curfew," I added, taking a few steps toward the winding staircase in a clear dismissal.

Big mistake.

His glass slammed against the back of my head with a dull thud that radiated pain through my skull, only emphasized by my knees hitting the hardwood floor. I groaned, looking at the glass as it sat innocuously on the floor beside me. He must have upgraded, because this one had a thick, heavy bottom on it to keep drunks from spilling it over. The old ones just shattered. Placing my hand on the back of my head, I lifted my gaze to clash with his as he hovered over me.

"Did I give you permission to walk away from me?" he snarled, spittle flying from his lips and onto my face. I hated that I recoiled. I hated it more that he noticed. "You wait until you're dismissed to leave my presence. Do you hear me?" His face turned purple; the unpleasant color of his skin made the silver scars stand out. A vein throbbed in his forehead and a small piece of me wished the vein would burst, but I was never going to be that lucky, was I?

His fist gathered the fabric at the front of my shirt, and he lifted me to my feet with ease. I resisted the urge to cower under his cold gaze. He examined my face, as if looking for evidence that I was doing drugs or becoming a criminal or something. My blood ran cold as he inhaled deeply, letting his eyes roll back and fall closed as he focused on the scent clinging to my skin. *Her* scent. When his eyes opened, they were glowing blue in the dim light, and he smirked. "You went to visit that Delta bitch, didn't you?" He gritted his teeth as he released my clothes and shoved me backward so that I stumbled a couple steps.

"Yes, I did," I stated, trying to keep my cool as I snapped the bottom of my shirt to release some of the wrinkles he'd left in the cotton. I'd have pointed out that she had a name, but I didn't want the beauty of it repeated back to me by the horrid slash of his mouth. "Is that a problem?" My voice hid none of my disdain for him. I hated that he had learned her scent from my being around her.

Lucien rolled his head from side to side on his shoulders as if trying to relieve some unseen tension he was feeling. I was uncomfortable with the motion since it usually meant something bad was coming my way. Why did he have to be drinking when I got home?

"It is a problem, actually." He stared me down as I glared at him from the other side of the foyer. "Her family was down caste, and with good reason." Pointing toward the door in the vague direction of the Nocetti home, he looked as though referring to them caused him physical pain. "I want you to start seeing Jessica Barber."

I couldn't stop myself from staring stupidly at him, torn between outrage at his demand and vaguely hopeful he would spill some information. No one but the parents involved ever really knew the reason there was a fallout between the Nocettis and the rest of the pack, and my father had literally never spoken about it before. Not to me, anyway. "What are you talking about?" I asked him, putting more aggravation in my voice than necessary, hoping that pushing him would loosen his tongue. It demanded an answer from both proclamations.

He stared at me for an agonizing moment, as if he was sizing me up. "Well, of course *you* wouldn't know, but the Nocetti family betrayed our pack. They're lucky I so graciously let them stay in our territory and didn't throw them out. They're extra lucky that I didn't force them to be like the damned Omegas." He picked up his glass from the floor and looked at it with disgust, though I know his disgust was aimed at the lowest rank in the pack and not the glass itself. "Also, I've spoken with Dr. Reginald Barber, and we have both agreed that you need to mate with his daughter, Jessica."

I chose to ignore anything about the ginger monstrosity, opting for information about Cadence's family instead. "What did they do that was so horrible?" I pressed him further for answers I instinctually knew he wasn't going to give.

His cold blue eyes lifted to mine, and I vaguely wondered how I could possibly be related to him. I hardly looked like him other than our eyes, which I think he hated more than anything in the world. Like he had to look at his deceased mate every time he looked upon my features. There was a heavy pause between us as the tension in the room grew to nearly painful levels that made me wish I hadn't asked anything at all. Like lightning, his hand reached out and backhanded me across the face. My head whipped to the side with the impact, and I growled at the painful sting it caused, my teeth clashing together. "You should have died instead of your mother." His words stung, but it wasn't the first time I'd heard them.

I knew that was as good of an answer as I was getting and I stood there, staring at him without asking him anything further. I was aware that I had overstepped enough as it was, and I wasn't interested in getting any more abuse from him tonight. Instead, I waited for permission to go to my room, since it was now well after midnight, and I wanted to go to sleep.

Finally, Lucien looked away from me as if coming out of a stupor. "What are you still doing here? Go to bed, you worthless child." His expression as he glanced back and assessed me told me I was as useless as a slug he found crawling through his entryway, and I was more than grateful to get away from the scrutiny of his gaze.

I refused to run. Running from an angry dog only made it chase you down and rip out your throat. I learned long ago that hurrying away from my father brought worse punishment than taking my time and leisurely leaving his presence like I wasn't desperate to escape. That said, I wanted nothing more than to shift and take off up the stairs faster than he could call my name.

My long legs took me down the hallway toward my bedroom, halfway to the window at the end. While Cadence's room was soft shades of gray and lilac, mine was cobalt and black. Frowning, I looked around at the colors my father chose, masculine and powerful, he claimed. Frequently, I wondered why he didn't choose red for blood or purple for royalty. I figured he didn't want me feeling too passionate or kingly about anything.

I pulled my shirt over my head, tossing it into the dirty hamper beside my bathroom door. Confusion rattled in my brain as I once again tried to figure out what exactly the Nocettis had done, but I knew nothing further was coming from my father. I knew for certain that Cadence didn't know, because I would imagine she would have told me at some point. Alex didn't know anything; her father was one of the tightest traps of all. She knew all the ins and outs of the school drama, but that wasn't super helpful in this situation other than whispered rumors that I doubted amounted to anything at all.

What the hell was he saying about Jessica Barber? Amber eyes and ginger hair floated in my brain for a second before I shook the image away. That girl was horrible, the worst of the worst of entitled Beta families.

With a sigh, I looked in the mirror at my torso; white scars crisscrossed over my toned abdomen. It reminded me of who I would be when I took over for my father, and it wouldn't be a monster like him. I would do everything in my power to be everything he wasn't, including a better father. Shifting my weight, I turned away from the mirror, not wanting to see the worst of my scars that were spread over my back. Some of them were purple, and those were the ones I hated the most. They were fresher, stretched out and formed keloids over the past couple years since he'd last whipped me when I was sixteen. I'd done my best to stay out of his way since then, having learned all the places to easily avoid him. Initially, when he'd taken a break when I was fifteen, I thought it was because I was stronger and better able to fight him. Instead, I got a couple months off until he had a rack installed just for me in the dungeons.

I walked into the bathroom, picking up my toothbrush and aggressively brushing my teeth as if the mint would help me forget the demonic presence that slept just down the hall. He never did forgive me for what happened to mom, and I didn't anticipate that he ever really would forgive me either. Sometimes I couldn't even forgive myself for what happened, even though it wasn't my fault. I guess when something is pounded into your brain enough, you tend to believe it. Mom died giving birth to me, and my dad often screamed at me for murdering his mate while he beat me, especially when I was younger. It was something I could never forgive him for, no matter how much time went by. I lost her too, but my loss didn't matter.

Rinsing my toothbrush off, I tossed it into the glass holder with so much force the porcelain cracked. That didn't make me feel any better. I wasn't sure anything other than being in the presence of Cady could make me feel much of anything at all. However, the numbness that was taking over was much better than the rage I frequently felt at how terrified I was of my father. I shouldn't be afraid of being around him, I should love him. Frankly, I thought I'd be happier if he died. Sometimes, I wanted to be the one to put him into the ground myself.

Chapter 6

CADENCE

The next day after school, Ezra had to spend time studying in the library for an upcoming exam, giving me plenty of free time. As if moving on their own, my feet took me away from the school and in the direction of one of my favorite places in the world. It was over a mile away, but well worth the walk as I broke through the tree line of the forest I'd been wandering through. Axe Marks the Spot stood beside a sad looking grocery store. Things in the Delta and Omega world were not as well taken care of as the side of town that housed the Alpha and Beta families. It was just another thing to keep us separated from the pack members who actually mattered to the Alpha.

I walked into the building, giving a wave to the girl behind the counter. "Hey there, Ava," I greeted, offering a smile.

Ava smiled brightly, exposing a dimple in her right cheek. I wondered once again if I should ask her about getting a ride here after school every so often, but my social anxiety prevented that from being possible. While she was one of the few people who were actually nice to me in the pack, it didn't change the fact that she was still not my friend. She was also a Delta, which should put us on the same level, but that's not the way things actually were; I'd always be less than. Remembering that made me smile shyly before immediately going toward my locker.

My trusty axe laid in its place, waiting for me to pull her out and wield her like the glorious weapon that she was. Being a rather non-athletic individual with lackluster arm strength, I preferred a wooden handle over a metal one. The metal was heavier than I was typically comfortable with, and it was harder for me to get a good stick. On the other hand, my favorite hickory handled axe sunk every single time, provided I threw it correctly. It took a long time and extensive practice with my Grandpa Henry for me to get the muscle memory down to stick almost every single time. Bullseyes were more common than kill shots, but I wasn't going to complain as long as I could make an impressive throw.

I popped my earbuds in, "Bad Moon" by Hollywood Undead filling my brain as the pulsing beat soothed me. Closing my eyes, I relished the tune and lyrics for a moment before turning around to Ava walking away from lane five. I smiled gratefully at her as I noticed the wood was already dampened and ready to catch the sharp blade of my axe.

Keeping my earbuds firmly in place, I stood back several feet from the target and got into position. I always threw with one hand, finding it easier than putting both arms over my head. I realized long ago that I was consistently worried I would accidentally hit myself in the back of the skull with the blade in that position. It was an unnecessary concern, but it held me back nonetheless. I could hear my Grandpa Henry teasing me in my head, the ghost of his presence filling the place he created. Standing nearly completely sideways, I held my arm straight out in front of me, my hand gripped around the base of the handle with the blade facing the target. I didn't always throw this way, but it was the best for a warmup.

Pulling my hand back until my thumb grazed the back of my head, I took a deep breath to steady my limb and then threw the axe toward the target. The blade embedded itself to the upper left of the bullseye, causing me to press my lips together in annoyance.

"It's just a warmup, Cady. No need to fret. I know you'll hit that kill shot when it matters the most." The whisper of my deceased grandpa echoed to me from the past. He'd always encouraged me when I needed it.

I threw for so long I completely lost track of time. No one else came in while I was there, leaving me hours of peace and music blasting through my earbuds. Ava never bothered me, letting me do my thing as she'd grown accustomed to since she'd started working here.

At one point, I realized that it had gotten dark in the room, and I turned to see that Ava had turned off the lights behind the counter. That also turned down the lights in the waiting room that no one ever used. A tall man sat on the couch; the cover of *The Princess Bride* visible even in the dim light.

"How long have you been sitting there, dad?" I asked, grinning as I pulled the music from my ears and paused it on my phone. Setting down the axe on the table that sat behind my lane, I took a moment to take a long drink of water as his dark eyes lifted to meet mine.

"Long enough to see that you can aim even better than my father could." His quiet voice reached me and caused a furious flush to heat my face. He closed the book and stood, stretching his arms above his head. "And that's saying something. He had always been an excellent marksman and spent his life trying to make me as good as him. However, it seems that gene skipped me and went straight to you, my darling."

I laughed, walking over to put my favorite axe away in my locker. She was a gift from my grandpa, and I felt a small amount of sadness as I closed the door on her. "I miss him," I breathed, feeling the familiar pang of grief in my chest at memories of him.

"Me too, kiddo. He was a great man, dedicating so much time to bring enjoyment to the youth of his pack with this place. I think he'd have been very happy, just knowing that you come here so often. You keep his memory alive every time you pick up his axe." Dad smiled fondly, his gaze far off in his memories. "He built this place to bring some kind of recreation to the Deltas and Omegas, you know? He felt that being impoverished was no reason not to be able to have a good time," he explained, chuckling. A light that very rarely appeared in his brown eyes flickered, reminding me that there was life hidden in there still.

I smiled, remembering to spin the lock on the locker before linking my arm with my dad's. He guided me from the building, pulling out his keys to lock up behind us. "I know," I responded finally, tilting my face up toward the dark sky. Stars glittered far above us, and I wondered if they were watching us, like the guardian angels I'd read about in storybooks.

Dad led me to the car, something he took care of since it was such a necessity to get to work. "Do you mind going with me to the food pantry for a little bit? I told Georgia that I'd stop in so she can tuck her kids into bed," he asked after we both dropped into the car. The food bank stayed open later so that Omegas who worked late hours could still get food to feed their families with donations from anonymous Beta families who still possessed bleeding hearts. I'd never tell Alex, but I knew that her parents were one of those donors.

I blinked at him for a moment before nodding. "You never have to ask, dad. I'm always willing to pull my weight in this pack." I gave him a small smile. I would never be convinced that my father didn't pull more than his fair share of weight.

The smile he gave me did not cover up the tiredness in his eyes. "Thanks, kiddo," he said, pulling out of the lot and driving into Omega territory toward the food bank.

We arrived home late, the minutes creeping toward midnight. I immediately went into the bathroom, brushing my teeth with my eyes closed. I fell on top of the blankets, too tired to get under the covers before falling asleep.

I found myself on the top of a cliff, gazing out at the expansive ravine below. A river cut through the center, winding between the mountains surrounding it. I wondered how long this river had been here, cutting through the mountain until it formed the ones I could see today. The feeling of time slowly ticking by gave me a wistful feeling. I wrapped my arms around myself as a cold wind danced around me, shifting my hair around my shoulders even as the rain made it stick to my skin. My toes gripped the grass that tickled the soles of my feet. I found myself wishing I could predict these dreams so I could start wearing appropriate attire.

Glancing around, I wondered when he'd be arriving. He never approached, always appeared. That was the funny thing about dreams; they were so mysterious.

"Remember me?" I closed my eyes, letting the smooth timbre of his voice wrap around my brain. Chills tingled over my arms and legs as his presence approached. It was immense, growing stronger every time we met here. "I was wondering when you'd show."

Turning, I glanced up at his face. "How could I forget my dream guy?"

The corner of his mouth quirked upward; the expression was so slight I almost missed it.

"Besides, I was here first," I whispered, the words swept away by the wind. He still seemed to hear it, tilting his head to the side.

"I meant before tonight. You haven't been back in weeks. I was starting to think my imaginary friend abandoned me."

It was a weird thing to say. Something he always said if I didn't dream him up every couple nights. I disregarded it as something my self-conscious was doing.

Maybe because I felt like a side character in my own life sometimes, my mind was playing it out in my dreams. How ironic, since he was the imaginary friend.

"It's been twelve years. Why would I abandon you now?"

His eyes grew stormy, the distrust brewing behind them again. He always wavered between believing in me and not. I tried not to let it hurt my feelings, though if anyone could hurt their own feelings, it would be me.

"You wouldn't be the first to abandon me," he murmured, the sadness making his words sound heavy in my ears.

I reached out, gently brushing my fingers over his cheek. He stiffened, pulling back for a split second before melting into my touch. It was like he was a frightened animal, no matter how powerful he seemed.

The rain was slowing to a drizzle, sunlight peeking around the clouds and slowly warming the air around us.

"I will never abandon you."

He nodded, his expression growing tense before he glanced over his shoulder. "I've got to go."

"So soon?" My stomach twisted. I didn't want him to leave.

"Yes. I'm being summoned."

I inhaled, pulling my hands to my chest and clutching them together. "Don't forget me."

He had turned, was walking away. His motions stopped, though he didn't look at me. "Dream of me and I'll be there."

I jerked upright in bed, my clothes stuck to my skin. Gasping for air, I pushed my hair out of my face and pressed my hand to my chest. Just like I always did after these dreams, I tried to picture the face of the boy I saw, but it was gone. The features of his serious expression sifting out of my consciousness like sand through my fingers.

CHAPTER 7

CADENCE

The next morning, the dream forgotten, I rushed down the stairs and plopped into my usual seat at the kitchen table. Dad was there, reading his book as usual.

"Good morning, Cade." He glanced over the novel to look at me with a smile.

"Good morning, dad," I responded, pouring myself some cereal and milk in a bowl.

I was dunking the sugared wheat clusters, making sure they were all coated when he spoke again. "Cadence, I am keeping the clinic open later than normal tonight. Alma called this morning to say that she's pretty sure that the baby is coming today. Since she was correct the last two times, I have no doubts that this baby will keep the pattern," he said, putting down the book to take a sip of coffee.

Looking up at him, I nodded and took a bite of cereal. "Is there a reason you're telling me this?" I gave him a playful grin.

His eyes lifted to meet mine, a twinkle of humor in them. "Yes. Can you go to the food pantry and make sure that the stock is rotated so the older stuff goes first? Also, William's sixteenth birthday is tomorrow, so Molly is going to be coming around nine to pick up more supplies than usual. I already okayed it with Georgia," he explained, putting down his mug and standing to put it into the sink.

"Sure, dad." I averted my gaze. Delivering babies took a lot more supplies than ordinary ailments and I couldn't help but worry how much it would dwindle the meager things my dad could afford to purchase. "Do you want me to get a job or something? So that we can buy more things for the clinic? I don't want the Omegas to suffer because our Alpha is too cruel to fund medicine for them." I put down my spoon to give him my full attention.

Dad paused at the sink, his back to me so I couldn't see his face. I was sure that my words hurt him, but it was a reality we faced; that all the Omegas faced.

"I want you to enjoy your high school experience," he stated curtly, still not looking at me. "You're still a child until May fourteenth, and you should get to be one until then."

I stood up, trying not to be frustrated with him. "But dad, it's not like I'm immune to the suffering of the Omegas, I see it every day." My hands formed fists and I hated myself for the tears that burned my eyes. "It's not fair that you have to single-handedly fund a clinic because Lucien won't allow the Omegas to go to the pack doctor."

He did turn to face me then, his dark hair bristling with his rage. "You are a *child*. I will not discuss finances with you. You will not get a job because I need your help with the food pantry. I do have donors for the clinic, we are fine financially. I am your father, and I will provide for you until you Ascend and move on to an academy." His mug hit the bottom of the sink with a loud thud before he left the kitchen.

The conversation was over, and I did not feel resolved, though I knew that he was not going to entertain any further discussion. I looked down at my half-eaten bowl of cereal and winced. The thought of eating anything else made my stomach turn, but I couldn't waste the food. There were children two blocks away who would give anything for this amount of sweetness, and that thought had me sitting down to finish the last of it. Guilt made the sugary cereal taste like ash, and it took everything in me to swallow every bite until I could rinse out the bowl and place it into the sink for later.

Dad's words hung heavy in my soul as I finished getting ready just in time for Ezra's honk that announced his arrival out front. The last thing I wanted to do was go to school and pretend like dad and I hadn't just had a spat about something so incredibly difficult. As I put on my backpack, I decided I'd make him dinner and take it to the clinic after I did my job at the food pantry. It was the least I could do for him.

ALEX

It was third period Chemistry class, one that Ezra and I had together without Cadence. As we walked toward our class from his locker, the anxiety emanating from him felt stifling.

"If you keep chewing on your lip like that, you'll soon be drinking your own blood. Do you think that'll make you an upir?" I asked, glancing at him for the third time since we'd started our trek to class.

Ezra released his lower lip, now fuller than usual from the amount of gnawing he'd been doing, sighing heavily as he lifted one hand to muss up his golden waves. I eyed him, hoping that if I stared long enough, he would break and tell me what was weighing so heavily on his mind.

"I had a confrontation with my father last night." He was still not looking at me and instead staring one thousand miles down the hall. It was obvious that he was not mentally present in the school, instead absorbed in memories of the past. I let him stew, knowing that waiting was typically the best method of getting him to spill his secrets.

I turned into a stairwell and out of the mass of students filling the hallway on their way to class. Leaning against the railing, I glanced over the ledge to be sure that there was no one else in the stairway before turning back to him. His pale blue eyes were staring over my left shoulder, though they weren't focusing on anything.

"What happened?" I finally broke his intense internalization so that he actually looked at me.

He appraised me for a long moment, his lips pressed firmly together and exposing a dimple under his lip. Closing his eyes, he whispered, "He insists that I date Jessica."

"Barber?" I asked, unable to stop the growl from grating the word.

"That's the one." Opening his eyes again, I saw a fire burning within them that told me just how furious he was about it. Ezra couldn't hide his emotions even if he had to. "He is pretty much forcing me into mating with her regardless of who my actual mate is. He seems to think it would be good for the pack if the doctor's daughter is the Luna."

"That's the most ludicrous thing I've ever heard."

He sighed again, rolling his eyes as he leaned back against the wall, tilting his head back against the white painted bricks. "I know. It's absolutely insane, but he was pretty insistent that this was the path to follow. I don't think I have a choice but to at least take her out on a couple dates until Cadence Ascends and we know the truth." He sounded more defeated than I'd ever heard from him.

My jaw dropped in a rare show of surprise. "Have you told Cadence about this?" I whispered, knowing for certain that he hadn't. She'd definitely have said something to me about it.

"No, not yet," he muttered, as I knew he would. "I'm half afraid to, honestly. The last thing I want to do is hurt her."

I frowned at him. "Well, you're going to have to get your shit together and tell her. This is insanity, but you have to trust that she will understand as best she can."

He scowled at me as the bell rang. "I know that. That doesn't mean I want to see her face when I have to tell her."

Picturing Cadence's smiling face made my chest hurt. That girl was the light to my darkness, and I knew for certain that this would eat at her. "I'll be there when you tell her, but I'm not going to be the one to do it." I gave him a face that said I meant those words. "And you can't take as long as you did to tell her that you're in love with her."

A small twitch of his mouth exposed a dimple in his left cheek. "I won't. I just . . . don't want to face the consequences of not following my father's orders on this. I've avoided being whipped for over two years and I don't want to face that again," he whispered, and I could see the agony and trauma etched into his face. "That feels so selfish. I hate that about myself."

I shook my head. "It's not selfish to not want to be abused by your father, Ezra."

He winced. "I knew seeing my dad talking to Reginald Barber at my Ascension would be trouble."

Frowning, I turned from him and moved toward the doorway before someone stepped into it and obstructed my path. Scowling at the roadblock, I snapped, "What the hell do you want?"

Jessica smiled at me, exposing more teeth than was necessary and I couldn't help but notice that it was almost too wide. As if I needed more reason to think that this girl was straight up vile. "My father told me this morning that he spoke with Lucien yesterday evening," she crooned, turning her creepy beaming smile on Ezra who shuddered beside me.

"Can you get out of our way? Your caricature of a smile is creeping me out. Did you get extra teeth implanted into your head to have that effect or are you just naturally repulsive?" I took a couple steps forward, encroaching on her personal space and causing her to flinch back a step. I smirked wickedly in response to her obvious wariness of me and took another large, stomping step forward. Jessica lurched backwards and almost tripped over her own feet.

Jessica glared at me and gave Ezra a simpering look before turning and walking toward the class that we all, unfortunately, shared. The three of us walked into the class and Mr. Clemens looked up from where he was reading a textbook to the class. His bushy mustache flickered like a snowy caterpillar as he took in the three of us.

"Take your seats." His reedy voice grated my frazzled nerves. "Jessica Barber, you have detention with me after school for tardiness."

Jessica looked like she might burst, her face turning an unhealthy shade of purple as she stormed toward her seat. I glanced at Ezra and tried to hide a smile. Being friends with the prince sure had its perks sometimes.

CADENCE

The bell rang, signaling the end of third period. Mr. Rutger, the trigonometry teacher, packed up and disappeared from the classroom as usual to get to the cafeteria. I put all of my things together and glanced behind me before standing, ignoring the whistles from Brody and his friends behind me. One of them told the others to cut it out, but I wasn't sure who spoke. Unable to get out of the classroom fast enough, I quickly walked into the hallway and allowed the crowd of students to swallow me. Hugging my book to my chest, I made my way toward the cafeteria to meet Ezra and Alex. Ezra was waiting for me just outside of the cafeteria, smiling warmly when I approached.

"Hey there, Cadybug," he said, pulling his arm from behind his back and handing me a crimson amaryllis.

Gasping, I took it from his hand. "Where were you keeping this?" I asked, grinning at him as I tucked the stem behind my right ear.

"I have my sources." He leaned down and pressed a chaste kiss to my lips. Gripping his shirt, I yanked him into another kiss when he tried to pull away.

He chuckled against my lips and we both ignored someone whistling as they walked past.

"Okay. Let's eat," I said, finally letting him go and walking through the door.

My eyes scanned the room, finding Alex already seated at our usual table. She frequently held the table for us so no one braved booting us out of our spot. It was unlikely that anyone would, but stranger things have happened. Ezra and I grabbed our food from the line and sat down with Alex.

"So, Cadence, do you want to hang out after school today?" Alex asked, glancing at Ezra before shifting her gaze back to me.

"I can't tonight. I'm going to the food pantry this evening and then I think I'm going to stop at the clinic to take dad some dinner. We fought this morning and I want to make it up to him."

I frowned as somebody stopped walking behind me. Craning my neck, I looked up at Brody, Kyle, and Jason. After an awkward pause, I finally broke it.

"What?"

Jason smirked at me, leaning down to look directly into my eyes. "How is daddy doing? Still running himself ragged so your mommy can be the pack's biggest freak and freeloader?" he asked, his tone cold and disarming.

I blinked at him, unable to suppress the shock I felt at such an unexpected series of questions. "What?" I repeated, this time in surprise instead of annoyance.

Jason's emerald eyes sparkled with mischief, and I stared at him, waiting for the point of this conversation. He leaned closer to me, his mouth brushing against my ear as he whispered, "You are this pack's biggest disappointment. I can change that if you wanna shack up with me."

I recoiled from him, chills of disgust erupting over my skin at the feeling of his breath on my neck and in my ear. "No. Hard pass." I wrinkled my nose at him.

"Knock it off, Jason," Kyle muttered, crossing his arms over his chest as an uncomfortable expression curved his mouth into a frown.

Brody looked as angry as usual, though it was the first time I'd seen it directed at Jason. "Dude. Did you really bring us over here to say that?"

Jason shrugged, straightening and winking at me before walking away. Kyle and Brody glanced at his retreating form, both looking uncomfortable. Brody opened his mouth as if to say something before grunting eloquently and stalking off, Kyle following behind.

Ezra and Alex looked confused, and I frowned. "Why do I get the feeling that he was making fun of me? What was that with the other two?" I wondered aloud, rolling my eyes and returning to picking at my grilled cheese.

"I don't know that was," Alex muttered, causing Ezra to press his lips together in inadequately suppressed rage, the dimple below his lip appearing.

"Whatever. It doesn't matter. I'm *definitely* not interested in Jason Barber," I muttered, pulling apart the sandwich despite having suddenly lost my appetite.

Another person stopped at our table, this time across from us. Jessica stood with her hands on her hips as she looked at the three of us as though we were a freak show and she'd paid good money to peer at us with her superiority.

I raised a brow at her as she stood there, waiting to be acknowledged. "What do *you* want? I didn't want to talk to your brother, and I don't want to talk to you," I snapped, my tone harsh and uninviting.

Jessica, ignoring the cues that she was unwanted, sat down across from Ezra and leaned forward onto the table, giving him a wide smile. It didn't go unnoticed, even to me, that she pulled her elbows in, pressing her breasts together to emphasize her cleavage. I looked between them, unsure what was happening.

"Oh, I just figured I'd swing by and visit my new boyfriend." She shifted her eyes directly to me.

I immediately glanced at Ezra who looked stupefied. Alex, on his other side, looked upset, but unsurprised.

"*Jessica . . .*" The warning was apparent in his tone.

"See, our fathers got together and decided that they were arranging our marriage. Dad, you know, the pack's doctor, told me this morning that he suggested to Alpha Lucien that Ezra and I be married on May fourteenth. Don't you think that's the perfect day for a wedding?" Her eyes glittered with malice as she stared me down across the table.

It felt like a boulder had been dropped into my stomach, every beat of my heart ached as the pain of it breaking filled my chest like a balloon. I opened my mouth to speak, but nothing came out of it but an odd sort of choking sound.

"Not really," Alex spoke up, ever the cool cucumber. "Since an Ascension is already on the books for that day. You know it's supernatural law that no other events can be held on the day of an Ascension. Even holidays are delayed if there's an Ascension that day."

Jessica smiled brightly, tapping her long, red fingernails on the tabletop. "Perhaps, but father informed me that if it's an Alpha's wedding, it can supersede any Ascension for those involved. Since Ezra will be the Alpha, that means it applies to him."

Ezra finally spoke up, standing and leaning forward over the table, his hands pressing against the top. "Except, Jessica, that I am not an Alpha. Only the next one. There will be no wedding between us, and definitely not on Cadence's birthday." His voice was low and menacing.

A hush fell over the cafeteria as those around us finally realized that something was happening at our table. I stood, refusing to be a spectacle because of this when I'd been nothing but mocked for entertainment my entire life. It was futile, though. Everyone's attention was already on us. Jessica stood across from me, disregarding Ezra to stare me down.

"This isn't over, Cadence. You are a coward, and cowards never win." Her amber eyes bored into mine.

I lifted my chin as I regarded her, my friends bolstering me as they always did. "And you, Jessica, will never truly have won Ezra. Even if you do marry him and you get to take my place at his side, just know that you will never have his heart. *That*, will always belong to me."

With that, I turned and stormed from the cafeteria to find a bathroom. I desperately needed a good cry.

Chapter 8

CADENCE

I spent the rest of my day in relative silence. My friends did not attempt to force me to talk to them, which was wise. Truly, I just wanted to get the entire day over with so I could go to bed and wake up tomorrow with a fresh outlook. Unfortunately, I had too many things to do. I went home to make a quick dinner that I could transport to dad.

I whipped up stir fry, letting it cool while I gathered the things I needed to study as I hung out around the food pantry. When I was mostly ready to go, I scooped the dinner into three containers, taking two with me and leaving one in the fridge for mother in case she left her room while I was gone.

I tossed my bag over my shoulders, heading into the attached garage to get my bike. Our home was right on the invisible line that divided where the Omegas resided and the Deltas. The food pantry was set up directly in the middle of the small area of pack territory that belonged to the Omega families.

Biking along the streets, I kept my eyes straight ahead. Seeing the dilapidated houses and duplexes that the Omegas were forced to live in made me feel overwhelmed with sadness for the families dwelling in squalor. It was never for any particular reason, typically the poverty was generational; the Omegas went to our school, but they were less likely to get into larger academies because they couldn't afford the application fees. Potencia Sui Generis did not have an application fee, but it was so prestigious that your grades had to be exemplary to get in. Everyone wanted to get into PSG, including myself.

The streets were immaculate despite being rundown, the Omega community always pulled together to keep their area of the pack clean and orderly. Everyone did their part, picking up any stray trash and helping each other get their lawns mowed when anyone had extra time or extra money for gas. Sometimes, William Jones would go around with an ancient manual push mower to clean up yards after school. That was often how our own lawn was mowed. None of the buildings had graffiti, but there were plenty of murals on the sides of businesses that some of the artistic volsifis did to add some cheer to the downtrodden.

I pulled up in front of the pantry, my bike squealing as I hit the brakes and unceremoniously dropped it against the brick wall of the tiny building. As backward as it may seem, I was never overly concerned about things being stolen from this part of the territory. Much like my grandfather, I always assumed that if it was stolen that the thief clearly needed it even more than I did; especially those who have nothing and know the value of such a mode of transportation.

Walking into the building, a bell tinkled above me as I pushed the door open. Georgia called from the back, "Be right out!" I smiled at the few people who were there and waiting in line for their rations, holding empty boxes in their hands.

I moved behind the counter, waving a greeting to the next person in line. "Hey, Ms. Jones. I hear that someone is celebrating a birthday tomorrow." I reached out for her empty box as she pushed it across the counter.

She smiled warmly, her blue eyes sparkling with mirth. "Cady, dear. How many times must I tell you to call me Molly? I only need a couple more eggs than normal for the cake. I've been trying to save the ingredients to make his favorite meal. He really enjoys chicken stir-fry. Unfortunately, I wasn't able to get enough chicken to make it this year. I'm going to make a vegetable barley soup instead."

A twinge of guilt twisted my gut as I took in the sadness that flickered behind her eyes. Our family had grown accustomed to vegetarian meals years ago. Meat was too difficult to obtain at times, but dad had made friends with a human janitor who also raised chickens. He often sent him home with poultry and eggs in exchange for medicinal guidance when he needed help and couldn't afford healthcare. My mind shifted to the two containers of stir-fry sitting in my bag and the right choice was obvious.

I gave Molly a sad smile and nodded. "I can definitely empathize with that. Sometimes resources are hard for us to get on this side of the pack."

Before anything else could be said, I walked into the back and put together Molly's box. Underneath the small bag of flour, I placed the container with my meal and covered it so she couldn't find it too early and give it back to me. I was familiar with William and his lanky frame; he definitely needed that meal more than I ever would.

Walking back to the counter, I smiled warmly at Molly and set the box down on the counter. "Please wish William a happy birthday for me. I'm not sure when I'll see him next." I pushed it toward her and nodded as she said goodbye and departed.

It didn't take long to work through the line, and I was grateful we had enough rations to help everyone who arrived for aid. Georgia and I always worked well together and filled our time in the back with idle chitchat until everyone left. The last person shuffled out around six-thirty, the bell above the door announcing their exit. She immediately turned to me with a smirk on her face.

"So, what was this I heard about you being our future Luna?" she asked, putting her hands on her hips and eyeing me with such glee that I shifted on my feet.

"Hmm . . . you know how the grapevine is," I hedged, taking too long to answer.

One of her brows quirked upward; she wasn't fooled. "I do know how the grapevine is. Usually, the truth is hidden somewhere in the rumor. So, spill. Are you the future mate of our darling Ezra Wolfe?" she pestered, her tone indicating that she would tolerate none of my nonsense.

I sighed heavily, resisting the urge to roll my eyes. "You know I won't know until I Ascend at the earliest. Though, Ezra certainly seems to think so, since he keeps telling people that I am. I think that's a bold claim. I can't imagine there is any way I'm going to be the next Luna." I leaned back against the counter and rested my hands against the edge.

Georgia looked me over, scrutinizing my face before she finally spoke again. "You remind me a lot of our late Luna. Have I ever told you that?"

I made a sound of surprise. "No, you've never mentioned that. How could I possibly remind you of her?" I leaned forward slightly in keen interest. I'd never heard a ton about the prior Luna of the pack, but I was definitely curious to know more about Ezra's mother.

Georgia turned away from me, a faraway expression coming to her face. "Giselle was a gorgeous woman. Tall. Plump. She was picked on in high school, but she always kept her head high. Her face was almost ethereal. She really was the only person who could soften that creature we call an Alpha. It was like she held him in a spell, that she was so pure and true that it purified his darkness." Her forehead creased, wrinkles forming around her eyes as her face fell at some memory she was reliving. Then she brightened, a wistful smile curving her mouth. "Ezra is the spitting image of her. It's uncanny. What reminds me of her is your unending love for people. You care so deeply that it directly affects you when others are hurting. You're like your father, that way. You'd give your own skin if it meant that someone else could be saved, and that's not something most people can say about themselves," she mused, turning her brown eyes to me, "I'd be honored to have you as our next Luna. There couldn't be anyone better for the position." A small smile appeared on her face and caused faint wrinkles to appear on the edges of her eyes again.

My face flushed to a level that was uncomfortable and I averted my gaze. "Thanks for that, Georgia. I'm afraid you speak too highly of me. Besides, Alpha Lucien and Dr. Reginald Barber are trying to force Ezra to be with Jessica."

Georgia snorted in indignance, rolling those dark eyes. "Jessica Barber? There could not be a worse choice for Luna. I think she'd make life harder for our Omegas than even Lucien has, and that's saying something. Lucien represses our desire to accept our wolves, and I doubt she would do any differently. Most of us hope that Ezra will dissolve the unspoken rules that criminalize shifting."

I pressed my lips together, unable to disagree with her. "There are other choices. Like Alex," I rebutted, shrugging despite the sick feeling that entered my stomach at the thought of them together. "And I know that Ezra wants to remove those restrictions. He's mentioned it in the past."

Georgia snorted again. "Ezra sees Alex like his kid sister. Always has. She has her own job anyway, becoming the future General of the Guard." She grabbed her coat and pulled it over her shoulders. "If you become the Luna, the pack will rejoice; especially us little folk down here in Omega territory."

She walked past me, pausing for a moment to pat me on the shoulder. "Thank you for coming down to help. I really appreciate it. You can close up around ten; everyone should have been through by then." She gave my shoulder a small squeeze before walking out the door.

I looked after her for a few moments, frowning at the conversation we had. "There's no way I'd be a good Luna for this pack," I whispered to myself before turning and walking into the back.

It was slow work, looking through all the goods and checking expiration dates. Anything expired was typically what the volunteers ended up taking home to their families, since food was typically good even after the stamped date. Packing everything expired (there wasn't much) into a box and putting it in the corner, I longed for music to keep me company. Around nine-thirty, I succumbed to my desire and put my headphones in, the strings tickling my chin and forcing me to pull them out to untwist the wire so it didn't grate my nerves. "Satellites" by Sleeping with Sirens filled my ears as I took it upon myself to go through the new donations and organize them on the shelves.

Every few moments, I'd peek from the back to see the waiting area empty before disappearing into the back again. As ten o'clock came around, I quit bothering to check the front and focused on getting all the recent donations put away. I was pleased to see how many there were, and how most of them appeared to be new purchases and not just things that had been sitting in a Beta kitchen until the expiration came too close for comfort. My lips twisted as I saw a box with the mailing label still on it. The Wilkins' address popped out at me and my mind drifted to Kyle and the way he'd looked at me at lunch. Sighing, I pushed it to the back of my mind so I could focus.

Collapsing the last box, I put it in the main room where the cardboard was stored for later use. We tried to keep the extras in case someone forgot a box or didn't have one to bring. Closing and locking up all the doors, I hummed along to "Memories" by EarlyRise while I gathered all my things. My stomach grumbled hungrily, but I ignored it as I typically did. The feeling would fade before long anyway.

I was tossing my backpack over my shoulder when a splash of color caught my attention. Sitting on the seat of my bike was a stunning amaryllis, the petals wide open in a proud display of crimson. Tilting my head to the side, I reached out and picked it up, looking for a note and finding none. Figuring it was a gift from Ezra as an apology, I found it odd that he didn't stop in to see me. Maybe he didn't want to bother me while I was working. I sighed heavily and pulled my phone from my pocket to send him a quick text.

> You're forgiven. Just don't keep secrets from me, okay?

Hitting send, I watched the blue bubble appear before shutting off my phone and tucking it into the back pocket of my jeans. I hopped on my bike and started riding down the sidewalk. The clinic wasn't far away, but I felt the need to get there quickly. I was certain dad hadn't eaten all day. He was typically so busy, he didn't get the chance. With the amaryllis safely tucked behind my right ear, I hopped off the curb to ride on the street.

It only took a few minutes to get to my destination. The building looked as run down as all the others. A sign on the window beside the front door said "CLINIC" in large, red letters. Dad had asked me to make it a few months prior to replace the last one I'd made. Every year or so, I had to make a new sign for the place as the old one faded and yellowed in the sun. The door was unlocked, the bell ringing above my head as I entered the building. Inside, it was much brighter than it looked from the street. Dad was meticulous, and the nurse that helped him, Alice Jones, kept the place sterile and professional.

Unable to put them anywhere else, Dad's degrees hung on the wall behind the registration desk: one from Potencia Sui Generis for magical medicinal studies and one from SUNY Upstate Medical University for human medicine. I'd asked him once how he'd managed to attend two schools at the same time. He insisted that they only overlapped a little. I assumed it just took a little while. Callum and I weren't born until our parents were in their forties. They were still pretty young, but it was uncommon to wait that long in Scarlet Moon. Ezra told me once that other packs were often into their fifties before having children so they could be established. Waiting that long wasn't so strange when the average lifespan of a volsifi was three-hundred years.

I jumped as a baby crying broke into my thoughts. Placing a hand over my racing heart, I took a deep breath before dropping my backpack onto one of the waiting room chairs to fish out dad's dinner. Taking a seat, I pulled out my phone to see no response from Ezra and frowned.

Dad's voice came from the back, causing me to smile. "Congratulations, Alma and David. It's your first baby girl," he said. Then, quieter, "Alice, I believe I heard the bell ringing. Could you go see who it is?"

Footsteps came my way and I hurried to stand with my container of stir fry. The door behind the desk opened and a pretty young woman appeared, her thick chestnut hair tied in a braid that hung down her back. Green eyes, just like her brother's, sparkled in greeting above the blue surgical mask she wore. "Hi, Cadence! I'll let your dad know you're here." She nodded her head to me before disappearing again as the door closed with a loud click.

Plopping back into my seat, I looked at my phone again and was relieved to see a message from Ezra at last.

Ezra

> I appreciate your forgiveness, though I don't deserve it. No more secrets.

My lips pressed together as I typed out a response.

> Of course, you deserve it. I'm sorry I reacted the way I did. I just wish I didn't hear it from her.

I was about to put my phone away when it vibrated again.

Ezra

> I wish you hadn't either. It won't happen again. I love you.

I smiled at my phone, biting down on my lower lip.

> I love you too.

Satisfied with that, I put my headphones back in and put on "Alright" by Charlotte Sands. Closing my eyes, I tilted my head back and let the guitar intro lull me into a pleasant peace.

Just as the song was coming to an end, I heard the door open and lifted my head to see my dad approaching me. He had a tired smile on his face and that made me sad. I wished I could relieve more of the burden on him. Standing, I held out the container of dinner to him and his brows raised.

"Thank you, Cade. I appreciate you bringing me food, since I'm going to be here a little while longer to make sure Alma's able to go home in the morning." A rough edge to his voice betrayed just how exhausted he was, pulling my heartstrings.

I nodded, knowing better than to say anything about it now. "I figured it would be a late night. Babies are never predictable."

He chuckled and nodded, brushing his fingers through his hair and making it stick up awkwardly in the front. "No, they are not. Neither are teenagers, it seems," he mused aloud, his dark eyes dropping to the container of food in his hand. It was a sad excuse for dinner, but it was better than nothing. "Thank you again, Cadence. You should be getting home, though. It's already late and I worry about you. I'll watch you on that app thing and make sure you get home safely, okay?"

Dad pulled me into a tight hug, squeezing me so hard I could barely breathe, and I did my best to squish him just as much. He laughed again, pulling back and ruffling my hair. "I love you, Cady."

"I love you too, dad." I picked up my backpack and tossed it over my shoulders. "I'll text you when I get home if I remember."

He smiled and shook his head. "You and I both know you won't remember. That's why we got this ridiculous app," he muttered, pulling his phone from his pocket and wiggling it at me.

I nodded, walking toward the door. I turned back to him and smiled. "Try not to stay out too late." Without waiting for a response, I left the clinic and hopped back onto my bike for the couple mile trek to my house from the heart of the Omega's territory.

The sky was overcast, sporadic rays of sunshine broke through the covering to stream down to the ground around me. Beneath my feet, the grass was damp and leaving little drops of water on the pink paint on my toenails. I didn't remember painting my toenails. Maybe Alex did and I forgot.

"Remember me?"

The smooth voice made my breath catch in my throat and I turned to see the boy walking toward me. Though calling him a boy was unfair. He was at least a year or two older than me. Even as I thought it, I wasn't sure why or how I knew that. Even as I tried to focus on his face, it didn't really appear. It was like I could see him better if I was turned away, but it still wasn't concrete.

The clouds shifted away from the sun, the light sparkling around the small clearing as the water drops shined in ethereal prisms.

"How could I forget my dream guy?" I murmured, clasping my hands in front of me.

I reached out and touched his arm, but it lacked substance. It was like holding on to a vaguely corporeal cloud.

"I know."

He slid his arm from under my grip to hold my hand in his. His fingers were long, the larger knuckles making them look thicker than they actually were. Raising my hand, he gently pressed his lips to my knuckles. A deep rumble echoed in his chest, making my entire body tremble in response.

"I'm grateful for your constant presence. You are the sun in my stormy life, even if my brain conjured you so long ago. Sometimes I wonder if I have multiple personalities and you are the better of the two."

I swallowed, not sure how to respond. "Sometimes I wonder that too. Like maybe I created you so that I could have one person I could truly talk to about anything. Since you're a figment of my imagination, you're a piece of me. That comes without judgment." My voice cracked as I spoke, and I felt his grip tighten on my fingers in response.

"Is everything alright, Hathor?"

"Why do you call me Hathor?" I deflected his question with one of my own. "You've called me that for years, but you've never told me why."

He was silent for so long, I thought maybe he'd vanished, and I hadn't noticed. I shifted my fingers, but they were still entwined with his.

"Because she was the Egyptian Goddess of many things, but some mythology says she was the protector of dreams. She carried the sun on her headdress between two cow horns. Your presence makes me feel like the sun is shining. It's like the sun only feels real when I'm here with you. She was maternal and associated with beauty, love, dancing, and music. It's said she was also one of the most powerful goddesses."

I felt my forehead crease. "That's a lot of meaning in that name, Silas."

He chuckled and I bit my lip.

"And why is it that you call me Silas?"

I flushed, feeling the heat in my cheeks. "Because we meet near a forest, and that's what Silas means," I said, gesturing behind him to the tree line that was always partially hidden by fog.

He turned to look where I was pointing, then burst into laughter so loud it startled me. The sound was rich, coming from deep in his chest. It echoed in the ravine behind me, giving it the effect of being surrounded by him.

He sighed as his laughter died off. "I haven't laughed like that in a long time, if ever," he said, squeezing my fingers. Leaning forward, he gently pressed his lips to my forehead. "I hope whatever topic you're avoiding turns out okay," he whispered, his breath tickling my face.

An annoying beeping sound was filling the space around us and I looked around. "Do you hear that?" I asked, using the distraction as a convenient excuse to continue ignoring the topic of my problems.

He shook his head. "No. I don't hear anything but your racing heartbeat."
I scoffed at him, pulling away as the world started to dissolve around me.
"Don't forget me," I called out as consciousness pulled at me.
"Dream of me, and I'll be there."

Chapter 9

CADENCE

The next day, Ezra and I walked into the school as normal, ignoring Brody as he whistled at me. Looking back, I noticed that Kyle was not joining in on their buffoonery. A frown appeared on my face, and I had to resist the urge to glare at them. Walking to my locker, Alex met us on the way with a gleeful smile on her face that told me she had gossip to drop on us. Salt, rose, and patchouli followed her and my body relaxed.

"I heard that Jessica was caught cheating in Trig and earned herself a detention," she whispered conspiratorially, practically grinning from ear to ear with glee.

I glanced at her before shoving my bag into my locker. "Good for her. That's the least of what she deserves." I closed the door with a sharp bang. Turning toward her, I hugged my book to my chest. Ezra huffed behind me, and I glanced at him, scowling as he grinned at me.

Alex smiled broadly like this was the greatest news in the world. "What she needs is to find a guy so she can leave Ezra alone. Wouldn't that be lovely?" she inquired, her hazel eyes flitting over Ezra's shoulder. I turned to see her looking at Jason as he and Brody continued to watch the three of us from down the hall, though Kyle had disappeared. I rolled my own eyes at both of them before turning my back. "It's a shame Jason's her brother, because they would be a perfect, horrible couple."

Leaning against my locker, I let my eyes drift over the students wandering toward their homerooms. My eyes settled on Jessica Barber and her two friends, Allie and Joy, as they sashayed through the hall toward us. It was as if speaking of the demonic spawn herself truly did bring her forth. Growling in my throat as Jessica's amber eyes locked onto Ezra, I glowered at her in the hope that it would force her to walk away. It didn't.

"Hey, Ezra. Do you have any plans for this weekend?" she flirted before sinking her teeth into her lower lip as she appraised him. I wondered if she actually thought that move was attractive when she did it. The way she ogled him disgusted me on a visceral level and I stared at her around Ezra's broad frame while Alex glared at her and her friends.

Ezra, not skipping a single beat, turned to me and moved back a step so I wasn't hidden behind him. "Cadence, want to spend the weekend with me?" He ramped up the charm like he actually needed to woo me.

I smiled brightly at him, nodding enthusiastically. "Of course," I answered, shifting my gaze back to Jessica. I dropped the smile and put on the surliest expression I could manage.

Ezra smiled politely at Jessica, causing a flush to redden her cheeks. "Sorry. Looks like I have plans."

Jessica looked as if she'd been slapped before she pouted in Ezra's direction and leaned toward him. "You'd seriously rather spend time with this fat butterball than me? You know that your father wants us together," she whined, batting her lashes in his direction as if that would make him realize he'd want to be with her instead.

My jaw dropped and I felt shame as my face flushed with humiliation. Of course, she'd go for the fat dig. I wasn't surprised she'd be that unoriginal, but it didn't make it sting any less. Closing my jaw with a sharp click of my teeth, I considered just walking away from the entire situation but hazarded a glance at Ezra first. I was pleased with the steely glare he leveled on Jessica.

"Get off of me. If there was ever any chance you had with me, which there wasn't, you just killed it with that comment." His voice was low and gravelly with rage; he was giving her a warning with his tone. I felt warned, and he wasn't even leveling any of his judgment on me.

Jessica floundered, seemingly speechless from the harsh rejection. It seemed she didn't move fast enough for Alex, who didn't hesitate any longer and gave the redhead a shove. "He said back up, bitch," she snarled as she continued advancing and invading Jessica's space.

Frantically backing away from my best friend who was officially in attack mode, Jessica stumbled over her own feet. "I didn't mean it," she pleaded, her voice a hushed whisper as she cowered from Alex. Jessica's friends, the ever-loyal posse that they were, ran down the quickly emptying hallway as the threat of a physical confrontation lurked in the near future.

"Didn't mean it, my ass." Alex backed Jessica against the lockers across the hall. "You will never speak about Cadence that way again. And you *will* get far away from Ezra. He's taken and not interested in vile people like you."

Jessica was wide eyed as she shuffled sideways to get away from a fiery Alex. The blonde backed up, allowing our mutual enemy to slide away from her before walking away in a hurry. "Oh yes, do run, and jump, and skip. Coward!" she called to her retreating back. I may have been the only one to appreciate the Sleepy Hollow quote but didn't have time to relish that.

Ezra and I could only watch helplessly as she backed directly into Mr. Rutger, who seemed to appear out of nowhere. His brown eyes seemed to glow as Alex whipped around to face him with a muttered apology. Mr. Rutger looked her over for a moment before he got a wide smile on his face that was equal parts disarming and charming.

"Not a problem, Miss Pierce. Hopefully there's not a problem here?" He put his hands out to the sides to gesture to the group of us. His gaze flickered down the hall to Jessica as she hurried around a corner and disappeared before returning to Alex as she continued to stand in front him.

"There's no problem," I assured him, unable to stop myself from speaking. "Just a misunderstanding," I added as his dark gaze swept to me. I felt my breath catch in my throat as he examined me closely for what felt like an extraordinarily long time before his easy smile returned and he nodded.

"Very well. Hurry on to class, then. I do believe you are about to be late."

The late bell rang. Alex and I linked arms and walked toward our home-room as Ezra split apart from us and hastily moved in the opposite direction with Mr. Rutger following him.

After lunch, we all found ourselves in Mr. Bowman's class in our usual seats. Alex, just behind me, leaned over her desk again to whisper in my ear. "I will never regret being in this man's class. He is a god among men, I swear. Look at those biceps when he comes in, my goddess!"

Mr. Bowman swept into the room just as the bell rang. We had finished *To Kill a Mockingbird* and had moved on to *The Outsiders*. I was definitely a fan of the movie, having had a celebrity crush on C. Thomas Howell and Patrick Swayze since I'd first seen it a couple years ago. I hoped that part of our lesson would be to watch the movie again.

We all watched, a couple girls giggling in the back, as Mr. Bowman slid the last couple feet toward his desk and hopped up to sit upon it. He gave us a brilliant grin that had most of the girls in the room swooning and sighing around me. I had to admit, a part of me could not get past how attractive he was, but I still didn't understand how some people could just swoon over someone because of their looks. What if he was actually a total troll in personality? I was also supremely distracted by Ezra sitting directly in front of me. I reached out and tugged on one of his golden, rogue waves. He glanced over his shoulder at me with a grin.

"Alright. *The Outsiders*. Did everyone read the assigned chapters over the weekend?" He clapped his hands together as if he didn't already have everyone's rapt attention.

Various answers came from around the room, and he chuckled as he stood up. "I'm pleased with your honesty at the very least, though I wish more of you had at least attempted to finish the assignment." Rubbing his palms together, he eyed the classroom with a swing of his head. "Who read the first four chapters? Raise your hand."

Hesitantly, each of our trio raised our hands as well as some random others around the room. I was smug in the pettiest of ways that Jessica was not one of the ones who raised her hand. It took quite a bit of restraint to not smirk and played off the action by rubbing my lower lip inconspicuously like it had an itch.

"Okay. Good. At least half of you care about your education. Good to know. This is why I love my job," he said, the sarcasm laid on thick. "Since we are on the subject of how much I love my job, does anyone know why exactly I got into teaching English? I'm hoping if you understand my motives, maybe you'll bother to do your homework." His silver eyes scanned the room before landing on me and a flush of dread immediately heated my face. "Cadence?" he asked me, nodding his head in my direction.

I looked down at the cover of my book, staring at the leather jacket printed on it. Before I could put myself together enough to respond, I heard a voice muttering behind me. "Of course he would pick the butterball. His favorite holiday must be Thanksgiving." I wasn't sure if Jessica meant to be quiet or not, but she wasn't. I slid down in my seat in shame as a couple other people laughed, wishing a giant hole would open up in the floor so I could jump into it. Facing Kuorir, the God of Death and the Underworld, seemed like a much more pleasant experience than being humiliated in front of an entire class over something beyond my control.

I heard Alex whip around to face the ginger wench in the back of the class with a snarl that made chills erupt over my arms. My eyes lifted to Mr. Bowman's and his steely stare levelled at me like he was trying to decide if he wanted to intervene or if I would stand up for myself. His gaze swept over me slowly as if he was sizing me up and I suddenly wasn't sure if I wanted to measure up or not. Deciding that I didn't want to be a spineless wimp, I sat upright and straightened before turning to face the bully in question.

"Please, Jessica. Is that the best you can come up with? You already used that fat insult today. Maybe you should just admit that you're jealous you don't have big boobs and leave it at that?" I gave her a slight shimmy of my chest before turning my back to her as her jaw dropped and more students laughed than before.

My lips pressed together in a desperate attempt to hide the grin that wanted to display itself on my face, and I noted that Mr. Bowman was hiding his own with a thumb pressed into the corner of his mouth.

Jessica huffed behind me for a moment before she finally responded. "I'm not sure having big tits is worth jiggling like the world's biggest jelly mold."

I didn't even have time to react before Ezra stood up and turned around to face her. "Drop it, Jessica. Quit pretending like you have any standing in this pack. Cadence is your future Luna, so perhaps you should do your best to stay on her good side. You don't want her remembering moments like this when she has your life and future in her hands, do you?" He spoke calmly, as if he was telling her the weather. Again, I wasn't sure that I wanted him claiming that if we weren't sure, but I didn't stop him. Undermining his authority wouldn't help any of us, especially since his thinly veiled threat seemed to have its desired effect.

Jessica's mouth snapped shut with an audible click of her teeth, and I glanced back to see her face blushing a red that contrasted starkly with her hair as she sunk down into her seat. *It must suck to be rejected by the prince twice in the same day. I wouldn't know.*

Finally, Mr. Bowman stepped in and gave Jessica a final warning before continuing. "Back to the lesson. Why do I teach English? I need to inspire you to actually care. If that's possible."

There was a resounding silence throughout the room, no one speaking a word and everyone waiting breathlessly for the answer.

"Because I enjoy how one piece of fiction can mean something different to every single person who reads it. It's like how being able to see how someone sees art tells you a lot about them, and I enjoy getting to know people in their truest capacity. I'm fascinated by what makes someone who they are. Now that you know, maybe you'll put a bit more care into your work, yes? Start seeing the joy in learning about yourself and others."

I stared at him for a moment, taking in his profile carefully. He had a straight nose, high cheekbones, and expressive thin lips. His words resonated in me as if he was pulling that explanation from my very soul. I also enjoyed learning about people on a deep and intimate level. It was easily one of my favorite things.

"That's . . . beautiful," I responded breathily, ever the awkward troll that I was.

Jessica's harsh voice rose from behind me, pulling me from my thoughts like a bomb. "Wow. Just when I thought you couldn't be any more of a freak, you just keep surprising me."

Mr. Bowman gave me a look I couldn't interpret before dismissing Jessica to the principal's office and resuming his lesson once again.

Chapter 10

CADENCE

It had been a couple of weeks since Ezra and I had shared our first kiss . . . and a couple more. It felt like anytime he got the chance, his lips or hands were on me. It felt like he couldn't ever get enough contact with me. I didn't usually mind. Sometimes it was overstimulating, but most of the time I found myself enjoying it.

However, I did wonder if I was broken, because no matter how much I enjoyed the sensation of him touching me or kissing me as his hands wandered over my back, the last thing I ever wanted to do or thought of was taking it further than that. Alex was hellbent on being the first person to know if we decided to "do it," as she so eloquently put it. I wasn't in a rush, though, and Ezra didn't seem to be either. I really just enjoyed exploring his soul through his kisses. It was like I could read his mind when his mouth was on mine, but maybe that was part of being mates, though I still wasn't convinced that we were.

I frowned in the mirror at myself, trying desperately not to make those typical, weird faces as I applied my mascara. I was disinterested in wearing a ton of makeup today, deciding only to accentuate my unique eyes. The splash of blue that broke up the solid blackness of the rest of my left iris deserved all the attention that it got. I tried to ignore the creeping feeling that something about me felt . . . off today. Heaving a sigh and ignoring my gut, I used a hair dryer brush to beat my damp hair into submission. It was naturally a tighter wave, but I preferred it to be straight; it appeared smoother that way. Ezra and Alex occasionally convinced me to wear it more naturally, but it was a battle they didn't often win.

The holiday break was starting tomorrow, and I was dreading being away from Ezra for Novzima. His dad always threw a huge party for New Winter holiday on the Alpha Estate, and my family had been disinvited and banned most of my life; ever since my twin, Callum and my grandma were taken. Though I had asked my dad several times why we weren't allowed to even go to the party like literally everyone else, he never really gave me an answer.

Pushing that thought out of my brain with violence I could only muster against myself, I instead got dressed and went downstairs. I felt oddly flushed but disregarded it; perhaps it was from the blow drier. Goddess knows it gets incredibly hot. I'd also chosen to wear a sweater and that surely did not help, no matter how thin it was. I was almost to the bottom of the stairs when I turned and went back to my bedroom. Shedding the sweater, I decided not to torture myself with the overstimulation of being too hot. I pulled on an oversized band tee, "Set It Off" emblazoned in white across the black fabric. A smile teased my lips as I remembered the concert Ezra and Alex took me to for my seventeenth birthday. We rarely left the pack territory, it was frowned upon, but occasionally we would sneak out to see our favorite bands live or movies. The nearest city that held any kind of event was hours away, but it was always worth the drive.

Dad was already gone for the day by the time I got downstairs, but he left out a box of cereal and the milk on the table as if I couldn't have gotten that for myself. I resisted the urge to roll my eyes as I took advantage of his attention. At least he cared, unlike mom. I tried to avoid her gaunt face and haunted eyes as much as possible. You never knew when she was going to lash out. The woman hadn't shifted in years, and you could tell by her atrophied muscles and the way her eyes were lifeless. I refused to live like that. I knew that Callum was her child, but he was my twin. We shared a womb until we were born and then we shared everything after that. Dad told me all the time that we couldn't sleep if we weren't in the same bed, even as infants. After he vanished? The nightmares came.

Pulling myself out of the memory lane of horrors I was wandering along in my brain, I hurriedly ate my cereal so I'd have time to brush my teeth before Ezra arrived. Everyone knows that milk makes your breath unpleasant (something about bacteria or whatever; I hate biology), and our kissing was too new to have anything less than the freshest of breath. I'd even started carrying breath strips and gum. The thought of having halitosis was enough to make me never kiss anyone again, no matter how much I enjoyed it.

Fortunately, I did have enough time to brush my teeth. I was just putting the toothbrush back into the cup when I heard Ezra honk the horn. Still feeling overheated, I neglected to put on my jacket and instead slung it over my arm as I hurried out the door. Over the past several weeks, the rain had turned into snow and thick flakes were released from the clouds to dance to the earth . . . and my hair. There were already a few inches gracing the ground, and I knew there would be more of it later. Snowman snow was my favorite, though it wasn't the best for driving. Fortunately, Ezra was an excellent driver for having only a couple of years of experience. He was as meticulous with driving as he was with everything else he did. I had to believe it was partially those golden boy tendencies he had.

Hurrying toward the car, I was careful not to slip on the slush that instantly formed on the ground under my boots. Darn this northeastern mountain weather. It was always so erratic and emotional; you never knew what you were going to get when you walked outside. One of my favorite things was when the sun was shining brightly, but it was frigid outside. It felt like mother nature was trying to trick you, and I enjoyed the game. Walking outdoors sometimes felt like a shock to the system. Today, the bite of the breeze felt amazing on my arms, and I felt vindicated in my choice of not putting on a coat.

As I plopped into the car, I glanced at the look on Ezra's face. His voice sounded as concerned as his eyes looked when he asked, "Aren't you cold? Your face is really flushed."

"It would have to be a lot colder than this to chill my already frozen heart." I gave a beaming smile as he shook his head.

"Whatever," he responded simply with a deep chuckle that I swear I could feel in my bones. It made me want to grab and kiss him.

Leaning over, Ezra closed the space between us as he read my mind. He pressed his lips to mine for a moment before jerking away from me. His blond brows furrowed as he examined me, taking in my face like he was looking for something.

"What?" I was concerned that something was wrong with me or my breath. I resisted the urge to breathe into my hand to check or immediately put in a breath strip.

"Do you have a fever?" He reached out to touch my forehead with the back of his fingers. "You're so hot."

I flushed, confused. Deciding to play it off with humor, I gave him a flirty smile. "Thank you."

He sighed and straightened, glancing at me out of the corner of his eye like he wasn't sure if I was messing with him or not. Letting it drop, he put the car in gear and pulled away from the sidewalk.

The drive was quiet other than "East & West" by In Her Own Words playing on the radio. I tried very hard not to fidget in my seat. It was impossible not to notice that Ezra was deep in thought, though the content of those thoughts was what really bothered me. While I felt like something was off with me, his noticing as well did not make me feel any better. Despite knowing him most of my life and being very, very close with him and knowing he would never judge me, it didn't mean that his judgement wasn't of the utmost concern to me. His thoughts and opinions mattered to me very much, and I was concerned he thought something was wrong with me. Though rationality told me he was probably just worried I was sick, that didn't stop my stupid brain from worrying about the worst.

Thanks, anxiety.

Ezra seemed to relax by the time we got to school, and Alex only pointed out that I looked flushed and left it at that. Brody only made one lewd comment during trigonometry before lunch, leaning over his desk to murmur in my ear. I ignored him as I always did if he said anything that crossed my boundaries of comfort. I knew that he was only hitting on me so he could make fun of me with his stupid friends, Kyle and Jason, if I fell for it. No one was interested in the butterball . . . only Ezra, and I still didn't entirely believe that most of the time.

After fifth period, I was on my own once again and heading downstairs to Species Cultures class. It was easily the most interesting class since Mrs. Walker often ignored direct orders to keep us completely sheltered. Alpha Lucien was of the firm belief that we were volsifi and that was the only species we should bother to know anything about. Mrs. Walker had taken frequent vacations around the world, meeting and learning about other species before settling down with her mate in the pack.

I'd just entered the stairwell when a hand grabbed my shoulder, nails digging into my flesh before I was pushed back against the wall. Glaring upward, I expected to see Brody and was unpleasantly surprised that instead I was staring into angry amber eyes.

"Listen up, freak. You're to back away from Ezra. He's *mine*, and that's an order from the Alpha," she grunted, spittle flying from her mouth and onto my face in moist flecks. It was physically painful to not wipe the speckles away from my flesh, and I forced all that agony into a glare as I looked up at her.

My brain frantically shuffled through anything to say, and I came up blank. Instead of saying something witty or condescending, I stared up at her with a furiously empty expression. Her mouth curved into a wicked smirk, and she backed up a little bit, allowing me to take a breath I didn't know I'd been holding.

"Oh, so you have nothing to say when you don't have your guard dogs backing you up. I'll keep that in mind. You're a spineless weakling if you don't have Alex and Ezra to fight for you. Now I know to attack you when you're alone." She took a couple more steps back as her smirk dissolved into a glare. "I mean it, bitch. Stay away from him. I'll make sure to get close to him at the Novzima ball. The one you won't be invited to," she threatened before cackling loudly and making me jump as the volume of it ricocheted around the stairwell.

She turned and stomped down the stairs away from me and I took a couple deep breaths as my eyes lifted toward the ceiling in an attempt not to cry. I couldn't let her win, and bursting into tears would definitely give her an undeserved win. Wiping my face, my hands shook with the need to wash her germs from my flesh, but now wasn't the time. I didn't need a detention for being late on top of this.

Pulling my headphones from my bag, I put on a song and let "Fade with Me" by Attack Attack! guide me to my class. Along the way, my fingertips subconsciously brushed over the callus on the heel of my palm. I wished I had an axe to throw, the music not quite cutting it.

As I walked into the class, I paused the music and made my way to my seat in the back of the classroom. Placing my notebook on the desk, I ruffled the edges of the pages, the sensation soothing to my brain as they shuffled against my fingertips. Pulling the buds from my ears, I tucked them into my pocket and stared down at the plain red cover of my notebook.

Mrs. Walker stood up at the front of the class, moving to stand in front of the whiteboard. Gesturing behind her at the word written in black, she asked, "Does anyone know this word and who it refers to?"

No one volunteered an answer at first, including myself. Alex and Ezra were the only two I knew of who had any knowledge about other species. Ezra because he'd met some of them and Alex because her father thought it was important in case of war. Brody was also preparing to be a warrior, though I wasn't sure what his parents bothered to teach him.

A girl at the front of the class raised her hand. "Elv-aff?" she asked, flushing pink as Jessica giggled at her.

Mrs. Walker glared at Jessica before responding, "Close. It's pronounced El-va-fay. This species, while similar to human depictions of fairies, differs in various ways. They do have wings, their color and shape typically corresponding to something about them, like their gift if they have one. They tend to have magic relating to earthly elements even if they don't have a particular gift outside of that."

She paused, looking over the classroom. "Does anyone know anything about the royal family?"

Again, no one raised their hands and she scowled. "The current king of the elvafe is Ramses Sayed. His son, Meruem, will turn twenty-one in June and is preparing to take his father's place on the throne next summer. They live in the Stargazer Kingdom, the door of which is located not far from here. It is somewhere in the Appalachian Mountains in Pennsylvania, though the exact location is heavily guarded. Only an elvafe can access any of the kingdoms using their earth magic.

"This is typically the point in the lesson where I would show you the royal family, but the elvafe are distrustful of technology and therefore have no pictures anywhere I've ever been able to find. King Ramses has one son, Prince Meruem. Meruem is often called the Dark Prince for his ruthlessness in battle and execution style. He is incredibly powerful and has the gift of natural disasters, including storms like tornadoes, blizzards, earthquakes ... If you can think of it, he can do it. It has been said that his favorite is lightning and that he executes criminals by striking them in front of the gathering kingdom to keep the populace in line. It's this rumor that's earned him the moniker of Dark Prince. He is the future King of the Elvafe."

The students were silent for the rest of the class.

I could not wait to escape the stuffy building that felt as if it were closing in on me. All of the students crowding around me made me feel like I was buried alive in a sea of people – of hot bodies all focused on themselves as they bumped into me on their way to the freedom of the outdoors. I couldn't wait to join them, but my frustration was climbing and short circuiting my brain. Frozen at my locker, I stared at the spines of my textbooks as I waited for the calamity around me to lessen a bit before I could pull myself together enough to make my exit.

Things quieted down and I felt nothing but relief as I shut my locker door. Glancing around, I looked for those familiar blue eyes and found them approaching from down the hall. As usual, Ezra's golden appearance made my breath catch in my throat and my heart felt several sizes too big for my chest. I calmed down once we were together, but when his baby blue eyes met mine ... he was my salvation, forever rescuing me.

He approached; his smile wide and crinkling the corners of his eyes as he gave me an appraising look. "You're not wearing headphones today," he commented, happiness painting his deep voice. "It will be lovely to have your conversation as we get to leave this hellhole."

Ezra's hand found mine, our fingers lacing, his thumb brushing over my knuckles, as he walked beside me toward the parking lot for students. "Some days are better than others," I told him, as if he didn't already know that. This guy knew me better than I knew myself most of the time.

His fingers gently squeezed mine as he led me to his car so he could drive me home. As usual, I asked him, "Want to hang out for a bit?"

A deep sigh left him as he gripped the steering wheel until his knuckles turned white, distress apparent in his expression and actions. "I can't. The stupid Novzima party is tomorrow, and Lucien wants me home tonight so I can be at 'peak performance' tomorrow in front of all his cohorts." The displeasure in his tone was palpable, emphasized by the inhuman growl in his voice. I barely even flinched when he referred to his own dad by his first name. I did have to resist the urge to shift away from his tone and aura, fighting all my instincts that told me to run from the angry Ascended wolf. I placed my hand on his as it gripped the gear shift. Immediately, the tension building within him relaxed and he gave me a small smile of appreciation.

"There's no one in this galaxy like you," he whispered tenderly, the tension still visible but less oppressive. He always immediately got amped up when his father was mentioned. The reasons why were obvious, though he still refused to talk about it. He hadn't spoken about the abuse he faced at home in years. "I'd be lost without your touch," he added, his voice so quiet that I almost missed it.

A flush warmed my cheeks more than they already were and I resisted the urge to fan myself as heat crept up my neck. "You say that as if you don't have that same effect on me," I murmured, brushing my knuckles over his high cheekbone, eliciting a low growl from him. My hand immediately pulled away on its own, unsure what that noise meant.

"Please don't stop," he pleaded, his pale blue eyes shifting to my face. I could see the need for physical contact there. "It's calming."

I nodded and shifted my fingers through his loose waves, giving them a gentle tug as I combed through them. A small smirk curved my lips as I made them even more disheveled than they usually were.

"I wonder what craziness Alex is going to get into over the weekend." I changed the subject, shifting my gaze out the windshield at the snow falling from the sky and doing an elaborate dance as the wind shifted the flakes about.

Ezra chuckled, shaking his head against my hand that rested on the back of his neck. "Who knows. She was talking the other day about another date with that guy she's been seeing."

"The nipple bruiser." I tried to think of his name, but it was hard to keep up with all of Alex's flavors. I never understood how she could keep them all straight or had the energy to entertain them all. The idea of even speaking to that many people made me tired, though no one would be surprised that I'd rather take a nap than forge multiple romantic relationships.

Another smirk graced Ezra's face as he nodded, a dimple forming in his chin. "Is that his name, then?"

I nodded in answer even though he wasn't looking at me before allowing us to sink back into silence. I was preparing to spend the rest of the drive fantasizing about Ezra's eyes and the way he looked at me until he spoke and startled me out of my thoughts.

"You should come to the Novzima party," he stated suddenly, glancing at me as his fingers gripped the steering wheel harder. Clearly, the idea gave him just as much anxiety as it should.

"I'm not sure that's a great idea. You know that we are pariahs. I'm just grateful that your dad didn't force us out of the pack. I'm not sure I want to push those tiny gracious buttons and try to encroach on his turf." I pulled away from him and turned to stare out my window. The idea of looking Lucien Wolfe in the face made my stomach twist uncomfortably.

I was startled when Ezra's hand landed on my knee, the tips of his fingers digging gently into my thigh. "You're my mate. He's going to have to get over it at some point. You are the rightful Luna to this pack regardless of his wishes. Whatever my father's opinion of you is, the Goddess clearly sees things differently. If I have to choose who to take orders from, it's Levende."

The sound of the Goddess' name on his lips made a shudder trickle down my spine. There was power in that name. I responded with a deep frown, still not looking at him. I didn't have the heart to tell him that I could never be the Luna. I was too broken, uncertain, and terrified. That was a big responsibility and allowed no room for my weaknesses. My self-consciousness could potentially cause catastrophe.

"Come on, Cadybug," he begged, using his childhood nickname for me as he pulled into my driveway. "It's a masquerade ball. No one will even recognize you," he pleaded with me, his sky-blue eyes burning into mine.

"Yes, it's not like I have unique eyes or anything," I replied sarcastically, staring at him with all the intensity that I could muster, imprinting my gaze into his memory.

Ezra's serious face broke into a wide smile, showing off his white teeth. They'd be perfect if one of his front teeth wasn't slightly overlapping the other, just enough to notice. I found it endearing despite how much he'd always hated it. Finding myself grinning stupidly in return, I got lost for a second before sighing heavily. "Okay. What about my scent? That would be easily picked out if he's looking for it," I pointed out, still trying to find any reason not to be in the presence of the Alpha.

"There will be hundreds of people there. There will be so many smells, he could never pick out just yours." He waved a hand as if that was a silly concern.

I sighed again, narrowing my eyes at him for a moment before rolling them. "Fine. What color are we wearing?" I opened the car door to get out.

"Red, of course." His devilish gaze was twinkling as I got out of the car and left him behind as I walked into my mostly empty house.

CHAPTER 11

EZRA

Arriving home, I was not surprised to see servants and extra hired hands running around like mad, setting up for the party. Standing in the middle of the foyer was my father, watching as several people stood on ladders and on the twin arching staircases to decorate the massive evergreen tree he'd gotten. It was the first thing to see when entering the manor through the front door.

Truthfully, Novzima was one of my favorite holidays, simply because the house actually looked alive for a few days before the festivities were over and the whole thing was taken down. Then the estate might as well be a museum about a man with no love in his heart. The plain, white walls were always bare, the only thing to ever decorate was a lavish portrait of my mother above the fireplace in the drawing room. Her golden waves danced about her shoulders, blue eyes glittering with mischief. Her scarlet lips were tilted up in a polite smile as she gazed down at anyone sitting in the stiff, white chairs.

Lucien turned as I approached him, giving me a steady glare before turning back to the tree as the gold and silver ornaments were placed all over it. "Are you ready to celebrate the beginning of a new year and the oncoming winter, Ezra?" His tone indicated he didn't really care how I felt. Everything endearing about our relationship was just for show, to assure everyone that Lucien actually had some kind of soul in that body of his.

I nodded, not bothering to give him a true answer as I shoved my hands into my coat pockets. Glancing around the hall, I frowned as Omegas and Deltas bustled around us to set everything up. The looks on their faces made me uncomfortable, the twinkle in their eyes gone after years of being trampled on by the Betas and my father.

Lucien turned to me again, scowling. "I've spoken with Dr. Barber again. Jessica is your date tomorrow," he ordered, the frigid look in his blue eyes daring me to speak against him.

Looking at him, I steeled myself before giving my head a slight shake. "No, father. I do not have a date to the party tomorrow." My voice left no room for argument. I knew he'd behave if anyone was there to witness, since he couldn't have the underlings talking poor about him or knowing the truth about our lack of love.

His jaw clenched, a muscle ticking near his ear. "Fortunately for you, you do have a date. Her name is Jessica Barber. She will be here at six o'clock sharp. I sent her father a swatch of your tie so that you may match."

My brows raised and the look of triumph on his face showed me the glory he felt at catching me off guard. "Well then, I hope she has a fun night dancing on her own. I do not have a date," I repeated, leaning forward slightly and placing my hand on his upper arm before walking away from him. I knew I'd pay for that move later, but I didn't care. I was growing weary of his meddling.

After spending one of the longest nights of my life locked in my room and studying, the day of the party had finally arrived. It was the Eve of Novzima, and I was excited to spend the evening lost in the festivities with my lovely mate. I resisted the urge to sigh, the black and crimson vest corset that was customary formal wear for men wouldn't allow for that much expansion of my lungs. I stared into the mirror, adjusting the tie knot and the wrist cuffs of my dress shirt. The corset made my lean torso more exaggerated, and I fidgeted with the golden false buttons down the front. As I shifted, the slacks felt snug against my thighs. I would not let my discomfort dull the need to see Cadence. Fortunately, I'd planned things with Alex ahead of time and she'd found a dress for Cadence and a matching mask for me. I had no doubts that she would be the most beautiful woman at the ball and easy to spot among the other attendees, though maybe that wasn't the best thing.

Going downstairs, the catering service my father hired was bustling around, making sure everything was of the utmost perfection, so they didn't face the wrath of my father. There would be other packs here to join us, mostly members of the Volsifi Council and their families. We had to maintain peace between us and stay strongly united. To show weakness would give the other species reason to intervene and stick their noses where they didn't belong. The Volsifi were on good terms with most of the other species, but remained in a cold war with the Elvafe for reasons that were lost with time. I'd asked my father several times, but he never gave an answer as to why. He wasn't one for being very helpful in the most necessary of times, so I wasn't surprised when he was stubbornly silent on this supposedly trivial matter.

It wasn't long before our home was full of people, some I recognized from Council meetings, most I didn't. I paced around the party, doing my part to smile politely at our guests so I didn't have to deal with Lucien and more of his shit later; he still hadn't doled out his punishment from last night and I wasn't eager to add to it.

A man I vaguely recognized as Arthur Greaves from the Harvest Moon Pack stepped into my view. I looked up at his face, one that looked many years older than Lucien's.

"Jolly Novzima, Arthur. I heard you just celebrated your one hundredth birthday last week. I hope it was a wonderful day," I said coolly, eyeing him as he moved to stand beside me.

"Jolly Novzima, Ezra. I did. It was quite lovely, yes. I'm sorry I missed your Ascension last month. My daughter just had *her* first daughter the day prior, and I wanted to return to my pack to see her." Arthur's explanation was unnecessary, and he knew it. He was well aware I didn't expect any of the Council members to hang around after the meeting that morning. "She waited until she was fifty. Something about wanting to be established first. Like that's the woman's duty." He scoffed in disgust.

I looked at him with a raised brow. "I think that's perfectly reasonable. Not everyone can start as young as you, Arthur."

He eyed me. "No. Your father was even younger. He's still a young pup, wielding so much power for his age."

I made a humming noise in vague agreement, pointedly ignoring the jealousy in his tone.

"What of you, Ezra? Going to settle young and bear children immediately?" he imposed, eyeing me sideways.

I shrugged, tucking my hands into the pockets of my slacks. "I'm not sure, Arthur. I think that my opinion is not the only one that matters when children are involved."

Arthur scowled at me. "Whose opinion are you looking for, Ezra? A good mate will do what she's told regardless of her wishes. The man decides the children, especially if he is king."

I refused to deign to look at him, keeping my expression neutral. "My body isn't the one carrying the children, Arthur. Who am I to force that burden upon someone I will love as much as my mate?"

"Did that Cadence put that mentality into your skull, boy?" Arthur growled, clearly displeased with my disagreement.

This time I did look at him, leveling him with a glare. "I came to that opinion on my own, Arthur. Though I do hold Cadence's thoughts in the highest regard."

Arthur chuckled humorlessly. "Quite smitten with her, it would seem."

I didn't give an answer, just continued staring at him.

"Be careful with that harlot. She could be dangerous, and I don't want to see you getting hurt."

My blank stare changed to show my confusion and offense. "Don't pretend to care about my well-being, Arthur. Everyone knows you're hoping to overthrow our rule and take over as King. Perhaps you should focus your midlife crisis on other things, like actually ruling your own pack."

Arthur gritted his teeth, eyeing me with malice. "Lucien was a fool for letting her live." The words were snarled, angry. Even if I was going to question his words, I didn't have the chance before he vanished into the crowd.

Alex arrived at my elbow, distracting me from the conversation, the green in her mask bringing out the green in her hazel eyes. She approached me, the emerald gown swishing around her and the glitter sparkling in the lights. I looked around her, hoping for a glimpse of Cadence and she laughed.

"She's not here yet," she said, her eyes glimmering behind her mask with mischief. "Well, she is, but she asked for a minute alone outside."

I sighed, running my fingers through my hair and glancing as a second figure approached. It took a moment because of the mask, but I recognized him and gave him a nod. "Ivan, are you the mystery man Alex has been seeing?" I asked, a grin slowly appearing on my face.

Alex slapped my arm, and tried to glare at me, though she couldn't hide her smile. "I haven't been keeping him a secret, you just haven't asked."

Both of my brows raised as I appraised her. "Cade and I both asked, and you were tight lipped, Alexis Mae Pierce."

Her face wrinkled at the use of her full name and Ivan laughed. "Well, now you know!" she said, grabbing his hand and pulling him away and leaving me in solitude once more.

I was standing in the entranceway, looking up at the tree that stood between the two arching staircases with unseeing eyes; the red and gold decorum going blurry as my gaze shifted into my mind, getting lost in my thoughts. I ignored the cold wind blowing into the hall as more guests arrived until I heard the whispers all around me. Confused, I blinked the haze in my eyes away before turning around and feeling my breath seize in my lungs.

In front of me stood Cadence, her face flushed with the cold under her mask, her lips parted slightly as she looked up at me. I could never miss the sparkle in her eyes, the splash of blue turning violet as she gave me a heated look that spoke of stolen kisses and late-night murmurings. She was right, the mask could never hide her unique eyes from me. It took every ounce of strength not to grab her to me and crush my lips with hers.

Cady was gorgeous with her dark hair in thick ringlets, half pulled up into a pile on the top of her head. The mask was the color of true red, bringing out the stain on her lips. The dress–*the dress*–was jaw dropping, hugging her curves in the perfect way as the red satin slid over her full hips to the floor with a slit up the side to show a peek of leg as she walked toward me. The deep neckline cut down between her breasts, showing ample cleavage that made my teeth sink into my lower lip and a curse shiver through my barely functioning brain. It was something so unlike anything she'd have chosen herself and I knew I owed Alex all the praises in the world.

If I ever had my doubts that Cadence was a woman and no longer a girl (I didn't), those were quickly dashed against the rocks of my crazed male hormones. This image was in sharp contrast to the little girl I met fourteen long years ago who arrived at the same Novzima party in her red dress and dark pigtails.

There were whispers all around us as she walked up to me and I stood there like a bumbling idiot, searching desperately in my brain for something to say. "I–uh–like your . . . you look beautiful," I stuttered finally, any suave comments I may have had lost as I gazed into her gleaming eyes that were barely hidden by her mask. I had to keep reminding myself that there were others around us and that we weren't alone, my hands shoving themselves in my pockets so I didn't reach for her. I swallowed around the dryness that had suddenly formed in my mouth and shook my head. "Do you want a drink?" I held my arm out for her.

A shy smile lingered on her mouth during my entire stupid fumbling of words, and I wondered if she knew how gorgeous she was or the spell she had cast on me. Her fingers gripped my arm and we walked into the dining room where there was a feast laid out on the long table. Several bowls of punch sat along another counter, the crystal glittering in the light as we walked toward them. She looked over the hors d'oeuvres, plucking up a small square of almond cake with raspberry icing and sugared cranberries perched on it, a classic Novzima dessert, and popping it into her mouth. Chewing happily, she returned to my side as I handed her a glass of hot winter berry punch. She plopped a cinnamon stick in her mug, swirling the deep red liquid before taking a sip.

Her eyes widened and a small moan escaped her that brought a smile to my lips. Cadence downed the rest of the drink, her eyes closed as she savored the taste. When she finished, I took the mug from her hands and placed it in a bin for dirty dishes.

"Ready to dance?" I asked her, holding out my hand. She smiled and placed her hand in mine. I wanted to sweep her into the ballroom where Novzima celebratory symphonies played. The melodies were reminiscent of the Christmas hymns that humans used, something we learned long ago when we'd tried to mingle with them.

Something moved quickly behind Cadence, and before I could see or stop it, steaming red punch was dumped over her head. Cadence did nothing but drop her hand from mine and close her eyes as the hot liquid doused her from above, ruining her hair and dress as it coated her from head to toe. Looking around her, I saw Jessica just behind Jason, her arms crossed over her chest and a pleased smirk on her lips. When she noticed me, her lips twisted down into an ugly scowl.

"Figures I'd find you by the food table with the porker. You could at least *try* to hide your cheating, Ezra Wolfe," she snapped, popping one hip out.

Jason grinned at Cadence as she turned to glare at them. She didn't even give them the satisfaction of attempting to wipe the punch from her face, instead raising her chin. "You'd have to be dating Ezra for him to be cheating on you." I was surprised by the steadiness in her voice.

Jessica stepped toward her, lifting her crimson dress so it didn't drag in the punch. I couldn't help but notice how the color clashed aggressively with her orange hair. "Ezra and I are betrothed, and you'd do well to remember that. It's been determined by our fathers that I am to be the next Luna of this pack. I will not allow some low ranked, overstuffed, ugly bitch from a traitorous family to take my place next to him. Ezra is far too good looking to be with a commoner like you," she ranted, her face getting closer and closer to Cadence's.

I opened my mouth and stepped forward to interject, but I didn't have to. Cadence beat me to it.

"If the only things you care about are ranks and looks, you will be sorely disappointed when you're ninety years-old, your looks are gone, and your Beta children cut you off because they cannot tolerate the hatred in your heart," she retorted, jabbing one finger in Jessica's face. In this proximity, I noticed the slight tremor in it. "Is your soul so rotted by your hatred that you can't even see Ezra for everything he is? If all you can see in him are his looks and status, you're no more deserving of him than I am."

With that, she slammed her shoulder against Jessica's and stormed out of the room. I went to go after her, but Jessica's talons found their way into the flesh of my wrist. Stopping, I turned to look at her and saw a pleading look in her eyes and her lower lip pushed out in a pathetic pout. "Let go of me, Jessica."

I suddenly realized the silence in the room. Glancing around, I noted everyone staring at us and realized that the entire scene had been witnessed several times over. Pressing my lips together, I stared at her while she floundered for a response.

"You've been promised to me, Ezra. And I want what's mine." She wrapped one arm around my waist and pressed to me. Revolted, I went still as stone and continued to look down at her with the blank expression I presented to my father.

Jessica's lower lip popped out in a pout, putting on a show for everyone watching us. She lifted her head, pursing her lips as if she were going to kiss me and I raised my chin up and out of her reach.

"Get off of me," I demanded, my voice low and as menacing as I could make it. "I will never be with you. I would rather take my own life than spend it with you. The grip of death and facing Kuorir is much preferred to being chained to you."

She loosened her grip, a stunned look on her face. "How could you say such horrible things to your future mate?" she whimpered, her eyes glimmering with tears.

I scoffed at her. "Stop with the fake waterworks, Jessica. You're not my future mate. No matter what schemes our fathers concoct, they cannot force the hands of the Goddess." I pushed her off of me and walked away to find Cadence.

CADENCE

Leaving the confrontation, I felt hot and uncomfortable, and not just because of the hot punch that was growing colder by the minute. My first move was to go upstairs and away from the majority of the partygoers. I was certain that some had trickled upstairs, but I could just ignore them. Grabbing my bag, I pulled out my phone to aid in that task. Some liquid had gotten in, but it was mostly on my headphones. The cord was sticky with the sugary drink, but I couldn't stop. The need for music was overwhelming me and I jammed the wet headphones in my ears and plugged them into my phone. My heart shattered as they made a horrid static noise before shutting off entirely, my connection to the solace I needed was gone and I couldn't afford to replace them.

I ripped the cord out of my phone and tossed them onto the floor to crush an earbud with the toe of my pump, the destruction causing a smidgen of relief. Closing my handbag with a snap, I continued through the halls in search of a bathroom to at least wash my face. The sticky heaviness of my dress was getting to me and humming a tune was not helping.

I was worried at first that I wouldn't be able to find the bathroom in this gigantic building filled with long hallways, countless stairs, and huge rooms. This had been the Alpha's manor for centuries, and thus was set up for endless visitors and meetings through the ages. Old money and lavish houses passed down from generation to generation until it ended up in the hands of Lucien Wolfe, though he didn't deserve it.

As I was walking through yet another upstairs hallway and cursing myself for storming off and not bringing Ezra with me, I heard water running behind a doorway and I paused to wait for the room to become available. Unfortunately, when the heavy wooden door opened and revealed Lucien himself, my heart stuttered in my chest. I did my best to give him a pleasant smile and hide the fear that sent a tremor down through my fingers, hoping my mask would keep my identity hidden until he moved past me to return to the party. As it seemed, my luck was so poor that I rolled a zero on a twenty-sided die for all events this evening. For those who don't know, that's a critical failure in Dungeons and Dragons.

Lucien's frigid blue eyes landed on my face, examining me as if he could look through the mask to my identity hidden beneath. In actuality and much to my dismay, it would seem that he could.

"*You,*" he snarled, one long, pale finger pulling away from the crystal tumbler in his hand and pointing at me as he stormed across the wide hall toward me. Involuntarily, I backed up until I was pressed up against the wall behind me, the surface cold on my wet, bare back. I could feel my skin sticking to the paint and it made me wince. "What are *you* doing here?" His icy eyes glared daggers into me.

"I was invited," I whimpered, immediately wanting to kick myself for throwing Ezra under the bus. Though, on second thought, I supposed Alex could have invited me as well.

"*Invited?*" A cold smirk curved his cruel slash of a mouth as he glared down at me, his eyes as empty as his soul. I realized I'd never truly been afraid until this moment, my eyes wide as I looked up into his, sensing nothing but hatred for me. "You will never be invited here, you *abomination.*" His voice was low and menacing and chilled me to the bone.

Shamefully, I cowered away from him, cringing as his aura washed over me and making my heart thump painfully against my ribs. I wanted to be stronger and have more of a spine in the face of confrontation like I did when Ezra and Alex were with me. I wanted to be able to stand up to him and question why he hated me so much. Instead, I withered at his words, trying to turn my face away from his.

That move must have angered him more, because he aggressively grabbed my chin with his free hand, forcing my eyes to look up into his as his fingertips dug into my face. Shifting his grip, he held onto my jaw as if shattering it in his hand would solve the world's problems. I figured it might just solve his problems anyway. "You are an abomination, and you come from a family of traitors. You are not welcome here, and you should be grateful I didn't force you and your worthless family to leave the pack when I found out about your family's transgressions." His tone was quiet and dripped a venom that made my eyes water and my heart squeeze. I was fairly certain I'd rather he was screaming at me.

"My son, as worthless as he is, deserves better than to be seen around this pack with the likes of *you*," he scolded, his volume raising as he towered over me, his face coming within a couple inches of mine. I no longer wished he was yelling at me. The smell of black licorice wrapped around me, and every inhale pulled more and more of the acrid scent into my nostrils until I was suffocating with it. "Leave him alone. I will not have some monstrosity such as yourself mingling with the future Alpha. My grandchildren will not be atrocities like you. He already has a mate that I've determined is more appropriate for the role of this pack's Luna. Jessica Barber is far superior in every way, and I will not stop until Ezra realizes that."

With a sneer of abhorrence, he released my jaw while attempting to push me away from him. The back of my head slammed against the wall behind me, throwing stars into my vision. His soulless, pale eyes stared at my left eye with such detestation that I cowered away from him. "And you're offensively weak, too. You don't deserve to belong to the Scarlet Moon pack if you can't even keep your spine straight in the face of your Alpha," he chastised, glaring at me. "If I'd had my way, you would have been slaughtered when I found out about you. Taken out to pasture and . . ." He pulled the index finger of the hand holding the glass across his throat in a horrid gesture, sloshing the green liquid inside of it dangerously close to the rim of the tumbler. "Just like what I hope happened to your worthless brother. Culled to keep the weak from growing and soaking up resources like useless sponges only to reproduce and create more hopeless invalids."

"I am *not* worthless. I'm intelligent and I will accomplish something with my life. My father is brilliant and did not deserve to be down caste because of whatever *you* decided that he and my mother did wrong. My brother is alive, and I will find him once I Ascend and can escape the walls of this *pack.*"

Lucien looked at me appraisingly, making it obvious he detested what he saw. "The audacity in you to speak to me like that. I will not have it." He walked away from me before glancing back over his shoulder. "Try not to go diving into punch bowls like a pig in a sty. I know it's hard when your worthless parents can't afford to feed you, but do try." He looked me up and down, taking in my sticky appearance. "It doesn't bode well for your already poor status in this pack. Leave my home at once and do not return. You will never be welcome here."

As he walked away, I did my very best to maintain my composure until he was out of sight. Hurrying into the bathroom, I tried to calm myself down, my breath coming out in wheezing squeaks as I leaned over the sink. Have you ever been upset to the point that you were past crying? Because that's where I was as I dry sobbed, clutching my chest as agony ripped through my lungs. I was hyperventilating, having a panic attack as I did my best to come back down from the anxiety that was taking me to new heights of fear.

Too hot. I was too hot, and it was so stuffy in this bathroom, I was sure I would suffocate and die before long if I didn't do something. My gaze shifted around the room before landing on a window above the toilet. Hurrying, I walked over and climbed onto the toilet and tore open the window with so much force the pane rattled in the frame. Cold air rushed into the room as if it had been vacuum-sealed and I gasped and gulped at the frigid wind as it blew over my face. Closing my eyes against the onslaught, I felt the calming effects of the drastic change in temperature, the steam doing its part to open my lungs so I could–wait, steam?

Opening my eyes, I looked down at my bare arms as steam rose off of them in thick waves as if I were standing in a hot shower. Blinking, I stared down at myself in horror as steam wafted from the already ruined satin. It was the first time I'd actually looked at the dress, and the color made it seem as if I were skinned, just pure muscle on display. A chill ran down my spine, raising goosebumps over my arms . . . but they weren't there because I was cold. I was terrified of myself.

EZRA

After scouring the downstairs and not finding even a glimpse of Cadence, I realized that she must have gone upstairs if she didn't leave. I sincerely hoped that she hadn't left in that soaked dress.

Heading across the foyer to search upstairs, I saw my father coming down the staircase. When I noticed the glass of Bismuth in his hand I glowered at him. He glared right back at me with the look of which I was very familiar. He was royally pissed off, and his sights were set on his darling son. The last thing

I wanted to do was talk to him, but as he was directly in my path, it was an inevitability.

"Son, what did I tell you about hanging around that . . . *female*?" He clapped me on the shoulder with his free hand and smiled brightly at me as if he weren't speaking my worst fears aloud.

Hiding my real horror at knowing he'd found Cady before I could, I casually shrugged his hand from my body. I laughed lightly, pressing my thumb against the corner of my mouth to occupy it so I didn't punch him instead. "And what did I tell you about how I wasn't going to stop?" I responded curtly, dropping my hand and putting it directly into my pocket. It was better to put my fist away than make a scene by slugging him.

Lucien chuckled in turn, the action not meeting his eyes as he did it. It never did. That smile was for show, so no one was aware that we were in the midst of a confrontation. "Get her out of my manor before I have her removed, and then spend the rest of this evening with *Jessica*." The blue of his eyes flashed with a fury that mirrored my expression.

I gave him a hard look, dropping all the jovial pretenses and leveling him with a glare. "Fine on the first, but I'm leaving with her. I will not be spending any time with Jessica."

I immediately went up the stairs before he could say anything further, slamming my shoulder into his on the way. Walking down a few long halls I went to the bathroom everyone unfamiliar with the estate ended up in and knocked. I knew it was occupied due to the glow on the hardwood and hoped my inkling was correct. Inside, I heard a thud, a curse, and shuffling as footsteps approached the door.

"Who is it?" I recognized Cady's voice despite the undercurrent of panic and confusion that tainted the normally melodic tone of her speech.

"It's me." I placed my palm against the door. "You've been gone a while, and I was making sure you're okay." My forehead rested against the door, almost as if I could sense her doing the same on the other side. "Please let me in."

I could hear her swallow, her hesitance speaking volumes more than any words could say. I could only imagine what my father had said to her after what he'd spoken to me, and I wanted to soothe her. Cady's breaths seemed sharp and short, as if she had just gone for a sprint that left her breathless and my concern grew exponentially.

"Something's wrong with me, Ezra," she fretted, her voice seeming even closer than it had been before. I hated that piece of wood more than just about anything at that point. It was in my way.

"There's nothing wrong with you, Cadybug." My voice was barely above a whisper, though I knew she could hear me. The party was far below us, the music floating up to us as if from a dream.

There was the snap of the lock coming undone just before the door opened, letting me know to pull back slightly so I didn't fall into the room on top of her . . . as appealing as that thought might be. As the door opened, the dim hallway was bathed in a warm glow from the lights in the bathroom and I frowned as I took in Cadence's appearance. While she had already been soaked downstairs, she was now even more disheveled. Her face was flushed, and her chest heaved as she panted.

"What happened?" My eyes widened as I took in the look in her eyes.

Her hands balled into fists at her sides and her cheeks grew even redder with an emotion that her mask effectively hid. Backing into the bathroom, she made room for me to enter before shutting the door behind me.

"I told you. Something is horribly wrong with me!" she snapped, sounding angrier than I'd ever heard. It took longer than I'd care to admit, realizing that she was embarrassed and alarmed and that was why she was lashing out at me.

I held my hands up, palms out in a gesture of surrender. "Cadence, there is nothing wrong with you. I do want to know what happened, though." I tore my eyes off of her to look around the room. Everything looked fine other than the window being open, something I didn't notice until I felt a cold breeze blow over me. By the end of December, it was quite cold this far north in the Adirondacks.

She looked at the window and frowned before walking over and climbing onto the toilet. I waited for her to tell me what was going on, but figured she needed fresh air first. Why else would the window be open? However, I was quickly proven wrong.

Nothing happened at first, just Cadence staring down at me, her gaze as anxious as I felt, as she stood on the toilet seat. Then, a breeze came in along with a small flurry of snowflakes. Her skin glowed slightly as the cold air touched it, just before steam arose from her skin in small plumes. My eyes widened as the snowflakes blowing in melted in the heated air around her, falling in a mist onto her skin, the drops sizzling as they landed against her flesh. I felt my jaw drop open as I watched in a mix of horror and utter fascination.

"I told you. There's something wrong with me!" she repeated, taking my surprised expression and translating it into disgust. Cadence's hands came up to cup her face before removing the mask and whipping it across the room. It hit the mirror above the sink with a heavy thud before landing on the counter. As she sobbed into her hands, her skin seemed to glow brighter, and my forehead creased in concern. "Is this normal? Does this happen to every Volsifi before they Ascend?" She lowered her hands as her lip pushed out in a sad pout. Mascara was pooled under her eyes, the tears leaving tracks in her makeup.

I blinked stupidly and found I couldn't answer her question. I was too distracted by the flash of violet in her left eye that left me speechless as we gaped at each other. I'd noticed the color earlier but disregarded it as being under the mask. Stepping closer to her, I gazed into her eye, noting the sparkling glitters that shimmered in that now violet splash in her left iris and I opened my mouth again to finally answer her, "No . . . I didn't go through anything like this . . ."

"I really am an abomination!" she howled, covering her face with her hands again, her shoulders shaking with sobs.

"No, you are not!" My words were firm as I reached out and placed my hand on her shoulder. I didn't know how else to console her.

I did my best to contain the gasp as her flesh nearly burned my palm. She was so hot, it felt like she should be hospitalized for a fever. Ignoring the discomfort against my skin, I pulled one of her hands from her face to help her off the toilet. She didn't fight me, fortunately, and I guided her from the bathroom and through the maze toward my bedroom. The longer I held onto her skin, the harder it was to ignore the heat that caused a pulsing ache in my flesh. If I hadn't seen what happened when the cold touched her with my own eyes, I would assume she was just sick with fever sweats.

Once we were in my room, she stood awkwardly as I dug through my dresser to find clothes she could wear. I nearly grabbed sweatpants before thinking better of it and getting her some shorts and a thin, dark t-shirt instead.

Holding out the clothes to her, I gestured at the door behind me to my private bathroom. "Do you want to take a shower and try to relax before I take you home?" I reached over to lock my bedroom door.

Biting her lip, she nodded and took the clothes from me. When she turned around, my gaze dropped to what looked like a dark blur along her spine. "Cadence, do you have a bruise on your back?"

She turned her head to look at me, the mark disappearing in the shifting light. "What? I don't think so." She arched her back to look over her shoulder.

"It must have been a shadow," I muttered, shaking my head. "I'm sorry."

Cadence smiled sadly and nodded at me, turning away and exposing her bare back, no bruise or dark mark in sight. Just before she disappeared into the bathroom, she stopped and gave me a sincere look over her shoulder. "Thank you for everything," she whispered and closed the door before I could respond.

Shortly after the bathroom door closed, "Puzzle Pieces" by Framing Hanley drifted to me through the thick door. The sound distorted further as she turned on the shower, and I pulled out clothing for me. My outfit had also been ruined with the punch incident, and I tossed it into a heap on the floor. After hours of discomfort, I opted for sweats and an ancient t-shirt as I propped myself up on the bed to wait and text Alex.

Several songs later, the music paused and she reappeared in my room, her bare toes digging into the carpet as she stood in the doorway in my clothes. I looked up from where I lay on the bed, shutting my phone off and setting it aside as I sat up to gaze at her. Honestly, seeing her in my clothes was way more appealing than even the dress had been. Standing awkwardly, she uncomfortably tugged at the waistband of my shorts where they seemed to be a bit too snug for her liking. I gave her my oldest and loosest pair, hoping they would be the most comfortable. I wasn't sure anything could make her at ease in that moment, though.

"Do you want to go home or stay for a little bit?" I glanced at the time. It wasn't very late, and she had more than enough time to return to her house before her dad began to worry. I was certain he'd be concerned about her returning home in my clothing, but I would deal with that when the time came.

She paused, gazing at me for so long I began to wonder if I'd overstepped before she finally spoke. Her voice was husky and sent chills over my flesh. "I'd like to stay."

Cady's gaze shifted from me to a shelf above my dresser, a small giggle causing her somber expression to crack. She reached up and pulled down a crocheted llama, examining it. "I can't believe you've kept all of these. Especially this one." She pointed to the first stuffed llama on the shelf. "It looks like a constipated horse," she commented, laughing, and causing me to chuckle.

"Of course, I've kept them. You made them for me. They're my most prized possessions." I stood up and pulled down the one she pointed to, a hand-stitched llama made of lavender and gray fabric. "You gave this one to me when we were ten. It's the first Novzima that we exchanged gifts," I reminisced, holding out the hand-stitched stuffed llama. "You said you made this as soon as you found out that llamas are my favorite animal."

She smiled fondly, putting the one from last year back on the shelf and taking the one I was holding from my hand. "Yeah. I remember. I found a sewing kit in the garage and cut apart a dress to make this. Dad was unsure if he should be proud, horrified, or angry." Another laugh came from her, the sound sparkling in the air around us like music.

"Probably all of them. I was proud and touched that you would think so highly of me that you would cut apart one of your favorite dresses to make it for me." I gazed at her as her eyes lifted to mine. "That's when I knew for sure that you were the most important person in my life." Leaning down, I pressed a gentle kiss to her forehead. When I pulled back, she was blushing, a shy smile on her face. "Plus, you work hard to earn the yarn to make everything you put together. I would never throw it away and waste all of your efforts like that."

Her cheeks flushed a delicate rose color that made me brush the back of my hand over her skin. "You're too kind to me," she murmured, her eyes shifting around my head before landing back on mine again. "I do appreciate it."

I gave her a smile, booping the tip of her nose with my thumb. She gazed at me for a moment longer, her eyes widening for just a moment before her gaze tore from mine. I looked to the side, following her attention.

"I didn't even notice these when we walked in," she breathed, walking across the room to a backless shelving unit where several amaryllis plants were in various stages of bloom. The daylight lamp was currently off, letting them rest for the evening. "They're beautiful." Her fingers gently danced over crimson petals. Stiffening, she turned to me with wide eyes. "Do you grow all the flowers you give to me?"

I nodded once, shrugging. "Yeah. They're exceedingly hard to buy. They're not a common flower to regularly purchase, so I've been cultivating these for years now."

She blinked at me as if she were having trouble determining my words.

Turning from her, I sat on the edge of my bed and reached over into my nightstand to pull out a small gift. The wrapping paper was white with red amaryllis flowers, her favorite. Her eyes widened slightly as she came over and dropped onto the bed beside me. "Jolly New Winter," I whispered, using the loose English translation of the holiday name.

Cadence looked up at me and smiled. "I didn't bring your gift because I thought we were getting together with Alex tomorrow," she rebutted, both of her hands in her lap.

I chuckled. "We are, but I couldn't wait. I'm too excited about my stroke of brilliance to wait another day."

She shook her head, grinning. "You're so impatient. Alex will be displeased with you," she chastised, taking the gift from my hand and gently untying the ribbon with a slowness that made me anxious.

"I *am* impatient, and you're the worst with unwrapping. Just tear the paper, it's not like you'll ever reuse it," I grumbled, pointing at the package as she loosened the tape and unfolded the wrapping.

Her dark gaze lifted to mine and she tilted her head slightly. "I'll have you know that your gift is exactly this size and maybe I will reuse the paper," she teased, plucking the tape from the other end and sliding the box out of the paper and placing it beside her on the bed.

My eyes widened in exasperation as she continued to look at me instead of the gift in her hand. "Cadence, you're driving me mad," I grunted, unable to keep the levity of humor from my voice.

Finally, she looked down at the box in her hand and gasped. "You got me wireless earbuds?" The incredulity was apparent in her breathless tone. "Ezra, this is amazing and perfect!" She threw her arms around my neck and gave me a hug. "Thank you so much," she gushed, pulling away again and opening the box to pull out case containing the white buds.

"I figured this was better than those wired ones you had. They always got caught in your clothes and you've complained about accidentally ripping them out when you're throwing axes and . . ."

"Ezra, it's amazing. I don't need any justification. Thank you." She dabbed her eyes.

"Please don't cry," I murmured, reaching out and touching her face.

"I'm just so happy." Her words were the brush of a whisper.

Leaning my forehead against hers, I smiled in contentment. "Me too, Cadybug."

I inhaled deeply, absorbing her delicate scent of white florals, berries, and sandalwood. It was intoxicating. Suddenly, an idea occurred to me, and I abruptly stood and grabbed her hand. "Follow me."

Cadence seemed almost wary as we hurried down the hallway into a long-abandoned bedroom. When we were both inside, I closed the door behind us and grabbed a blanket that was draped elegantly over the foot of the large bed. Tossing it onto the floor to block the crack, I made sure it was sealed before flicking the light on.

Looking at her, she stared at me with confusion written all over her face.

"I don't want anyone to see the light on in here." My voice cracked with the effort of holding onto the emotion swelling in my chest. "This was my mother's room."

Cady gasped, her hand pressing against her chest as her eyes darted around the large space. I let my own eyes wander, taking in the dusty mauve of the walls that danced with the deep ash color of the hardwood floor. Every piece of furniture was ornate, elegant. The wood all matched, from the four-poster bed to the nightstands to the dressers. My gaze dropped to Cadence. She tiptoed around the room, gently touching the carefully velvet mauve bedspread with her fingertips before finding a pile of books still on the nightstand. They'd been there for over eighteen years, but just like everything else in the room, they were spotless and meticulously cared for.

"Why did she have her own bedroom? I know why my parents sleep apart, but I thought your parents were happy . . . before . . ." Her voice trailed off as she clutched her hands in front of her waist.

I frowned, looking up at the gray tulle that hung over the windows as my hands found their way into my pockets. I felt vulnerable, exposed. "When she was pregnant with me, she was very sick. She had headaches and frequent fevers that kept her bedridden and miserable. Her sleeping schedule was erratic, and my father didn't want to disturb her every time he went to bed. So, he'd check in on her here and then go to his own room on the other side of the house. He said he put her here so when she screamed, he wouldn't have to listen to how much I was torturing her."

Cadence gasped and I refused to look at her. I didn't want to see the horror, the sympathy, on her pretty face. "Ezra."

The way she spoke my name was a pained breath, a kiss against my aching heart. This wasn't where I wanted this impromptu visit to go. "Anyway, he's held this as a shrine for her ever since. That's not why I brought you here, though. I wanted to get something for you."

Still avoiding her eyes, I went to the closet and pulled down a box from the top shelf. This was covered in dust as though the things in the closet didn't matter. Lucien kept the room anyone could see from the hallway perfectly clean and cared for, but her personal things inside this room were as abandoned as her memory. Everything was a show.

I held the box carefully, looking at her for the first time before gesturing for her to come closer to the door. Handing her the box, I swept to the dresser and looked inside, pulling out pants and a shirt before meeting Cadence at the door. I put a finger to my lips and shut off the light, replaced the throw blanket on the bed, and waited at the door with one ear pressed to the wood. When I was certain no one was coming, I opened the bedroom door and guided Cadence back to my own space.

Back in the safety of my room, I released a breath I didn't know I'd been holding. Turning to Cadence, I saw her eyeing the box suspiciously. I took it from her, brushing the dust onto my floor before putting it on my bed. The pink cardboard was aged, yellowing in the corners. I flipped the lid open and displayed a pair of black leatherette loafer pumps with a chunky heel and a bit of a platform. They were very obviously from the nineties, but I didn't think she would mind.

"I think they'll fit you," I said, picking up the left one and handing it to her.

Cadence's confusion did not ease as she took the shoe from me and stared at it as if it were the world's hardest puzzle. When her eyes lifted to me, her brows were furrowed, a line formed between them. "They're cute, but I don't know why you're showing them to me."

I grinned. "They're for you. You can't go outside barefoot. There's snow on the ground."

Her brow smoothed as her expression dramatically shifted to surprise. "I can just wear the heels Alex put me in," she said, gesturing vaguely at the floor behind me.

"They're ruined, sticky, and probably uncomfortable. You can't dance in those."

"I am *not* going downstairs to dance with those people."

I chuckled, shaking my head. "You're correct. You are not. We are going outside. I want to show you something."

When she continued hesitating, I gave her the lounge pants and t-shirt from my mother's dresser. "They may smell like cedar, but they will fit you better. I think my mom was about the same size, judging by the few pictures I've seen."

Cadence frowned, her eyes shimmering as tears formed. "I feel bad wearing her things."

I put my hands on her shoulders, squeezing gently. "Don't feel bad. From what the staff here have told me, she would have loved you."

She continued frowning but wandered into the bathroom and quietly shut the door.

CADENCE

In the bathroom, I felt like I could breathe again. I felt touched by his sharing things about his mother with me, no matter how incredibly sad it was. He was right, her clothes did feel better than his, still fitting a bit snug but without the crushing feeling his clothes gave me. The lounge pants traveled to the floor, catching under my heel. I eyed them, the deep blush color made my toes look pink against the yellowed tile beneath them. The colors blurred together as tears filled my eyes and I sniffed.

Plopping onto the toilet, I put my face in my hands and wept quietly. I thought I'd gotten it all out while I was in the shower, but it seemed I wasn't out of tears quite yet. Using some toilet paper, I gently dabbed my eyes and stood to look in the mirror so I could frown at my reflection. My nose and cheeks were splotchy and red, my mouth looking swollen from crying in the heat of the shower. Rolling my eyes, I turned away from myself and regretted looking. How Ezra could be so cordial and affectionate when I looked like a swamp monster, I'd never know.

Pulling together all of the bravery I could muster, I opened the door to face him again. He looked up from the amaryllis flowers, smiling brightly as he handed a crimson bloom to me. The expression made smile lines form from his nose to the corners of his mouth. Ezra looked so happy that it felt infectious. I felt my mouth curve in a smile of my own and I accepted the flower to brush my

123

thumb over the smooth petal. The urge to press my nose into it was strong, but I knew it was pointless. Amaryllis didn't have a smell, though Ezra's teakwood and amber scent clung to the petals regardless, as if his presence had been absorbed into the precious flower.

"Come with me again," he said, reaching for my hand.

I looked at his hand for a brief moment, taking in the smooth swirls of his fingerprints and the softness of his long, tapered fingers. His middle finger had a callus on the side of his knuckle from years of writing tools pressing there. Reaching out, I placed my hand into his and let him guide me from the room.

He guided me through the upstairs hallway. Doors were placed along it, though I didn't know where any of them went. Ezra stopped beside a small table sitting in the hallway. It was far from the only one, and I wasn't sure what was special about it. Much like the rest of the house, there were no pictures, but a tall glass vase held carved crystal flowers that draped over the top in brilliant blue facets. On either side of it was a gray marble bowl, black veins tracing across the sides, filled with royal blue palm stones. They were smooth and opaque, and I wanted to reach out and touch them. Ezra slid the bowl to the side and gently pressed against the surface of the table. A button I hadn't seen pressed down into the wooden surface and a deep grinding sound came from the wall just beside me. I watched as the wall opened like a door, swinging outward until the hall we'd walked down disappeared behind it.

I turned to look at Ezra, but he only grinned. "It leads out the back. When the house was built, servants lived in the home and used these passages to get through the house without being seen. My father, the monster that he is, insists they're still used so he doesn't have to deign to look at the omegas that work for him." As he spoke, his grin faded until his lips pressed together with displeasure. The action made a shallow dimple appear in the left side of his chin below his mouth.

I sighed. "Don't worry. It won't always be that way. You will do great things when you become the Alpha," I reassured him, reaching out to grip his upper arm gently. My thumb smoothed over the soft, thin fabric of his shirt.

He nodded, though his expression didn't change as he led me into the dark passageway. The door shut behind us, throwing us into darkness for just a moment before lights lit up to show an unfinished hallway. I could see the lathe and plaster from the rooms on either side of us between the beams that supported the walls. Relief flooded through me at the lack of cobwebs. At least it was cleaned regularly, it seemed.

Ezra guided me through the passages, occasionally taking turns and leading me down steps until we reached a wooden door at the bottom of a stairwell. He turned to me with a smile before opening the door and leading me into the driveway that was wrapped around the side of the house. It took me a moment to orient myself on an unfamiliar side of the house and with the snow coming down around us.

Behind the house, to my left, the roof of the Crest could just be seen over the trees. It was the hub where The Guard trained and held their meetings. It was at the very peak of the mountain and shielded the Alpha family if there was an attack from the other side of the mountain. Guard members took rotations, spending a full twenty-four hours working there before returning to their families.

I was confused, looking back to Ezra. He flashed a grin at me, his eyes crinkling with mirth as he turned his back on the Estate and led me into the forest toward the Gardens of Ascension.

The forest was pretty barren at this time of year, but the flurries still caught on the branches on the way down. We laughed as we tore through the crisp underbrush, no longer caring about how much noise we made. Our footsteps crunched loudly, the only sound in the abandoned forest.

"Just a little farther," he called back to me, glancing over his shoulder. The moonlight caught his blue eyes and they glittered with a sense of mischief.

A stabbing pain was pretty persistent in my right side by the time we broke through the tree line and into the Gardens of Ascension. I'd never been there when we weren't watching someone Ascend, and the emptiness of it felt like a blend of magic and eeriness I couldn't quite grasp. The bushes that lined the walkways were bare, their branches lying dormant for the frigid winter.

I was pulled away from my thoughts as a song started playing. Turning, I saw Ezra holding a small speaker that blared "Infinitely Falling" by Fly by Midnight, a brilliant smile displayed on his face. His eyes sparked, displaying his emotions proudly for me to see. Love, affection, warmth that left my skin tingling as he looked at me.

He put the speaker down before extending his hand to me. It was an upbeat song, not really one to slow dance to. A laugh rang through the trees, brought from my lips as he grabbed me around the waist and started dancing in warp speed. He guided me expertly in the steps as though this were the most normal thing in the world. Instead of matching his movements, I kept falling behind and being dragged as laughter had me nearly doubling over.

Ezra laughed with me, the sound contagious as we fed off each other's giggles. He spun me and I went up on tiptoe to attempt it smoothly. I lost my balance on the frozen ground, and he caught me, arching me backward into an elegant dip as his mouth dropped to my throat. His lips pressing to the pulse point on my neck made me gasp.

When we both straightened, he looked into my eyes. The laughter had left his face, but his blue eyes still sparkled with it as he gazed into my face. My mouth popped open with the intensity of his stare.

"Ezra," I breathed, sliding my hands up his sides and making him shiver under my touch.

"Cadybug."

A smile danced at the corners of his mouth just before he dropped it on mine. I closed my eyes, getting swept up into the rapture of his kiss.

CHAPTER 12

CADENCE

The next morning, I plopped down at the table next to my dad. As I settled in, eyeing the over easy eggs on my plate, he put down the book he was reading and smiled pleasantly at me. I peered at the cover to see the title.

"*Pale Fire* by Vladimir Nabokov? Doing some light reading this morning?" The sarcasm was heavy in my tone.

"Yes. It was my favorite in high school and reminds me of a simpler time. How was the party last night?" he asked before picking up his coffee and taking a sip.

I shrugged, smashing my eggs into a yellow mess before scooping some onto my fork. "It was beautiful, of course. Ezra gave me my Novzima gift already." I smiled fondly in memory of the earbuds.

Dad chuckled, shaking his head. "That boy couldn't keep a surprise if his life depended on it. How many more years do you think Alex is going to tolerate him giving gifts to you before the designated exchange the next day?" He spread homemade jam on a slice of toast before taking a bite.

I laughed in response. "Probably an indefinite number. She knows how he is at this point, and I think she's given up changing it." I looked up from my plate as he slid a small gift across the table toward me.

"That girl will never give up on anything. You know it as well as I do." He paused for a moment, looking down at his plate before giving me a bright smile. "Here's your gift from your mom and me," he said, his eyes glittering with mischief. Neither of us mentioned that mom definitely had no part or interest in the gift.

I shook my head, swallowing the bite in my mouth to say, "Dad, you really didn't need to get me anything."

He shook his head. "Of course I did. You're my baby girl, and you deserve the world. I'm sorry that this is all I could get you." He waved his hand in a clear dismissal of my concern.

Carefully, I opened the package to find a silicone cover for the case to my earbuds. "You and Ezra conspired!" I pulled the earbud case from the pocket of my pajama pants and fit the scarlet cover onto it. I smiled happily at it, flipping open the case just to look at the tiny devices hidden safely and charging inside it. "Thank you, dad."

Standing, I walked around the table to give him a hug and dropped a kiss onto his thick, graying hair. He chuckled, standing from the table and depositing his dirty dishes into the sink. As usual, he wasn't worried about receiving a gift from me, even though I always had one for him.

"Dad, you have something to open too," I said, standing and plucking his gift from the pile. I never saw the point in purchasing wrapping paper, so I always decorated some butcher paper I get from the food pantry in exchange for helping out there and wrapped the gifts I made in that instead. Dad's, as usual, I drew ornamented Novzima trees and holly berries on. Handing it to him, he beamed at me and sat back down at his usual seat to carefully open the wrapped package.

As he pulled apart the paper, his smile grew. Pulling the navy blue knitted scarf from its wrapping, he immediately wrapped it around his neck and let the ends hang to his navel. "Thank you, Cady. My old one was getting rather threadbare." He gestured to the scarf hanging by the door; it was the one I'd made him a couple years prior.

"I noticed. You were past due for a new one." I laughed as he picked up the ends and inspected them closely, a frown of concentration creasing his brow.

"You know, Cade, you've gotten quite good at crocheting," he praised, and I didn't miss the edge of emotion that caused his voice to warble. "I'm proud of your craftsmanship, and you should be too."

I nodded, trying not to tear up as he reached for another hug. I stood up into the embrace and wrapped my arms around his middle. "Jolly New Winter," I whispered, afraid that if I spoke too loudly it might shatter the moment.

"Jolly New Winter, my darling." He pressed a kiss to the top of my head. "Unfortunately, I've got to get to work. I'm putting a full day in between the food pantry and the clinic."

I nodded as I pulled away and he ruffled my hair. "Do you need help today?"

He shook his head and shuffled to the front door, still wearing the scarf. Pulling on his coat and shoving his feet into boots, he sighed heavily. "Alright. I'm off. I love you, Cady. Have fun with your friends today, okay?"

He pulled open the door as I responded in kind. Just about to step out into the cold, he chuckled and loudly greeted someone with a booming, "Jolly New Winter!" The door shut behind him for just a moment before it opened as Alex walked in with Ezra right behind her.

Alex came hurrying over to me, throwing her arms around mine and locking me into an embrace. "I'm so sorry I wasn't there. I'd have punched her in her stupid, smug face," she wailed in my ear, causing me to wince. I looked over her shoulder with wide eyes to Ezra for help and he pressed his lips into a thin line in response, the dimple appearing beneath his lip.

"It's okay. Karma will come for her, I'm sure," I murmured, struggling to shift one arm out of the crippling hug to pat Alex on the back while subtly trying to blow her wild, blonde curls out of my face.

Alex pulled back, looking me in the eye. I could see just how upset she was when I gazed back at her, the emotion overwhelming me. "Yeah. Here's karma, and it's coming for her." She held up her left fist and shook it angrily.

I put my hand over her white-knuckled fist and gently pushed it down. "That's not necessary, Alex. Seriously, she'll get hers at some point. No one can be that awful and get away with it forever." My tone was earnest in the hope that she would let it go.

That was a foolish desire, because she just glanced at Ezra who looked blankly at her. It was a moot point; I could tell with that look that they were communicating silently. Frowning, I pulled away from Alex and decided to abruptly change the topic and interrupt their little nonverbal convo before they could make too many decisions without me.

"Alex, think fast." I tossed the package at her.

Their concentration broke as Alex turned to catch the flying gift, dropping her gaze to the decorated paper. "Aww, you drew gifts on my gifts," she gushed, brushing her hand over the wrapping with a touched smile on her face.

I rolled my eyes. "I always draw gifts on your gifts. You like puns."

I grinned as I picked up Ezra's and handed it to him instead of throwing it. "Yours won't tolerate a flight, no matter how brief," I told him when he gave me a curious look.

His brow furrowed as he looked at the gift, dancing llamas adorned the paper with colored lights around them. "Didn't you make me another llama?" he asked, not hiding the touch of disappointment in his voice.

Shrugging, I gave him a teasing grin. "I guess you'll have to open it and find out."

Both of them tore into the paper to find their individual gifts. Alex pulled out a deep purple colored sweater that I crocheted with a loose weave to display whatever she decided to wear under it. She squealed and gave me another crushing hug.

Ezra grinned as he tore off the top of the makeshift bag I'd created, pulling out a crocheted llama as expected. This time, however, I made it into a plant pot with a glittering succulent inside. "Ah, so that's why it couldn't be thrown." He grinned at me before giving me a hug as well, though his was much gentler.

Alex grinned and handed me a card that I carefully opened. Inside it said, *'Enjoy another year of your music streaming!'* It was the gift she'd gotten me for the past several years since her and Ezra went in together to get me a smart phone. It took me a month to get over such an extravagant gift. I still didn't think I deserved it.

"Thank you." I hugged her and did my best to make it as bone crushing as hers. I knew it wasn't close, but the effort was there.

When I pulled back, she turned to glare at Ezra. "You already gave her your gift, didn't you," she accused, narrowing her eyes and scowling.

Ezra flushed heavily and walked into the living room while whistling in the least innocent way possible. I threw my head back and cackled, as she chased him down to punch him in the arm and he cursed at her.

Night had fallen and I found myself alone again when Ezra and Alex were summoned to their respective homes. Sighing, I put in my new earbuds and smiled when the noise announced they'd turned on. Putting on "She's Quiet" by The Home Team, I threw on a light jacket and made my way out into the night on my bike. The cold air whipped my face as I went, causing me to briefly close my eyes and inhale the scent of rain approaching. It was such an odd winter with only a small snow flurry for Novzima that was quickly washed away by freezing rain.

I was almost to Axe Marks the Spot when a tall figure stepped into my path, waving their arms. I screeched to a halt with a yelp and stared up into the green eyes of William Jones.

Pulling one earbud out to pause the music, I scolded him. "William! You gave me a heart attack!" I pressed a hand against my chest to ease my racing heart.

His eyes widened in shock and he shook his head, his chestnut hair flopping into his face. "I'm so sorry, Cady. I just wanted to stop you so I could thank you for that food you sent home with my mother. She was so surprised, and I just appreciate it so much," he rushed, throwing his arms around me.

I blinked back the surprise and patted his back gently. "It wasn't a big deal. I was just happy I could make your birthday special. Anyone would do that for someone else."

He pulled back and gave me an exasperated look. "No, Cadence. Most people wouldn't do something like that. I know that was your dinner, and you didn't have to give it to me instead." He took a deep breath and blinked furiously. "I saw you coming and . . . your family means so much to us, and I just had to let you know." He wiped his eyes with the sleeves of his shirt, taking a large step back from me. "Anyway, I happened to look out and see you coming and wanted to make sure that I let you know how much we appreciate you and your dad," he added awkwardly, dropping his hands to his sides and pulling the sleeves over his fists.

I smiled at him and nodded. "Of course, William. We appreciate you guys, too."

We stared at each other for one anxiety fueled moment before he waved. "Anyway–uhh–good night. Please be safe," he stuttered, hurrying back into his house and shutting the door with a loud click.

Staring after him for a long minute, I tried to discern my feelings. Unable to do so comfortably, I decided to just pop my earbud in and pick a new song.

I slipped my phone into my pocket as "Worst In Me" by Bad Omens filled my ears and made my brain happily sing along. Hurrying toward my destination, I wanted to get off the street before I had to communicate with anyone else. Emotion was choking me as I aggressively blinked to try to allay the tears before they fell, but the cold air blowing into them wasn't helping. By the time I pulled up in front of Axe Marks the Spot, my cheeks were damp with tears that burned down my cold flesh.

I yanked my keys from my pocket and unlocked the door. It was times like these that made me truly grateful that my Grandpa Henry thought to add the stipulation that I was allowed access whenever I wanted when he passed on this place. Figuring I didn't need to lock the door behind me, I flicked on the lights and went straight to my locker. The dial of the lock spun beneath my deft fingers before I flicked the release and pulled it open to display my babies to me.

Reaching in, I went straight for the black hatchet, the ancient language glittering silver along the handle. At the bottom where the heel of my palm rests, an amaryllis was carved in. I smiled as I ran my fingers over it, my mind traveling back to when it appeared there.

"That wasn't there before, Grandpa. Why is there an amaryllis on there now?" I asked, looking up into his dark eyes.

Grandpa smiled down at me, holding it out for me to take in my tiny hand. "Because you're eight years old now and more than capable of wielding this weapon, which means that it's time I handed this down to you," he answered, crouching in front of me. "And whenever I see an amaryllis, I think of you and that smile you have on your face right now."

I wiped the tears that burned my eyes, looking down at the small hatchet that was my perfect size. "What do the words mean?" I ran my fingertip over the silver etchings in the black coated metal.

Grandpa shook his head. "I don't know. The translation has been lost with time. This hatchet has been passed down the Nocetti line for centuries."

I nodded, staring down at the weapon for a long moment before turning my gaze back to his face. He gave me a wide smile, the motion causing light to flicker over the silver scars on his face. "Thank you, Grandpa."

I came back out of the memory; "Ghost" by Parachute was now blasting into my ears and I bobbed my head in beat to the song as I walked toward aisle five, where I felt at home. It was Grandpa Henry's favorite number and lane, and I inherited it from him. Pulling out the bottle, I soaked down the wood as I danced around the small, fenced-in area. Feeling comforted in solitude, I hummed along to the words.

I picked up my hatchet by the very bottom of the handle and in one motion, spun on the spot and released the small weapon in the direction of the target. With a heavy thud, the blade sunk into the kill shot in the upper righthand corner. I danced toward the target and stood on tiptoe to rock the hatchet until the wood released the blade. Singing along, I danced backward to the starting position when a prickling sensation wormed along my spine. Feeling like eyes were on me, I immediately stopped singing and froze in position.

I was suddenly overwhelmed with the feeling of no longer being alone and my fingers tightened around the metal handle of the hatchet in my hand. It was raised to my shoulder, and I slowly lifted it into a throwing position before turning around toward the glass door. I realized that the decision to leave it unlocked might have been made in poor taste. Just as it came into my vision, I saw a shadow of someone leaving and the door swinging closed. My heart hammered in my throat as I pulled out one of the earbuds and found myself drowning in the silence. Gasping for air, my eyes scanned the room before settling on something red in my locker. Frowning, I walked over slowly, each footstep making me feel like I was one closer to a horrific discovery.

Stopping in front of it, I stared at the red flower laying on the bottom of my locker. Reaching out, I picked up a perfectly bloomed amaryllis with shaking fingers. A note had been sitting underneath it and I whimpered as I read the words, *'You ignored me last time. I'll make sure that doesn't happen again. I'm watching you.* "The amaryllis fell from my hand, dropping onto the floor at my feet and laying there innocently.

My favorite flower was being used against me, and I had no idea who would do such a thing.

Unwilling to part with my weapon, I closed my locker door and spun the dial before hurrying outside. I glanced around, but no one was there as I locked myself out of the building. Once I was outside, I realized that I'd left the lights on, but didn't care enough to go back inside. Never did I want to be home more than right that second, so I put my earbud back in my ear in a meek attempt to soothe my frantic mind. "Faint" by Linkin Park blasted into my senses as I hopped onto my bike and scurried home. Fortunately, I didn't see another soul until I saw my dad the following morning.

Chapter 13

EZRA

After exchanging gifts with the girls, I got a text from my father that urged me to return home for a discussion with him. As much as I did not want to talk to him, I felt that defying him so close to the party wasn't in anyone's best interest; it definitely was not in mine.

The drive home had me so anxious that nausea was creeping in. Attempting to breathe through the nerves wasn't helping, so I attempted Cadence's trick of music. However, after only a few seconds, I clicked the radio off again and resolved that silence was the better choice. As I drove through the Beta's territory, I wrinkled my nose at all the mansions that dominated this part of town. It was a far cry from the Delta's part of the pack, where there were small to mid-sized homes and most of them were a bit worse for wear. Here, where the Alpha could look out from his estate and have a view of his minions, the mansions were all pristine. You could hardly tell from the outside that even some of the Betas felt unrest under the thumb of my father. Having gathered donations from many of the Beta families to deliver to the Omega food pantry, I'd heard my fair share of distaste for how he ruled the pack.

As I made my way along the last street, the Wolfe Estate loomed on top of the hill that had a perfect view of the rest of the pack. It was ridiculously large, surrounded by immaculate landscaping that gave us very little in the way of privacy. That was a point of contention for my father, though he never made a move to change it for fear that it would make more reason for people to attempt to peek into our lives. He couldn't have that.

I pulled my vehicle into the garage between my father's sports car and an SUV that he drove in the winter, overindulgences that were not needed. Dread overwhelmed me as I made my way out of the garage and toward the front of the home. There was entry into the estate through the garage, but my father trained me to use the front door so he always knew when I was coming and going. Just another way for him to have control over me.

Walking into the large entryway, my father was waiting for me. In his hand was one of those crystal tumblers filled with the vile emerald liquid that always spelled hell for me. His eyes were colder than normal as he looked me over before grinding his teeth in disgust.

"How many times must I tell you not to see that girl? I can smell her stench on you." His voice was clipped and short with the rage I could see in his eyes. "You're going to start courting Jessica Barber. I've arranged a date for you tomorrow evening after school, and there will be no arguments from you."

My hands clenched into fists at my side as I stared at him, looking him in the eye while I acknowledged to him and myself that Cadence was more than worth this fight. "No. I will not stop dating Cadence, and I refuse to so much as speak to Jessica."

Lucien stared at me for a long time, my breath coming in short bursts as I resisted the urge to run from him; to stay facing his fury. A storm was coming, and this was the calm announcing its impending arrival. We continued to look at each other and I refused to look away from his gaze despite the gamble that decision was. I learned long ago that my father, as wretched as he is and no matter how little he deserved it, was given a gift by the Goddess.

Taking a deep breath, my father took a couple steps toward me and stopped just out of arm's reach. "You will stop seeing Cadence, or you will be punished, son," he threatened, his voice smooth like velvet despite the tremor of displeasure he had at the word "son". Every hair on my body raised in response to that tone, knowing exactly what trap I was walking into.

I continued to meet his gaze. Looking away would fare far worse for me. "Punish me, then. I will not stop seeing her," I announced, my tone confident and even as I willingly signed up for hell.

Lucien stared me down, his nostrils flaring as he processed exactly what I was saying to him. A muscle in his jaw twitched before his eyes widened. I refused to flinch as his pupils dilated until nearly all the blue disappeared around them. "Very well." His tone remained eerily calm and relaxed. "You know what to do. Go lay down on the rack."

A chill rolled down my spine as my mind fuzzed over, a dull ache pulsing behind my eyes. I didn't bother fighting his control, I knew it was a pointless battle and would only make my headache worse. My legs moved of their own volition, taking me across the entryway to a plain, white wall. I dragged my hand over the invisible latch that opened the wall and exposed a stone stairwell down into the blackness below. Without hesitation, I walked against my will down into the frigid hell that awaited me.

As I made my way down the long, winding staircase, torches lit by magic on the walls until I finally reached the bottom where a room of tortures awaited me. The rack sat against the far wall, and I walked past various other devices, including the chains I'd been hoping he'd hang me from. He reserved the rack for when he was especially displeased with me.

If one didn't know any better, it would almost look like I was laying on a ladder that was tilted at an angle with leather straps hanging from it. My instincts wanted to argue against the movements of my body as I laid down on the bars with my hands over my head. Muscles rigid as my body automatically fought the puppeteer guiding me, the pulsing in my eyeballs becoming harsher. Stabbing pains fired through my brain as though I was being electrocuted and my body quit thrashing against Lucien's magic. I held perfectly still as his fingers, nimble with extensive practice, strapped me onto the ancient torture device.

"You're making me do this," he muttered to himself as he tightened the ropes until they bit into my flesh. Removing my shoes and socks, he made sure I wasn't going anywhere. Once I was tied in place, my body relaxed as he relinquished control of it. I knew it was pointless to try to escape. Any attempts had ended up causing me more suffering in the past. He was too good at tying the straps for me to move any of my limbs.

I said nothing in reply, resolving to myself that it wouldn't be any good. Instead, I just laid there with my head to the side to watch as he positioned himself at the base of this horrid device and gripped the crank. "Remember that this is entirely your fault. If you would just obey me like a good child, I wouldn't have to do these things to you." His voice was completely deadpan as he repeated the phrases he'd said thousands of times throughout my life. He said them as if he was bored and reading them from a script, and in a way, that hurt more than the actual torture.

His knuckles were white as he gripped the crank and began to slowly turn it. At first, it wasn't too bad. Lucien always took it slow, not wanting any of this to be over too quickly, of course. My back popped as the rack pulled at my wrists and ankles, stretching out every joint in my body. He kept slowly turning the crank, my joints starting to scream after a solid minute of him winding the rack. He just kept staring at me while he inflicted the agony, his blue eyes dead. I saw no hint of emotion in him while he kept going until my eyes started to blur with tears despite my furious attempt at blinking them away.

Finally, he stopped and released the crank to turn away from me. While he was walking to a table, I did my best to control my breathing with overstretched lungs so I could adjust to the strain on my body. He quickly put together a concoction in a large metal bowl on a wooden table a couple feet from me. I knew what he was putting together, so I closed my eyes and did my best to relax my body in preparation for the agony that was due to follow.

When his shoes scuffed against the stone floor, I opened my eyes to see him standing over me with a metal whip. It looked like a thin, disembodied spinal cord with spikes protruding out of each vertebra. His hands were protected with gloves as he held up the silver whip and showed me how it glowed with liquified monkshood. Without giving me any time to prepare, he flicked his right arm, and I felt the bite of the whip as it sliced through my shirt and into my flesh. A cry of agony passed unbidden through my lips as the effect of the monkshood kicked in immediately, my raw back exploding with a fiery pain that made my vision bleed black around the edges.

"The monkshood will slow your healing," Lucien informed me, still using that deadpan tone that proved to me just how little he cared about hurting me. "You won't die, that would be too much of a blessing for me," he added like it was some kind of reassurance. I squeezed my eyes shut in a failed attempt to block everything out.

The sound of metal on metal had me preparing for the worst just before another crack broke through the air and searing anguish tore through me again. Over and over again, he whipped my back until I was sweating with a mix of excruciating pain and the effect of the monkshood coursing through my veins. My heart was pounding a crazy pattern in my chest, beating out of rhythm as the poison tainted my organs. Nausea swirled through me, and my head pounded by the time he finally set down the whip on the table with a heavy thud of metal against wood.

"This is all your fault, you worthless child. You will obey me, or more of this will be in your future." His voice sounded faraway as if I were sinking into a deep ocean. With a thud that jarred my screaming body, I cried out when the rack suddenly released and dropped me onto the stone floor. Suffering tore through me like a raging fire and I writhed against the cold flagstones as my body struggled to heal the lashes and poisoning.

As if in a dream, I heard his footsteps walk away from me, getting farther and farther away until the door at the top of the stairs slammed closed and plunged me into darkness.

CADENCE

The next morning, I found myself sitting alone at the table with only a note from my dad to keep me company. It told me that he was going to be at work all day at the clinic and wouldn't be coming home until late in the evening. I spent a significant amount of time trying not to think about what happened last night, deciding that ignoring the situation was going to be my way of handling it.

I'd just brushed my teeth when a horn honked outside, and I hurried out the door to find Ezra waiting for me. As I buckled up my seatbelt, he turned and smiled at me. "Good morning, Cadybug," he greeted, eliciting the first smile from me in nearly twelve hours.

"Good morning, Ezra." I gave him a warm smile before looking out the window as he drove toward the school. I inhaled deeply, closing my eyes and relishing in the scent of teakwood and amber.

"We need to talk about Jessica," he minced out, his tone ominous. I turned to look at him, noting the way his jaw twitched as he resisted the urge to grind his teeth.

I pressed my lips together between my teeth, unsure how to respond to a sentence like that and instead going with the option of silence. Ezra glanced at me warily before sighing heavily and turning his attention back to the road.

"My dad, since seeing you at the party, is doubling down on me being with Jessica. He's insisting that I not see you anymore. I've tried to tell him no, but he's not listening to me." Ezra stared straight out the windshield, the steering wheel complaining loudly as he tightened his grip on it until his knuckles blanched.

I scowled out the passenger-side window, crossing my arms over my chest. "Well, if he's being that persistent, then maybe you should." I tried very hard not to sound snippy. I knew it wasn't his fault. "Some things aren't worth the fight," I added, trying to soften my words.

I heard him actually grind his teeth that time and I turned my gaze to him.

"You are always worth the fight. I don't want to do this, Cadence, but I think I might actually have to bend to him this time."

"You say I'm worth the fight and you defy him a lot. Why is this the time you're listening to him, Ezra?" I huffed and leaned back in my seat.

"Cade, I can't fight him on this one. I won't stop seeing you, but I have to at least put on a front of courting Jessica," he implored, the pleading in his voice catching my attention.

My eyes burned with tears that refused to fall as I dug my fingernails into my palms. "You've spent so much time convincing me and yourself that I'm your mate, but maybe Jessica actually is." I hated the petulant childishness tainting my words.

He snarled at me. "Cadence! I don't have a choice! I have to meet him at least halfway on this."

I flinched at his volume and tone of his voice, looking over at him with wide eyes. He had never spoken to me like that before. It was then that I noticed his posture, sitting up straight and away from the back of the seat.

"What happened, Ezra?" My gaze bored into the side of his face.

"Nothing, Cadence. I just have to do this."

Now it was my turn to growl at him. "Damn it, Ezra. You have to talk to me about this. Something is wrong, and I deserve to know what it is."

He stared blankly at the road as we made our way to school, making my anxiety skyrocket. I'd just opened my mouth to say something when he finally spoke up.

"He whipped me for disobeying his orders. He whipped me with a silver whip soaked in monkshood to slow the healing process," he whispered, so quietly I almost didn't hear him.

Horror and revulsion tore through me as I continued to stare at him. I couldn't think of any words to say, but this reveal had me noticing other things I hadn't previously: the sweat on his brow, how his breathing was shallow and quick, the fact that he still couldn't put pressure on the wounds. "I don't . . . I can't . . ." I put my hand to my mouth as my stomach twisted.

"Don't say anything. I'm fine. This isn't the first time he's done this, and it probably won't be the last either," he muttered, the steering wheel complaining under his intense grip again.

He pulled into the school, aggressively throwing the car into park before getting out. I followed suit, reaching out and taking the backpack from his hand before he could complain and tossing them both over my shoulder. Ezra glanced at me before walking into the school, his lips pressed together in a slash of discontent.

"How long will the monkshood be in your system?" I asked quietly, looking up at him as he gingerly made his way through the hallway and trying his best attempt not to bump into anyone.

"A couple days," he grumbled, not elaborating any further and causing me to drop it for now. "My first date with Jessica is tonight."

I couldn't ignore the punch in the gut those words brought me, and I bit the inside of my cheek to hold back the tears that threatened. We made it to my locker where Alex was waiting for us. Always the perceptive one, she looked between us.

"What's going on?" Her hazel eyes examined Ezra closely, but he didn't answer. Instead, he grabbed his backpack from my shoulder and left us to go to his own locker downstairs. Her gaze fell on me.

"Lucien is forcing Ezra to date Jessica. Ezra tried to stand up to him, and Lucien whipped him with a silver whip dipped in monkshood." The words left me in a rush that left me breathless. "Their first date is tonight," I added, hating the way my voice trembled on the last word.

Alex looked just as appalled as I felt.

After English class, our group broke apart and I found myself seemingly alone in the stairwell. Halfway to the bottom, someone gave me a hard shove between my shoulder blades and caused me to stumble down a couple steps. I whipped around, about to tell whoever it was to be more careful when I saw Jessica's smirking face.

"Watch your step, klutz. Maybe if you weren't such a cow, you'd be a bit more graceful," she admonished, crossing her arms over her chest.

I scowled at her before hurrying the rest of the way down and onto the safety of the first floor. Hustling through the halls, I only had the safety of the classroom in mind. The doorway appeared in front of me, but a sharp tug on the back of my head stopped me and pulled me backwards. In an alcove, I was shoved backwards into the shadow where Jessica pinned me against the wall. Giving in, I didn't bother to struggle and instead gave her my angriest glare.

"Stay away from Ezra. You might think you have some kind of claim on him, but you don't. He's mine," she snarled, getting closer to my face than was necessary.

I frowned at her, leaning my head back against the wall in mock relaxation, as if this didn't bother me at all. She pressed her forearm into my chest to hold me in place, clearly not trusting me at all. "Jessica, I don't know if you're aware of this, but Ezra is a sentient being with free will. I cannot claim him, and neither can you."

I felt the sting of the slap before the action fully registered, the tingling pain covering the majority of my cheek. "Keep your greasy paws off of him, Cadence Nocetti. Just keep your face in the bucket of fried chicken where it belongs." She practically bristled as she jerked away from me and disappeared into the crowd.

Taking a moment to regain my composure, I let out a dry sob when I knew she'd be out of earshot. When the bell rang, I hurried back into the now empty hall and walked into class. Mrs. Walker didn't say anything to me, instead deciding to just jump into the lesson.

"Okay. We talked about the elvafe. Now it's time to talk about the upirs. Who knows anything about Upirs?" She stood at the front of the class and walked along the whiteboard.

Jessica raised her hand and then immediately started speaking without being called upon. "Upirs are like human vampires. Drinking blood and being deviants at night," she answered, a smug look on her face.

Mrs. Walker shook her head in disappointment. "That's not correct. Anyone else? No one?" Her gaze drifted around the room, taking in all of her students. I slid down in my seat a little as her eyes wandered over me before she sighed. "Upirs don't necessarily follow any particular human lore you've read about from whatever media you've ingested. Upirs do not need to drink blood to survive; in fact, they typically eat food just like we do. However, they can drink the blood of their inamorate attached, their form of our mate bond, and that gives them their ultimate power."

The teacher paused and looked around, letting that information sink into us students before continuing. "When Upirs Ascend, they form crimson tattoos that cover their bodies, similar to those humans receive from lightning strikes. When their magic is activated, their tattoos glow red with power."

I raised my hand, completely fascinated with this topic. "Do they shapeshift or fly?" I asked once Mrs. Walker gave me her attention.

A small smile curved her lips. "Not every Upir can fly. It depends on their power level and what abilities they have. Like Volsifi, the Goddess Levende can give any supernatural being one special gift. Sometimes that's the ability to shapeshift, but typically it is not. Most Upirs are bound to travel by foot," she answered, giving me an approving nod before continuing the lesson.

"Are there any prominent packs of Upirs in the world?" Jessica inquired, speaking as she raised her hand and earning a scowl from Mrs. Walker.

After a moment, she nodded. "Yes. The Shadowvale Coven in London is currently the strongest group of Upirs in the world. They have a young prince who is your age and next in line to take the throne from King Dargan Oliver. I've heard that he is quite studious, very bright, and very powerful."

Mrs. Walker turned, picking up a small remote on her desk and hitting a button. A picture flashed on a projector screen as it lowered from the ceiling. I sat up in my seat, leaning forward as three people came into focus. Two of them looked to be in their mid-thirties while the third looked like he was my age.

"In the picture, you can see King Dargan and his wife and inamorate attached, Queen Victoria." Mrs. Walker pointed to the two sitting in the front of the image, their deep complexions and dark eyes standing in stark contrast against the pale blue background. Standing behind them was the teenager, his mahogany eyes telling me his soul was one of the oldest I'd ever seen. The corners of his mouth were tipped down in a sadness that bled into my heart.

A hand rose up before she could continue. "Has he Ascended yet? What's his gift?"

Mrs. Walker shook her head. "No, he will not Ascend until April twenty-first."

Another student in the class raised his hand, sounding more concerned than I thought was necessary. "What's his name?"

With a raised brow, Mrs. Walker smirked. "Terrence Oliver."

At the end of the day I stood around waiting for Ezra at my locker. Alex bailed, telling me that her dad was summoning her for physical training, and she couldn't keep him waiting. I frowned, watching the school slowly empty as I leaned against my locker, earbuds in place and "Crutch" by Set It Off blaring in my ears. After several minutes and consistently checking the time on my phone, I straightened up and started heading toward his locker.

Ezra's locker was a decent walk from mine. As I descended the steps and entered the hallway downstairs, I could see from down the hall that he wasn't where I'd expected him to be. Concern caused my brow to furrow, and I wondered if he'd left already. Opening the app the three of us used, I saw that Alex was already in Beta territory and Ezra was still at school. My teeth sunk into my lower lip, and I glanced around the hall before my eyes settled on the boy's restroom. Steeling my resolve, I decided it was better to check since he looked less than okay that morning.

Walking into the restroom, I was surprised to find Kyle hovering over Ezra who was slumped on the floor. My eyes widened as I hurried over and fell onto my knees beside them. "What happened?" I pulled my earbuds out of my ears and shoved them into my pocket.

Kyle looked panicked as he glanced at me, his hazel eyes expressing just how worried he was. "I found him this way. We need to get him to Dr. Barber." He started reaching for Ezra's shoulder.

Automatically, I reached out and grabbed Kyle's arm, my fingers gripping his forearm. "No. We can take him to my dad. He's at the clinic today. I know what's wrong with Ezra, and we can't take him to Barber." I met his gaze as he looked up at me again, refusing to back down.

He seemed to hesitate, his lips forming a thin line before he nodded. "Okay. You know him best." He pushed his dark curls off his forehead before reaching down and picking up one of Ezra's arms.

"Just be careful with his back," I murmured, bending low to lift Ezra's other arm over my shoulders.

Kyle nodded, doing the same and we both stood. It was awkward, since both Kyle and Ezra were several inches taller than me, but we slowly made our way through the school toward the student parking lot. The building was pretty well cleared out at that point, no one lingering behind and the teachers having mostly left already. Once we got outside, I realized how grateful I was that Lucien got nothing but the best and we could unlock the car with the button on the door. With great effort, I got into the SUV and heaved Ezra in behind me while Kyle helped from outside.

Once Ezra was settled on the backseat, I moved to get out of the car before Kyle spoke up. "I'll drive. Stay back there with him," he stated, closing the door before I could begin to argue with him.

He bolted around the car and jumped into the driver's seat, pushing the button to start the engine. "Do you know how to get there?" I asked, meeting his hazel gaze in the rearview mirror.

Kyle had the decency to look ashamed as he shook his head. "Unfortunately, I don't," he admitted, putting the car into drive and pulling out of the parking lot.

"Just head into Omega territory and I'll guide you from there." I held Ezra's head in my lap, my fingers working through his damp curls. He was completely still, making me extremely nervous and causing me to check his breathing multiple times.

Pulling out my phone, I texted my dad that we were on our way and that it was an emergency. I was certain that he would be watching our journey through the app, and I knew he wouldn't respond more than the "waiting" that I got from him. We both knew that emergencies did not allow us to ask tons of questions.

We stopped in front of the building, my dad and Alice waiting for us on the sidewalk. The car was barely parked before my dad pulled open the back door and looked at me. I almost didn't see the glimmer of worry in his eyes as he took in Ezra's condition. Kyle was at his side, helping him pull Ezra from the car to carry him into the clinic with Alice opening all the doors for them.

Once Ezra was on a table and dad looked him over, he paused to ask, "What happened?"

I swallowed, glancing at Kyle warily before answering him. "He was whipped. Silver dipped in Monkshood." My voice choked with the tears I was desperately holding back.

Dad's black eyes immediately looked at me, the whites completely visible around his dark iris in surprise. I glanced at Kyle who looked equally horrified by this. Already in this, I plowed on with my explanation. "Lucien is forcing him to date Jessica Barber. He refused, so Lucien punished him last night by whipping him. I think it's his back; he wasn't leaning back against the seat of his car this morning."

Without needing to speak, dad and Kyle immediately worked together and flipped Ezra onto his stomach on the table. Alice handed dad scissors so he could cut the black t-shirt off of him. I could see that it was drenched, the fabric peeling away from Ezra's skin. As his back was exposed, we all collectively gasped in shock and horror at the sight of his ruined flesh. Dad counted fifteen lashes aloud, the angry, purple flesh torn open in crisscrossing lines that covered what looked like hundreds of old scars in various shades and levels of healing. Some were old enough that they were white while others were fresher, still purple and raised.

Covering my mouth, I resisted the urge to vomit and swallowed the saliva that pooled in my mouth. Kyle looked grim, his jawline twitching as he jammed his hands into his pockets. Dad looked angrier than I'd ever seen him as he leaned down to inspect the rips in Ezra's flesh.

"There are tiny pieces of silver embedded in these wounds, meaning that Lucien used a whip meant to fall apart to inflict more lasting damage. That would make it incredibly hard to heal these wounds, even for a volsifi, that fact being compounded by his use of monkshood—" His murmur cut off as he straightened and grabbed gloves. "I need to remove the silver immediately."

When Kyle and I didn't move, he looked between the two of us and sighed heavily. "Listen, I know he's your friend and you're concerned. However, for sanitation purposes, I'm going to have to ask you both to step outside. I will take care of him, but it will be a slow process. I have to remove all the silver and administer an antidote for the monkshood."

I paused and looked at my father, wondering if he'd lost his mind. "There is no cure for monkshood," I contradicted, eyes wide.

Dad paused and looked at me with a frown as Alice rushed around, preparing the room for their work. "Of course there is. I'll explain later. You need to get out. Our time is limited." His stern tone left no room for argument.

Kyle wrapped his hand around mine, pulling me from the room and shutting the door behind us. He turned to me, his eyes wide and swirling with emotions I couldn't define. "I know it's hard, but I think you should trust your father on this." He reached out to wipe tears from my cheeks that I hadn't even realized were there. "He's an excellent doctor. My father has said for years that removing your dad from the position of pack doctor was the stupidest thing Lucien has ever done."

Sighing, I nodded and turned toward the waiting area. As I sat down, Kyle sat beside me, and we stayed silent for a long moment before he spoke up. "I was thinking about what you said in there. About Ezra being forced to date Jessica to keep him away from you. Do you think Alpha Lucien would back off if you were dating someone else?" He leaned forward and put his chin in one hand as his elbow rested on the armrest.

I looked at him in surprise, furrowing my brow. "Maybe, but I don't know anyone who would be interested in pretending to date me." I leaned back and stared at him as he chuckled.

He shrugged, sitting upright and looking back at me. "I'd do it, if it meant keeping Ezra from being punished like that." As he finished his sentence, all gaiety fell from his face; it left him looking at me with such intensity that I wasn't sure if I felt seen or uncomfortable. "I also would enjoy getting to know you in the process," he added, the corner of his mouth tipping upward minutely.

Blinking, I found myself completely dumbfounded. "I don't think your friends would appreciate that idea," I rebutted, my voice monotone with the shock of this conversation. "This is absolutely absurd." I suddenly found myself pacing in front of him, that hazel gaze following me intently.

After a few minutes, he must have gotten tired of watching me track a trail in the carpet because he stood up and gripped my upper arms. I looked up into his face as he gazed down at me earnestly. "I cannot watch the future Alpha of my pack be tortured for something like this. I also never hated your family despite all of the Betas being influenced to turn against them. My family never agreed with Lucien's decision to ostracize your family, and I would love to get to know you." Without saying anything, I continued to stare at him as though he were speaking in a foreign language.

Sighing, he released me and glanced away, seemingly collecting his thoughts as he looked at nothing in particular. "Listen. I think you're a beautiful girl. I also know that you and Ezra are an item, and I will not do anything to overstep your boundaries. I'll take you out on dates in public to give the illusion that you and Ezra are truly not together so that Lucien will leave him alone. I will not kiss you or even hug you, if you don't want me to. We can be friends who go out." His tone said he was imploring me to take him seriously. "I feel like I was forced to lose the chance to know you because of the stupid caste system and my even more stupid friends."

I felt uncomfortable with this entire proposal and took a step away from him. "I feel like this is some kind of joke." I wrapped my arms around myself, creating a shield against him.

Kyle stayed silent and I glanced at him, expecting anger and instead finding sadness. "Why would I joke about something like that?"

"Please. You do know who you are friends with, don't you? Brody is always pretending to be interested in me, and Jason? He's such a jerk," I retorted, pulling my shoulders up toward my ears as though I could hide inside them if I pulled them up high enough.

Kyle did look angry then, his nostrils flaring. "Jason is a notorious asshole. I make no excuses for him. Brody is more complicated than you might think."

He rubbed the back of his neck and pulled his shoulders up in a mirror of discomfort. "I won't speak for either of them. I'd stay away from Jason, though. He has some kind of agenda that neither of us are in on. If Brody wants to tell you about his shit, then he will. It's not my job to speak for him."

I nodded, glancing toward the door that led to Ezra. Sighing heavily, I dropped my shoulders and relaxed the stress in my body. "I'd do anything to save him from this. Anything. I'd even let him go completely," I whispered, the door blurring as my eyes filled with tears.

"Cadence." His voice was hushed, pleading, and very close to me. I turned my head to look up at him, his face only a few inches from mine. "Let me do this for you." His hands were wrapped around mine, cool to the touch and soothing to my overheated fingers. "For both of you."

I nodded, letting the tears fall and leaning my forehead against his chest as his arms wrapped around my shoulders.

Hours later, Kyle and I were sitting in chairs beside each other, both leaning back and staring at the ceiling. It was getting late, both of our stomachs growling with hunger, but neither of us moved. As one unit, we both leapt to our feet as the door opened and my father walked into the hallway. I tried not to look too hard at the blood on his white coat, but the dizziness swept through me anyway. Kyle seemed to notice and wrapped his arm around my shoulders to steady me again.

"He's alive and stable," my dad informed us, looking between us with a frown on his brow. "I wasn't sure he was going to make it for a moment, the damage from the poison was extensive. We made a salve out of the soot of the sacred datura flowers that were burned under a full moon mixed with activated charcoal and clarified butter. Now he's on an IV drip of fluids and a concoction of vitamins to start the healing process. It will be a while before he's back to one hundred percent, but he's alive."

Kyle and I glanced at each other. I was so relieved that I burst into tears and put my face in my hands, though I took comfort in Kyle's hand rubbing my upper arm. Dad was quiet for a moment before speaking up again, "I don't think what happened to Ezra should leave this group. While I think it's repulsive what Lucien did, there are too many members on his side to try to make him pay for his actions right now."

Dad stepped closer, the smell of his aftershave embracing me as much as his arms did and my body quit trembling as he held me close to him. "Kyle, I'll trust you because your parents have been nothing but courteous to us. They've also gone above and beyond to help the Omega community, and for that I appreciate them. Please don't betray my faith in you, son." He jostled me as he placed a hand on Kyle's shoulder.

"I would never betray your family. I have the utmost of respect for you and Cadence," Kyle assured him, his voice somber and ringing with such truth that I pulled away from my dad to gaze at him. Kyle was looking my father in the eye, a glint of something resembling pleasure in my father's approval of him.

"Good to hear, Kyle. Please give your parents a hello for me. I saw you brought Ezra's car here. Can the two of you take it to my house so I can easily take Ezra to it when he's ready to leave here?" he asked, looking between us. The two of us nodded before leaving the clinic.

Kyle drove me to school, where he got into his car and followed me to my house while I drove Ezra's. I pulled it into the garage where my father's car usually went, not needing to have people asking questions. When I exited the garage, Kyle was parked in the driveway and was standing in front of it. His hands were in the front pockets of his jeans, and he leaned back against the hood of the car as he looked at me, concern etched in his features.

"Are you okay?" His quiet voice reached me through the silence of the night.

I considered my answer, looking up to the clear winter night sky, the stars twinkling above like they were watching this interaction and offering their moral support with their soothing beauty. *Goddess, what trajectory was my life taking?*

"No, but I will be," I responded, dropping my gaze back to him. "I always end up okay, even if it takes time to get there."

He nodded, straightening up and walking toward me. "I can understand that. I can't imagine what challenges you overcome all the time."

"Do you want to come in? I can whip up something for us to eat. I'm sure you're as hungry as I am," I offered, trying not to feel uncomfortable with admitting that I need to eat to someone who looks like he was chiseled from the material of the gods.

His smile widened and he nodded, revealing perfect, white teeth. "I'd be honored. I'll even help cook."

Kyle was surprisingly capable in the kitchen, and I couldn't stop myself from asking about it. "Do your parents not have servants like other Beta families?"

A chuckle came from him as he shuffled the chicken around in the pan. "No. The families that didn't agree with Alpha Lucien on how he treated whatever feud happened with your family tend not to unless they pay them well. The downfall of the Nocetti family really opened their eyes on how fleeting the status of Beta could be. My parents, like many others including Alex's and Brody's, decided not to enslave the Omegas and instead donate money and supplies to their causes."

I paused for a moment before asking, even though I knew the answer already. "And the Barbers?"

Kyle stiffened for a moment. "They have many and pay them horribly. I've heard that their punishments are some of the worst, and Dr. Barber has many servants who work for him at the Beta clinic."

Frowning, I looked at him for so long that he turned to look back at me. "Most of the Betas do not agree, but so many are afraid to go against Lucien that they don't donate anything like my family, the Pierces, or the Griffins," he continued, listing Alex's and Brody's families.

Heaving a sigh, I stood beside him at the stove and grinned as I changed the subject. "Well, Mr. Wilkins, I am impressed with your cooking. Maybe *we* should hire *you*," I teased, watching the line between his brows smooth as he smirked.

"Maybe you should. I make a mean omelet, and I'd love to make one for you sometime." He pulled the pan from the stove and dumped the food onto two plates I'd grabbed earlier.

The meal was comfortable, our conversations spanned over childhood memories and favorites. I enjoyed hearing his stories about combat training with Alex and how she nearly always got the upper hand over him, no matter how he tried to beat her.

"Oh yeah, she can throw me over her shoulder onto my back like I'm a pillow. Just *slam,* onto the mat, and then I'm tapping out right after. She's fierce and I'd hate to be on her bad side." He laughed as he put his fork on his empty plate and leaned back in his seat.

"What about Ezra?" I shifted toward him and put my chin on my fist, my elbow resting on the table like a true lady.

Kyle sighed, his grin still in place as he looked into the distance of his memories. "Ezra . . . he can take on just about anyone. He's leaner, like me, so he's more of a slippery fighter. We are fairly evenly matched in hand-to-hand combat, but when he has a sword in his hands?" He exhaled in a sharp woosh. "He's unstoppable. He wields a sword like it is part of his body. Watching him fight that way is like watching an elegant dance."

My eyes widened, fascinated by the glimpse into the lives of my friends I'd never gotten to see. I had no idea that they were such impressive warriors. "That's–I never knew any of that," I whispered, wondering how much else I didn't know about my favorite people.

He nodded, curls falling into his face and causing him to sweep them off his forehead. "They're quite impressive. Alex's dad didn't get to the position of General by happenstance, and Alex is just as brilliant as him. Maybe even better."

I slumped into my chair, exhaustion hitting me like a heavy weight. Kyle's perceptive gaze immediately caught my expression, and he stood up and carried the dishes to the kitchen. I heard the water turn on as I laid my head on my arms on the table. What felt like seconds later, his shadow fell over me and his hand gently gripped my shoulder. "You're going to have the worst neck ache in the morning if you sleep here." His voice was hushed, coming to me through a haze of sleep.

Grumbling, I forced my eyes awake to see his hazel ones not far from mine. With a smirk, I realized that he was laying his head on the table in front of me. "Maybe I like having neck pain," I mumbled, my words slurring. It had been such a long day, and it was well after midnight.

Kyle chuckled, gently squeezing my shoulder again. "No one likes neck pain. Want help to your room?"

Exhaling, I nodded and sat up straight with his help. When I stood, I took a couple shuffling steps before he swooped my legs out from under me and picked me up. "No, I'm too heavy," I grumbled, my arms automatically going around his neck.

"Don't be ridiculous," he admonished, his voice not even sounding strained as he carried me upstairs. When he paused, I pointed down the hall to my open door and he carried me into my room. Gently, like I might break, he laid me down and pulled the blankets over me. "Good night, Cadence," he whispered, turning and leaving my room.

Seconds later, I heard the front door closing and the electric lock engaging as my eyes shut and I plummeted into a dreamless sleep.

CHAPTER 14

EZRA

A s I came out of a fog of sleep, the first thing I noticed was my heart banging painfully inside my eyeballs. While consciousness slowly crept over me, I realized that the agony encompassed my entire body and not just in my eyes. Groaning, I tried to sit up before I realized that I was actually laying on my stomach and my back was on fire. Wondering if my father had finally snapped, placing my body onto a funeral pyre, I inhaled but there was no trace of smoke. Another grunt escaped me as I opened my eyes to see David Nocetti sleeping on a cot not far from me. That was unusual.

My arm felt like it was made of cement as I pulled it up to feel my face, checking if I was actually alive. Why my muddled brain thought that would tell me anything, I'll never be sure. What it did accomplish was assuring me that even my skin was aching, each individual cell fed through a paper shredder. Maybe I'd been resurrected as Flat Stanley, and someone decided my trip around the world was over and it was time for my demise?

Agonizingly slowly, I moved first my toes and then rocked my legs from side to side. My body was coming to life again. With every new awakened body part, I wished I could just face Kuorir, the God of the Underworld, and just pass off into my next life. I pushed my torso off the bed, but the screaming of my back came out through my mouth as I did. I flopped onto the bed and writhed in pain, grunting. Unfortunately, that caused even more agony to tear through my entire body until I was sweating profusely, and nausea rolled up my throat.

Before I could register what was happening, an emesis bag was against my mouth as I dry heaved until bile came up. A gentle hand combed through my hair, soothing me as my vomiting slowly eased.

"Is he okay?" a male voice asked behind me as the person in front of me pulled the bag away from my mouth.

"He's fine, I'm going to pump painkillers and nausea medication into his IV," another male voice answered, one that I could almost recognize through the haze of pain.

"Do you want music to distract you?" Cadence's voice came to me, the words distorted and rippling as they moved through the fuzz of my brain.

"Yes," I breathed, wanting something to focus on other than how my body felt.

Suddenly, her eyes were in front of me, and I latched onto them, the very visage of them grounding me in sanity. A piece of plastic was pressed into my ear, one of her earbuds. Immediately, the song changed from something heavy to something more mellow; I found myself drifting on the melody and lyrics of "Fearless" by Pink Floyd. It was one of my favorite songs of theirs, and it was easier to let go of the pain and melt into the vision of colors and dreams of night-colored eyes with a splash of daylight.

CADENCE

I kept one of the earbuds, floating on the same song as Ezra while his face and body relaxed almost immediately. Gently, I reached out with my fingertips and wiped away the creases in his forehead while he drifted into unconsciousness. Pulling up the chair I'd been dozing in, I sat beside him and held his hand. Feeling eyes on me, I looked up to see Kyle watching us with an indiscernible look on his face. I was just about to ask him what was wrong when he caught me staring at him and smiled sadly at me instead.

Unsure what to do with my feelings, I buried them, dropping my gaze to Ezra's face. His jaw was working, proof that the painkillers hadn't quite set in yet. The music swelled to a crescendo in my ear and I wanted nothing more than to take the agony he was feeling so he didn't have to.

Settling into my seat, I glanced over Ezra's back, still covered in the salve, to Kyle. Our eyes met and he gave me another sad smile before leaning his head against the wall and closing his eyes. It was the middle of the night and sleep took me quickly as another Pink Floyd song swept over me.

EZRA

The next time I woke up, David was walking around, the music no longer in my ear. While I was still in pain, most of the agony had dwindled into something aggravating rather than debilitating.

"How long has it been?" My voice croaked with lack of use and thirst.

David turned, not seeming surprised to see me awake. He had a syringe in his hand and injected more medicine into my IV. "It's Tuesday," he answered, giving me a sad smile. "And not the same Tuesday you came here. It's been one week. I've kept you sedated since the night you woke up while Cadence and Kyle were here on Wednesday night."

"Wilkins? Why was he here?" The confusion was making my head pound.

At that, David was mildly surprised. "He helped Cadence bring you here. He knows what happened but swore to keep everything between the group of us." He frowned at me. "Cadence told me last week that your father informed the school you went out of pack territory for emergency meetings with him to explain your sudden absence. He has not reached out and seems unconcerned about your condition, though I'm sure that does not surprise you."

It really didn't. I wouldn't have been surprised if he was disappointed that I'd survived. Frowning, I looked at David as he poked around at my back, the pressure causing stinging pain to pierce through my body. "I think I have to do it . . . date Jessica," I muttered, wishing there was a way out of this.

"I know that, son. Cadence knows that, too. She will want to speak with you after school. If her and Kyle keep to their routine, they should be here momentarily." He confused me once again by mentioning Kyle.

"Kyle Wilkins?" I asked again, wondering if I was hallucinating.

David nodded. "That would be the one. He's been here just as religiously as Cady has."

Flabbergasted, I wondered if I actually had died and woken up in an alternate universe. I didn't feel any relief as Cadence walked into the room, Kyle following behind like a bodyguard. That was my position. What the hell happened while I was unconscious?

Excusing himself, David walked out of the room and shut the door. I grunted as I forced myself into a sitting position. Despite doing nothing but sleeping for a week, I felt completely exhausted, and my body was aching with every motion, the muscles screaming after so much disuse.

Cadence stepped forward, pulling up a chair so we were closer to eye level. "How are you feeling?" Her tone was cautious, clearly uncertain about what to expect.

I sighed and rubbed my face with my hands, the movement taking way more energy than it should have. "Like I was attacked by a grizzly with poison tipped claws," I grumbled, dropping my hands into my lap and wincing as the action jarred my back.

Cady nodded sympathetically, looking at me as if she wanted to say something I wasn't going to like. Did she end up with Kyle while I was out? Was that revenge for what I had to do with Jessica? Internally, I shook my head to clear those thoughts. It was unfair to assume such things of Cadence. She would never do that, and I knew better than to think it.

"I have to date her." I wished the cobwebs in my brain would clear so I could think clearly.

"I know." The sadness was clear in her tone and on her face. "I know you do. I can't watch you go through this. You might not survive next time." A pause as a crease formed between her brows. "I have a suggestion, a possible answer to truly get him off your back."

My eyes narrowed before glancing at Kyle who stood just behind her. Kyle didn't shift his weight or look guilty. He just looked back at me with an open expression that didn't reveal anything.

I didn't say anything, just focused on Cadence as she fidgeted uncomfortably. "Kyle and I are going to pretend to date while you pretend to date Jessica. That way, your father will be completely thrown, and he won't continue this torture," she said, each word coming faster until she said the last and inhaled sharply. Her face was crinkled in what I could only assume was a mix of worry and guilt. "He may think it's an act, but he won't care as long as the show is there for the rest of the pack."

"No," I snapped immediately, glaring at Kyle. "Was this your idea? What about Brody? Isn't he your bestie or whatever?" I snarled at him and watched as he pressed his lips into a thin line, though he didn't avert his gaze or look sheepish.

"Brody will survive. I'm doing what's best for Cadence, who doesn't deserve to be under the scrutiny of your father more than she already is, and for the future Alpha of my pack," Kyle responded, his voice cool and even. "I will not put my hands on Cadence if she doesn't want me to, so you can relax about that. She also willingly agreed. We both think it's the best way to get Lucien to stop meddling," he added, "I will not watch you go through this again when I can do something about it."

Opening my mouth, I was going to speak before I snapped it shut with a click of my teeth. "Fine, but I'm not happy about it. One step over her boundaries and I'll end you," I threatened.

"Not a problem," he agreed, dropping hazel eyes to Cadence who looked up at him. "I have combat training. Are you okay?"

My body stiffened painfully at the intimacy that had formed between them in just a week.

She nodded, but said nothing as he turned and left, closing the door quietly behind him. I could vaguely hear David talking to him, but the pounding of my heart was covering the actual words they said. "I feel betrayed," I muttered, not looking at Cadence.

"Please don't feel that way. It's not real. We will be going out as friends, nothing more. It will just look like we are dating to outsiders," she assured me, her voice pleading. "I don't want to hurt you, but I can't watch your father continue to do this. I saw the scars. I know this wasn't the first time."

I sighed, pushing one hand through the greasy waves on my head. "It's not. He's never given me so many lashes before. It's usually just one or two at the most."

My eyes shifted to her, and she frowned at me. I wasn't sure what she expected, but I wasn't pleased with Kyle going on dates with her. At least it was better than Brody. "I'm sorry. I'll adjust. I know it's for the best. I don't need my father targeting you further," I ground out, the words sounding as forced as they felt.

She nodded, standing up and lifting her backpack from the floor. "I'm not worried about me. I'm worried about you, and you look like you're about to fall over. I'm sorry for springing this on you," she said, bending down and pressing a gentle kiss to my lips. "You're the only one I want, Ezra Wolfe. Don't forget that while we drag ourselves through this hell. In just a few months, I'll Ascend and then we will have all the answers."

She gave me an appraising look, memorizing my face as I looked up at her. Her eyes looked haunted. "I love you." Her words were a whisper as she leaned down and pressed her lips against mine. I heard a thud as her backpack hit the floor and her hands were on the sides of my neck as our kiss grew more desperate. Wincing, I wrapped my arms around her waist and pulled her flush against me and kissed her until we were both breathless. It still didn't feel like enough.

Chapter 15

CADENCE

The sun had returned for an unseasonably warm February, melting all the snow and turning everything to frigid puddles. Alex's Ascension Ceremony was quickly approaching, and her nerves over the entire thing made me feel guilty for not being more thoughtful. Over the past couple weeks, Lucien had left Ezra alone while he healed and the circles beneath his eyes grew paler until they disappeared altogether. However, this morning when he picked me up, he had news.

"Father mentioned to me yesterday afternoon that he set up a date with Jessica for tonight," he grunted when I got in the passenger seat. His fingers gripped the steering wheel with anger that he'd barely kept beneath the surface. "He also told me that if he catches me giving too many rides to you that I'll get a repeat of my last defiance. I spoke with Kyle after combat training last night and he agreed to start picking you up and dropping you off for school." The words were strained and painful, like they physically hurt him to say.

Ah, so that was the reason for so much rage. I nodded, deciding it was best not to say anything further and looking out the window. February was upon us, and now the plans we had made to look like we were no longer a couple were starting to take root. I was solidly disappointed. As much as I enjoyed Kyle's company, I didn't like being away from Ezra, and watching him with Jessica was going to be pure torture.

He parked and opened the door for me as usual. I moved closer to him and whispered, "I wish we didn't have to do this."

Ezra nodded, averting his gaze. "I hate it too. I love you, and I know that this hell will be worth it."

To hide the whispers around us about Ezra's disappearance and the usual accusations about him hanging out with the pack's traitor, I popped my earbuds in. "February" by No Love For The Middle Child came into my ears, soothing my frazzled brain while I continued our conversation through text.

> Where do you have to take her? Hopefully somewhere that you can ditch her, so you don't have to be stuck for too long in misery.

I sighed, making a disgusted face at the end of the sentence.

He read my text and responded with, *Moony's*, the name for a pizza and arcade place in Beta territory. It was where the teens hung out to keep out of trouble. I'd never been there, and I felt a piece of my soul break as I waved goodbye when we reached the door instead of at my locker. Frowning, I hugged myself tightly as I walked into the school by myself for the first time in my life. I hated every minute of it.

There were stares and raised eyebrows as Ezra stayed behind while I walked ahead. Girls looked at me appraisingly, impatiently waiting for my reaction to finally being ditched by Ezra Wolfe. I knew there were bets on how long we would last, especially as I watched money changing hands in the hallway. We'd started rumors of our breakup last week, but that didn't help prepare me for this walk of shame. Even though it was all fake and Ezra and I were still together, it didn't make the judgment any easier. I could see some girls telling me things, but I thankfully couldn't hear them snicker as they turned their backs on me. My fragile grip on sanity was loosening by the moment, the pressure of teenaged criticism much more painful than I could ever have expected it to be.

Maybe things would be okay after all, and I felt more like that as Kyle split off from his group and approached me when I entered the main hall through the school. He smiled brightly at me before his eyes shifted to the buds in my ears. Nodding to me, he allowed me to take his arm and walked me directly to my locker. Glancing back at Brody, I saw his nostrils flare as he looked at Kyle and me, though Jason looked even more mutinous. That confused me, since I figured he would be happy about Ezra and his sister. Their union would make him Alpha rank, after all.

Turning away from them, I let Kyle keep me company while I gathered my things. When I'd gathered my stuff and placed my backpack in my locker, I shut it and turned to face Kyle. He blushed furiously as he raised his hands to waist level and crossed his arms in front of him before extending them out to the sides like opening double doors. Blinking, it took me a second to figure out what he was saying before it registered. Pulling the plastic buds from my ears, I placed them back into their case while smiling happily.

"That's really close. You have to make an 'R' with your fingers like this," I instructed, raising my right hand and making a fist except for my index and middle fingers. Then I crossed them in the ASL sign for the letter R. "Then you do the motion you did," I added, making the sign for 'ready' and grinning as he copied. "That's perfect. You know sign language?"

His blush deepened until his neck was as scarlet as his cheeks. "No, actually. I saw you and Ezra signing before, and I thought it might be good for me to learn it, too. I want to be friends, and I figured I should learn to speak to you in both of your languages." He shrugged as if to make the statement casual and jammed his hands into his pockets.

I flushed in return, my eyes widening as I saw Kyle in yet another new light. "We use Pidgeon Signed English, PSE; enough to discuss while I turn my hearing off. I appreciate the gesture, though, more than you know. You're kind of incredible, you know that? How are you single?" I teased, taking his arm as we walked toward homeroom.

"Oh, I don't know. Just never found someone at the right time," he muttered, staring straight down the hall as he walked with me.

After school, Kyle met me at my locker with a broad smile. He leaned against the locker beside mine as I stuffed everything I needed into my backpack. "So, Cadence, would you like to go on a date tonight? It's Friday night, and Moony's will be packed. We can go there and play some arcade games and share pizza? How's that sound?"

I paused in the act of zipping my backpack, glancing at Kyle and finishing the task before he noticed. Unsuccessful in my attempt, I watched the frown form on his face. "What's wrong?"

"Ezra is taking Jessica to Moony's tonight. Also, I've never been there and don't think I'd be super welcome in Beta territory." I remembered Lucien's threats the night of Novzima and shuddered.

Pursing his lips, Kyle seemed to ponder for a moment while I shut my locker. Just as I was about to throw my backpack over my shoulder, he pulled it from my hands and tossed it over his own. Giving him a small smile, I placed my arm in his as he guided me toward the back exit that led to the student parking lot. I could almost ignore the stares from our classmates as I looked up at him. "Well, that's a terrible idea then. The last thing you need is to see the two of them. I think you'd be more welcome than you'd think at Moony's, but not tonight. What do you like to do for fun?"

He unlocked his car and opened the door for me while I considered my options.

When he climbed into the driver's seat, I mused aloud, "I actually spend a decent amount of my free time at Axe Marks the Spot."

Kyle gave me a curious look. "What is that? Pirates? Tell me how to get there while you explain."

Biting my lip, I tried my best to forget where Ezra was and indulged in new experiences with Kyle. Maybe we really could be good friends. "It's an axe throwing place my grandpa built after my grandma died. He needed to be able to be home with my dad while he was a kid, and he worked too many hours when he was logging." I sighed. "So, he used his trade in a different way, building a place that anyone was welcome to, but that was really for the Deltas and Omegas. When he was alive, he accepted whatever you could afford to throw there, which was sometimes nothing. He even had lessons for those who really wanted to be good at throwing." I smiled fondly with memories of my grandpa.

Kyle glanced at me, the corners of his mouth lifting. "You must be pretty good at throwing, then," he said, a teasing lilt to his voice.

I laughed, gesturing to where he needed to turn and soon, we were pulling into the lot. It wasn't far from the school. "I'm alright," I replied vaguely, hopping out of the car once he parked.

He met me in front of the car, looking down at my hand before holding out his own. "If you want to," he assured me quietly, lifting his hazel eyes to meet mine. As the sunlight struck them, I could see how the outer ring of blue bled into amber and I found myself momentarily struck by how pretty they were.

It took a monumental amount of effort to push aside the insecurity that told me he was messing with me and place my hand into his. Our fingers automatically laced together as I led him into the building. Walking inside, I took a deep breath, inhaling the woody scent of the building. Ava, as usual, was behind the counter and looked up as we entered. Seeing Kyle, her entire face lit up as she leaned forward on the counter.

"Hey, Kyle." She gave him a smile so bright that even I was nearly blinded.

I glanced at Kyle just as she pulled his attention, expecting him to flirt with her. I felt my heart drop as he turned toward her for just a second. Raising his hand to wave, he said, "Oh. Hey, Ava." Then he turned back to me, and I felt bathed in the glow of his attention again. "So how do we do this? Axes are not my specialty, so I have no training in throwing them," he said, completely ignoring that Ava existed.

Dumbfounded by his complete disregard for the beauty behind the counter, I glanced at her and found her pouting behind him. He didn't seem concerned in the slightest, and I was pleasantly surprised. Realizing he asked me a question, I flushed. "Oh! Yeah. I'll show you."

Turning, I spun my combination on my locker and pulled out my favorite hatchet and an axe. When I turned around, Ava was approaching holding another axe by the head and handed it to him. He gave her a polite smile and a thank you before immediately turning back to me. I noted her confused frown before she walked away.

"How does the business run now?" His question pulled my attention to him.

"Oh, the same as it did before. By donations or whatever you can afford to give, typically. The new owner decided to keep my grandpa's policy on that." I gave a small shrug. "We can't typically afford to offer anything." My face heated even further with the humiliation of it, but Kyle didn't seem judgmental in the slightest.

"Awesome." He pulled out his wallet and dropped a hundred-dollar bill into the donation box. I balked at him, but decided it was best not to draw attention to it. I'd never seen anyone drop that much money into that box. Approaching me again and still ignoring Ava's existence, he gave me a broad smile. "So, what do I do, teach?"

Blushing, I walked over to my typical lane number five that Ava had already soaked for me. I gave her a thanks, but she didn't seem super accepting of it tonight. Pressing my lips together, I took my stance and showed Kyle how I always hold my axe, since that's what he was throwing. He watched me intently, and I hoped I made a decent shot. Doing a practice throw, I chucked the axe at the target and smiled with satisfaction as it landed in the bullseye with a satisfying *thunk.*

Kyle looked thoroughly impressed as I walked over and shifted the axe up and down by the handle until the wood released its hold. Turning around, I saw him looking at me with something I hadn't seen in him before. It was a look that Ezra gave me sometimes before he complimented me, and I wasn't sure how to read it. His smile wasn't present, just a steady gaze and a hungry look in his eyes that made my heart thump heavily in my chest and butterflies to flutter in my stomach before guilt coated them in concrete. When he caught me gawking at him, he immediately smiled warmly and moved to the line where I had been standing.

"You're taller than me. You might benefit from moving back a step." I gestured to the three blue lines on the floor. A red one was at the edge of the mat, a sign to not cross it while throwing.

Kyle nodded, flicking his head to move a wild curl from his eyes as he took the stance I did. Automatically, I reached out and adjusted the axe in his hand, so he was gripping the bottom. "Here. You'll never get a good stick if you hold it higher than that unless you're close to the target. You'd whip it right into the floor with that hold," I instructed, chuckling as I adjusted his grip and the position of his arm.

"Show me what to do?" He glanced over his shoulder at me. I slid my hands over his forearm to move it in the motion his limb needed to take for a successful shot, including giving him a rough estimate on where in the throw to release the axe.

He nodded. His face was serious as he stared down the target. I took a step back, watching his form as he did what I told him. He took a deep breath . . . and threw the axe straight into the floor where it bounced once and lodged itself into the fencing that separated the lanes. Glancing back at me, I saw his face flush as he expected me to laugh. I was more than familiar with that expression since I gave it frequently, though I wasn't sure why someone as confident as him would have it. I dislodged the axe from the fencing before walking to him. "You let go of it too late." I got into the stance and mimicked the motion and told him the exact position to release it.

With a deep breath, he nodded and took the axe again, gripping the handle tightly in his fist. Doing the same thing, he tossed the axe, and it stuck in the wood just outside the far line of the target. Cheering, I threw my arms into the air. "That's great! You got it to stick!"

"Sure, but it's not even in the rings," he stated simply, gesturing to the axe before going to retrieve it.

"Mmhmm, but a stick is something to be proud of, especially on your second throw," I retorted. He finally grinned back, stepping aside so I could take my next turn.

Eventually, I switched to my hatchet, preferring the lightness of it to the heft of an axe. Kyle showed interest in the amaryllis carved into the handle and I told him about my grandfather carving it for me. He seemed surprised that that was my favorite flower, and I shrugged.

"It reminds me of the time before my twin, Callum, was taken. He and my Nan on my mom's side were taken right before Heart's Day." I referred to the love holiday that happened toward the end of February, right around Alex's birthday. "So Novzima is the last happy holiday that I remember, and it reminds me of the last time that we were happy and celebrating."

When I glanced up at him, he was looking at me with such fervor that I felt the breath whoosh from my lungs. His hand covered mine as he turned the hatchet to get a better view of the amaryllis engraving. "That's beautifully tragic." His hand was warm around mine as his fingers gently held them. "Thank you for sharing that with me."

We both looked up and our eyes met, his shifted between mine, focusing on my left where the splash of blue resided. "Your eyes are so fascinating. Gorgeous and mesmerizing." His voice was hushed in the quiet between us. The scent of rainfall in a forest wrapped around me like an embrace and I inhaled the essence of him.

I was just about to speak when Ava walked over with keys jingling. "I'm closing up for the night. Can you lock up, Cadence?" she asked, snapping her gum as she popped a hip out.

Startling, I looked over her just as Kyle did. Glancing at his profile, I saw the tightness of his jaw and the annoyance in his eyes.

"Yeah, I can lock up. Thanks, Ava."

I side eyed Kyle as she snapped her gum again and left.

Kyle softened as he turned back to me, his hand dropping away from mine. The moment was ruined, but I was okay with that. It was getting way too intense for me. "Are you hungry? I'm starving."

He flicked his sleeve off his watch, glancing at the time. "Sure. Want to come to my place? Dinner should be done by the time we get there, and my parents would love to meet you."

My eyes widened with the horror of meeting Beta parents. I know he said that they were on our side, but that didn't mean they wanted my riffraff self to be at their *house*. Pushing the fear aside, I let myself live for once. Giving him a shy nod, I whispered, "Sure."

The drive to his house was pleasant as we talked about plans for the future. I learned that he also wanted to go to PSG, the famous supernatural academy. We discussed sitting together and writing our entrance essays until he pulled into a driveway of a very sizable home. Struck by its beauty, my jaw dropped as I leaned forward to look out the windshield. Even in the darkness, I could see how elegant the landscaping was. Winter roses practically glowed under small spotlights embedded in the lawn, their blooms strewn through the deep green leaves of their bushes. Trellises framed each side of the stoop, and I could only imagine what vines would climb the white wood in the spring and summer. Small evergreen bushes stood on either side of the house like sentinels keeping watch over the precious winter blossoms. Swallowing hard, I nearly changed my mind when he opened my door and held out his hand to me.

"Do they know the truth?" I breathed.

Kyle shook his head with a frown. "No. I told them we were actually dating, but they won't expect us to be touchy or anything. They've been asking when they could meet you for weeks, so try not to worry too much. They're ecstatic."

I nodded, weaving my arm through his as he led me through the front door. The entranceway was large and gorgeous, deep greens decorated the walls, the staircase a pale ashy hardwood and what felt like thousands of family pictures covered a large portion of wall space. There were plants everywhere, vines hanging from swinging pots or climbing up poles planted in every available corner.

I looked at all of them in awe while Kyle chuckled. "My dad absolutely loves horticulture. He did the landscaping outside as well."

Before I could respond, a woman entered the room, drying her hands on a towel. She stopped in the doorway, her dark curls bouncing around her shoulders. Kyle was the spitting image of this woman, so I could only assume she was his mom.

"Cadence, this is my mom, Natalie. Mom, this is Cadence Nocetti," Kyle introduced us, sweeping his arm between us.

I didn't know how to respond, so I pulled my arm from his and held my hand out to her as she beamed. "Oh, finally! Welcome to our home!" My hand was pointedly ignored as she pulled me into one of the tightest hugs of my life. Her strength rivaled even Alex's firm grip. "We are a hugging family, but I guess I should have asked." She pulled away, still gripping my upper arms. "Goddess, you are a pretty girl."

My face heated, the red splotches making me decidedly less pretty. Kyle's response did nothing to allay my embarrassment. "I told you she was beautiful, mom."

She pulled me into another hug. "You did. But I didn't realize how much of a young woman you've become since I saw you last. I'm so glad you're here," she enthused, practically dragging me by the hand into the dining room. "Kyle never brings home any girls. You're the first, and I'm so excited that it's you. I was worried for a while it would be that awful Jessica Barber, since he was friends with Jason." She made a face of disgust.

Was friends with Jason? I glanced at him, but he didn't seem all that concerned or like he'd even noticed her saying it.

I smiled awkwardly, overwhelmed and confused as she guided me to a seat, Kyle sitting beside me. "I hope you like roasted chicken," she said as a man walked into the dining room holding a platter displaying a large chicken. His ashy blond hair was perfectly coiffed, and his blue eyes glittered as they fell on me.

"I do," I replied, giving the man a shy smile in response to his beaming one.

"It's a pleasure, Cadence. It's been a long time since I've seen you, despite how much I run into your father. He's a good man," he effused, plopping into a seat across from Kyle while Natalie sat beside him. "My name is Chuck." It seemed almost like an afterthought as he dished food onto Natalie's plate.

The dinner settled into casual conversation as everything was passed around and I took small servings despite the sheer volume of food at the table. Kyle leaned over and assured me in a whisper that I could eat my fill, that no one would judge me or go hungry if I ate enough. I nodded and did take more, just enough to sate my hunger without filling me completely. Despite his reassurances, the trauma of my weight dug deeper than he could ever relieve.

I was asked standard questions by his parents, but I didn't feel interrogated. There were plenty of anecdotes and family stories shared by the three of them and I felt completely comfortable. Briefly, I wondered at just how *normal* it felt. It felt refreshing to be accepted by adults that weren't Delta or Omega families who loved my dad. I felt seen and appreciated, and Kyle looked at me like I was the most interesting and pretty person he'd ever seen; I didn't know how to feel about that, though. I didn't even know if any of it was real.

After dessert, Kyle's parents went into the kitchen and dished out portions for me to take home for my parents and Kyle practically shoved them into my hands. I didn't want to be rude and thanked Natalie profusely for everything they'd done for me, allowing me into their home.

Kyle and I chatted the whole way home. He walked me to the door, his gentle stare searing into me as I stood there awkwardly. I felt him examine my features like I was the finest piece of art he'd ever seen. "Thank you for everything tonight, Kyle. It was perfect, and I appreciate you getting me out of my head. It would have been a horrible evening without you," I said, using my thumb to unlock the front door.

Kyle smiled, reaching out to gently stroke my cheek. "Of course. I look forward to our next date."

With that, he returned to his car. After ensuring I was in the house, he drove away.

I was in my house for a total of two minutes before my phone vibrated in the pocket of my leggings. Wondering if Kyle forgot something, I was surprised to see Alex's contact photo instead. Pleased that she decided to call, I smiled happily and answered.

"How was your date?" she asked immediately, her tone vague.

"How did you know I was on a date?" I retorted flippantly as I got myself a glass of water.

She sighed impatiently. "The app, of course. Plus, I heard from Brody during training that Kyle was skipping out to be with you. He's livid." A twinge of amusement colored her tone.

I couldn't help but be pleased by that. As far as I was concerned, Brody deserved to be angry. He was a constant pain in my rump. "It went well. We threw axes and then he took me to meet his parents for dinner at his house. Though I wouldn't really call it a date. More like friends hanging out."

Alex was silent for a long moment; so long, in fact, that I said hello before she finally responded. "I can't decide if you're willfully ignorant or genuinely unable to tell how people feel about you."

I frowned, walking upstairs to my bedroom where I plopped into my desk chair, propping my feet up on the bed. "What are you talking about? He said that he was doing this as a friend."

Another frustrated sigh. "Kyle is totally into you. He might be doing this as a friend, but that doesn't mean he isn't hoping you'll fall for him in the process. Before you and Ezra officially became a thing, he was asking Ezra how he felt about you and they got into a scuffle about it during training. My dad kicked them both out for it."

I felt my stomach plummet into my gut as I sat upright. "You can't be serious."

"Why would I joke about this, Cadence? And I also overheard Jason telling Brody that he was the one who suggested that Jessica end up with Ezra. I think he orchestrated the whole thing, but why, I have no idea." She was agitated, her voice rising as she continued, "Brody was happy about it, though. He wants Ezra out of the way, because he's had eyes for you forever."

Scowling, I crossed the arm not holding my phone over my chest. "This is too fantastical to believe. I can barely believe that Ezra is interested in me romantically, let alone Kyle and Brody, too. I'm pretty sure Brody and Jason are, at the very least, making fun of me when they're 'hitting' on me. I'm still not convinced that Kyle's intentions are pure either."

Alex groaned and I could picture her rubbing her face in response. "I'm pretty sure they aren't. I just never told you about any of this because it never mattered before. It was always just Ezra. You didn't seem interested in anyone else. Now, there are other pieces on the game board, and I want you to know where everyone is standing on it. You're the queen, surrounded by kings who want to checkmate you to win the game of your affection."

I made a disgusted face. "I think you're being ridiculous." I snorted, shaking my head. "That's not even how chess is played."

Yet another sigh at me. "Well, I'll be here to talk whenever you want, but that time isn't now. We are about to be interrupted," she said, amusement returning to her voice. "I love you, Cady. Remember, I just want your happiness. Please keep your heart safe."

With that, she hung up and left me staring at my phone. Then, I was startled as the electric lock downstairs shifted and a notification popped up on my phone that Ezra unlocked it. If it weren't for the electric lock they'd bought us a year or two ago, I'd have been terrified I was under attack. I heard footsteps thundering up the stairs and I swiveled in my chair to see him barreling through my doorway, panting. His blue eyes looked strained; a tightness was present in the way he held his mouth. I almost missed the crimson amaryllis in his left hand.

"How was your date?" I asked, regurgitating the question Alex asked just moments earlier.

Ezra shook his head, his mop of frazzled curls bouncing. His blue eyes glowed as they looked me over. "Terrible. How was yours?"

I couldn't hide my glimmer of a smile, quirking the corner of my mouth upward. "It wasn't bad, though I'd hardly call it a date. It was more like friends hanging out in public."

Pain flashed across Ezra's face, there and gone so quickly I almost missed it. He had no right to be upset about Kyle; it was just as important for me to seem otherwise occupied as it was for him. I also had no right to be upset about Jessica, but that didn't stop me from feeling unhappy with the whole thing.

"I hate her. The only thing I could think about the entire night was how much I wished it was you and not that troll," he muttered, gentling his harsh tone. "Cadence, I hated every minute of it. I hated being away from you. Please forgive me for everything that's already happened and everything that's going to."

I stood, pressing my lips together and nodding. "You have nothing to apologize for. It just hurts."

He sighed, stepping into my personal space. His scent of teakwood and amber came with him. "Please know that I won't enjoy a single moment of it. I understand if you'd rather be with Kyle instead of going through all of this. He is a genuinely good guy, and he would treat you well. I'd make sure of it."

Shaking my head, I gazed up at him. "I don't. I want to be with you," I whispered, watching the relief cross through his eyes.

"Can I touch you?" Ezra asked, glancing at my mouth.

I nodded, and he reached out, tucking the amaryllis behind my right ear. I leaned into his touch as his arms wrapped around me. "Kiss me?" I countered, my voice a small prayer.

Ezra chuckled quietly. "Of course," he murmured, dropping his mouth to mine.

CHAPTER 16

BRODY

It had been several weeks since Ezra had returned to school from his absence. The story was that he was out of town for meetings with the council, but I wasn't buying it. I'd seen the look on his face, the way he was sweating and wincing every time he moved. Lucien had been doling out his usual punishment for a crime Ezra may or may not have committed. None of us spoke about it, but Jason had told those of us who trained at The Crest that his father had read in Lucien's mind about what he did to his son.

As often as Ezra and I had fought in the past, I didn't hate the guy. I did hate what Lucien did to him. Even with my rage, I couldn't imagine doing that to someone I was supposed to love more than anyone else in the world. The idea of laying my hands on Cadence to cause her physical harm made me sick. I'd done stupid things, but I could never intentionally harm her.

Even as the thought occurred to me, a feeling of guilt wrapped around my stomach. I just wanted her so desperately I could barely stand it.

The guilt twisted further as I walked into the Crest for training with Kyle. He stood on the mat when I entered the room, his sword already in his hands. The metal of the blade flashed in the glaring lights from the ceiling as he went through the motions. While Kyle was not a god with a sword like Ezra, it was still impressive to watch. My chakram blades were already in my hand, the handles together to form a circular blade around my fist.

Anger flared through me as Kyle's hazel eyes landed on me and he gave me a crooked smile, flashing his perfect teeth. He was perfect, and a part of me hated him for it. Not as much as the part of me hated him for getting Cadence. I didn't even care if it was fake, like Alex had told me. I wish she hadn't entrusted me with that information. It burned me more than thinking he was dating her for real.

Without thinking, I lunged at him. Kyle's eyes widened in surprise, a flash of white surrounding his iris before he raised the sword in defense against my blade. I split them apart, holding one in each hand and spinning in an offensive attack. Kyle deflected, his lighter build aiding him in evading my strikes.

"Dude. What the hell?" Kyle panted out, avoiding another attack as I backed him into a corner. "What is your deal?"

I snarled at him, baring my teeth before pulling away from him. "Damn it!" I shouted, resisting the urge to throw my weapons. It was the first time I'd ever wished a spear had chosen me instead of my chakrams. It would feel so nice to embed a blade into something to release some of the anger always simmering under the surface.

Kyle stayed silent, the tip of his sword resting against the ground as he eyed me warily. His lips pressed together in confusion. His uncertainty of what was wrong made the whole thing even worse.

"*Her*. Of all the women you could pretend to date, it had to be *her*."

Kyle blanched, his eyes wide with horror. "How did you know?"

I sighed, putting the blades into one hand, clicking them together so I could rub a palm over my hair. "Alex. I confronted her when I first heard about it. I think she intended to make me feel better."

Kyle audibly swallowed, glancing away from me before meeting my gaze again. "Did you tell Jason?"

I shook my head, glaring at him. "No. I don't trust Jason. I haven't told anyone. I've just been stewing in my fury."

Pressing his lips together, Kyle failed to hide a grin. "That sounds pretty par for the course for you, Brody." He paused, sighing heavily and crouching. He kept a palm on the handle of his sword like he was slowly pushing it into the floor. "I'm sorry I didn't tell you. I didn't want to risk Ezra's safety by telling anyone."

I paused, staring down at the floor. "It's not like that's the only reason. I've seen the way you look at her, too. I'm not a moron, as much as I may act like one."

Kyle snorted in response.

"Yeah. I know."

"It's not like I'm holding her hostage. If you want to attempt to date her, you can. She's free to make her own choices. I'd maybe take a different approach, though." Kyle's words were guarded, as if he didn't want to say them.

I looked at him, but his expression was blank. Unreadable.

I know he didn't want me to, but maybe I *would* make more of an effort.

CADENCE

Corana, or Heart's Day, was almost here, and you could feel the frenzy in the air. Hormones swirled around me in the hallways, like a thick, cloying perfume that never dissipated. I found it equal parts dizzying and nauseating. I was still confused as far as intimacy was concerned. The holiday of heightened fertility and celebrating love really emphasized that for me, as Alex gushed about her glorious relationship with Ivan. Kissing and cuddling was all I really needed, despite the world's assurances that I needed more than that. I was just as lost in exploring Ezra as a person during our secret meetings at my house. He gave me zero pressure for more than I'd originally offered. In fact, we'd never discussed it again. He seemed perfectly content letting things exist naturally. If he didn't, he certainly never let on.

Kyle was also a perfect gentleman, only holding my hand in public and never crossing the boundaries I'd first set in place.

Unfortunately, I was not blind to the pheromones surrounding me, especially from Alex. I'd stayed later than normal, choosing to study in the library for a change of scenery.

I was minding my own business at my locker, jamming my books into my bag at breakneck speed so Ezra or Kyle could save me from this personal hell that reeked of teenage romance even after everyone left for the day. One earbud was balanced carefully in my right ear, blasting "Volcano" by Emily Hearn at an almost unbearable volume to compensate for the other one being absent.

A hard smack landed directly on my ass followed by a painful grabbing of the stinging cheek. My book bag hit the floor beside me as I startled, knowing instantly that the offender was definitely not Ezra or Kyle.

Embarrassment flooded my cheeks with heat as I quickly turned around to face my attacker. Brody's face was inches away from mine, leering at me. My stomach clenched with nerves. I jumped away from him, slamming my back painfully into the open door of my locker, the door jamming against my left shoulder blade. My nerves tightened in my gut like a vise. I was never a fighter, removed from karate as a child for evading my sparring partner instead of engaging. Callum had been excellent and continued going until he was taken.

Brody took advantage of my overwhelmed body, wrapping an arm around my waist and hauling me toward him. With his other hand, he slammed my locker door shut, the noise fraying my already overloaded nervous system. I could feel the panic gripping my heart, the erratic beat drumming in my ears. He was so much taller than me, my neck craning painfully as I stared at him with wide eyes. Brody kicked my bag out of the way, pinning my body against the locker. The knob bit into my injured shoulder, sending icicles of pain shooting down my arm. He banged on the door next to my head, startling me further. My eyes roved over the empty hallway, cursing myself for staying so late. I couldn't even call for Ezra or Kyle, my phone sitting in the bottom of my bag, now ten feet out of reach.

"Hey, there, Cady," he said, his breath wafting over my face. He smelled of smoke and hot cinnamon, and though it wasn't an unpleasant smell, my stomach twisted as a core memory found its way into the recesses of my brain. New scent aversion unlocked. "Heart's Day is coming, and I want you to be mine."

I felt like I was hyperventilating, suffocating under his scent as it wound around my sinuses. It locked itself in, the spiciness of it making me feel hot and uncomfortable and my vulnerable position made it even worse. Looking into his dark eyes, I saw the same intensity I received from Kyle and Ezra, only this was dark. Twisted. Wrong.

"No," I said simply. That single word was a full sentence, and I didn't need to back it up with excuses. He didn't deserve any for being like this: overbearing and forceful.

"Come on, Cade," he growled, pressing his pelvis against me. My relief in his lack of erection did not ease my skin feeling like it might actually crawl off my body and run away to a bleach bath to cleanse myself of his touch. "I've never wanted anyone as badly as I want you," he murmured, his breath fanning over me as his nose slid up my neck, the action both foreign and unwelcome. The complete opposite of Ezra's intimate touch.

Chills erupted over my skin, and I cringed away from his heat and the overwhelming aura he put off. Unfortunately, my back was flush with the lockers, the chilled metal doing nothing to ease the sweat oozing out of my pores. Bad intentions wafted off of him like an acrid stench and I just wanted to escape. Cold tentacles of fear tickled their way down my spine before curling in my gut like a coiled snake. I overheated, like I was baking in the sun for too long. My head throbbed as the air around me became thick and stifling.

Brody began to pull away, his confusion morphing into fear as he gazed into my eyes. He focused solely on the splash of blue in my left iris, his dark eyes widening until I could almost see my reflection in their obsidian depths. The black of his irises lightened to a deep brown as glimmers of light flickered over his face.

I was burning up. I needed to escape to the frigid air outside. Without thinking, I growled at him, snarling and snapping like a rabid dog. "Get away from me," I seethed, the words sounding almost inhuman.

Fortunately, Brody was backing away from me, but he wasn't moving fast enough. I was a caged animal, and I needed to get out of this situation *now*.

EZRA

I was on my way through the halls, a bit further behind schedule than even Cadence was. I spent my time in the gym, waiting for her to text me and let me know she was done studying in the library. Jessica was blessedly busy. I had the evening free to spend with Cadence, but after I hadn't heard anything for a couple hours, I decided to go searching for her. It wouldn't surprise me in the slightest if she'd gotten so hyper focused that she lost track of time. I was halfway to her locker, the abandoned halls feeling almost apocalyptic and giving me a weird sense of dread. However, I realized that maybe it wasn't so much the halls causing me concern when I heard voices coming from the hallway above me.

Clambering up the stairs, I clung to the strap of my backpack as I hurried toward the voices, one of which was undeniably Cadence. She was yelling at someone, but I wasn't sure who. I automatically assumed it was Kyle and fury pulsed through me. As I made it to the top of the steps, I found Cadence in an altercation with Brody. He was backing away from her and she was . . . glowing? Her skin was flushed and emitted a gorgeous golden glow. Her skin glittered with magic as she lifted her hands up toward Brody, her palms facing him in what I assumed was a placating gesture.

"I am not and never will be *yours*," she shouted at him, her voice wavering as if she were shouting through a brutal wind. Her hair lifted off her shoulders, the thick, dark locks waving as if caught in the wind. As she got to the last word, an arc of golden lustrous light left her hands as she thrust them forward. The magic hit Brody like a physical blast, lifting him off his feet and throwing him into the lockers behind him before he dropped to a crumpled heap on the floor.

Without hesitation, I ran over to them, my shoes slapping loudly against the tiles. Brody groaned and put his hand on the back of his head before he jumped to his feet. His shirt was visibly charred and smoking slightly, though he seemed completely uninjured. Clearly off balance, he wavered slightly, using the lockers to steady himself. Dark eyes widening with horror, he stared at Cadence like she was a wraith appearing to him in the night.

"You're a *monster*," he whispered, his voice barely carrying over to us as I stopped at her side. His hands shook with fear, and he didn't even attempt to hide it. "And yet, I know you'll still be mine," he snarled, his lip curling up with anger and disgust. "This isn't over."

He turned and stalked down the hallway. Cadence and I watched him leave, breathing a sigh of relief when he didn't look back.

Chapter 17

CADENCE

I could not get out of the building fast enough. Hearing Ezra calling after me did not slow my pace in the slightest. The walls were closing on me, my feet carrying me from the school at lightning speed until I escaped the hell my world was turning into. I didn't know what was going on with me, but I felt like my life was careening off the track and I was lost on how to stop it from happening. Instead, I was running and hiding like the coward I was.

Jamming my earbuds in, I was relieved to find "Chaos" by Hollywood Undead just starting. I shut the world off and disappeared into my own brain, far from the people around me. Unable to stop myself, I fell into beat with the music blasting into my ears. It was like a slice of heaven wrapped its arms around me as I dropped into the endless abyss of rhythm and lyrics. The notes hugged me like a tangible thing. It was my own peace found in the chaos awaiting me, a gift from the Universe like a cure to the plague of my internal thoughts.

I had no idea where I was going until I was there. Axe Marks the Spot appeared in front of me, like an oasis. The faded sign like a pirate's map out of a Caribbean fantasy. It was yet again my salvation when I was losing traction of my life. Ezra was already being forced away from me, and after today, I was sure that he'd be out of reach completely. Mate or not, he couldn't settle with a monster, especially when he had other options. Because that's what I was now, I was sure of it. The pack would rebel, and his father would rather take us both out than let his son mate with someone like me; he'd made that abundantly clear. I tried to shake that thought from taking root in my subconscious; that was a despair I couldn't let myself sink into.

Walking through the doors, I gave a nod to Ava before heading to my locker. I spun the combination into the lock and opened the door to find my prized possessions waiting for me. Pulling my hatchet from her fabric case, the black metal gleamed happily in my hand. For a moment, I thought the carvings actually glittered golden, though when I blinked, they were back to the etchings I'd always known.

I made my way to the appropriate lane and grabbed the water jug before I realized that Ava had already dampened the wood for me. Turning, I met her gaze, quietly saying, "Thank you," to which she nodded. At least she seemed to have forgiven Kyle's slighting.

"Help" by Papa Roach took over as I stood behind the second line in front of the target. Taking a deep breath, I did my best to relax my muscles and remove the jitters that still lingered in my fingers. Shifting my grip, I made sure my pinky held most of the pressure at the very bottom of the handle and pulled my arm straight back over my head, tossing the axe toward the target. It flew through the air, rolling a couple times before sinking into the wood with a heavy *thunk* just to the right of the bullseye. Pressing my lips together, I sighed inwardly before walking over and yanking the damned thing out of its deep seat in the wood.

Getting into position again, I threw it repeatedly until I was consistently hitting bullseyes. And then I quit using the standard practice position, doing spins and underhand tosses, whipping the weapon at the target, sinking bullseye after bullseye. After an hour, my arm began to protest. I promptly ignored it. I was not done relieving my mental stress, so it would have to wait to rest until I was good and ready to.

Pausing for a moment, I gazed down at the amaryllis carved into the handle of my weapon. Thinking back to Grandpa, I desperately wished that he was with me. I could talk to him about anything, even confusing boy things. Pressing my thumb gently against the sharp blade, I enjoyed the twinge of pain. It was grounding in a way that nothing else could be. Without aiming first, I turned quickly and whipped the hatchet toward the target, face relaxing with pleasure as it embedded itself right into the kill shot in the upper righthand corner.

The hatchet was a bit harder to pull out of the kill shot than the standard size axe since it was so much lighter and lodged above my head. I stood on tiptoe to rock it until it finally relinquished its hold on the wood. As I turned around, I nearly threw the thing when my gaze landed on someone standing right behind me. Rage immediately took over my senses as I ripped one of the buds out of my ear, the song continuing to play, and glared at Ezra.

"You can't sneak up on people who are wielding weapons," I snapped at him, unhappy with his stupidity. "I could have killed you before I even realized it. You, of all people, should know that."

Ezra's eyes practically glowed with an emotion I couldn't pinpoint as he stared down at me, his hand wrapping around mine as I gripped the hatchet as if it was the key to my salvation. Pulling me against him, his blue eyes pierced my soul. At his nearness, I could see all the fractures of color that made up the total hue of his irises. There were so many shades of blue, broken pieces fitted together so they appeared like pale sapphires; his eyes were as beautiful as he was. I was lost in them as his focus remained on mine, and I was having trouble determining just what he was thinking or feeling.

"You don't usually come here. . ." I started, though he successfully cut me off.

With no warning, he yanked my body flush against his and pressed his mouth to mine. This kiss was not like our other kisses. Those were gentle, loving, exploratory. This kiss we shared was ravenous and captivating. His lips seared mine with a delicious heat that made me feel breathless and entranced. I was lost in him as his mouth moved against mine, his tongue invading my space as he claimed me. His free arm moved around my waist, attempting to pull me tighter against him, our contact broken only by the weapon held in our combined fists.

With a growl, he pulled completely away from me and ran his fingers through his waves. It took me a second to figure out why I was suddenly so incredibly cold and empty. Blinking slowly, I shifted my eyes to him and attempted to clear the fog in my brain. It was so lonely out here, outside of his grip; achingly isolated and exposed.

Without a word, he turned and walked toward the exit. I knew I should follow. I had a moment of uncertainty; I was never the type to idly obey orders. However, if I wanted more kisses like that, I didn't have much of a choice. My decision was made. I put my weapon back into my locker before exiting the building to follow him outside.

The car ride was awkward. Stilted. I had been surprised that it was nighttime already when I'd walked outdoors. I'd even needed to lock the door behind me, Ava already gone for the night. It's incredible how much time passes when you're trying to run from your own feelings and insecurities. Frighteningly enough, I still wasn't ready to face them. My right arm ached as I lifted my elbow against the door of the car so I could prop my heavy head on my closed fist.

"Cadence, what was that?"

Ezra pulled over suddenly on one of the back roads that led to my house. We were completely surrounded by trees here, the lack of any streetlights making me feel isolated and alone. The privacy the forest provided made this moment seem so much more intimate than I was prepared for it to be. My eyes drifted to the trees outside of the car, wondering what living things resided in their sheltered domain. The Adirondacks were the place I'd always call home, no matter how much I pretended I wanted to leave.

"I don't know why you're asking *me*. You're the one who attacked my face with yours." My response was snarky and wholly unfair. I knew what he was asking, but I wasn't ready to talk about it. Hell, I wasn't ready to think about it.

Ezra turned to stare at me from the driver's seat, his face cast almost completely in shadow. From what little I could see of his expression, he was not amused. It was a few moments before he gathered his composure enough to say as much. "You know that's not what I'm talking about. What happened at the school?"

I didn't want to remember what happened at school, to face what my body did without my control or permission when I was scared and alone. However, when I looked into Ezra's darkened face, his eyes and their expression hidden in the shadows, I knew I couldn't run from anything forever. Even if I wanted to, Ezra would never let me hide. It was sort of his specialty, to force me to be a reasonable almost-adult.

"I don't know. I felt trapped and afraid, and then I just got so hot and there was a blinding light and . . . I don't know what happened."

I put my face in my hands, rubbing at my temples as I tried to remember the incident step by step, but it was like my mind blocked itself from reliving it. Dropping my hands to my lap, I tipped my head back against the headrest and stared at the ceiling, the charcoal lining looking pitch black in the sheltered darkness. Ezra flipped the headlights off, a sure sign that he wasn't planning on leaving this empty road any time soon.

"Did you have any control over it?" His voice was quietly probing. He was trying very, very hard not to throw me into panic mode. I appreciated his concern, but I'd already been there for hours.

"No. I felt cornered and stuck. His smell was so overwhelming to me, and I just needed to get away from him. It was like my body took control of the situation on its own and removed him from me." My fingers shook with the memory, and I clasped my hands together to hide the tremors. However, his sharp gaze noticed anyway.

I was startled when his hands wrapped around my own and he leaned toward me. "I don't understand why this is happening to you, but we will find out. I'll do my best to help you." His voice was hushed between us, a whispered caress against my fried nerves.

Despite my initial reservations, I was starting to appreciate the little bubble of peace that we had here. Even as I struggled in silence, it wasn't so bad when I was with him. I briefly wondered if my need for him would bite me later. Brushing that aside as a possible mate effect, I looked at him for a moment before turning my head to gaze through the windshield at the road ahead of us. It was a black tunnel leading away from us, the moon nearly gone, a mere sliver in the sky. I always appreciated that the moon was so reliable, always waning and waxing without fail or stutter. It reminded me that Alex would be Ascending on a new moon, one of my favorites to watch.

"Let's focus on getting Alex through her birthday first," I said quietly, suddenly wishing I wasn't the last one to turn eighteen in our group. Ezra Ascended on November third, Alex on February twenty-fifth. I had until May fourteenth.

Every Volsifi had a large ceremony to celebrate their Ascension; a huge bash where the birthday Volsifi would dress to the nines and shift under the rising moon in front of the entire pack while wearing a sacred robe that shifted with them. Volsifi, unlike cult classic werewolves, could shift regardless of the lunar cycle. They could even shift during the daytime if they chose. Naturally, some were better or faster at shifting than others, but no one knew that until after their very first in front of the entire pack.

It was a nerve-wracking experience to say the least. I was wholeheartedly not looking forward to it. No one ever had a problem, but if anyone was going to, it would be me. It seemed like I was consistently an issue for everyone around me.

Ezra sighed in exasperation, glaring at me. "There's something different about you, and I'm determined to know what it is. I just want *you* to know and remember that there is nothing wrong with you, no matter what you might think or anyone might say to you. Being different is not equal to being a villain or a monster."

I exhaled sharply, pulling my hands from his. I turned my face away. I didn't want to see the hurt in his eyes if there was any. Instead, I pressed my heated forehead against the cool glass of the window and tried my hardest to relax.

Listening as Ezra moved behind me and flicked the headlights back on, I closed my eyes tightly. Picking at the thick skin beside my nails, I absently thought about how I needed to trim it as he pulled onto the road and drove toward my house. We said nothing else for the entire duration of the car ride. I muttered my thanks as I hopped out.

Dad was already home and in bed by the time I got there, so I got something quick to eat before scurrying to my bedroom for the night. I only hoped I could get some semblance of sleep.

Rain poured around me, thunder echoing through the ravine. Lightning flashed, lighting up the darkness and exposing the trees that surrounded me. Another rumble of thunder made the earth shake under my feet, nearly knocking me down. I gasped, reaching around for something to keep me upright.

My hand landed on his shoulder; his shirt soaked through as the boy's arms wound around my waist. They were impossibly strong for a dream, gripping me with such pressure it almost felt real. His face buried in my neck and he inhaled deeply as if he could smell the scent on my skin. His fingers dug into my flesh through my drenched shirt and he clung to me as if I was the only raft in a storming sea.

"Remember me?" he whispered, the smooth depth of his voice making me shiver.

"How could I forget the man of my dreams?"

He trembled against me as though my words caused a physical reaction in him. "It has been a long time. I thought you'd abandoned me, Hathor."

"I would never abandon you, Silas."

He nodded, one hand reaching up to tangle in my dripping hair as the rain slowed to a steady drizzle. I slid my hands up his arms, wrapping them around the back of his neck and letting him shudder against me until that ceased with the rain.

"I've had a very bad time without the reprieve your presence brings."

"I'm very sorry. I don't know how to force these dreams. I didn't realize my inner voice needed me so much."

He chuckled, the rumble in his chest vibrating against mine as he pressed to me.

"I didn't realize I'd need my imaginary friend so much either." A pause. "What do you do when you're not with me?"

"I live my life."

He nodded, pulling back as if he were going to look at my face, but he turned his head and looked over the ravine as rays of the sun broke through the black clouds. "See what you do? You bring the sun, warm the earth. You really are my better half. I should let you take the reins more often."

I smiled, glancing down at my toes in the mud. "Maybe you should."

He lifted his eyes to the sky as though looking for a sound only he could hear. "It's that time again. Don't forget me."

"Dream of me, and I'll be there."

Chapter 18

CADENCE

eart's Day fell on a Friday, and I could hardly stand being in the school. Girls giggled over flowers and gifts while boys strode around, puffing their chests in a show of toxic masculinity that made me want to retch. The only giggling female I could tolerate was Alex, and a giggling female she was.

Alex was collecting pink camellias like crazy. They were the sacred Corana flower, symbolizing love, adoration, and longing. There was a long table in front of the office where you could buy a camellia, at a ridiculous five dollars apiece, and fill out a card so it could be presented to whomever you bought it for after lunch. Due to my tight budget, I never bought a camellia for anyone and only ever received one from Ezra and Alex. Two were plenty for me. In fact, it was too much. I was fine with being a Corana pariah.

In stark contrast, my blonde best friend was a camellia hoarder, and I couldn't be mad at her blushing face as she strutted around after lunch with her large, and growing, bouquet. She often received extra as an early birthday thing, something she milked endlessly.

Toward the end of the day, the camellia deliverer caught up to me, and I smiled politely, holding out my hand in preparation for my two flowers. However, I was quite surprised to be handed a bouquet of close to twenty of them. Alex, standing beside me, looked quite perturbed as I gawked at the flowers in my hands.

"Who are all of those from?" Her eyes were wide with disbelief and curiosity. If it were anyone else, I'd think they were jealous, but she seemed just as baffled as I was.

Digging through all the stems, I found five cards. The first two were from Alex and Ezra with cute, handwritten notes. The third was from Kyle, promising me another date in the near future. The fourth was an awkward half apology from Brody that made me roll my eyes. The fifth, however, was a completely different beast. As I read the words, I felt dread sinking deeper into my soul, like icy tendrils wrapping around me.

Don't worry, my love, I haven't forgotten you. You'll be mine.
No one will keep us apart.

A shudder ran down my spine as I stared at the handwriting on the card, the fancy cursive elevating the already threatening words. How one single person sent more than one camellia was a question all on its own. I pulled the card from the large bouquet and handed it to Alex, watching her face pale and her hazel eyes widen.

"I don't like that. Who would write that? What do they mean they haven't forgotten you? Have you gotten something else?" she trilled, the horrified confusion obvious in her expression as students bustled around us, blind to our inner turmoil. The bubble of fear was amplified by the mundane chatter surrounding us. How could everyone be so unaffected? Did they not see what was happening?

My eyes scanned the hallway, but no one paid any mind at all. I swallowed the lump in my throat and immediately stomped over to a garbage can lingering nearby. As if the bundle of camellias were burning my skin, I threw them into the bin and turned away like they might bite me. I held onto the three Kyle, Ezra, and Alex sent me, clutching their stems like a life jacket in a stormy sea.

"I don't know, but I don't like it."

Gazing down at her own camellias, I could tell that Alex didn't think they seemed as sweet and innocent anymore.

"Don't let this ruin your day." I placed a hand on her shoulder and gave her a small squeeze.

Alex looked around before meeting my eyes. She gave me a small smile, but the expression didn't reach her eyes. I could see within their swirling colors that she was concerned, and not just for me. That card seemed to imply just as much threat to Ezra or Kyle since everyone thought we were together. I'd already decided that I didn't want to tell anyone else. Ezra had enough concerns in his life without me laying anything else on him, and Kyle was only doing us a favor and didn't need to be dragged into my drama.

Changing the subject, I linked my arm through hers and gave her a wide smile. "So, where are you going to school after we graduate here?" I nudged her ribs gently with my elbow.

Alex paused, eyeing me sideways before answering. "Goddess, I don't know," she muttered, rolling her eyes. "My dad wants me to go to a volsifi exclusive school like Havermoon, but I think I'd rather go to one of the mixed campuses. We are so closed off from the other species here, and I want to go and learn about them and meet new people who aren't so . . . wolfy."

I nodded as we walked toward our next class. "Yeah, I want to learn about the other species even more than Mrs. Walker manages, and not just be in-undated endlessly with volsifi culture. There are things to learn from other species as well." I kept my voice low. It was a sensitive topic among most of the pack, the isolation constantly enforced by Lucien's rule. The old-school volsifi preferred to keep things segregated, thinking that broadening horizons was a foolish, new-aged belief. Because volsifi were perfect, right? We couldn't possibly learn anything from anyone else, and heaven forbid that love be shared between species. Especially since interbreeding was strictly forbidden by the High Table.

"We should go to the same place," she suggested after a moment of contemplative quiet. "I was thinking of going to Potencia Sui Generis Academy like my dad."

"I was just looking at their website the other day," Ezra commented, appearing behind us and throwing his arms over both of our shoulders. "I also agree. We should all go to the same place." His warm smile was relieving, his blue eyes glittering. I could tell we were both letting go of the tension of last night.

Well, if he was going to just let it go, so was I. No need dwelling on the past if it was done. It wasn't going to help us. Even though it was super important that we talk about it, I wasn't interested in looking at my faults and shortcomings with a microscope. No thanks.

Later that night, I found myself alone in my bedroom. Sitting at my desk, I stared at my laptop screen, pretending to read a report for English class. Instead, my fingers practically itched as I forced them to ignore the fact that there was a website for an academy that I so desperately wanted to attend.

With a heavy sigh, I finally caved and looked up the site for Potencia Sui Generis Academy. The webpage was mostly straightforward with the crest and the name of the academy in the header. Beneath that, there was a banner with various links you could follow to find further information about the school and the application to get in. The colors appeared to be teal, navy, and champagne. That's a color scheme I could get behind, for certain. I did love teal . . .

I needed to go to this school. Pulling my phone from inside my bag, I texted Alex and Ezra, letting them know that I was applying for PSG. After a moment of thought, I texted Kyle as well and received a response instantly. He was applying too. Setting my phone aside so I could concentrate, I went about filling out the application.

The application process was straightforward, just like everything else about the school, it would seem. The most daunting part? An essay explaining why *you* should be accepted and what you wanted to accomplish by attending such a prestigious academy. Talking myself up was not one of my strong suits, but I would do my best. I'd never wanted anything as badly as going to a school with the only two people who were always by my side, especially when my father was an alumnus.

It was the early hours of the morning by the time I finished my essay, at least the first draft. Once I got started, it seemed like the words spilled onto the page. Editing would be a nightmare, but I decided that would be morning me's problem. I fell into bed, determined to fix the three-thousand-word essay with a clear head.

Morning came too fast, as it usually did. Yawning, I sat up and stretched so deeply that my vision sparked with stars when my arms finally relaxed again at my sides. Collapsing back onto the bed, I rubbed my eyes until the flashes and heaviness in my head passed and I could get up. I was on my way to a hot shower when I glanced at my laptop and noticed something that made me stop in my tracks.

"No." The whisper came forth unbidden as I read the words on the screen, something that seemed to seal my fate like nothing else could.

'Thank you for submitting your application! Due to an increased number of applications . . .'

I quit reading, unable to fully process anything other than the fact that I sent a word vomit essay about my life and how I wanted this more than I wanted oxygen to a poor admissions clerk at the most prestigious supernatural academy in the world. I felt the blood drain from my face as I plopped unceremoniously into the chair at my computer, my eyes no longer focused on the screen.

I heard the doorbell ring downstairs but left it alone. I knew my dad would get it, and I couldn't handle dealing with another living being at the moment. Unfortunately, that visitor was for me, and she burst into my room with the kind of determination that only Alex could manage. In her arms were an incredible amount of clothing bags, and my dad followed her in, carting even more. I blinked stupidly at my friend as she dumped all the black bags onto my unmade bed and my dad followed her lead before leaving as the doorbell rang again.

"That'll be Ezra, he was right behind me." She pointed at the pile on my bed, counting all of the black hangers as she puffed a wild curl out of her eyes.

"What are you doing here?" I asked ungraciously as I stood and gestured at her and all her clothing bags that seemed to take up an inordinate amount of space.

Alex finally stopped and looked at me, examining my face as her forehead creased. "I need to try on dresses for my Ascension Ceremony next week," she admonished haughtily.

"Were these plans finalized at any point?" My eyebrows raised as Ezra stepped into the room, hauling even *more* bags. I turned to look at him as if he could help me. "Where was I when these plans were made?"

Ezra unloaded his arms onto my already overflowing bed. He lifted both hands, palms facing me in a placating gesture. "Yesterday at lunch?" It was phrased as a question, like he was uncertain as to whether the answer would get him bitten or not. "Alex asked if she could come over today to try on her dresses and said she wanted me here, too." I could tell he wasn't sure why she wanted his opinion. As someone who exclusively wore T-shirts, undone flannels, and jeans, I understood his point.

Alex sighed in exasperation, pinching the bridge of her nose. Clearly, she was beyond tired of this conversation and my inability to remember something so important. "Listen, I need support. This is nerve wracking."

That it was.

"Listen, I'm sorry. I didn't mean to lash out. Let me go to the bathroom and get myself together, and then I'll be back and one hundred and ten percent supportive, okay?" I ran my fingers through my thick hair, flipping the part to the other side before walking to the bathroom and pulling myself back together. This was not about me, and I wasn't going to make it that way.

Several hours later, Alex had gone through no less than fifteen dresses. Each one was standard white, though some of the underskirts were a different color, and every dress was a different style. The purity aspect of the Ascension Ceremony was preposterous, but we all still kept with tradition.

Alex stood in front of us, looking defeated. She was wearing a gorgeous dress that hung to her knees in a very flowy skirt, the empire waistline emphasizing her thin figure that she worked hard to maintain. As she shifted and turned, the fabric of the skirt glittered and flickered multiple pastel colors as if it were made of magic itself. It was easily my favorite out of all the dresses. In fact, I suspected Alex thought so too, since this was the fourth time she'd put it on and stared at herself angrily in the mirror.

Ezra looked at me, a helpless expression on his face. The sparkle in his eyes faded twenty minutes and fifteen dresses into this adventure. He was way out of his element here, and it was painfully obvious, even to me. I could tell that most of the dresses looked nearly identical to him, since he wasn't one to notice the minute details that his eye wasn't trained to see. Ezra was adamant that every dress was perfect while he sat there in dark blue jeans with a dark grey T-shirt and a navy flannel that was completely unbuttoned.

The glittering bodice of her current dress captured my eye as she did a small spin, the skirt fanning out around her in a swirl of pinks, lavenders, and blues. It was breathtaking.

Standing, I approached cautiously before going to my jewelry box. Inside, I pulled out a comb that belonged to my maternal grandmother, Margaret, and turned to show it to her. Alex's eyes lit upon it before widening.

It was a gorgeous heirloom, the diamond encrusted leaves fanned across the top of it, each spray ending in a pale tanzanite that glittered purple in the light of my bedroom. Pulling all her crazy, blonde curls over one shoulder, I tucked her hair back behind her ear and used the comb to keep it off her face. Her eyes sparkled as much as the comb and her dress as they met mine in the mirror. I looked at our reflection, myself in burgundy leggings and an ancient gray T-shirt with holes, and her looking like she needed a fist full of flowers to walk down the aisle.

"You're stunning. I couldn't imagine you wearing anything else for the ceremony," Ezra marveled in an awed whisper, his eyes wide. The sparkle had returned to his blue gaze.

He was right. She looked every bit the Ascending volsifi that she was.

"If you wear anything else, I'll never speak to you again," I beamed, only partially joking.

CHAPTER 19

ALEX

The rest of the weekend flew by with the three of us hanging around Cady's house and watching movies while stuffing our faces with popcorn. Early on Sunday, my father texted me and told me I needed to be at The Crest by lunchtime for more combat training. While I didn't want to leave, I did not want to anger my father more than I had been of late.

Instead of heading home, I went straight to the gym. I typically left clean clothes in my locker so that I didn't have to worry about forgetting things. Wishing I hadn't put on such thick eyeliner, I stared in the mirror as I plaited my hair into a thick braid that hung down my back. Wondering who I'd be sparring with today, I made my way into the gym to see Brody waiting for me.

"Fancy seeing you here." He wrapped his fists as he stood in the middle of the mat.

I scowled at him, wrapping my own fists. "Don't act like we don't have bones to pick, Brody," I bit out, taking a brief moment to stretch out my limbs.

"What the hell were you thinking when you attacked Cadence at the school like a rabid animal?"

Brody sighed, having the decency to look ashamed of himself. "I know. Kyle and Ezra already got on me about it. I don't need more of it from you." He rubbed his hand over his cropped hair. "Haven't you ever wanted someone so much that seeing them with someone else makes you angry?"

I quirked a brow, shaking my head. "No, because typically I accept rejection and move on."

He bared his teeth, exposing his gap as he took a step closer. Even though he was several feet away, his sheer size was a lot to take in. If I were anyone else, I might have flinched away from him. But I'd put him down more than enough to feel confident he wouldn't hurt me. It didn't matter that he was well over six feet.

"It's not that easy, Alex. There's just something about her that draws me to her."

My eyes widened. Ezra and Kyle had both expressed very similar feelings, and I was concerned about what exactly that meant for Cadence.

"Did you ever consider that being aggressive isn't the way to win her over?" I threw back, stepping forward and meeting him in his space. My head tilted back to meet his eyes. I was close enough that his oppressive aura was overwhelming. I pushed my own out to compensate. "Hasn't it occurred to you that maybe being nice to her would be better than being a possessive dick who makes crude comments all the time?"

The look on his face told me that no, he hadn't actually considered that at all. His gaze was no longer on me, he was looking through me and focusing on his thoughts. "Are you telling me that women don't actually want someone like that?"

I heaved an exasperated sigh. "Sure. Some girls do when a relationship is already there. You gotta read the room, dude. You have no defined pleasantries with her and no rapport. The only thing she knows about you is that you're very tall, very demanding, and that you disregard people's boundaries. She actually only recently realized you weren't making fun of her."

His head flinched back like I'd physically assaulted him. "What? She didn't realize I was being genuine?"

"No, Brody. When you're a giant ass and constantly say gross things to someone, they think you're being an obnoxious pig." I reached up and flicked his forehead, causing his brow to furrow as he glared at me.

Brody's expression relaxed and his dark eyes moved over my face, taking in my aggressive disposition. "How do I fix this?"

Rolling my eyes, I shoved my hands against his chest. He stumbled back a couple steps. "Talk to her? Apologize? Quit being possessive over someone who currently doesn't like or know you? There are many options. Figure it out."

He frowned, a crease forming between his brows as he lost himself in thought again.

"Listen, let's just spar like we're supposed to. I'm not giving you lessons on how to woo my best friend. I want her to be happy, and if you want to be the one who makes her that way, you need to figure your shit out."

I turned on the stereo and faced him. Brody was still locked in his trance, staring at the floor. If I focused hard enough, I was certain I could see smoke coming out of his ears. With no warning, I threw a solid punch into his side.

Let the sparring begin.

CADENCE

At school on Monday, not much happened until after lunch. After English class, Alex and I dawdled on our way to my locker, taking a detour to the restrooms. We took a long moment to fix our makeup, giggling about the guys she was seeing, and deciding who was the better fit. Ivan was clearly her number one. She focused on the bedroom, and I forced her to think outside of it. Maybe that's why the two of us worked so well as friends.

"Okay, but Ivan does this thing–"

I sighed and rubbed my temples. "Alex, what do they offer you in conversation? Or personality?"

Alex looked baffled. "What draws you to Ezra and Kyle?"

"You're assuming I am drawn to Kyle?"

She rolled her eyes and gave me an exasperated look.

"Kyle is very sweet. He's observant and picks up information on me very quickly so he's always doing the right thing. Ezra is . . . Ezra. He's thoughtful and intelligent. He's always been there for me. He knows all my history because he lived it with me. He's comfortable to be around."

Alex was watching me closely. "And Kyle? Is he comfortable to be around?"

I examined her face. "Yes, but in a different way. It's also entirely pretend. We're just friends, so Kyle shouldn't really be part of this discussion."

Alex made a thoughtful humming noise, putting her makeup back in her bag.

When we finally exited the restroom, we found Kyle and Brody in a heated discussion right outside the door. I frowned as their raised voices assaulted my ears. Why did people feel the need to be nose-to-nose in an argument? Personally, I didn't enjoy arguments, and I definitely did not want to have them within spitting distance.

"You need to back off, Brody. I know you're not the greatest at taking hints, so let me spell it out for you. Cady is not interested in you. She's made that abundantly clear, and that's not going to change no matter how many times you tell her that her ass looks great in jeans and leggings and sweater dresses . . ." Kyle's tone was sharp and whipped out of him like a physical weapon. I very seldom saw him that way and couldn't deny the way my heart rate picked up.

Brody appeared nonplussed by Kyle's words. The smirk that played on his lips didn't budge as he looked directly into Kyle's face. "I don't know if you've noticed or not, but Cadence is very smart and completely capable of making her own decisions without you forcing your possessive opinion down her throat," Brody shot back with a shrug of his wide shoulders.

My mouth fell open as Kyle stepped even closer to Brody, clearly unbothered by Brody towering over him. Emotions were ramping up quickly and I could tell they were moments from throwing fists, or worse . . . shifting. I could taste the tension as the air thickened between them, though no more words were spoken as they kept their gazes locked in some kind of test of wills.

Swallowing down any insecurities that threatened to choke me, I glanced at Alex who was looking between them like she wasn't sure which one to pull out of the argument. Both males were puffing out their chests and I could almost hear the ticking of the testosterone bombs that were counting down to ruin. Shaking off my fears, I stepped between them. It wasn't an easy feat to do since they were chest to chest at that point and I had to jam myself between them. One hand on each chest, I shoved them both away from each other and they both stumbled slightly like they hadn't noticed my presence until then. Kind of rude, since they were arguing about me and all.

"Just knock it off," I snapped, glaring between the two of them as they gawked at me like they just remembered that I existed at all. Frowning, I tried not to cross my arms and sulk like a petulant child and instead fueled my anger. "I am not a prize to be won. I will not stand here and watch you argue over me like I'm some kind of property."

Piercing Brody with my gaze, I admonished him directly. "Especially you." Shoving my finger into his chest, he actually took a step back as if I were the scariest person he'd ever seen even though I was over a foot shorter. "You have no right to stake any kind of wolfy claim on me. You've done nothing but be a sex crazed pig. Shape up or you will be nothing more to me than an enemy."

I gave each of them a hard look again before turning away and wrapping my arm around Alex's. Glancing back, I saw Kyle flip Brody off. Rolling my eyes, I held his elbow when he extended it, appreciating him standing up for me even though I wasn't ready to thank him for it.

Alex paused, removed herself from my arm and approached Brody. She punched him in the arm with enough strength that he winced and rubbed at the spot. "That, is not what I meant. Remember what I said. Figure your shit out."

I stared at her with wide eyes, confusion rippling through me. Glancing up at Kyle, his expression was blank as he watched the scene finish unfolding.

Alex returned and grabbed my elbow. She yanked me down the hall as Mr. Bowman appeared among the crowd. "Alright, everyone. Break it up," he called out, waving his hands in an attempt to disperse the students who had been thirsting for a fist fight. Goddess, people could be such Neanderthals.

The three of us moved down the hallway, leaving the crackdown of a teacher behind us. Glancing behind him, Kyle swore under his breath. "I have to go back that way. I forgot that I need to stop at my locker."

"Okay. I'll see you after school?"

He grinned at me, leaning down to press a kiss to my forehead. "Absolutely."

Watching him go, I sighed wistfully.

"Yeah. There's nothing there." Alex's sardonic voice broke into my thoughts, but I chose to ignore her. I wasn't ready to think that she might be right.

I spun the lock to my locker and stopped in my tracks at the amaryllis laying in front of my books. Alex leaned around me to look at what had stopped me before reaching in and picking up the amaryllis. My brow furrowed as I took in the card attached with a red ribbon just like the ones from Heart's Day. Reaching out, I lifted the paper to read it and gasped as I took in the words scrawled artfully across it.

Don't keep me waiting too long. Patience isn't a virtue I possess,
but you will be.

Dropping the card as if it had bitten me, I took a step back and looked at Alex's confused face. She picked up the card and read it, her jaw dropping as she took in the words. "Even if you wanted to contact this person, you don't know who they are. How do you expect any returned feelings if you remain anonymous?" She gripped the amaryllis in her fist, crushing the delicate petals. Some of the scarlet attempted to break through her fingers, but she showed no mercy as she threw the amaryllis into the nearest trash can.

"I don't know, but I really don't think I could find it in me to be interested in someone who insists on leaving me creepy notes regardless," I mumbled, slamming my locker shut and leaving her behind as I went to my last class of the day.

After class, I went to my locker to gather my things. I knew that Alex had to go to training with her father right after school. I also knew that Kyle would be looking for me to take me home. However, I was disinterested in being in such a confined space with anyone. I was still fretting about the note I'd found earlier and was not ready to talk about it.

Opening my locker, I was horrified to see yet another amaryllis sitting among my belongings, the note attached making a lump form in my throat. Picking up the paper, I saw the words that made my eyes sting with tears that I refused to let fall.

It was very rude of your friend to ruin and throw my gift away.
Here's another. From my heart to yours.

Tossing the amaryllis away, I hurried out of the school among the throng of students also escaping the confines of Harlington High. I needed to get the hell out of that building, the walls were suddenly closing in on me. Despite the size of our volsifi school, it was suddenly an iron maiden, the doors shutting to pierce me with the stems of amaryllis that were left as "gifts" from someone who was clearly watching me much more closely than I thought.

It was several miles from the school to my front door, but I figured that I could use the exercise and fresh air. Taking a long walk wouldn't kill me and it would be good to get some steps in. I had never been more grateful to have worn sneakers to school; though when it started raining, I wished I'd worn boots. Glancing at the gray sky, I closed my eyes as I popped my earbuds in. Clicking through my app, I found "Voices" by Motionless In White and put it on. It was living rent free in my brain, and I needed to play it out of my head.

I was part way home, grumbling at myself as I stomped along the sidewalk in the freezing rain. My phone buzzed in my pocket, and I pulled it out to see a text from Kyle asking where I was and if I was okay. I responded with the walking emoji. He sent a frowning emoji and asked if I wanted him to pick me up. There was nothing I wanted more than for someone to drive me home, but I didn't want to talk about the amaryllis or my feelings. I stupidly told him no and put my phone back into my pocket.

I was just changing the song playing through my earbuds when I heard a car approaching and slowing down. Confused, I looked up as a shiny, orange SUV pulled up along the sidewalk and the window rolled down. I peered through the window as Brody leaned over to look up at me. His face looked concerned, uncertain.

I scoffed, rolling my eyes and started stomping away from him. I heard a car door open and a second later, a hand was on my shoulder.

"Cady. Stop. Please."

His deep voice was rough with emotion, and I scowled as I turned to face him. The rain poured around us and my brain itched with a memory just out of focus.

"Why?" I snapped, crossing my arms over my chest and staring him in the eye.

Brody seemed almost cowed as he pulled his hand away from me suddenly. "Because I need to apologize. For everything."

"Don't worry about it."

I turned on my heel and started storming away from him again. The wind whipped around me, throwing my hair in my face and making it cling to my cheeks. There was silence, and I almost thought he had actually left.

A warm, dry coat was thrown over my shoulders, the hood flicked up to shield me from the downpour. I stopped, stiffening as the smell of wood smoke and spicy cinnamon enveloped me completely. If I wasn't so thrown off, I'd almost feel comforted. But I wasn't supposed to feel comforted by his scent.

Turning, I looked up into his pleading face. "Just let me drive you home and get you out of this storm. I can smell the electricity in the air, I don't want you to get hurt."

I glanced down at my soaked sneakers and the way my jeans were drenched up to my knees. The stubborn streak in me really wanted to tell him to shove off and leave me be. But the temptation of a warm car was too much to resist as my teeth rattled together.

"Fine," I muttered, walking back to his car.

Relief flickered over his face before it vanished. He ran ahead of me, opening the car door so I could get in. The heated seats were already on, and I relished the tushy toaster as it ate through the chill that had sunk into my bones.

Once he got into the car, he immediately pulled away from the curb in the direction of Delta territory. The ride was awkwardly silent for several minutes as he drove through the streets toward the back road that led through the forest. I'd put my earbuds back into my pocket when I'd gotten into the car, and now the anxiety was settling in for the quiet car ride.

I couldn't take it and said the first thing that had come to my mind. "Why did you decide to pick me up?" I slid my palms over my thighs to try and work out some of the tension coiling inside my limbs.

He was silent for so long that I wondered if he'd respond. "Kyle suggested it. After you texted and told him you were walking, he called me. Told me that you weren't interested in help from him, and that it was a convenient excuse for me to talk to you and give you a legitimate apology."

I balked at him as though he'd just admitted to knowing the secret to everlasting life.

"Oh," was all my genius brain could think to say.

His teeth tugged at his lower lip as he ran his palm over his short, soaked hair. "Listen, I'm sorry for being such an idiot, Cadence. It's just that, you drive me crazy. You're just so, you, and I just . . . I can't stop . . . I need . . ." He grunted in annoyance.

His knuckles gripped the steering wheel as he stuttered through his apology. I could tell that he'd practiced an apology all afternoon and that it still wasn't going well for him. I'd almost feel sorry for him if I wasn't so annoyed by his previous actions. I could still feel the force of his body pressed against mine and a shudder rolled through me. I desperately hoped that he wouldn't notice.

He did.

"I just, your body is so amazing, I just want to grab you and do everything with you. But I can't, and I just don't know what to do with myself. I don't like not getting what I want."

I blinked, looking out the passenger window. "That's a really . . . weird way to apologize, Brody." Instantly, I felt regret. He was really trying, and I was disregarding that. I just couldn't get past his repeated sexual assault, no matter what he said at that moment.

Glancing at him, I saw color creeping along his cheekbones as my words settled into his brain. Goddess, I was even embarrassing *him*. I turned away from him to watch the blur of trees rushing outside the window. I didn't expect him to answer, so when he did, I jumped.

"You're right. I apologize for that too." His words were so quiet that the sound of the engine almost hid them from me. I turned back to look at him once again, but his dark brown eyes remained trained on the road ahead.

I let the silence gnaw at me and wished it would just swallow me whole as we drove along the road toward my house. On high alert and distinctly uncomfortable, all I could do was dig my nails into my palms. Embarrassing myself again wasn't something I was interested in, and I figured that letting my anxiety build was better than subjecting either of us to any more awkward conversation.

Finally, I guided him to my house, and he stopped at the bottom of the driveway. Grabbing my bag, I made a hasty escape before I could say anything else that would humiliate me further.

Like a gentleman, he waited until I was safely in my house with the door shut and the lights on before he pulled away and drove toward what I assumed would be his own home. Leaning my back against the front door, I put my face in my hands and groaned as my brain forced me to relive my stupidity on repeat until I dragged myself to bed.

Sitting at the dining room table, I looked across the checkerboard at my twin brother. He stared back at me, quirking one pale brow up so it hid behind his shaggy, pale bangs. His eyes twinkled with the glory of knowing he was winning, the blue of his irises so clear it was almost startling when you saw the splash of black that marred his right eye. If you didn't know any better, you'd assume he had an eye injury that caused his pupil to bleed into the sky blue, but I did know better. He was my complete opposite, even in the splotches that interrupted the color of our irises. The only thing we had in common was pale flesh.

I eyed the black circles on the board in front of me, well, what was left of them anyway. Frowning, I narrowed my eyes and jumped one of his pieces before smirking smugly. He was just about to move and end the game when a heavy banging from the front door caused us both to jump.

Nan, her blonde hair so much like mom's, looked up at my pap with a horrified expression on her face. Callum looked as confused as I felt by everyone's reaction. It was just a visitor, right? Nan looked at the two of us, her blue eyes flickering violet as she gestured for us to hide in the crawl space behind our bed. Grabbing Callum's hand, I pulled him from the table and rushed to drag him into our favorite hiding spot.

Unfortunately, the door blasted off its hinges before we could move more than a couple steps. Nan screamed, "No! Don't take our babies!" The sound caused me to pause and look at the aggressive looking men who stomped into the house. I wasn't sure who I was looking at or what they were doing there, but I knew that I needed to escape them. Nan was still screaming until one of them made a hand motion that silenced her voice. Grabbing her throat, she looked terrified as another man snagged Callum despite my desperate attempt to hold on to his hand. A strangled

cry escaped my brother, fear apparent in the sound. Pap picked me up and ran with
me, but on the way a wooden arrow tore through his chest.

"Run, Cadence! Run!" he screamed, dropping to his knees as his hands
hovered over the wooden tip of the arrow, the tip glowing purple. I reached for the
arrow, but he pushed me from him, knocking me down. Unable to speak, Pap just
gestured to the back door, signaling for me to leave.

"We have one of them. Leave the other. We aren't to steal them both," a
gruff man shouted, causing me to look over my shoulder as the men took my
grandmother and twin away from me. Nan was bleeding from her face, and I
didn't understand why. Confused and afraid, I sat next to my Pap's body and
sobbed.

Sitting upright in bed, a strangled sob came from me as tears poured down
my face and dripped onto my shirt from my chin. "No, not Callum," I wailed,
reaching for my earbuds like my mother taught me back when she still cared.
Pushing them into my ears, my hands shook as I found the playlist that con-
tained just one song that would loop endlessly until I no longer needed it.
"Flying Dreams" by Katie Campbell blasted into my ears, the gentle melody
and repetitive lyrics immediately calmed me. It was the song she'd played every
time she would rescue me from my nightmares until she couldn't be bothered
to leave her bed any longer.

Laying back against my drenched pillow, I winced before moving to the
other side of the bed to escape my sweat puddle. Curling on my side, I let the
words flow over me while my hands gripped my upper arms painfully. A new
day would come, I was sure of it. I knew I'd see my brother again, some day.

When I woke the next morning, there was a single red amaryllis sitting on
top of my closed laptop.

CHAPTER 20

CADENCE

The next few weeks passed by like leaves caught in the breeze. I blinked one too many times and they were gone. Most of me knew that it was the effect of being on high alert for these things, but now I felt like I was seeing amaryllis everywhere. It seemed like anywhere my eyes went an amaryllis was there. In the designs on other people's clothing, in the holes in the drop ceilings of the classrooms . . . just, everywhere. I hated it. It was making me feel like I was being watched no matter where I went.

Sitting in my last class and trying not to hyperventilate, I almost leapt out of my skin when my phone vibrated in my pocket. I stared out the window at the forest outside the school, wishing I had already Ascended so I could escape into the wildness of it and live as a wolf.

Out of the corner of my eye, I saw Kyle pull his phone out of his pocket and look at it. Glancing at him, I saw a very confused expression unfold on his face before he looked up at me. I forced myself to relax before I glanced at the text that had come through. My eyes widened as I looked at the picture that came from an unknown number–a picture of me, sitting in this class. It was obviously taken through the window of the door a moment before it was sent, my gaze was staring unseeingly at the teacher within it. My eyes shifted from myself to the back corner of the class where a large red X was drawn over Kyle, and I couldn't shake the feeling of dread that flooded my system.

The fact that I didn't notice anyone there when I had been looking at the teacher made my pulse skyrocket further. The door was right beside the whiteboard where Mr. Redmond was giving his lecture on genetics. My heart then dropped even *further* when a series of amaryllis pictures appeared, my phone vibrating relentlessly in my palm as text after text came through. The first several were pictures of the amaryllis where I'd found them scattered through my life, then just a generic one from the internet that kept coming on repeat. I was horrified that the first one was taken in the food bank, the amaryllis the one I thought had been given to me by Ezra as an apology for not telling me about Jessica.

"Ms. Nocetti! Put your phone away. This is your only warning," Mr. Redmond reprimanded, throwing his heavy biology book down on the desktop with a loud bang that made me startle yet again. I really hadn't needed that extra emphasis on his words. I'd already gotten the point.

Just as I hit the power button to turn my phone off, a text with actual words came through that made the hairs raise on the back of my neck.

Unknown

> I'm coming for you. Kyle should watch himself. You're mine.

I sat on the edge of my bed that evening as Ezra practically paced a rut into my carpet while he stormed back and forth across my room. His brow furrowed to such an extreme that I vaguely worried it might get stuck that way. Alex perched on my desk chair; her hazel eyes trained on the floor as she lost herself in thought. What those thoughts were, I could only guess, but I assumed it had to do with the bomb I'd just dropped on them about the text. Kyle was sitting on the floor behind Ezra, his eyes staring unseeing into an unknown distance.

When I'd turned my phone on, there was nothing new from the unknown number. I was quite grateful for that fact, but I still honored my promise to Alex and told my group about the incident. As I looked at the texts still hovering on my screen, I felt chills break out over my flesh all over again. While I hadn't wanted to drag Kyle into it, it seemed I didn't have a choice since he got a series of photos of us together, including ones taken through the blinds of us in my kitchen and dining room. There was even one of him lying me in my bed the first night Ezra had been in the clinic.

Ezra opened his mouth to speak, a furious expression on his face, when Alex stood abruptly.

"Hold on. I need to catch him before he rings the doorbell," she said in a rush as she darted out the door.

The three of us looked around at each other in confusion. No one said a word as the front door opened and hushed voices could be heard speaking. Then the door closed again, the lock thrown in place and alerting my phone that it had been locked manually. I was becoming more and more grateful to Alex and Ezra for granting me technology.

Alex appeared in the room, Brody towering behind her. My heart shuddered in my chest as the baffled expressions on the faces of Kyle and Ezra mirrored my own.

Alex glanced around at us all before frowning and plopping back in my desk chair. "I invited him because he knows everything. He received a warning text after the incident in the hallway with Cadence and told me about it. I trust him."

There was stunned silence as Brody shut my bedroom door behind him. He sat on the floor beside Kyle, and they glanced at each other before the conversation started again as if it had never been interrupted.

"Who the hell could it be?" Ezra seethed, digging his fingers into his hair and tugging on the already distressed waves. He'd been running his fingers through them since I told them about the texts over an hour ago.

"My money is on Jason," Alex spoke up from the chair, her eyes lifting to mine.

"Jason?" Ezra and I echoed, both of us unsure as to why she would come to that conclusion.

"Yeah. Jason. The guy who's been putting you and Jessica into your fathers' heads and leaving Cady free. I think that Cady and Kyle getting together set him off. It clearly had an effect with Brody since he made a move in the hallway."

Brody grunted in response, leaning his head back against the wall. As a disgruntled look appeared on his face. I don't think he liked being reminded of his actions against me. I could empathize since I didn't either.

I stared at Ezra as he lowered his hands, clenching his fists at his sides before releasing his fingers as his movements suddenly stilled. It was like I could actually see the wheels turning in his mind as he mulled over her words, pondering that maybe she was actually correct in her guess. A scowl pulled down the corners of his mouth as he must have concluded that she might be on to something.

"That would make sense. Everything started happening right around the time Ezra Ascended. That's when Jason started talking about an upgrade in status when Ezra and Jessica get together," Brody commented from the floor. "He's been growing more distant since November."

"Why would Jason care about me, though? It's not like there's anything there that he could claim," I said, frowning. "I'm hardly a catch in regard to status. My family is so outcasted that it would probably knock him down to my status to be with me."

Brody growled at me. "Maybe in regard to status, but there must be something else about you. I know I'm hardly the only person interested in mating with you. I've felt drawn to you since we were kids, and even more after I Ascended. While I don't know what Jason's motive would be, it probably isn't status."

There was a slight lull in conversation as Alex stood and began pacing in Ezra's place.

"When did you start getting these texts and the flowers? Why didn't you tell us when it started?" Ezra demanded, dropping into the desk chair and leaning forward on his knees to stare at me at eye level.

"November. I thought the first couple amaryllis were from you. It was the day I wasn't talking to you because Jessica was the one to tell me about the arrangement."

Ezra looked sheepish and dropped his gaze. I frowned, reaching out and touching his hand. He immediately intwined our fingers.

Kyle sat upright at last, crossing his legs underneath him. "Well, whoever it is, they're very persistent." He glanced at his phone again.

I had seen the text messages he'd received, and the words had chilled me enough that I would remember them until I was in my funeral pyre.

Unknown

> Back off Cadence. She's mine. I will slaughter you and mark her with my scent if that's what it takes. This is your only warning.

Shuddering, I tried to not dwell on the text threat he had gotten and instead tuned back into the conversation. Kyle was now up and pacing, tapping his chin with his index finger as he walked and Alex dropped down beside Brody.

Kyle frowned. "Jason has not forgiven me for dating Cadence. No one knows the truth outside of this room but David. I haven't told Jason about our arrangement. Since he'd technically be in the Alpha circle if you and Jessica work out, I'm assuming that's his prerogative for forcing his father to approach yours, Ezra. That's if he did, anyway. Reginald Barber might want in the Alpha circle all on his own and be orchestrating the entire thing."

I felt completely gobsmacked. "But why would he threaten you? That doesn't make any sense," I gasped, shaking my head. "In any case, I think we need to end this arrangement before something happens to you, Kyle. Maybe we should take these threats seriously."

Kyle stopped his pacing and looked at me with a bewildered expression. He clearly never considered that option. "Cadence, I will absolutely not back out of this arrangement. Lucien is still very much a threat to Ezra, and my job as a Beta is to protect the Alpha. In any case, I'd still want to hang out even if we weren't pretending to be dating, because you're an excellent friend. I don't think that would fly with this guy either." He aggressively gestured at his phone.

Alex paused and looked at Kyle. "Maybe it's not even a guy? Would Jessica be capable of this?" She pulled her hair into a bun, using one of the pens laying on my desk to stab it into place.

Silence followed that, and we all stared at each other. It was like we all had the answer within reach but couldn't quite pin it to the corkboard of red lines we'd made.

"Maybe we should talk to your dad, Alex," I suggested, rubbing my hands over my denim clad thighs. "Maybe this is bigger than we can handle at this point."

Alex pressed her lips together and gave me a look I could only interpret as pity. "Unfortunately, stalking is taken even less seriously in this world than the human world. This person hasn't technically done anything to anyone other than make threats and maybe a case of breaking and entering, which we have no real proof of. I don't think my dad can do anything unless an act of violence is made against one of us." She rubbed her hands over her upper arms. I noticed for the first time that she was wearing the sweater I crocheted for her for Novzima. I instantly felt like a terrible friend for not realizing and appreciating it.

Nodding, I accepted her words as truth. Stalking was unheard of in this pack, and I couldn't think of a single instance where it had happened previously. It was highly possible that they wouldn't do anything, especially given that *I* was the victim. I trusted that Alex would approach him if it would do any good at all.

I groaned, throwing myself back on the bed and glaring at the ceiling. Why do all the weird and terrible things always have to happen to me? My phone buzzed beside me, and I frowned, sitting up and looking at the one-sided conversation with the unknown number.

Unknown

Ding dong. Delivery.

What followed was a picture of my dining room table, a bouquet of amaryllis sitting in the center of it that were definitely not there when I'd arrived home. A gasp tore at my throat, and I stood up, hurrying downstairs to see if they were actually there and hoping that it was an altered image. My footsteps pounded down the stairs as I realized I truly did not care if I bothered my mother, maybe it would be better if I did. Anxiety ripping at my insides like a feral beast, my socked feet slid on the tile as I rounded the corner into the dining room, horror making goosebumps break out over my flesh as I stared at the red mass of amaryllis in an elegant vase on the table. Their petals glittered ominously under the ceiling light as I gaped at them, barely hearing Ezra, Kyle, Brody, and Alex arriving behind me.

I looked at my phone, checking to see if anyone had accessed the electronic deadbolt to the front door and saw that it had remained locked since Brody had arrived at the house. Things were escalating quickly, and the realization that I had no idea what would be next made my head spin. It felt like I wasn't safe anywhere, not even in my own home. The violation of the whole thing made me want to scream.

"What the hell is this psycho going to do next?" Alex fretted. Her voice was hushed behind me as the five of us stared blankly at the offensive amaryllis that seemed to take up an inordinate amount of space in the small room. They'd have been beautiful if it weren't for the entire situation attached to them. The fact that they were placed there made them a bad omen.

I stomped toward the table, grabbing the entire collection and carrying them into the attached garage. My gaze landed on the large, green bins beside the door, and I threw the whole thing into the first one so aggressively that the vase shattered and sprayed glass everywhere inside the plastic bin. The loud bang and tinkling aftershock of the mini explosion echoed all around me in the concrete room, giving me a small smile of satisfaction within the storm of horrors I'd found myself in.

I picked up the lid from the floor and jammed it on top as if leaving it off would allow the amaryllis to float back up into the house like a ghost, haunting me forever. Inside, I knew it was absolute craziness. This wave was over, though something else would quickly follow. Things were happening in rapid succession, and all I could do was wait until the next event. Maybe that was the hardest part about having a stalker; the fact that you couldn't really anticipate anything without holding your breath and watching for everything. Something about feeling unsafe and knowing you couldn't do anything but react seemed so much more sadistic than a physical attack. The slow mental torture of waiting for the next thing was driving me to the edge of madness.

I hated waiting to react. It didn't appeal to my need to plan out my life with ridiculous care and attention to the finer details. Realistically, I knew that most of my plans would never come to fruition, but that didn't stop me from making them all the same. Without a path to follow, life was chaos while you were lost in the forest of decisions.

It didn't take much effort for me to convince everyone to stay with me for the night. I even broke my dad's rule about closing and locking my bedroom door, refusing to leave us possibly exposed to some psychopath in the night. Especially since dad was over an hour away working a twenty-four-hour shift.

I scowled at the ceiling in the dark, Alex beside me on the bed while Ezra, Kyle, and Brody bedded down on the floor. They refused to leave my side in case something happened, especially since I had yet to Ascend. It put me at a serious disadvantage. You gained your full strength when you Ascended, sometimes even gaining a special ability as a gift from the Goddess, Levende. It wasn't always obvious either, sometimes it took a while for you to realize you even had one. Ezra was fairly sure he didn't. I'd never thought to ask Kyle. It was considered rude to ask about gifts in this pack. Lucien frowned upon expressing exceptionalism when it was his underlings.

Sighing heavily, I turned to stare at the door in the darkness, my back to Alex. Alex immediately pressed against my back, throwing an arm and a leg over my waist and attaching to me koala-style. I smiled to myself, trying to slow my thoughts so I could slide into the lovely abyss of sleep. However, my brain frequently failed to work that way without forcing myself to focus on something specific.

Using my usual go-to of counting sheep, I finally sunk into the darkness of sleep.

The familiar cliff was in front of me. Rain immediately soaked my tank top, causing the cotton fabric to cling to my skin. My shorts were not enough clothing and I shivered in the onslaught of rain. Looking up at the sky, I saw lightning

flashing in the clouds as thunder rumbled loud enough to vibrate my bones. A frown appeared on my lips as I glanced around the small outcropping. It was one of the first times I hadn't arrived first.

The boy stood at the very edge of the cliff. He was wearing a cloak of sorts, his head downcast as he stared into the ravine. His hands clenched into fists at his sides, and I worried that he was going to jump. Panic rippled through me as I held my hands against my chest as if that might warm my frozen fingers.

"Remember me?" I called out, hoping he would hear me over the raging storm around us.

Fog danced around his cloak as he turned toward me, his eyes ravaging my face as though it was the first meal he'd seen in a decade. His gaze danced down my body and he swept the cloak from his shoulders to wrap it around mine. The outside had water beading over the deep red fabric, running down the outside of it like rain against a windowpane. The inside was dry and warm from his body heat as it covered me completely.

"How could I forget the woman of my dreams?"

I found solace in his voice as it danced in my ears. I wished I could hear him speak forever. I felt vaguely guilty, like I was cheating on Ezra with this man. It was a silly notion. Did it count if he was only in my head?

"I'm sorry I've been gone. There's been a lot happening. I wish I could control these dreams," I said, relieved as the rain started to slow. The thunder rumbled farther in the distance, becoming less frequent.

His mouth pressed into a thin line. "What's happening?" His tone became dark, causing a shudder to ripple through me. I wasn't used to him sounding so displeased.

"It's nothing. Everything will be fine."

"Hathor. Talk to me."

"There's nothing to discuss, Silas. There's no point in talking about my waking life in my dreams."

He scowled. "Of course, there is. That's the point of dreams. To work out problems in your waking life."

"Will you tell me of your problems?" I asked, earning a scowl in response.

"There is nothing my waking or sleeping self can do about my problems. They exist and will continue to exist regardless of what I do. Let me help with yours."

I sighed, pulling his cloak tighter around me. "There's nothing you can do to help me with mine. Everything happening is outside of my control."

His face darkened. I didn't like that look on him. The walls came down behind his eyes and I was thrown out into the cold again. He was blocking me out.

"I suppose that I, of all people, can understand that."

Looking around, his expression tensed. I could see a flicker of fear behind his eyes as they returned to my face.

"I must go. Don't forget me."

"Dream of me, and I'll be there," I whispered as he vanished into a fog.

My memory of his face deteriorated with him.

CHAPTER 21

CADENCE

The five of us were on high alert and always in communication in case anything happened. The amaryllis and their disturbing notes were always creeping on the edge of my consciousness. I felt like I was slowly losing my mind. Jumping at every little thing became my increasing reality, and while I probably shouldn't have, it felt like my bedroom was my safe space. The stalker had been in my room, but I chose to ignore that. I needed one place that felt okay.

I was sitting on my bed, finally getting around to reading the book Ezra had bought me. My earbuds were in, blasting "Flying Dreams" by Katie Campbell. It was the lullaby from the movie, one that had very special importance to me as it reminded me of my childhood when my mother still cared. *Mrs. Frisby and the Rats of Nimh* turned out to be fairly different from the movie. I pursed my lips to the side as I finished the last page and closed the book. Holding it against my chest, I closed my eyes and thought of Ezra. I could so easily picture the happy smile on his face when he saw how surprised I'd been. The sparkle in his eye and the way his cheeks creased when he smiled.

My phone vibrated against my knee, and I shifted so I could pull it from under my leg. The electric lock had been unlocked by Ezra, then locked again. My forehead creased while I wondered if it was a fluke. A knocking sound startled me, and I pulled out my earbuds as Ezra's voice called my name through the door.

I couldn't erase my confused expression before I opened the door to Ezra panting on the other side. He straightened when he saw me, that smile I'd just been picturing gracing his face.

"What are you doing here?" I asked, moving out of the way so he could come into the room.

Ezra didn't speak, waiting until I closed the door before he grabbed my face and kissed me with so much emotion, I thought I might drown in it. My back pressed against the door as he leaned against me. His hands slid to the back of my neck, supporting my head as he tilted it backwards.

"I needed to see you," he mumbled against my mouth, not breaking the kiss.

I let myself drown in him, gripping his flannel overshirt in my fists at his sides and using the fabric to pull him closer to me. My skin felt alive under his touch as his hands slid down my sides and under my shirt to tease along the waistband of my leggings. His hands felt cool against my lower back, soothing my feverish skin as his lips brushed over my jaw and down the side of my neck.

"Ezra," I breathed, tilting my head to the side and sliding my hands under his shirt and brushing my fingertips over his back. I slowly traced the ridges of his crisscrossed scars . It was like reading a map, one that guided me through his childhood of trauma and left him the man he was today. The man who loved me.

"I love you." His voice was hushed, a breathy declaration against my skin.

"And I love you."

Ezra pulled back, examining my face as he brushed his fingers over my face. I left my hands against his back, gliding my thumbs over his scars.

"I'm sorry I didn't text first. I didn't even know if you'd be alone, but I needed to see you. We haven't had a moment alone in months and it was eating me alive."

I shook my head. "You have nothing to apologize for, Ezra. You never have anything to apologize for."

He swallowed, pressing his lips together. I removed one of my hands from his back to poke the shallow dimple beneath the left side of his lips. That cracked his serious expression, and he gave me a half smile.

"You arrived just in time. I just finished the book you got me."

His smile widened, finally reaching his eyes so they sparkled with mirth. "Yeah? Was it better than the movie?"

I laughed, shaking my head. "No, but it was good in its own right."

He nodded, pressing a kiss to the tip of my nose. "Good. Then it was a gift well given."

I stood on tiptoe and kissed his lips before sliding out of his grasp. Plopping onto the bed, I held the book against my chest. He sat next to me, reaching out and brushing his fingers through my hair to tuck a lock behind my ear.

"I've been thinking of you every day, Cadybug. I miss when things were easy."

My lips pressed together, and I looked down at the floor. "I miss it too. Kyle is great. He's very much a gentleman. I appreciate everything he's doing. I just wish I didn't have to be apart from you at the same time."

He sighed, pressing his forehead to mine. "I understand, though Jessica is still a troll and always will be. She is the bane of my existence, I swear."

I laughed, but it was breathy and half-hearted. He placed his fingers on my chin and tilted my head toward him. His lips pressed against mine again for a moment.

"Do you remember why I started calling you Cadybug?" he asked, a smile teasing his lips.

I genuinely laughed that time, tilting my head back. "How could I forget?" He lifted his chin toward me. "Tell me the story again?"

"I will always retell it for you." And I did, feeling like I traveled back in time.

I was in a small clearing in the forest not far from the school. I barely ever skipped, but Jessica said some nasty things about my new dress in class, and I just couldn't deal with the rest of my day. I could still hear her sneering voice in my head.

"Ew. Look at that dress. Clearly your dad bought it used. The pattern is disgusting and the ugly, frilly lace at the bottom is practically yellow. I bet that dress is older than my dad!"

It was stupid, the most ridiculous of insults, but it really hurt me. Dad wanted to get me something special for my tenth birthday and stopped to pick it up for me after working a thirty-six-hour shift. I really liked the lavender and gray swirl of flowers on it. My favorite colors. The lace made me feel girly and pretty, but now that felt foolish. It was still my favorite dress, but now it was tarnished by Jessica's mean comments.

I lay on the ground, staring up at the clear blue sky through the branches high above. The warmth of the sun kissed my face and made me feel a little better. It was like knowing that no matter what, the sun would continue to shine, spreading love and light throughout the world. I reached up my hand, letting the dazzling rays dance through my fingers. It was like the golden light made my fingers sparkle with gold, and I smiled. A gentle breeze whispered through the trees, brushing my hair across my face and tickling my cheeks. Holding my breath, I let the breeze sing me its song. It was a beautiful melody, the sound of a symphony as the trees' leaves played their own musical instruments. I felt magical for a single moment before I remembered . . .

I was alone, and I felt every bit of it. I spent so much time alone that I could barely stand it. Ezra and Alex tried to hang out when they could, but it was hard for them. I lived so far away from the Beta and Alpha sections of the pack's territory. Sighing heavily, I scowled at the sky like I wanted to scowl at Jessica. It didn't make me feel any better.

The sound of footsteps broke through the singing of the birds and bugs around me, startling me out of my daze. I sat up and glanced at the surrounding trees. Facing the direction of the school, I found myself hoping that it wasn't Mr. Hammond coming to lecture me about skipping school. I was supposed to go to the nurse, but I just kept walking until I found myself here.

Ezra appeared through the trees. I breathed a sigh of relief, sitting back and watching him approach. He wasted no time sitting down beside me and raising a brow.

"You know she's just a dumb girl, right?" he asked, looking downright grumpy.

I played with the frilly lace at the hem of my skirt. "I know that, but it still hurt my feelings."

Picturing my dad's face, I felt sick to my stomach with guilt. He was so happy to be able to bring me a gift that he knew I would like, and now I didn't know if I could ever wear it again.

Ezra's blue gaze watched me closely, examining my expression. Taking a deep breath, he held it for a moment before letting it out in a huge sigh. "If you could be any bug, what would it be?" he asked, his face completely serious.

I blinked at him. "What?"

He grinned, his eyes sparkling with humor. "You heard me."

Letting my eyes roam, I pondered it. A ladybug hummed, floating down until it landed on Ezra's knee. I looked at the orangey-red of it and counted the two black dots.

"A ladybug."

He raised a blond brow. "Why a ladybug of all things?"

I smirked smugly at him. Now who was distracting who? "So I can give people good luck when they see me and I land on them." I gestured to the ladybug crawling over his knee and down his calf.

"I don't know if that's a thing . . . I think that hurting a ladybug gives you bad luck for a while."

I shrugged. "That's fine, too. I'd be okay with cursing people for hurting me. I'd start with Jessica Barber."

He threw his head back and laughed. "You're vicious, Cadybug."

My face heated and I glanced at his face before looking back at the ladybug on his leg. I put my finger down in front of it, letting it crawl onto me. "That's the first nickname anyone has given me other than Cade or Cady," I said quietly. I felt touched. My eyes stung as tears threatened.

"I'm glad I was the first," Ezra whispered, pulling me back to the present.

I grinned. "You've taken a lot of my firsts. You should start saving them for others," I retorted.

He smiled, exposing his almost perfect teeth. I looked at them, a smile curving my mouth at the one front tooth that slightly overlapped the other.

"I'd happily take all your good firsts. I'd just as happily take all your lasts."

I lifted my eyes to his, looking between them and the contented look they held. "My lasts?"

"Your last first kiss. Your last hug. Your last partner. I want to be with you forever."

Reaching up, I gently slid my fingertip down his nearly perfect nose. It hooked ever so slightly. Ezra was perfectly imperfect. I loved it about him. My fingertip grazed over his jawline and a hungry look pushed out the expression of contentment. Pausing, I examined his face closely.

"I want that too," I finally replied, my hand finding its way into his golden waves.

It was as if a flood gate opened, and he kissed me with a ferocity that left me breathless. His weight pushed me backwards as he leaned over me. One of his knees landed between my thighs, keeping him from laying on me as he continued kissing me ravenously. I reciprocated his fervor, my arms wrapping around his neck and pulling him down against me.

The next morning, I was grinning stupidly. Ezra stayed for a little bit after kissing me so intently, I thought I'd fall apart at the seams. It was glorious and I felt like I might have been glowing. It took effort not to think too much about it and focus on Alex's upcoming Ascension, cementing her place as a volsifi. That night, as the new moon rose, Alex would shift for the first time in front of everyone in the pack. It was no ordinary Tuesday, and it was impossible to focus.

Fortunately, not much occurred during the day. The only thing that stuck out as unusual was the fact that Jason seemed to be everywhere I was. The coincidence fried my nerves, but over the course of the day, I learned to ignore the feeling.

Kyle took me home after school so I could quickly get dressed before the ceremony. It was customary for female volsifi to wear dark dresses and male volsifi to wear dark slacks and button-down dress shirts. The only person who dressed in white and to the nines was the volsifi who was Ascending, symbolizing rebirth. Today, that was Alex.

I dressed in a simple black dress that hugged me in all the right ways, according to Alex. She said that's why she'd bought it for me, and I wasn't going to complain. She'd purchased me clothes for too long for me to refuse the gifts now. I wore black tights underneath and my knee-high leather boots that I enjoyed during the cooler months. Being February in the northern Adirondacks, it was pretty cold out, though it didn't seem to bother me as much as it used to.

Conveniently, Kyle had brought his own clothes and changed in our downstairs bathroom. Dad was hovering as well, dressed in all black just like

Kyle. I wondered vaguely if mom would bother to go when she suddenly appeared behind my dad like a ghost. Her blonde curls were pulled up in a loose updo that revealed her slender neck.

My mother was gorgeous, and I looked nothing like her, though I wish I did. Her thin figure was dressed appropriately in a black dress to match my dad, but she didn't have the same warmth in her blue eyes as he did. I think a part of her died when my twin brother and grandmother vanished. While I couldn't imagine how hard it would be to lose a child and a parent at the same time, that didn't stop me from slowly building up resentment over how she'd vanished on me and dad, too.

"Are we ready to go?" Mom's voice broke the silence, holding an alto melody that was captivating to everyone around her. That was something dad had always said; her voice could bring a dead man back to life with its gorgeous richness, then they'd die all over again when they got a glimpse of her physical beauty. He wasn't incorrect on that statement.

I nodded, reaching out to Kyle. He wasted no time in putting his hand into mine and squeezing my fingers; he'd become one of my people in the past couple months. I craved his closeness as much as I did Ezra's or Alex's. My mom's pale blue gaze, so much like Callum's, dropped to our connection, a frown furrowing her brow before being wiped away. If I hadn't been looking at her with wide eyes and waiting for a reaction, I would have missed it completely.

I led Kyle from the house, wanting to get out of the tense atmosphere my mother created. I loved my mother, but she also unnerved me in a way I couldn't quite explain. I took it personally that I lost my twin brother, grandmother, and mother in the same day. Part of me resented her for not being able to pull herself together for me, like I wasn't worth being present for in the absence of my twin. Dad had no problem being a parent to me, even though he also lost one of his children. In fact, my dad never stopped being there for me, his love never shifting or waning due to his grief, like he needed to hold me closer after seeing how quickly you could lose someone. My mother had faded into the background like a specter, haunting our house; he had come forward to be a stand-up father every chance he could.

Kyle and I drove separately from my parents, not wanting to be trapped in a vehicle with them. The drive to the Alpha's estate felt like it passed in a blink, my concern for Alex dominating my thoughts. It took me a few moments to realize that my hand was still in Kyle's, balanced on the gear shift between us.

Shifting ceremonies were held in The Garden of Ascension off to the side of the Alpha's estate, buried beyond a winding road up a large mountain where there was no way a human could stumble across it. While we were pretty well segregated from humans where we were, there was always a chance a curious person could find their way to our tiny town up near the border to Canada. Volsifi usually tried to find mountainous terrain where a wolf could possibly belong so as to not raise suspicion, and we always kept our high schools separate from the humans. We did not hide in plain sight like some of the other supernatural species.

Twilight was upon us as Kyle parked at the garden. I paused and looked at him for a moment, taking in his features before reaching out to brush the backs of my fingers over his jawline. I paused halfway through the action, my eyes widening as he looked at me with an equally stunned expression.

"I'm so sorry." My cheeks felt hot as the sun as I pulled my hand away.

"Don't be sorry," he reassured me, grabbing my hand and nuzzling his cheek against my fingers before kissing their tips.

We stared at each other for a long moment before he cleared his throat and looked away. "Now I'm the one who's sorry. That was inappropriate." He gently placed my hand in my lap before pulling away.

I stayed silent, not sure what to say. My gut swirled with a confusing amount of concrete coated butterflies, and I shook my head. "Don't be. I didn't hate it."

A low chuckle stirred the air between us as he shook his head, rubbing his chin with his left hand. "Thank the Goddess for that. I'd be unhappy if you *hated* my touch," he murmured, causing those butterflies to shed some of the stone encasing their wings.

Oh no. I was in trouble. I tried to remember kissing Ezra. It had made me happy, and still did, but I couldn't stop the conflicting feelings developing.

Kyle exited the car, walking around the front to open my door for me as he always did. Taking a couple deep breaths, I tried to pull myself together before he opened my door. Reaching in, he took my hand and helped me out of the car before shutting the door and locking it behind us. Looking up at the darkening sky, I bit my lip as anxiety took over again. Sensing my unease, Kyle took my hand in his, our fingers automatically lacing together as he patted my arm. "No need to worry. Ascensions always go well." He gently squeezed my hand.

Easy for him to say. He already did this last September.

We walked into a large, stone building that looked out over the sprawling gardens stationed behind it. In the summer, there would be flowers coloring all the bushes that grew along the paths within the garden. In February, it was mostly winter roses, various winter berries, and evergreen bushes that broke up the bare branches of the hibernating flora. In the middle of the currently barren garden was a large stone dais called the Ascension Pedestal that was slightly elevated so every volsifi in attendance could see the Ascending. Tonight, was Alex's turn, and she didn't share a birthday with anyone else in the pack.

Occasionally, there were two volsifi shifting for the first time at once and they shared the pedestal to shift together. Usually there was only one at a time. Twins were unheard of, other than me and Callum, of course. I was an exception, certainly not a rule. Something I heard often when I was younger. I'd also heard that twins were a bad omen, but my dad has repetitively vehemently denied that there was any truth to that.

Inside the building, a feast was laid out on sprawling tables along near-ly every wall. The Alpha and Beta families never cut any corners with any Ascension Ceremony regardless of where the Ascending fell in the hierarchy. Every volsifi got special treatment on their eighteenth birthday. This was pretty standard fare for every volsifi, no matter what pack. We learned long ago that every species does something special for their Ascension, though I didn't know what those traditions were for the others. Lucien insisted that learning too much about other species was unnecessary.

Kyle and I wandered along with our plates, serving ourselves before finding a table with Alex and her family. Ascension Ceremonies were the only time that the caste system was ignored for camaraderie. It was one of the few times that my parents could feel like maybe they still belonged to the Betas, though I knew we would always be Deltas unless Ezra and I were officially mated and he took his place as the Alpha. At that point, our entire family would become members of the Alpha rank. Ezra taking his place as Alpha wouldn't happen until after we finished at an Academy, though I was no longer certain we would be going together.

My eyes drifted around the crowd, hunting for any sign of golden curls, until Kyle nudged my arm and gestured to a corner where Ezra stood next to his father. His smile was pleasant, but I could see that there was no light in his gaze. Jessica stood on his other side, hanging onto his arm like a ginger leech. It made my stomach sink into my intestines, dimming the glowing feeling that had enveloped me just that morning. I forced myself to go find Alex and ignore my own feelings. We had to keep up appearances after all.

Alex looked nervous as all hell as Kyle sat next to her, shifting food around her plate instead of actually eating anything. I didn't blame her, since I was fairly certain I wouldn't be able to eat for weeks before my own Ascension. I sat on his other side, looking across all the people congregating in celebration. All of their eyes kept drifting to our table, making me feel like I was on display. It invoked every instinct in me to run and get the hell out of there, an unfortunate side effect of being the scum of the pack.

I was snapped out of my reverie as Brody came over and sat on my other side like a quiet sentinel. He moved so , it was remarkable, given his size. He flashed a smile at me, trying to maintain some semblance of normal. The only thing that made his teeth less than perfect was the gap between the two in the front. I felt awkward. I still hadn't adjusted to his presence and our issues seemed to be suspended above us. I'd accepted his apology, but I was still working on moving past his stupid actions.

Feeling a heavy gaze on me, I glanced around the room to find Ezra, who sat at the head table beside his father. I saw that he was already staring at me, and our eyes met. He examined me closely, as if trying to get a read on me and my mental state. The answer was not great, but he might as well have been thousands of miles away. His lips pressed together, the dimple beneath the left side of his mouth appearing. Jessica was gabbing beside him, not realizing that he wasn't paying her the slightest bit of attention. Ezra's eyes flicked to Kyle, and I noticed Kyle staring back at him, though I had no idea what they were communicating through that look. I tried to feign ignorance by taking a couple bites of food. Ezra and Kyle ended their intense stare down a moment later and Kyle turned to look at me instead, offering a small smile in comfort. It didn't help ease my confusion.

As time went on, our table filled up with people I knew, but wasn't close to. That was fine. I was okay with keeping to myself as I tried my hardest to ignore Brody's constant glances at me. It felt like he was continuously gaging my wellbeing, making sure I was okay. I wasn't. I didn't think that would change anytime soon.

A burst of raucous laughter broke out across the room. The four of us glanced over to Jason's table where he was guffawing with dramatic flair. His emerald eyes were focused on me, and I cringed internally. I didn't want his attention, it made me feel unnerved. Most people were afraid of the unknown, I was afraid of people.

Too soon, Lucien was standing from his position at the head table. He was dressed in a blue that bespoke his royalty, but all I could focus on was his cold glare as it lingered on me for a moment longer than I was comfortable with. We listened to his warning. We heeded it. So why was he still looking at me as though I was a wraith that had descended upon his pack?

Finally looking away, Lucien raised his hands to garner silence, his voice cutting through the leftover chatter of the large group of volsifi in the room, quieting everyone instantly. "Good evening, and welcome to the Garden of Ascension. Tonight, we celebrate Alexis Pierce turning eighteen and rising in status to that of a full volsifi."

Alex rose and adjusted her skirt, smoothing invisible creases as everyone's attention shifted to her. Sitting this close, I noticed the tremor in her fingers as she clasped them in front of her to calm them. I wanted to reach out and grab her hands and try to force any sense of ease into her nervous system that I could. However, knowing my place, I remained seated and left my hands in my lap where they belonged. Ezra eyed his father with no lack of disgust as he continued speaking, giving a speech for a girl that he barely knew and probably didn't like. I wondered if anyone else in the room noticed.

"With that, please join me and Alexis at the Ascension Pedestal." Lucien gave Alex a warm smile, but it didn't reach his eyes. In all of my seventeen years, I'd never seen a smile reach his eyes.

Alex slipped out of her heels and dress so she was barefoot in a white slip, placing her clothing on her chair before walking to join Lucien at the doorway to the gardens. I was grateful for her that there was no snow on the path as we all rose as a pack and weaved through the labyrinth of sleeping flora toward the dais in the center. All along the paths leading to the Ascension Pedestal were tall, wrought iron candelabras that held thick, white pillar candles. This was customary for Ascension Ceremonies that occurred during the new moon, and it was my favorite. The large granite slab in the center of the gardens was approximately twenty feet wide, large enough for at least two volsifi to stand on for their ascension. Alex was climbing onto it as we approached, Kyle's status allowing us both to stand right at the edge of the platform.

Lucien stood next to Alex on the pedestal. Once she was ready, he handed her the ancient ceremonial cape, the white satin gleaming golden in the candlelight that lit the night in the absence of the moon. The cape was thick and heavy, the large expanse of white satin only broken by the outer edge cape that was embroidered with silver moons and stars that glimmered like the real things in the dim lighting. After situating the cape about her shoulders and clasping it at her neck, Alex pulled the hood up over her head and hid the glittering hairpin she'd borrowed. The hood fell down to her nose, shielding her eyes as she stared straight ahead. The slip she'd worn dropped to her feet, but the cape brushing the granite pedestal hid her naked flesh.

Lucien's cold gaze landed on Kyle, Brody, and me; I stared him down as I took Kyle's hand, our fingers locking together. On my other side, Brody put his hand on my shoulder and tucked against my back. It was more supportive than I'd have ever thought. Having been watching Lucien, I noticed the almost imperceptible flaring of his nostrils before he turned back to Alex. Once Lucien turned away, I glanced up at Brody to see fire in his dark eyes as he glared at Lucien's profile. I pressed my lips together, turning to look at Alex. She stood on the dais in the center where a separate slab of granite the color of blood symbolized the Scarlet Moon our pack was named after. The outer ring was the standard white granite, heavily imperfected with black and gray specks. I had to admit, it was a stunning piece of artistry.

Standing out there, the bitter chill of the winter air nipped at our noses and exposed flesh. I felt okay, my newfound warmth coming in handy for once. Shivering, Alex looked like she was about to have a heart attack at any moment; either that or a complete breakdown. Her nerves were all consuming as she stood before us, the moon high in the sky above. The next part was ingrained into us from infancy, it seemed. The words that spawned the Goddess Levende to bless us with Ascension. While we also mentioned the God of the Underworld, Kuorir, his purpose was to guide our souls in the afterlife until we could be reborn again into the hands of the Goddess in our next life.

The cape didn't move as a cool breeze blew through, though I noticed her legs tremble. No one talked about how it felt to shift for the first time, and if they did no one believed the stories as they were so varied. Ezra had assured her that it didn't hurt *that* bad, but some people said that it feels like you're being ripped apart and stitched back together. I wasn't sure who to believe, truthfully; both seemed like viable options. There was also the unspoken variable that it was different for everyone.

Alex stood in front of us, her arms wrapped around herself. Stripping was pretty standard for Ascending volsifi, but it was always jarring to experience it in such an intimate way. The cape shifted with the volsifi wearing it. The threads of the cape were made by satin threads soaked in moonlight for a fortnight and each pack had its own. They were all ancient heirlooms that had been passed down for centuries. I'd heard once that the volsifi cape had threads pulled from the sacred Datura flower, woven together from magic and moonlight. Both tales were mystifying, and I chose to be in awe of it regardless of how it was made.

Clouds shifted above; the dark circle of the new moon that existed among the stars exposed to us all as Alex stood beneath it on the Ascension Pedestal. Taking a deep breath, she held out her arms to the sides and tilted her face up to the moon. Her words did not betray her fear, coming across as strong and confident as Alex always sounded. The large hood of the cape fell from her blonde curls, the pieces she'd left down cascaded down her back, the borrowed comb glittering happily in the candlelight.

"Mother Goddess Levende, most precious divine Luna, I stand before you as naked as the day you and Kuorir, most divine Alpha, gave me life once more. I offer to you my body, my soul, my life on this night. Please grant me the gift of Ascension, so that I may shift into the glory of the wolf you have given me and so that I may join my pack as an equal," Alex called up to the moon, speaking directly to the Goddess above who blessed us with life after previous deaths. Ezra claimed that the Goddess would speak back to you when you called upon her during the ceremony.

A violent tremor wracked Alex's body a moment later, her head dropping down to look at all of us surrounding her. We all waited with bated breath, but the ceremony never went awry. Just as with all volsifi before her, Alex's eyes widened in surprise as another shudder made her tremble aggressively. Her hands rose to her cheeks as her bones shifted and changed in her face, her nose and mouth extending into a snout. Fur erupted over her flesh, as golden as the hair on her head. It was long and curly and looked as soft and luxurious as her human locks. It didn't take long for the shift to happen fully, and within a minute, she was standing on the raised pedestal on all fours. Just like her human form, Alex's wolf was gorgeous and stood out among the others that I'd seen. I felt breathless as I gazed upon her, and her hazel eyes shifted to meet mine. She looked . . . as proud as she should.

After a moment of adjusting, Alex raised her head to the moon above us and gave a long howl. As wolves shifted around me, more howls joined hers, filling the night with the sound of a large and ancient pack. Beside me, Kyle smirked and winked at me before he howled in his human form as he hurriedly removed his clothes. However, the sound shifted as he himself did. A blink later, I was gazing down at a large wolf, his fur curly and dark brown. His eyes were still hazel as they gazed up at mine and I couldn't stop myself; I reached out and touched his head, petting him behind the ears. A low rumble could barely be heard over the sound of the howling around us, but I knew it would have been a hum of pleasure in his human form.

Turning to my other side, a massive, black wolf stood beside me. Brody. His fur was shorter than a lot of the others, but that didn't diminish his sheer size. His head bumped against my navel as he moved past me to join Kyle on my other side.

Looking around me, my eyes found another wolf I'd seen before, his dirty blond waves and piercing blue eyes as captivating as the wolf standing beside me. I ignored the russet wolf who nuzzled into his neck before howling herself, the sound giving me chills of rage. Looking away, my gaze dropped back to Kyle, who gave my hand a nudge with his snout.

Before I could get too lost in him, he took off as the rest of the pack did with Alex leading the run. Around me were other teenagers who hadn't yet Ascended, including William Jones who waved awkwardly, and the children of the pack. Babies were kept at home during particularly cold ceremonies like tonight, so there was no one below the age of eight left standing around. Those of us remaining turned and walked back into the building and the promise of heat. The running portion didn't usually last too terribly long, and they would all be back soon enough so the celebration could continue.

CHAPTER 22

CADENCE

D ad, after promises that nothing would happen between the two of us and
an extra promise that the door would be left open and we wouldn't both
be in bed, graciously let Kyle spend the night, even though it was a school night.
I'd already been called out from school the next day; most students are absent
the day after an Ascension since they ran so incredibly late. Kyle's parents didn't
want him driving back home in the wee hours of the morning after dropping
me off. It wasn't without an incredibly uncomfortable conversation about being
"safe" that made me search the ground eagerly for a hole to hide in. I couldn't
find one, much to my dismay.

Kyle and I were still awake when my parents came home, watching movies
in the living room. My dad seemed relieved that we were barely cuddling, sitting
on opposite sides of the couch with my feet in Kyle's lap.

"No funny business," he instructed sternly, pointing between both of us
with a serious look on his face even though he was aware of the arrangement.

Kyle looked mildly horrified, and I wasn't sure how to feel about that until he spoke.

"I would never betray your trust, sir. Cadence will be just as innocent in the morning as she is right now. Although . . . maybe she's not all that innocent . . . she did choose this movie," he teased, gesturing at *Ten Inch Hero* playing on the television.

I looked at him with my mouth agape before tossing popcorn at him as he guffawed. "It's about a sub shop in California! It's a pun," I said incredulously, grabbing the bag of peach rings and throwing one of those at him for good measure before chomping on one and aggressively stretching it until it ripped while staring him right in the eye.

Chuckling, Kyle picked up the gummy from his shirt and popped it into his mouth to talk around it. "See? She's vicious. You can trust that even if I did try anything, I wouldn't survive the attempt. You raised her right, Mr. Nocetti."

Dad, unable to help himself, grinned and nodded. "Yes, I did. And it's David." He trudged up the stairs after my mother who'd disappeared as soon as they'd walked in the door.

After finishing *Ten Inch Hero* and then *Empire Records* (Kyle's choice), we found our way upstairs where I started digging several crocheted blankets from my closet. Standing on tiptoe, I struggled to yank them from the top shelf, grunting with the effort. Heat surrounded me as Kyle appeared behind me, his arms easily reaching the blankets and pulling them down. "Where do you want these?"

I pulled out a sleeping bag and tossed it onto the bed before grabbing a navy afghan blanket and unfolding it partially to lay it down on the floor for extra cushion. I looked up to find Kyle intently examining the stack of afghans with an intrigued look on his face.

"What?" I asked, walking over to him and picking up a purple and white one from under his nose to lay on the floor.

"Where did you guys get all these?" He unfolded the next one and looked at the colors and stitching.

Pausing, I blinked in confusion. "I made them. Why?"

Kyle looked up with an astounded expression that made me feel weirder than it probably should have. "These are incredible, that's why. The craftsmanship is impeccable, like the ones my grandmother used to make. Where did you learn? Where did you get all the yarn?"

Shrugging, I crossed my body with my right arm, rubbing my left arm awkwardly as I shifted my weight from foot to foot. "Practice. And Mrs. Jones gave me lessons while I was helping her work in her shop on weekends. I also get supplies that way," I responded sheepishly, wishing we could talk about anything else.

"Is that William and Alice's mom?" He moved to the next blanket and examined it closely. "How much work do you have to do to earn this much yarn?"

I nodded as he gazed up at me, still looking awed. "Yeah. That's their mom." I hesitated before answering his second question. "A lot. Yarn is so expensive. It took me a couple years of work to earn this much yarn. I also am given spools by some of the Omega families who can afford it for holidays and birthdays over the years."

I wasn't sure how I felt about it, but some of those heavy butterflies in my stomach flew a little lighter as he studied me with such intense reverence; like some of the concrete coating their wings cracked and disintegrated.

"Sometimes, I think this arrangement was the best decision I've ever made," he murmured, his voice quiet and tender as his eyes dropped down to the blankets in his lap.

I didn't know what to say to that, guilt still rolling in my guts as I finished making him a bed on the floor. As much as I hated sleeping with the door ajar, I refused to betray my father's trust and left it standing open. We climbed into our respective beds. Even in the dark, sleep wouldn't come. Hearing no change in Kyle's breathing, I assumed he was awake as well.

"Thank you. For everything. You've sacrificed your happiness to help me with something that gives you nothing in return."

He was silent for so long I thought he might actually have been asleep. My cheeks heated with that realization, wondering if I was actually okay with that. However, I was startled when he finally spoke.

"I sacrificed nothing to be with you. I've never been happier than when I'm spending time with you, especially in moments like this." His voice was hushed in the silence. Overwhelmed with the urge to join him on the floor, I rolled over and tucked the blanket around me before falling into a dreamless sleep.

I woke up slowly to the feeling of something brushing over my nose repeatedly. As I clawed my way through the layers of unconsciousness, I realized that it was brushing from my forehead, down the bridge of my nose before lifting and starting down the same path again. Furrowing my brow, I tried to figure out what was happening while lost in the haze of sleep. Hearing a giggle, I groaned and opened my eyes to find a pair of hazel ones looking back at me. One finger, the nail painted black, pulled away from my face before plopping down on my forehead and dragging down the bridge of my nose once more before bopping me on the tip of my nose.

Jerking backwards, I scowled at Alex as she cackled, the noise causing a grunt behind me. Turning around, I saw Kyle stirring from his position on the floor while Ezra stood leaning against the doorway and staring down at him with a look of discontent on his face.

"Good morning, grumpy gills," I muttered to him, causing his blue eyes to lift to me while I raised my arms above my head and groaned as all my muscles pulled taught and stretched themselves out.

"Good morning, Cadybug," he responded, smirking at me as he pushed off of the doorframe and reached down to help Kyle off the floor. "Good morning to you as well." The look on his face seemed nothing short of pleasant and I wondered if I'd misread his previously disgruntled expression.

It was late morning, and my stomach was grumbling unhappily. I stopped to brush my teeth in the bathroom before heading downstairs where the others were collected in the kitchen. Immediately, Alex thrust a shopping bag into my face where I found sausage, a couple cans of biscuits, and milk. I pulled out the sausage and milk and went about making sausage gravy while Alex pulled out the containers of biscuits to make. Kyle asked about coffee, and I pointed at it so he could start a pot. Ezra stood around looking pretty while the rest of us worked around him, apparently completely useless in the kitchen.

"Ezra, your privilege is showing," Alex teased, booping him on the nose with the spoon she was using to pop open the container of biscuits.

Ezra looked around helplessly, unable to really defend himself. While his father might be a dictator who made it known how he felt about the lower castes, that didn't stop him from hiring Deltas and Omegas as maids and cooks in his estate. The caste system was such a ridiculous sham.

"Come here and keep this going. I'll fry some eggs. Make sure you really get in there and keep scraping everything off the bottom. You don't want it to burn." I handed him the spatula.

Ezra's eyes exposed how uncertain he felt, but he ended up grabbing the utensil and stirring the creamy mixture in the pan regardless. Honestly, he was so anxious I was worried he might not be aggressive enough, but I let it go. No one liked being nagged.

255

It was about then that Brody showed up, unlocking the door with his own code and letting himself in after texting me to announce his arrival. He hovered around, helping with random tasks.

Pulling out an electric skillet, I got to work making everyone eggs to go with our incredibly unhealthy breakfast. I didn't care, it was one of my absolute favorites. Brody appeared at my back and I turned to face him. A small smile graced his lips as he held his hand out for the spatula.

"You're hosting. The least we can do is cook for you," he said.

Affirmations were mumbled all around as Alex tucked a mug of chamomile tea into my hand and nudged me out of the way.

In no time at all, we had a scrumptious breakfast put together and were sitting around the dining room table. Dad appeared out of nowhere, sniffing the air curiously as he walked into the room while pulling on his coat.

"That smells heavenly," he commented, gathering everything in an overnight bag.

I swallowed a mouthful. "There's extra, if you want some. I can fry up some more eggs if you want modified haystacks since we don't have any hash browns."

Dad was about to leave to work an overnight shift at the hospital, and he hardly ever ate well when he was working one of his twenty-four-hour shifts. He got too distracted being an emergency surgeon to care for himself. Typically, he put in hours here in the pack, working for little to no money to heal the lower caste's injured and sick. However, that wouldn't pay the bills, so he did overnight shifts in a human hospital as an emergency room doctor and donated anything extra we didn't desperately *need* to provide medicines and supplies for those who needed it. To say he was overworked so mom could stay home and be absent as all hell was the understatement of the year.

I hated their arrangement. It wasn't fair that dad had to practically run himself into the ground while she couldn't even get out of bed to parent me. Yet, it wasn't my problem how they went about making ends meet and dad had made that abundantly clear on numerous occasions. Dad also refused to let me get my own job, assuring me that I needed to focus on school to get into a good academy. So instead, I helped when I could around the food pantry and the seamstress' shop.

The reminder of that failure to get into the school made my stomach twist uncomfortably. All that work he did, and I botched the entrance essay into PSG. What a nightmare.

Dad politely declined, insisting that he was running late for the long drive into the human city to do a shift at a short-staffed emergency room. I frowned at him, hoping I had just missed him eating breakfast earlier. He gave me a reassuring smile, dropping a kiss onto the top of my head before he ran out the door.

"It kills me," I said simply, staring at the door like I thought there was a chance he might come back through it and reassure me that he wasn't over-working or starving himself.

"I know." Alex's eyes expressed her sympathy from across the table.

Ezra nodded knowingly on my left side as his hand found its way to my thigh. They'd both been there the times dad stumbled home in the late afternoon after working a long shift, too thin from not eating, and fell onto the couch because making it up to bed was too much effort. However, dad's gut was still in place. Hopefully it stayed that way. I hated to see the life drain from his dark eyes as the weight shed from his body.

Kyle pressed his lips together, his eyes dropping to Ezra's hand on my thigh as his cheeks turned red. I didn't know how to interpret that, so I didn't bother trying. His foot bumped against mine under the table as his gaze lifted to mine and held so long that Ezra cleared his throat and gently dug his fingers into my thigh. Pushing away from the table, I announced that I needed a drink and went through the doorway into the kitchen.

I was filling up a cup with water when Ezra appeared beside me. I glanced up at him, trying not to feel guilty. He gave me a half smile as he brushed my hair from my forehead.

"I've missed you," he whispered, brushing his thumb over my cheekbone. I leaned my face into his hand, causing his smile to widen.

"I've missed you too. I feel like we hardly ever see each other lately."

He nodded, his smile fading. "I know. How about we hang out one of these nights? I desperately need some alone time with you."

I smiled, placing my hand over his where it rested on my cheek. "I'd really love that. I love you."

His eyes sparkled with happiness, and he leaned down and pressed his lips firmly against mine. The kiss told me many things: that he missed me, that his love was still there, that I was still wanted and not cast aside. I kissed him back, trying to express everything to him that I couldn't put into words.

We shortly got back to the silliness of our day, and I tried not to dwell on my dad being a slave to the machine or my conflicting feelings on Kyle and Ezra. Maybe he wouldn't have to if my mom could heave her bones from her bed and be a presence in our lives. Last night was the first time I'd seen her in months.

"Dad texted. He needs me at training in an hour, so I unfortunately have to go." Alex pouted as she shoved her phone back into the pocket of her leggings. She looked out the window just as the sun fell behind the horizon and the glowing pink of the twilight sky disappeared with it.

Brody sighed, rubbing his face with his palms. "Yeah. I've been summoned to train with you. Can you give me a ride?" he grunted out, standing and half stretching as his hands pressed against the ceiling.

We all stared at him like he had four heads. "Didn't you drive?"

Brody rolled his dark eyes. "No. I needed to take a walk and decided to stretch my legs on the way here."

I blinked at him. "Brody, that's like, six miles. That's more than stretching your legs."

He grunted again, a smile cracking his serious expression and exposing the gap in his front teeth. "It's not more than stretching when you're six-foot-seven."

Alex pressed her lips together, raising her brows and shaking her head in disbelief before her expression grew serious again. "Ezra rode with me, so unless Kyle's going to give him a ride . . ." she added, pointing between the two of them.

Ezra flushed and glanced at Kyle before turning back to Alex. "No, unfortunately I have a date with Jessica tonight. Lucien informed me an hour ago. I've been ignoring it," he bit out, scowling and jamming his hands into his pockets. "So, I'll ride with you, Alex."

I stared at him, hating Jessica with an intensity that I could only associate with envy. Nodding, I shrugged one shoulder up as if it could shield me from the jealous hurt. Ezra frowned and approached me. He plopped on the edge of the couch beside me so he could face me, taking my hands in his. I didn't grip his fingers back. "I'm sorry, Cadence. I hate this as much as you do," he breathed, his tone earnest and pleading for my forgiveness; forgiveness for something that wasn't even his fault. I felt childish for taking it out on him.

"I know. It just hurts. You don't have to apologize for anything. I agreed to this."

Sighing, he leaned forward and kissed me on the forehead before dropping his lips to mine.

I kissed him back, but it stung in my chest. It was unlike the kiss earlier, when we were promising to spend time together and get back the feeling of falling in love. I didn't want to think of it as a kiss goodbye, and I tried my hardest not to dwell on it. Of course, he was sad. He didn't want to spend time with Jessica any more than I wanted him to.

Kyle sat rigidly on my other side, making me feel guilty. I didn't know what Kyle felt. We hadn't talked about it, but his reaction to Ezra kissing me in front of him didn't make me think he felt good about it.

"I'm so sorry this is how things are turning out, Cadybug," Ezra muttered, his voice thick. When he turned back, his eyes were glittering with unshed tears. "Just remember that I hate her with everything I am, and spending time with her only makes me miss you more. I will never marry her. I reserve that for you if you'll still have me when this is all over. I love you." A tear escaped, running down his cheek, and he angrily wiped it away.

"I love you too," I said, standing and closing the distance between us. Brushing a finger over his cheek, I wiped away a tear he'd missed. His hurt made my soul crack.

Alex stood, shifting her gaze between Ezra and I at the front door and Kyle sitting on the couch. "Just know, I will not pick sides. All I want is your happiness, Cadence." There was a sadness that even I could hear in her voice. "I'll see you in school tomorrow."

Brody stood awkwardly before abruptly walking out with a grunted good-bye. Ezra followed him out, looking so forlorn I wanted to tell him to cancel the entire arrangement. Alex gave me a sad smile as she departed after the guys.

Then the door was shut, and Kyle and I were left alone in a silence that seemed to yawn open for decades. Shifting forward, he turned toward me, his knee brushing against mine. I didn't feel the need to move it. He looked at me like he could see straight into my soul, like all of my thoughts and emotions were laid out in front of him and what he saw made him incredibly sad. Reaching out, he gently brushed his fingertips across the back of my hand, and when I didn't pull away, he took my hand in his and laced our fingers together.

"I'm sorry that you're going through this," he murmured, his voice like a balm that soothed my broken heart. And while his presence eased the ache in my soul, it would never mend the fractures within it.

Shrugging, I pulled my lips between my teeth and bit down on them, sighing heavily. "It is what it is. It's the best situation for Ezra's safety." I stood and kept a hold on Kyle's hand. "I'm not even mad at him. This just . . . isn't what I hoped for when we got together."

"No one hopes for this when they fall in love with someone." His voice sounded almost bitter, making me turn to examine his face.

"No. I suppose no one does." I frowned, staring at the floor. "I'm just sad. This hurts more than I expected it to. I'm happy I have you, but I'm devastated that I lost him in the process."

Kyle stood, combing his fingers through my hair. "You didn't lose him. You won't lose me either. I'll be here as whatever you need at the end of all of this. Okay?"

I nodded, unable to speak as I leaned into him. My arms wrapped around his waist, gripping his t-shirt, clinging to the safe haven he created.

"Okay."

We went upstairs to my room where we sprawled on my bed, his arm behind my neck as he snuggled against my side. My laptop was balanced on my thighs and tilted upward so that we could both see the screen. Kyle had encouraged me to check my emails for a response from PSG though we both knew neither of us would have a response yet. The several-months-long wait was upon all of us who'd applied, and I was aching with anxiety over it.

Not long after, Kyle had to leave, his parents summoning him home because of the school night. He'd kissed me on the cheek before he'd left, and I could feel his lips on my cheek long after he was gone. Now it was getting late, and I was hungry. The pizza we had ordered for dinner was long gone, so I wandered downstairs to get some food. I padded into the kitchen, opening the fridge and standing there, staring into the well-lit abyss for a long moment before shutting the door and sighing. Being indecisive was the pits, and this overwhelming sadness wasn't helping. I was going to go for the snack cupboard when something on the counter stopped me in my tracks.

Sitting on the gray counter was a gorgeous amaryllis. One would argue that it was perfect, blooming wide and open with velvety petals that almost seemed to glow in the dimness, they were so incredibly red. Horror filled me, surrounding me abruptly like I'd fallen in a tank of water that immediately came up over my nose. Panic gripped my insides as I closed my eyes and took deep breaths to attempt to keep the metaphorical piranhas of fear in the tank of water from eating me alive.

Opening my eyes, they fell on a card left on the counter. It looked just like the ones we got for Corana, like the one I'd seen all too recently. Confused, I picked it up and looked at the words written on it as my other hand lifted the amaryllis from the countertop. My heart seemed to slow in my chest and my fingers went numb as the card fell to the floor. I didn't need to keep looking at it to remember what it said. The cursive letters were burned into my retinas like they were a neon sign and not black pen on paper.

Tick, tock. Your birthday is coming. You will be mine. Kyle's blood will flow as red as these petals when I slit his throat for thinking you could be his.

I dropped the amaryllis like it might burn me, and it fell to the floor with a burst of crimson petals. I backed away from it, my hands coming to my mouth as my eyes scanned the house. I had locked the doors when my friends left, I was certain of it. Running around the house, I checked all the doors and windows, and they were all locked just like I thought they would be.

I was just about to call anyone to come save me when several texts came through from the same unknown number. There were pictures of me looking at the note and dropping the amaryllis to the floor followed by a message.

Unknown

> Didn't you like my gift to you? You shouldn't be such an ungrateful little bitch.

The photos were taken through the open blinds from the back door just behind me and I turned to look, seeing no one there. I closed the blinds with shaking fingers.

No longer hungry, I raced up to my room and quietly shut the door. I didn't want to bother mom, even though I should probably wake her and tell her about what happened. Instead, I decided not to tell anyone and laid in bed to stare up at the ceiling, not wanting to admit that things were getting even worse.

Grabbing my phone, I dialed a number and held my phone to my ear. It only rang once before Kyle answered.

"Cadence. What's wrong?" He sounded alarmed, like he magically knew something was wrong.

"I got another flower . . ." A choked sob caught in my throat, but I coughed to cover it.

I heard a turn signal click on the other end of the line. "I'm turning around right now. I'm on my way, okay? Lock yourself in your bedroom and wait for me, okay?"

I nodded before realizing he couldn't see me. "Okay," I whispered before hanging up.

It should have taken Kyle nearly twenty minutes to arrive at my house, but I heard the front door unlock in fifteen. Footsteps raced up the stairs before there was a knock on my bedroom door. As soon as I opened it, Kyle had me in his arms, squeezing me against him.

"Are you okay? You're not hurt, are you?" he asked, pulling back to look me over.

Reaching up, I put my hands on his cheeks and nodded. "I'm okay, just unnerved. I don't know how it would have gotten there because everything was locked. You had just left. Did you see anyone?"

Kyle shook his head before resting his forehead against mine. "I never would have left you here if I'd seen someone. I called my mom and told her that I needed to stay with you. I'll never leave you alone."

I nodded, wrapping my arms around his neck and letting him hold me against him. "Have you gotten any texts from them?"

Sighing, Kyle pulled back and walked toward my bed. Plopping down, he put his head in his hands. "I've been getting texts, but no physical notes or flowers or anything. I don't think he's going to actually do anything but these vacant threats."

Sitting next to him, I took one of his hands in both of mine and he turned to face me. "I don't know, Kyle. Maybe we should have an elaborate break up and quit seeing each other. I don't want something to happen to you because of me."

"No. I will not go running with my tail between my legs."

I caught my lower lip between my teeth and bit down until it stung. "I don't think you'd be a coward for that."

He shook his head. "I don't know if this person is serious or not. I can't give you up."

"What if they attack you? Or hurt you or something awful? I'd never be able to live with myself. Maybe it's time to notify The Guard."

"You know as well as I do that they won't do anything. Even if they took it seriously, The Guard have no idea how to handle something like this. This is unheard of here. Everyone knows everyone and no one would do something like this. We haven't had any new pack members in years that would stir things up, you know?" Kyle said, bringing my knuckles to his lips and planting a kiss on them.

My head landed on his shoulder as I curled into him. He pulled my legs into his lap, hooking them over his knee. His arm wound around my waist, pulling me close against him before planting a kiss on my forehead.

"I refuse to lose you. Don't ask me to leave you alone. That's a fate worse than death."

CHAPTER 23

CADENCE

Sitting at the lunch table, I shuffled my food around my plate while Kyle eyed me warily like I was about to burst into tears at any second. Fortunately, I'd already run out of tears over the past couple days, spending my evenings curled up in my bed and soaking my pillows with them. At this point, I was dried out, more mummy than person.

Hearing an obnoxious laugh across the room, I looked up to find Jessica watching me as she cackled and clung to Ezra's arm while he stared at her like she was out of her mind. A hand landed on my thigh and gripped it, breaking my attention and causing me to turn and look at Kyle who was still watching me.

"Don't pay them any mind, Cadence. It will only make things harder on you." Kyle's voice was soft and gentle as he rubbed my thigh with his thumb. I nodded and ran my fingers through my hair before wrapping my arm around his to lean into him while his hand remained on my thigh. His lips pressed against the side of my head before he whispered in my ear, "You really should eat something."

Glancing back at Ezra, I saw him watching me just as Jessica was gazing lovingly up at him. His jaw twitched and he stood up abruptly, causing Jessica to practically fall onto his suddenly abandoned seat. Picking up his tray, he tossed everything and dropped it off at the return before hastily exiting the cafeteria. Jessica flushed crimson, standing and leaving her tray behind as she ran to follow him.

Still not satisfied, I took a small bite before dropping the fork. Alex frowned beside me and shuffled food around on her own plate. I decided then that I needed to stop being such a downer. The past few days were plenty, and I'd ignored Alex while focusing on my own problems.

"So, how is it, being an Ascended volsifi?"

She turned wide eyes to me, seemingly surprised at my sudden attention. I tried not to let that hurt and failed. "Oh, uh . . . I'm not sure. It's cool being able to shift now. I wish we were allowed to actually do that, but I guess being able to is cool."

I frowned, trying not to be irritated about the ridiculous rule against shifting. "Is there any real difference?"

Alex and Kyle glanced at each other as if confirming their experiences were the same.

"Not really. I was expecting to have a wolf in my head or something, but it really feels like the wolf is just another part of me. Like I can change my body like I change my clothes. It's not really a separate entity." Alex shrugged.

We all stood up as the bell signaling the end of lunch rang, discarding our trays before walking into the hall. Kyle split apart from us, waving goodbye. Alex and I walked toward our English class. Falling into step beside me, she held her books to her chest and gave me no small amount of side eye.

"So, what's going on with you and Kyle?" She casually flicked her hair over her shoulder and examined me.

Glancing at her, I frowned. "What do you mean? You know all about the arrangement."

Alex scoffed and stared at me. "Sure. But I think both of you are catching feelings. I just want to make sure *you* know what's happening," she accused, causing me to pause in the middle of the hallway. Disgruntled words were said as other students diverted around me.

Everything suddenly clicked into place, causing my face to blanche. "Oh no," I whispered, looking at her with wide eyes. "I *am* getting feelings for him."

Nodding knowingly, Alex turned to face me, not bothering to move us out of the center of the hallway. "And he's fallen for you. *Hard*. He's a great guy, Cade. I think if you're having these feelings, you have some conversations to have. The three of you have been forced into this position, and it's totally unfair, but all three of you have the right to be happy. I don't know how that happiness looks right now, but I think you need to lay your cards on the table for them both, and it won't be easy." She reached out and tucked my hair behind my ear in such a loving way that I felt like bursting into tears.

I let out a shaky breath and blinked away the blur that appeared in my vision. "You're right, and I hate it." I let her take my arm and guide me toward our class.

After English class, I was trudging on my own toward Species Cultures when I was accosted in the stairwell again. Jessica was there, waiting to grab me and slam me back against the wall so hard my head bounced off it. Stars flashed in front of my eyes, and I blinked them away while she leaned close to me.

Her weight pressed against me as she leaned toward my ear so she could whisper directly into it. "Just thought you should know . . . Ezra and I slept together the other night after our date. He really is dynamite in bed. The things he did to me? Just—" She sighed a moan in my ear while my stomach revolted, threatening to empty all over her if she didn't quit putting so much pressure against my torso.

And then she was gone, and I was left to slide down the wall until I was sitting on the floor with my knees pulled up toward my chest. The betrayal cut me so deeply that I thought I might just be sliced in half and barely holding the two pieces together. Unable to do anything else, I numbly picked myself up off the floor and walked downstairs toward my next class. I walked through the doorway just as the bell rang and plopped into my seat. No effort was made to seem like I wasn't bothered by what I'd just been told. Jessica knew I'd be bothered, that's why she had told me to begin with.

Maybe I was deluding myself to think that Ezra was content with not having sex. Was this all orchestrated by him to get laid? *That's preposterous.* There's no way that Ezra would do something like that, he wasn't a vapid jerk.

Mrs. Walker stood up from her desk, breaking me out of my thoughts. Turning her back to us, she wrote the word on the whiteboard. "Sigh-ree-nah," she emphasized, turning around to face us again. Apparently, she had given up attempting to find a student who knew how to pronounce anything.

"Who knows what this species is?" She looked around the room before her gaze settled on me. I don't know what it was about my expression indicated that I was the perfect victim, but she called on me, nonetheless. "Ms. Nocetti?"

Frowning, I scoured my memories for something that would remind me about syrenas. My mind latched onto a conversation that Ezra and I had about mermaids once. "The water dwellers?" I asked, my face and voice exposing my uncertainty.

Mrs. Walker nodded, smiling at me before moving on with her lesson. "That's correct. They tend to create communities near bodies of water, though they don't have to live in water all the time. Most syrenas live on land and integrate with human societies while returning to the water for their festivals and celebrations. Does anyone know anything else about our aquatic friends?"

No one raised their hand, so she sighed and frowned at us.

"A decent portion of syrenas are skilled musicians and actors, excelling in the arts. Most celebrities you know and love are syrenas. However, when they get wet, their scales become visible, so they make great effort to hide from the humans during wet weather. Does anyone know where the largest community of syrena are located?" She looked around the room with a frown. Again, no one raised their hand, so she called on Jessica.

"How would I know? It's your job to teach this shit to us," she grumbled, sounding bored and cranky as she leaned back in her chair, crossing her arms over her chest.

Mrs. Walker made no attempt to hide her eye roll. "Sure, Jessica. Just thought some of you might have talked to your parents or cracked open a book. Silly of me to assume. You've also earned yourself a detention for that language."

Pulling herself together, she continued, "The largest community of Syrena are in San Francisco, California. It's called the Farallones Tributary due to its proximity to the Gulf of the Farallones. They are the largest congregation in the world, and also where King Kaito Mizu rules. The up-and-coming Prince, Calder Mizu, will be taking his place on the throne in four short years when he graduates from Potencia Sui Generis. I had the honor of meeting Mr. Calder when he was a child, he is a very brilliant young man who specializes in musical instruments."

Jessica scoffed, crossing her arms over her chest. "Instruments? It's not that hard to play one or two instruments." She rolled her eyes. "I can play piano and the clarinet, after all."

Abrupt laughter escaped Mrs. Walker and my eyes widened at that reaction. It took a few moments for her to stop laughing and she wiped tears from her eyes. "Ms. Barber, he has mastered playing one hundred and six musical instruments. Though he does specialize in the shinobue, a traditional Japanese flute. It was breathtaking to hear ten long years ago. I can only imagine how much he's improved since then."

Turning with the remote, she displayed a picture on the projector screen. This family looked much more pleasant than the upir royals. Four people were the focus of the photo: the king and queen sitting side by side with two teenagers standing behind them.

"Sitting down are King Kaito and Queen Erena. Behind them are Oceana and Calder." Mrs. Walker gestured at them, shifting my focus around the photo. My eyes caught on the prince, entranced by the easy smile on his face that exposed a dimple in his left cheek. His dark eyes were captivating under a fringe of thick, black hair.

The bell rang and jarred me out of my thoughts. I stood, grabbing my things and escaping the room before Jessica could catch me again.

In my last period, I plopped down in my seat next to Kyle who immediately looked up at me with a brilliant grin that lightened some of the load on my heart.

"Want to go out tonight?" He leaned toward me with a wink.

Sighing, I flipped open my bio book and glanced at him. "I can't. I have to work at Sew What tonight. Mrs. Jones wants the night off and I offered to cover for her."

Not to be discouraged, Kyle shrugged. "I'll come with you, if you want the company." That caught my full attention. No one had ever offered to go into Omega territory to help me volunteer before.

"There's no money to be earned, though."

Kyle looked truly offended. "Like I give a shit about money." Just then Mr. Redmond walked into the class and Kyle crudely signed in Pidgin Signed English, *"I'll drive you there. I'll walk with you to your locker."*

I chuckled, blushing slightly. Nodding, I signed back, *"It's a date."*

After class, Kyle and I stopped at both our lockers so we could leave for the day. Ezra wasn't at his, so I assumed he'd already left with Jessica. I pretended that it didn't sting my slowly breaking heart, but the ever-astute Kyle definitely noticed the change in my mood.

"Try not to think about it too much," he said when we were both belted into the car. "You know it's not real. Ezra and Jessica, that is."

Connecting my phone to the radio, I put on "Collide" by Dishwalla. I sighed with relief as the song played, leaning my head back against the headrest and closing my eyes. "I thought I knew that until Jessica told me something today before Species Cultures," I whispered, my eyes growing hot with unshed tears. "She told me that her and Ezra had sex the other night. Now I feel . . . shattered."

Kyle's hand found my thigh, giving it a tender squeeze. "You know you can't believe a single word she says. She's probably just trying to give you this exact reaction, Cady," he reassured me, being the voice of reason I didn't know I needed.

I stayed silent, getting lost in the song. After a long pause, he exhaled sharply and glanced at me. "Cadence. There is no way in this galaxy or the next that Ezra had sex with Jessica. He's totally and completely in love with you." His tone held a twinge of sadness. "She probably just wants you to give up on him so you're not competition anymore."

Grumbling, I put my hand on top of his where it rested on my thigh. "You don't have to be in love with someone to have sex with them," I countered, tucking my hair behind my ear and out of my face.

Another heavy sigh. "No, you don't. A lot of people don't, and that's okay. But Ezra? There's no way that guy is having sex with just anyone, Cadence. He's always mysteriously quiet when locker room talk happens."

I raised a brow at him. "And you? Do you participate in locker room talk?"

"Nah. Why would I want to talk to a bunch of coeds about what they're doing and I'm not?"

Both of my brows went up this time, and I was unsure how to respond to that. Fortunately, I didn't have to come up with anything when he parked along the street in front of Sew What. I led the way into the small shop, the front window decorated by William with bright paints that he insisted made the place look at least partway decent. I was inclined to agree with him.

The bell above the door jingled merrily to announce our entrance and Molly appeared from the back with a pleasant grin, her chestnut hair frothing around her shoulders. "Oh, Cadence! Thank you for coming. My old fingers need a break from sewing for a night. Also," she came closer, whispering conspiratorially, "Alice is working at the clinic tonight and I volunteered to take my sweet grandbaby for the night." She chuckled, glancing up at Kyle who stood just behind me. "Oh my, who is this strapping young lad?" she asked, appraising him with her eyes.

"Kyle Wilkins, ma'am." He bowed his head to her.

"Oh, pish posh. My mother was a ma'am. Please, call me Molly," she chastised, tucking him into a tight hug. He glanced over her shoulder at me with wide eyes and I giggled, covering my mouth with my hand as I leaned back against the counter.

When Molly pulled away, she glanced between the two of us before smiling wide. "So, what's the story here, Cady. You've never brought a boy here before. I'd have noticed one so handsome."

I ignored Kyle's surprised expression. "We started dating a couple months ago. I wanted to make sure he wasn't going to go anywhere before I introduced him to such an attractive woman, Molly," I teased.

Molly threw her head back and laughed gleefully. Kyle flushed and looked both pleased and embarrassed.

"There's no way I'm stealing anyone from a beauty like you, Cady. Now then, I'm going to go home and spoil my grandbaby. I left a list of tasks in the back for you to handle. Just get done what you can. Anything left, I'll take care of tomorrow." She grabbed her bag and her keys from the counter before walking out the door with the sound of the bell.

Kyle watched her go before turning on me with a wicked grin. "Boyfriend, huh? She did have one thing right; you are quite a beauty."

Rolling my eyes, I grumbled, "Ha. Ha. Very funny."

I went behind the counter and disappeared into the back where bags of clothes and blankets hung everywhere among supplies that cluttered the working surfaces. Amid all the calamity on her main table was a sheet of notebook paper with a long list of tasks on it, just like Molly had said.

Appearing beside me, Kyle looked at me with one of the most serious looks on his face that I'd ever seen. "I wasn't joking, Cadence."

Glancing up at him, I frowned and gathered the things I needed to sew some patches on a pair of pants. "I'm not sure what about me screams beauty," I muttered, plopping onto a stool at the table and beginning to sew.

Kyle scoffed, crossing his arms while leaning against the table and settling his gaze upon me like a weight. "I'm not sure what you could possibly think is ugly about yourself," he challenged, causing me to put the pants down so I could give him my full attention.

"The list is endless, Kyle. I'll start with my weird eyes. My nose is too thin, my lips are too full, my eyes are too wide and doe-like, and their color is off-putting. And don't get me started on all of this," I rebutted, grabbing my ample stomach rolls and shaking them.

Kyle continued to examine me before leaning down so he was only a foot from my face. If he were any closer, I'd have been staring at him cross-eyed. "First off, I think your eyes are the most stunning pair I've ever seen. Your nose is excellent for booping and kissing, which I've tried numerous times now and it's better every time. Your lips look like they're perfect for kissing, something I've been thinking about every day since we talked in the waiting room of the clinic. And your body?" He let out a low whistle, his eyes trailing over my entire figure as heat crept into my cheeks. I was fully clothed in a sweater and jeans, but he made me feel naked as his gaze raked over me. "Your body is utterly divine. Curvaceous and full and lovely," he complimented, his smile slowly growing as he straightened again, though his eyes never left mine again as he went on.

"Your body is what they modeled Aphrodite and Venus after. They were the goddesses of love and romance and sex, and they looked just like you. Full of love and plump with life. Your body has caused revolutions and ended wars. It was once the sign of wealth and power. Do not let children with small minds try to convince you that your body is not of the utmost perfection, Cadence Nocetti."

My mouth popped open at some point during his monologue and my face grew hot with an unattractive blush. "Are you making fun of me right now?" I resorted to my usual compliment reaction; disbelief. I wasn't sure I could accept that someone might actually feel this way for someone like me.

His forehead creased as he crouched in front of me, looking up at my face with concern and devotion. His hands skimmed up my calves, the heat soaking through my jeans on their way and leaving heated trails until they cupped behind my knees. "Why would I be making fun of you? I meant everything I said. I could probably come up with more if you really want me to."

Uncomfortable with such attention, I released an embarrassed giggle and Kyle's eyes widened in response. "Please don't. I don't know what to think right now," I whispered, watching as his hands shifted around to grip my thighs. Inhaling sharply, I stayed caught in his reverent gaze. He found my hands, lifting them to kiss each of my knuckles.

"Then don't think anything. Just accept that I'm telling you the absolute truth and nothing short of it," he murmured, his lips brushing against my knuckles.

I practically fell off the stool when the bell rang at the front of the shop. Clearing my throat, I allowed Kyle to help me up as he stood before practically running from the room to greet the customer. Surprised, I called out too loudly, "Oh! Hey, William. What are you doing here?"

William looked startled, then sheepish, running his fingers through his chestnut waves to push them out of his face and tuck his long locks behind his ear. "Mom sent me. She forgot a bag of fabric?"

274

I looked around the shop at the many, many bags of fabric before glancing back at him out of the corner of my eye. "Which bag?" A pause. "I thought she was taking the night off."

His cheeks flushed deeply; his green eyes flitted behind me as Kyle approached. "She said she had a project she needed to get done and forgot to bring the fabric home," William mumbled with a shrug, his voice cracking. "She said it is gold and in a canvas bag to keep the silk from getting staticky?" He shrugged again, untucking the hair from behind his ear.

Turning around, I poked among all the bags before finding a canvas one tucked on a shelf under the counter and pulling it out. Inside was a fabric that made me gasp. As the light slid over the folded up golden fabric, it looked like liquid gold spilling over itself and pooling against the sides of the bag. Blinking, I handed over the tote bag and he glanced inside before nodding. "That's the fabric."

"That must be for Lucien . . . I don't think even a Beta could afford whatever she's making with that," I gushed jealously, wishing desperately that I could see whatever creation was going to be born of the liquid gold.

William shrugged yet again; it must be a common move for him. "Mom didn't mention who it was for, but the Griffins are wealthy enough to afford something made of this fabric." He tucked the bag over his shoulder and walked toward the door. "Have a good night!"

The bell chimed after him as he left, and I looked at Kyle. He pushed his dark curls from his forehead and appraised my face before gesturing to the back. "Care to get back to work while I supervise?" A wicked grin slowly crinkled his eyes.

I rolled my own eyes and walked into the back while Kyle pulled his phone out. A flash of seriousness crossed his expression as he looked down at it and I pulled my brows together.

"Everything okay?"

He nodded as he pulled a speaker out of his pocket and placed it on a shelf. It turned on with a little tune that made me smile as I took my place at the table once again. A coy smile broke that serious face into something I was used to. Unfamiliar music filtered through the speaker, and I tilted my head as I examined his face as if it would hold all the answers. It was like he read my mind when he responded with, "'Perfect by Design' by NateWantsToBattle and AmaLee."

I blinked at him. "I didn't realize that we were close enough that you could read my mind." I looked away, taking a moment to pick up where I'd left off with patching the pair of pants.

Kyle shrugged and leaned against the shelving unit beside him, the speaker projecting the music over his head. "Music is your life and something you can't live without. It was an easy enough guess."

Narrowing my eyes at him, I perched on the stool again and prepared to begin sewing. He chuckled and leaned forward to watch what I was doing, though the heat of his gaze made me feel as though my fingers were fumbling. "Do you have to watch me so intently all the time?" I stressed, glancing up at him in mock irritation.

A laugh erupted from him, the sound coming from deep in his stomach and the hearty guffaw was infectious. As he caught his breath, he fixed me with a heavy gaze. "Of course. I'm intrigued by everything you do. From the way your lips move when you talk to the sparkle in your eyes when you're passionate about something." There was a small pause and I looked up to see the thoughtful expression on his face. "I also can't neglect to add how intelligent you are. I can't get enough of talking to you and learning everything about you. I'm like an addict, needing to know every piece of you. I don't think I'll ever get enough."

A furious heat crept up my neck as he spoke, and I resisted the urge to break the potency of the moment. I wanted to laugh, to blow him off, to refute the words that painted a picture of affection; most of all, I wanted to deny that he was telling me the truth. He couldn't possibly mean what he was saying, since I wasn't worth admiring in such a way . . . right?

The song changed and a piano melody filled the space. "Between The Trees? I didn't think anyone else knew about them." "Changed By You" was dancing around us, the simple piano melody and beautiful lyrics caressing my skin. It took a moment before I realized that the fingers brushing against my cheek belonged to Kyle and not the music. My own fingers stopped trying to thread a needle that was giving me problems. I was too distracted by the warmth of his touch to finish the task.

Turning, I looked up at him with wide eyes and his gaze met mine with that intensity I was slowly getting used to. It felt like I was the only person who existed when his hazel gaze examined me with such fervent veneration. The song was a confession, and as I stared up at him my heart hammered heavily in my chest. I was surprised to find that no nerves danced in my belly, the butterflies I'd felt before had shed their concrete shackles and settled among the flowers of love blooming inside my soul. Everything felt right, the pieces of the puzzle clicking together audibly as the sound of my lips parting filled the inch of space between us.

Kyle moved slowly, asking my permission as he paused and continued to drink me in with his eyes while mine dropped to his parted lips. I nodded so slightly, I was amazed that he even saw it as he closed the distance. When his mouth pressed against mine, the action was soft and gentle. His hesitation ended when my hand slid up his arm, tucking against the back of his neck and threading in his thick curls. Our lips parted and the kiss immediately became more heated as he leaned over me and his hands wrapped around my waist to keep me from falling backward.

Something bloomed in my chest, the petals unfurling and glowing with the passion that grew within me. His hands were hot against my flesh as they slid under the back of my sweater and his fingertips grazed up my spine. Tugging on his curls, a noise escaped our kiss that sent a rush of goosebumps over my entire body. He was between my thighs, our bodies pressed together so tightly I thought we might fuse as one being. Kyle's kisses were hungry, a dying man who'd finally found his oasis as he consumed me completely. I hadn't realized how desperate I was for his touch until he gave me everything I didn't know I needed.

A shrill sound paused the song, and he groaned in frustration. Pulling back from me, he dug his phone out of his pocket to glare at it. My fingers immediately reached up to touch my lips like I might memorize the feeling of his mouth if I pressed it into them. I wanted to remember their imprint until the world ended.

"Hey, mom," he grunted, his voice rough with disuse and I wondered how long we had actually been kissing. Silence encapsulated us while he listened to his mom speaking before responding with, "Yeah. I'm okay. I didn't realize what time it was." I checked my phone only to realize with shock that it was past midnight. More silence before he nodded. "Yeah. I'm with Cadence. I'm going to take her home first, of course. Love you, too. Bye."

With the mood broken, I cleared my throat and tucked my phone into my pocket. "I'll be ready to go in a moment. I'm sorry, I didn't realize how late it was." I stood as I put the project's bag back where I'd gotten it.

"Cadence." Kyle placed a hand on my arm to stop me. "I don't expect anything from you, not even another kiss. I know this is a difficult situation for you to be in, and I don't want you to rush or feel forced into any decisions."

I nodded, cleaning up the last of the fabric. "I just—need to think about things," I whispered, anxiety causing me to wring my hands, my gaze refusing to meet his.

He reached out, gently brushing the hair from my face and tucking it behind my ear. "Don't worry about giving me any answers. I am not asking any questions. Your presence in my life is all that I want." I knew without a doubt that he meant those words as my gaze met his. An adoring smile danced on his mouth before he placed his hand on my low back and guided me outside.

The ride home was quiet as we both mulled over our own thoughts, though it wasn't awkward. When I got home, he made no move to kiss me again and I was torn between being grateful that he wasn't pressuring me and disappointed that I couldn't feel him again.

CHAPTER 24

CADENCE

Finding out by the end of March that Kyle, Alex, *and* Ezra all got their acceptance letters did not help my mood in the slightest. I still had radio silence from PSG, and it was slowly eating me alive from the inside out. Maybe it was immature, but I was starting to resent the academy for not just ending the suspense already.

My only anchors were about to disappear to the Catskill Mountains and leave me behind. I tried not to feel so stupidly childish and whiny about it.

"Earth to Cady." Alex's voice broke through my thoughts and brought me back to the present. I blinked stupidly at her for a moment as she rolled her hazel eyes in mild annoyance. "Did you hear anything I just said?"

"No, I was–"

My words were interrupted as Brody stood up from a table across the room. He had his phone held up, displaying the screen to the cafeteria. "I got in!

Potencia Sui Generis, here I come!" he shouted, applause coming from around the room as he happily pumped his fist into the air.

I stared at him, feeling like I could vomit. Everyone around me was getting into PSG, and I was sitting around waiting for my rejection. I was a hopeless blend of anger and depression, slumping my head onto my hand to hold the weight of my stressed-out brain. I felt so betrayed by a school that owed me nothing that I couldn't even hold my own head up. Brody's eyes met mine from across the cafeteria. As he took in my stricken expression, his smile faltered. I didn't want Brody's pity, but I could see it clear as day on his face. My life was officially over.

Standing up abruptly, I only wanted to escape. Instead of making a grand exit like I planned, I ran directly into someone who was carrying a tray behind me. Fortunately, neither of us ended up covered in food, but his lunch was still dumped unceremoniously onto the floor at our feet.

"Oh! I'm so sorry!" I bent down to help him pick up the mess I'd made. Apparently, he had the same thought and our foreheads smacked together, knocking us both on our butts, rubbing mirrored spots on our heads. "Again, I'm sorry," I muttered, feeling hot with embarrassment. I was certain my face was flaming.

"No need." His green eyes were sparkling with amusement before I finally registered who I was looking at.

"William! Oh, Goddess, I'm so sorry. I'll pay for a new lunch," I sputtered again, horrified that I dumped a poor kid's lunch on the floor because I was running away from my problems like a child. I wondered if Jessica would have snide comments to say about this and my eyes automatically lifted and found hers watching me. An evil smile danced on her lips as she took in my humiliation with smug pleasure, though Ezra looked annoyed beside her.

"Again, no need to apologize." A pleasant grin carved his lips as my attention was drawn back to him. "It was an accident. No need for so much concern."

I nodded as he stood up, extending his hand to reach for mine. I hesitated for a moment as Kyle stood up beside me. Kyle reached his hand out to me as well, appearing agitated. However, William's face looked nothing but cheerful as he gazed down at me with his arm still extended.

After a moment's consideration, my hand slid into Kyle's, and he helped me up off the floor. If I hadn't still been looking at William, I'd have missed the flash of rage that darkened his gaze before it vanished into casual amusement again. Blinking, I figured I'd imagined it and disregarded it immediately. Why would this situation have made him angry?

Feeling eyes on me, I glanced at Brody who was also glaring unhappily between the underclassman and me. Ezra was also staring daggers. I could sense the wariness flowing off Kyle like a physical breeze. However, I hadn't expected to meet Jason's unimpressed glare, his arms folded over his chest as he stared murderously at the whole situation. Unable to deal with all the heavy emotions, I decided to just jump ship and fled into the hall while everyone stayed back. Lunch was almost over, and I needed to get to my locker for my books before my next class anyway.

That evening, I was at home with Alex. Ezra was training The Crest with Kyle, so the two of us got a rare opportunity for girl time. I lounged on my bed, my gaze fixed firmly on the ceiling above me. There were too many feelings going on inside of me that I didn't know how to name or deal with, so I pretended they didn't exist instead. I was the queen of healthy coping mechanisms.

Alex, on the other hand, wasn't fooled in the slightest. Her hazel eyes stared at me from my computer chair, drilling into the side of my head as she steepled her fingers in front of her mouth, elbows resting on her knees. I tactlessly ignored her, drumming the rhythm of "Bedroom Ceiling" by Citizen Soldier against my thigh as it played in my head while we sat in an uncomfortable silence that seemed to stretch on endlessly. Finally, Alex broke the bubble of tension.

"Why are you being so quiet right now?" she demanded, startling me with the sudden presence of a voice other than the song in my head. It had been externally quiet for so long that my psyche was adjusted to it and the sudden burst of sound ruptured my inner concert.

"What are you talking about?" I sat up to look at her. To release some of my nervous energy, I tucked my hair behind my ears and tugged at the ends, averting my eyes from her piercing gaze.

"Don't try to bullshit me, Cadence. Your silence is telling me everything that you're refusing to say out loud." I squirmed as her unrelenting glare made me feel like she was seeing directly into my brain and digging out everything I had carefully hidden inside of it.

"I'm not trying to kid you. I just feel like you, Kyle, and Ezra are going to take off and leave me here. You all got into PSG, and I haven't even heard anything back yet. I know my rejection is coming. Now that Brody got in, I just know that another spot is taken," I snarled, spilling my inner truths almost like they were pulled from my lips. "I don't think I can handle the four of you going off to school together while I'm stuck here like a worthless troll. I think if Jessica gets in, I might snap."

"Jessica didn't get in. I overheard her whining and crying about it to Ezra earlier today about how she got waitlisted. That's pretty much a rejection. Is there anything else?" she asked, pressing her steepled fingers against her chin as she surveyed me.

I didn't want to tell her anything. The last thing I wanted was to let her know about the moment Kyle and I had shared. However, as much as I tried to stop the words from escaping, I couldn't contain them while she was looking at me like that. "Kyle and I kissed a couple weeks ago. He said he doesn't want me to make decisions while I'm in the midst of emotional stress. The amaryllis keep showing up, and I think he's still getting threatening texts even though he's telling me everything is fine."

Alex's eyes widened and it was like a spell had been lifted from me. I took a deep breath and immediately pulled my gaze from hers like I'd been attempting while I spilled my guts. Standing up, I paced my bedroom like that would help me find solutions.

"Did you talk to Ezra like I'd suggested?"

"Of course I didn't. I'm afraid of losing him, of making a final decision. I don't want to lose either one of them. My growing feelings for Kyle aren't diminishing anything I feel for Ezra, and this is such a terrible situation."

Alex sighed and rubbed her temples like she was attempting to ward off an oncoming headache. "Did you tell Ezra or Kyle about the continuing harassment?"

I scowled at her, waving my hand in the air as if I could wave away the stress and trauma of the entire thing. "There's nothing they can do about it. I don't need to add more pressure to Ezra's shoulders. He's got enough going on."

"And Kyle?

"He doesn't need to deal with this either."

"It's not nothing, Cadence. Someone broke into your house *again* and left an amaryllis and a threatening note. You need to tell Ezra about this. He can help you." Her words were urgent. "You have to tell him about *that*. And if you don't, I will."

I stopped mid-step and stared at her like she'd suddenly grown an extra head. "Don't you threaten me like that!" I shouted, pointing a finger at her. "You can't just interfere–"

My words were interrupted by a short little tune played by my open laptop behind Alex. We both stopped and turned to look at it. I didn't even have to see the notification to know that it came from the Academy. It was like my senses knew that news of my future had just dropped into my inbox. My heart soared and my stomach felt like a boulder had just been dropped into it.

"I can't look at it," I gasped immediately, my heart hammering against my ribs.

"You have to look at it. I won't do it for you." Alex got out of my computer chair and stood behind it. When I didn't move, she gestured impatiently at my computer and exhaled sharply in a noise of frustration. When I still made no motion to open the email, she grabbed my shoulders before pushing me into my computer chair. "Open the email."

"I can't open the email." I ran my fingers through my hair in aggravation. "What if I'm rejected?" The last sentence came out as an anxious whisper, betraying my emotions completely.

"And what if it's an acceptance?" She gestured frantically at the open laptop, the screen of which stood there waiting. My desktop stared at me expectantly, the email icon taunting me.

With a heavy sigh, I aggressively rubbed my face with my palms before shuffling the mouse to wake it up and clicking on the icon. Within a moment I was facing my inbox. The name of the academy was there, but the only thing I could see in the minute preview was 'Dear Cadence Nocetti.' It wasn't much to go on, and the stress of finding out the answer to the question I'd been agonizing over was worse than the anticipation of the past several weeks.

Biting down on my lip, I glanced back at Alex, who was standing behind me like a reliable sentinel. She was preparing for whichever way this email was going to go, but I'd be lying if I said she didn't look hopeful.

Shifting my cursor again, I put it over the email and closed my eyes as I clicked on it. I heard Alex gasp behind me, but I couldn't look. She was waiting on me to give my full reaction.

Jerk.

Finally, I opened my eyes and read the email.

'Dear Cadence Nocetti,

It is with great honor that we write to inform you that you have been accepted into Potencia Sui Generis...'

I stared at the screen as time slowed down around me. Alex was tense behind me, holding back her celebration until the words had fully sunken into my brain. It took a momentous amount of time before I finally whispered, "I got in..."

"You got in," Alex chorused behind me, her hand falling onto my shoulder with a squeeze.

I stood up and looked at her eyes which shimmered with tears, the shock on my face slowly morphed into a smile. "I got in!" I screamed, throwing my fists into the air in celebration. "We are going to PSG together!"

Arms were thrown around me and we fell onto my bed in a jumbled heap as we shouted our celebrations.

CHAPTER 25

CADENCE

The next day I felt untouchable. The greatest thing had happened to me, and nothing could ruin it. Kyle walked beside me to my locker, my arm wrapped around his as I subconsciously stroked his bicep. Jason's green eyes tracked us like a predator us as we passed him. I didn't want any attention from him and the look he gave me made my skin feel uncomfortably itchy.

Shaking it off, we arrived at my locker, continuing a banal conversation as I spun the dial. It took a couple tries before I got it right because I was too busy discussing travel plans to get to the academy. It felt like things were finally looking up. I hoped things with Ezra would return to some semblance of normal as we would be hours away, out of the pack and far from the clutches of his overbearing and disapproving father. Though I didn't know what that would mean for myself and Kyle. It felt selfish to want to keep them both.

Opening my locker, I gasped as a dozen red amaryllis fell from the small space. Moving back, they all landed on the floor at my feet, the crimson color reminding me of fresh blood instead of the beauty of love and passion. My jaw dropped as I stared down at them all, but my stomach plummeted to the floor to join the pile as I looked at the note dangling from the shelf in my locker.

Kyle should watch his back. I'm coming for you.

My hand pressed against my mouth as I stared in horror at the note. Silence descended upon us as we stared at the puddle of flowers in the hallway.

I stared down the hall, my eyes meeting with Jason's as he watched the scene play out, his face tinged with mild amusement. Was this from him? His face gave nothing away as he shut his locker and turned to walk in the opposite direction.

My phone vibrated my back pocket, and I pulled it out to find a text from the unknown number. A frown crease my forehead as I saw a video attachment. Grabbing my earbuds, I put one in and hesitated as Kyle held out his hand for the other one.

"I'm in this too," he muttered. I couldn't deny that and handed him the other one before opening the text.

The video started playing, it showed Alex and myself in my bedroom, our clothes matching what we were wearing the day before and my heart squeezed inside my chest. Hearing the scene played back to me, I felt panic crawling inside my ribs as I heard myself confess, *"Kyle and I kissed a couple weeks ago."* The clip played on a loop for several moments as Kyle and I looked up at each other, my horrified face meeting his grim expression. My phone vibrated again, and we both dropped our gazes to the screen where a couple messages had come through.

Unknown

> How dare you do this to me? I am the only person you should be kissing.

Don't worry, Cadence, this will be taken care of. I still love you and will forgive you in time.

Congratulations on getting into PSG.

Turning around at the feeling of being watched, I saw Ezra observing the scene play out with concern. Jessica had been laughing, but noting his attention was not on her, she glared at me with such ferocity that I almost gasped. I might have, had my senses not already been deadened with the drenching of horror. Kyle moving beside me pulled my gaze from them. He reached into my locker and yanked the note down and shoved it in his pocket just as Mr. Rutger appeared beside us.

"Everything okay over here?"

"Yup. Everything's great. My boyfriend surprised me by stuffing a bunch of flowers in my locker. He's such a romantic," I gushed, smiling a bit too wide as Kyle's arm wrapped around my waist and pulled me close to him.

Mr. Rutger's brown eyes shifted between the two of us before he nodded briefly. "Very well. Make sure you clean those up before getting to class. You don't want to be late." He walked away briskly, disappearing around the corner.

Alex chose that moment to show up, eyeing the puddle of petals warily before looking up at me. The magnitude of her scrutiny made my fingers and toes feel numb and I knew what was coming. "Did you tell Kyle and Ezra about the others?"

"The others?" Ezra asked beside me, and I jumped at his sudden appearance. His expression was carefully neutral.

Kyle and I pulled the earbuds from our ears so I could place them back into their case.

I heaved a sigh as if breathing took a momentous amount of effort. "I've continued getting amaryllis, even since the ones you saw."

"And the one in your kitchen. You know, the one that managed to get there despite the doors and windows being locked." Alex gave me a stormy glare before turning to the men. "It was there after we left her house the day after my birthday."

I glanced between the three of them, feeling hot and uncomfortable and wishing I was anywhere but there.

"It was no–" I started, but Ezra cut me off.

"Why didn't you tell me it kept happening? I'd have come back and stayed with you." Ezra's voice was eerily calm and composed, making me innately aware that he was anything but.

Kyle's arm wrapped tighter around my waist as he looked at me, like he was afraid I was going to be stolen from him if he let me go.

Alex sighed and crossed her arms in front of her chest, her red lips pursing. "I wasn't told either. I had to practically pry it from her."

"Because it was nothing. And you couldn't come stay with me, it would ruin everything we are doing here." I pulled out of Kyle's grasp and stepped away from all of them. "It's just amaryllis. It's not like I'm being gifted dead animals or anything."

"Amaryllis with notes claiming you and threatening Kyle are not nothing!" Ezra shouted, causing the few remaining students around us to stop what they were doing and gawk.

I gave Ezra a look that allayed my anger before responding. "It's probably just a joke. I can't imagine that anyone is serious about all of this. I'm not impressive enough for anyone to go to all this effort."

I was concerned for a moment that both Alex and Ezra might spontaneously combust while Kyle's arm wound supportively around my waist. He understood why I didn't want to drag them into it. We'd discussed it in depth. We were in the trenches of this war together.

Alex and Ezra were getting red in the face and Ezra was visibly trembling with rage. I wasn't sure if he was mad that I was attempting to blow the whole thing off or my self-deprecating commentary.

"I can't with you," he stated, his volume lowering considerably. "Your ability to completely discredit yourself is infuriating on its own. Trying to sweep this under the rug like some kind of harmless crush is another level of maddening, Cadence. We need to do something about this."

"Like what? If we tell the principal or The Guard, they'll just blow it off and tell us it's a harmless issue. You've listened to those human podcasts with me before, right? The ones where people are being stalked and the cops literally don't do anything because they haven't *actually* done anything? The appearance of harmless flowers and text messages and notes does not a case make, no matter how threatening it sounds." I went to put my hands on my hips, my palms landing against the back of Kyle's hands as they sat on my waist. "And all three of you know that The Guard is not going to do anything about it. Even if this is serious and this person *does* do something, it's against me. They will do nothing to protect me more than they have to. Lucien has made sure of that." I looked between the three of them. None of them said a word in rebuttal as the late bell rang.

"Great. Now I'm mad, worried, *and* late," Ezra snapped, bending down to pick up the pile of amaryllis.

As he scooped them up into his hands, he cursed and dropped them again. I saw a bead of blood growing on one of his fingers. Putting it in his mouth, he glared at me for a moment before Alex sighed and removed her jacket. She wrapped up the bundle of amaryllis and looked at the stems to find them filled with pins. "Yup, this is just a casual crush for sure," she tossed at me, her tone thick with sarcasm as she dumped them in the nearby garbage can. Giving me one last withering look, she stalked toward our homeroom. I didn't say anything to Ezra or Kyle as I followed behind her like a kicked puppy.

So much for being untouchable.

293

ALEX

That afternoon, I found myself feeling restless. It was hard to pay attention as my brain processed everything that had been happening to Cadence, as well as her blooming relationship with Kyle. I wanted her to be happy, but it was such a sticky situation. Ezra and I were also anxiously waiting for the next incident to happen. We all knew it was a matter of time. Stalkers very rarely just decided that they were done being obsessive. While I understood why someone would be enthralled with Cady, I did not appreciate their way of expressing themselves. They hadn't even made themselves known. They were hiding in anonymity like a coward, and that didn't sit well with me.

Fortunately for her, she had me as a friend. I would cut a bitch for that girl, and I did not mean that figuratively. I'd kill someone for her and not think twice about it; slice a throat and wash my hands to eat dinner like nothing happened. It was something not many people knew about me: my bloodthirsty nature. You didn't grow up the child of the Alpha's number one warrior and not have a hunger for using a blade. I hid it under the guise of being a spunky girl with a taste for dramatic lipstick, but it was mostly a ruse, a way to get into the hearts of my targets so I could slice them apart from the inside like Hercules and the Hydra. The difference between Herc and I was that I was more ruthless.

I'd spent my life preparing to be the next Alpha's warrior, his numero uno Beta. I would gladly take my place among the ranks of Ezra's soldiers when he took the throne as the Alpha of our pack and the next King of the Volsifi. As if my bloodline wasn't enough of a reason to choose me, when my gift was outed, I'd be the obvious choice.

As for today, I was on a mission. Cadence was my sunlight, the humanity that was already keeping my inner wraiths on a tight leash. I knew that her companionship would be crucial if a war broke out. While I was confident in her ability to ground me, I was not confident in my ability to keep from turning into a monster on the battlefield; I'd needed to be pulled off of bloody and unconscious men more times than I cared to recollect. Even Brody and Kyle had fallen victims to the abuse of my fists. When I got my hands on my shurikens, the blades that fit between my fingers to give this kitty literal claws, I was unstoppable.

Since Cady was my sun, the gravity that brought my inner beast to heel, I was determined to keep her from being eclipsed. If she was hurting, the monster inside me rose up to lick her wounds and then slaughter the clouds that dared breath their shadows upon her brilliance. She was paramount to my sanity and had been since I met her when we were four. It was so easy to remember that day.

My father was already fine-tuning me into a killing machine at that age, giving me my first weapon when I turned three. He'd started with a sword, but it didn't fit me or my style. When I turned four, he took me to Axe Marks the Spot where Henry Nocetti held leagues for children to teach them how to use and throw hatchets. Since logging is our main business this far north, it wasn't unusual to start teaching children the ropes so they could replace the older workers when they came of age. This was particularly common in the Delta and Omega ranks.

I walked into the building, my eyes immediately settling on the twins that I'd heard my parents whispering about when they thought I was asleep. I'd never cared to pay too much attention, but looking at them was humbling. They were opposites, Cadence the darkness to Callum's light. Even the heterochromia in their irises were opposite, the blue of Cadence's breaking up the blackness and the black in Callum's looking as if his pupil bled into the blue.

I approached them and Cadence immediately smiled at me in greeting while Callum stood apart. He watched me warily, like he was worried that I would harm his sister. Cadence was absolute brilliance, her wide smile shining on me like a beacon in the darkness I hadn't realized I was cloaked in. I didn't understand why my parents were so wary of the twins, but I knew then that I could never be uncertain of her.

I stalked the halls, putting a sway in my hips as I stormed through the people swirling around me. My heels clicked loudly despite the chatter and slamming of lockers clogging up the hall. My teeth sunk into my lower lip as I got a couple appraising looks from those who noticed me. They'd all heard the rumors. I wasn't picky when it came to chasing affection. Having a warrior for a father did not allow for much in the way of hugs and love. I knew this about myself and didn't mind admitting it as a fault of mine, if you could even call it that. I also really enjoyed intimacy and exploring people's bodies. I had trouble believing that it was such a bad thing.

My eyes settled on my target at the end of the hall as Jason stood talking to a couple of his fellow assholes. Brody was noticeably absent. I walked right up to Jason, fisting the front of his shirt in my grip before pulling him from the throng and down to an abandoned hallway. He didn't fight me, unfortunately, as I dragged him into a dark area and pushed him against the wall. I wished he had; it might have made this confrontation even more interesting.

"What the hell do you want?" His emerald eyes leveled me with a glare as his arms crossed over his chest.

"I want to know what you're doing to Cadence." I got straight to the point. Having a long and in-depth discussion wasn't really my goal in this scenario.

Fury crossed his features for just a moment before he neutralized his expression again, a wall coming up behind his eyes to block me out. "What are you talking about?"

"I'm sure you are aware of someone sneaking into her house and leaving amaryllis everywhere with threatening notes. I saw you lurking around The Crest the other day, listening to our conversation. And those creepy ass texts? What is the plan?" I snarled at him, stepping closer and invading his personal space. He was several inches taller than me, but that didn't stop his Adam's apple from bobbing as he swallowed hard at the clear threat.

Jason held his palms up toward me. "I have no interest in the pathetic life of your precious Cadence," he denied, the words rushed and forced.

He was lying. I knew it as surely as I knew he was breathing.

"What are you planning next?"

He shook his head, though his green eyes glittered with rage. I wasn't sure what he was so angry about, but it made me feel deeply unsettled. "*I* am not planning anything," he rebutted, his words ringing true in my soul.

Confusion and alarm rattled me, but I kept my face appropriately ferocious. I curled my upper lip at him and bared my teeth.

Now it was time to use the other portion of my gift. I stared into his eyes, focusing intently on the green of his irises and the way I could see his pupils shifting as he assessed me. He was trying to figure out what was going on in my brain, that much was clear. I needed to know *who* was planning something. Just when I'd had a grasp on him and the wall started to break apart in his mind, a throat cleared, jarring me out of my focus.

Both of us turned to face Mr. Bowman as he came down the hall toward us. His silver eyes shifted between us as he asked, "Is there a problem here?" His posture told me that he was not going to tolerate any shit from the two of us.

The monster inside me snapped and snarled in my head. She made it difficult to answer with a lie and I forced a flirty smile on my mouth. Her rage did not want to be flirty, she wanted to rip his throat out for intruding. I managed it though; practice made perfect a long time ago. "There's no problem, sir," I lied as easily as breathing. It was an additional perk of my gift. I'd always been a smooth liar, but now I was a pro. I could tell falsehoods like they were reality, spinning others into a web of lies so deep they could never escape while I sucked the truth from them like a black widow.

I knew Jason would lie as well. Snitches get stitches after all, and he knew he didn't want stitches from me. He was a formidable opponent with a sword, but my small size gave me many advantages that his brute strength struggled competing with. Jason had always been envious of Brody and tried to emulate his fighting style, but Jason had never had the strength or size to appropriately pull it off. Ezra and Kyle knew of my prowess in combat, while Cadence was blissfully ignorant of what happened in the upper castes of the pack.

Ezra and I had decided long ago to keep her in the dark as long as possible. We were her silent sentinels, keeping her safe since we were young.

"No, there's not a problem," Jason answered right after me, an easy smile appearing on his face as he put his arm around my shoulders. I had to resist the urge to jam my elbow into his ribs and shrug his limb off of me.

Mr. Bowman looked between the two of us, suspicion apparent on his face. "Very well."

He nodded before walking away. It was apparent that we were to follow him out of there and disperse. Getting to the end of the hall, he disappeared into the crowd like a damn ghost, leaving Jason and I to split apart as if a bomb had been thrown between us. I tossed him a distrusting glare, narrowing my eyes as he did the same. Neither of us were done with this conversation, but he'd had a glimpse of what I could do, and he'd assuredly be avoiding me. Mr. Bowman threw a grenade into my plan, and I was not happy about it. Prick.

CHAPTER 26

CADENCE

It was the end of the day, and I couldn't stop fidgeting. The interaction with Ezra earlier reminded me that we really needed to have a heavy conversation. I'd put it off long enough, and I couldn't talk to Kyle until I'd talked to Ezra. Frowning, I pulled out my phone, texting Kyle that I was going to get a ride home with Ezra. Then I texted Ezra.

> Can you give me a ride home tonight? We need to talk.

It was rude of me to leave things so open ended for the next couple hours, but it was necessary. This was not a conversation to have over text. His confirmation came through while Kyle told me that he'd see me later for our scheduled date at Axe Marks the Spot.

At the end of the school day, I waited by my locker. "Raindrops" by PhaseOne and Escape The Fate pulsed in my skull, the techno interludes somehow easing my nerves as I picked at the strap of my backpack. Ezra appeared at the end of the hall, walking toward me. I was relieved that he had managed to extract himself from Jessica so I didn't have to see her before this conversation. Automatically, my arm wrapped around his elbow as he held it out to me.

The walk to the car was silent. When we both got into the car, I glanced at him while my gut clenched with anxiety. I could tell by the tension around his mouth that he was putting on the façade of being calm.

Taking another deep breath as he pulled out of the lot, my fingers found the start of a hole in the inner thigh of my jeans and picked at it. "I want to start this conversation by stressing that I'm completely in love with you. I miss you so much that it sometimes hurts to breathe. I hate you being with Jessica. I hate that she gets to spend all this time with you."

His jaw clenched.

"Spending all this time with Kyle, it's impossible not to notice that he's a genuinely wonderful person. You know that and have acknowledged it before, but I know that doesn't make this any easier. I enjoy being around him as much as I love being with you. I'd be lying if I said I wasn't developing feelings for him as well and it's just so complicated because it hasn't dimmed any of the love I have for you and it's like you're equal in my eyes," I rushed, the words coming out in a whoosh that was just as jumbled as I had expected them to be.

He remained quiet for several of my quick breaths, ramping up the anxiety in my gut as he mulled over my words. After a moment, I whispered, "I'm done."

Ezra nodded and inhaled slowly through his nose before exhaling through his mouth. "I know Kyle is a genuinely great guy. I also accepted in the beginning that it was a very real possibility that you would fall for him."

He paused, pondering what he was going to say as his knuckles turned white as he gripped the steering wheel. The plastic groaned under his clenching fists. "Ultimately, I just want you to be happy. I hate being away from you. I hate Jessica and spending any time with her at all. She's vapid, self-absorbed, and mean to you. All she cares about is status, and I hate being used for my status.

I'm trying to be okay with you and Kyle, but I'd be lying if I said it didn't sting like a bitch." The last word was ground out between clenched teeth.

I frowned at his profile, feeling my gut twist and my breath catch as I remembered what she'd told me in the stairwell all those weeks ago. The silence hung between us for several long moments before I broke it. "But you still had sex with her?" My voice was hushed with the embarrassment of mentioning it.

Ezra looked surprised and horrified. He glanced at me for the first time since he'd started driving. "Who told you that?"

My eyes widened at his lack of denial, my heart feeling like it was swelling inside my chest that was much too small. My lungs were squeezed as it continued to expand, making me unable to breathe as it grew until it shattered and rained fiery pieces into my already nauseated gut. "She did," I whispered, pressing my hand to my aching chest.

Ezra slammed his palm against the steering wheel so hard the horn honked, startling me so much that tears stung my eyes and panic made my heart race. "Damn her!" he shouted, turning toward me as he pulled up to a stop sign. I met his gaze, his eyes glowing with power and barely concealed rage. Whether it was at her for saying it or me for believing it, I wasn't sure. Either way, he didn't deny any of it. That hurt the most.

I didn't stop to listen to him, unfastening my seatbelt and lurching out of the car before it had even come to a complete stop. "Don't, Ezra!" I cried out, holding out my palm as if it could shield me from his words, from any further pain. "She was telling the truth the last time–" I gasped as pain seared through my throat. "Just . . . go be with her."

Turning away from him, I found myself in the copse of trees that separated the poor areas from the wealthy ones. I heard his car door open behind me as I oriented myself before taking off into the trees.

"Cadence!" His voice echoed through the trees, his footsteps thundering after me as I shifted through the underbrush and followed paths that I'd learned a long time ago. Unfortunately for Ezra, he very rarely went with me through the dense forest and was not as familiar with the layout as I was.

Losing him quickly, I looped around as much as possible, skirting around anything that would make excess noise. He'd never be able to hear the sounds of my steps over the pounding of his own, and I took advantage of that as I made complicated loops and spirals to drag my scent in a chaotic labyrinth through the forest. I heard a curse behind me as his footsteps stopped and so did mine. I tried very hard not to pant with the exertion of outrunning and outmaneuvering him as he stopped to listen for me. After a long minute, I heard him say from a distance, "This conversation isn't over, Cadence. I will see you later to talk further."

When he turned and walked away, I listened until his footsteps faded into the distance. After I felt safe to continue, I took off toward Axe Marks the Spot. My knees were weak, threatening to give out with every step until I tripped over a log as my vision blurred with unshed tears. Curling up on the ground, I sobbed openly as the sun winked at me through the naked branches above. With shaking fingers, I put my earbuds in and put on the song that happened to be already in the queue. "Dial Tones" by AS IT IS blared into my ears, soothing my soul as I let the waves of emotion roll over me in heavy waves that left me feeling battered and broken.

I couldn't stop thinking about Ezra's anger and I was furious at Jessica for telling me. The obvious reason that he was angry was because she had told me. I couldn't imagine he was ever going to; it had already been a couple weeks. Probably to spare my feelings. So much for that, I'd held onto that nugget of information because I was afraid of the exact confirming reaction that I ended up getting.

The sun was fading when I finally pulled myself off the ground. At this point, I wanted nothing more than to see Kyle and find comfort in his presence and the smell of rain that hung on his skin. Pulling out my phone, I texted him that I was on my way to our rendezvous point. I hurried through the woods as my fingers rubbed against the callouses on my palms. I was itching to get my hands on my hatchet so I could take my frustrations out on the target.

After several long minutes of stumbling numbly through the underbrush, I found myself escaping the shadows of the trees and trudging toward the only sacred place I'd ever truly had. When I walked in, Ava looked up at me then quickly dropped her shocked gaze back to the paper she had been looking at. It didn't occur to me that I probably looked like a drunk forest nymph. I went to my locker and grabbed the hatchet that called out to me. Pulling it from the case, my gaze immediately dropped to the carved amaryllis on the handle and stifled the wobble of my chin by sucking my lips between my teeth and biting down so hard they throbbed.

I pressed my thumb against the blade until a sharp pain echoed from the flesh and a small bead of crimson welled against the black metal. Smiling in satisfaction, I jammed my backpack into the locker and turned toward the target. Ava was walking away from lane five, the wood soaked and ready for my punishment. Honestly, I wasn't even sure who I was angrier at. Jessica for telling me and ruining the ignorant bliss I'd been living in or Ezra for betraying me so completely and not even having the nerve to tell me first.

I didn't even aim at the target. I just heaved the hatchet as hard as I could with a snarl. The blade of the hatchet embedded in the kill shot in what felt like a show of cosmic justice. It took a full body effort to wrestle the weapon from the wood it had chosen to meld with. After quite a few similar throws, I felt eyes on me and stiffened. Pulling out one of the earbuds, the music paused, her voice announcing their presence before my eyes spotted them.

Ezra and Jessica were at the counter. The fury that tore through me at the sight of him bringing my enemy into my safe haven was unlike anything I'd ever felt. When his blue eyes turned to me, I could see the apology in them and refused to accept it. Without saying a word, I turned around and threw the hatchet again, smiling happily as it embedded itself dead center in the bullseye. Stalking forward, I yanked it out and immediately threw it again.

I continued to ignore them, so angry that I didn't even realize right away that Kyle hadn't arrived yet. Pulling my phone from my pocket, I checked to see if he'd texted me and found nothing past the "on the way" text he'd responded with immediately. Frowning, I suddenly regretted not having the guts to ask Kyle to join a circle with me on the app we used to track each other's locations. I wished I could see where he was. Worry gnawed at my insides as I wondered if he'd been in an accident.

Pausing my music, I prepared to call my dad and ask if he'd heard anything when the sound of heels clicked toward me. Looking up, Jessica was standing in front of me and glaring.

"You just had to tell him, didn't you?" She didn't bother hiding the rage that burned in her eyes. "He screamed at me the whole way here and it's all *your* fault!" she wailed, stomping her foot and sounding like a disgruntled horse. Her mood immediately changed to barely suppressed gloating. "I'm glad I asked to come here, though. Seeing your distraught face was worth the headache," she simpered, pouting at me in false sympathy. "I was hoping you were here so I could rub our love in your face." She reached out and booped me on the nose and I gripped my hatchet so hard my knuckles cracked.

I glanced around to find Ezra but didn't see him anywhere.

"He went to the bathroom." Jessica snapped her fingers in front of my face to redirect my attention back to her. "You need to back off of him. I was hoping you'd disappear when I told you we'd had sex, but clearly, you're too delusional to realize you don't have a chance. Lucien had ordered our union, and who am I to deny the Alpha his desires?"

I scowled at her, averting my gaze as she continued to stare me down. I hated that she intimidated me so much when she was just a girl my age with no actual authority or power over me. She successfully made me feel beneath her. Confrontation was not something I was especially good at to begin with.

"You have no authority over his friends, even if you are in Lucien's pocket," I muttered, keeping my gaze away from her.

It was in avoiding her gaze that I realized my arm was bleeding. I frowned at the slice across my forearm, a straight line that was a couple inches long. My head tilted as my forehead creased with confusion. That was strange. I really should have noticed that happening.

"That's Alpha to you, butterball. I know you don't have the decency to hide under a rock, but you could at least show respect for your Alpha." Jessica's grating voice pulled me out of my thoughts, and I looked at her. She rolled her amber eyes, blowing a bubble with her gum and snapping it. "Where is Kyle, anyway?" Her eyes widened as realization struck and she laughed, tucking her tongue in her cheek. "Oh, he stood you up, didn't he? Seems you can't keep your clutches on anyone. I hope you lose Alex next."

Unfortunately, her comment had its desired effect.

I wondered if Kyle actually did stand me up, making me the butt of some mean and long-running joke between him, Jason, and Brody. Jessica was still cackling as she returned to her lane. She picked up an axe, holding it entirely wrong, before chucking it at the target and tossing it directly onto the floor several feet in front of it. I was so absorbed in my downward spiral that I didn't even glean any amusement from it.

Ezra reappeared behind her and leaned against the table placed behind their lane. I pulled out my phone and pressed play, letting the opening of "Ceilings" by Lizzy McAlpine wash over me. It did nothing to soothe my fraying nerves as I threw the hatchet at the target again. My heart wasn't in it, and the blade glanced off the wood before flopping onto the floor in defeat. I could empathize with that.

I heard voices over the music, and I turned around and saw Ava announcing that she was going to lock up and to head out. Ezra and Jessica returned their axes before leaving through the glass doors. Ava gave me a pitying look as she left. I took my time gathering my things, feeling so dejected that I could barely focus on anything. I pulled my jacket from my locker and went to throw it over my arm. The cut on my arm had already healed, leaving a silver scar behind. Thank the Goddess for volsifi super healing.

Ava was already gone, the front lot empty as I exited the building and locked up behind me. The weight of my backpack was nothing compared to the heft of my soul as I trudged around the side of the building in the direction of my home only to stop in my tracks.

At first, I only noticed Kyle's car sitting just outside of the ring of a streetlight. I processed unexpectedly seeing the car, blinking stupidly at it before taking another few steps in its direction. Standing in the halo of light, my brow furrowed at the empty vehicle. Then movement caught my eye as my gaze shifted over the top of the car, an unfamiliar set of eyes staring at me so intently that it felt like a physical touch.

My mouth popped open at the peridot stare that caught me in its sight, freezing me to the spot. The strange male looked like he was caught in the middle of doing something nefarious and I continued to blink stupidly at him. I didn't know *what* he was, or what he was doing there beside Kyle's car. Something about him felt off, but I couldn't place it.

"Cadence," he murmured, his voice carrying a resounding sorrow I couldn't comprehend, breaking the strange spell that had settled over me. The deep rumble of his voice seemed to vibrate my insides, drawing me forward around the side of the car toward him. The driver's side door was open, something pooling on the asphalt beneath the car. I couldn't discern what I was looking at and took a step closer, now within an arm's reach of the strange man. My attention wasn't on him, mesmerized by the slowly expanding darkness on the pavement.

He spoke again, pulling my gaze from the liquid collecting and spreading under the car. Lifting my head, I was entranced by those peridot eyes again, so green and so brilliant it cut through the haze and pierced me through the soul. "Cadence, please don't come any closer." The pleading in his voice caused me pause.

Frowning, a white, glowing orb resting in his palm captured my focus. Confusion tore through me. My body realized more quickly than my brain did, my chest tightening painfully.

I finally tore my gaze from his eyes to the dark curls that fell around his shoulders, his bare chest covered in black tattoos that I couldn't decipher in the darkness. But confusion truly settled over me when black wings unfurled from his back.

"You have wings." I pointed at them, as if they weren't obvious. My voice sounded hollow even to my own ears. "What are you?"

His face looked so sympathetic that it plucked aggressively at my heart-strings. "You weren't supposed to see this," he said regretfully, not answering my question. "Please turn around and walk away, Cadence. Save yourself from this."

I didn't even pause to figure out how he knew my name. Instead, I ignored his warning and stepped closer to peer at the ground below. Kyle was half out of the car, one leg on the floor by the pedals and the other twisted unnaturally underneath the vehicle as if he'd been attacked before he could even get out. His body was face-up on the ground, one arm at his side and the other flopped over his middle like he'd been thrown discourteously onto the pavement. His beautiful hazel eyes were staring up at me, empty and unseeing. I was so distracted by his vacant gaze that it took me a moment to see that his throat was torn apart, blood coating his entire torso and splattered on his face.

"Cadence," the stranger pleaded again, a warm hand pressing down on my shoulder and squeezing gently. "Please turn away. He wouldn't want you to remember him this way." His deep voice was attempting to soothe the shock that made my heart slow in my chest, but nothing could sugar coat the tragedy.

My eyes were as wide as Kyle's, staring down at him where he'd been tossed carelessly after being brutally murdered. Turning, I looked up at the man who held the glowing orb in his palm.

"That's his soul. I need to talk to him. Please. One more time," I begged, panic clawing up my throat and choking me.

He shook his head sadly, holding the orb against his chest. "You can't talk to him. His soul is recuperating from the trauma of death before facing Kuorir for assignment. He was a kind soul, he will get to rest in the Fields of Hope before being reborn into his next life," he murmured, those peridot eyes boring into mine.

"No . . . It can't be too late. I need to tell him I love him. Please. Let me talk to him."

The man looked as if I were breaking his heart as mine shattered, the pieces exploding outward and slicing my lungs to shreds. "You cannot talk to him. He is not able to speak in his current state. You need to let him be at peace." He reached out and brushed a tear from my cheek that I hadn't even realized had fallen.

Without another word, his wings spread wide, the black feathers glistening in the minute light from above. Touching one of the stones that dangled from his gauged ears, he gave me one last pleading look. In a blink, he was gone with a flutter of feathers and a gust of wind that blew my hair away from my face.

Finding myself alone, I turned back to Kyle's body and dropped to my knees beside him. Shock was giving way to panic, grief sweeping over me like a wave as the anguish stole the breath from my lungs.

Unable to breathe, I fluttered my hands over his ravaged body like I could save him and bring him back if I could only find the right place to touch him. The stranger's words were forgotten as heaving sobs started to rattle from my chest, tearing up my throat and leaving it aching in their wake. "No . . ." I whimpered, pushing his hair, damp with blood, from his forehead. My fingers left streaks in the crimson against his pale flesh. His skin was still warm, though it was cooling rapidly. "How long did you suffer?" My vision blurred as more tears filled my burning eyes.

Then, like a dam breaking free and unleashing a wave of anguish over me, I was suddenly drowning in the agony of misery. Unable to stop myself, I grabbed him, pulling his torso into my lap and cradling his head as it flopped limply against my arm. "No . . . Kyle . . ." I mewled, my voice cracking with the weight of the emotions piling in my chest.

I held him to me, clutching his body as if I could bring him back through sheer determination if I tried hard enough. But as much as I rubbed at his rapidly cooling flesh, his crimson life coating my fingers and soaking my shirt and jeans, he still wasn't coming back. I'd watched the reaper take his soul, been told it was time to let go, but I refused to believe it. I refused to accept that Kyle was stolen from this world, stolen from me. He was too good, too pure for such a cruel place as this, but I was going to be selfish. I wanted him back. I wanted to chase down that reaper and steal his soul; to return it to his body where it belonged and bring the light back to his eyes. But no amount of begging, no amount of wailing and crying and staring into his vacant eyes returned his soul to him.

His pale cheeks would never flush with life again. He'd never laugh, never smile, never cry or hurt or feel anything ever again. I'd never again feel his lips against mine, nor would we explore our life together. The harshest reality was that he would never know how I truly felt about him. I put off what I was afraid of, only to never have the opportunity to admit my love for him. Fear ruined my chance to tell him how I felt about him, and I would never forgive myself for it. I'd never know his reaction. I'd never be able to apologize for making such a mess of things, because no matter how much I loved Kyle, I'd always loved Ezra just as much.

So, I knelt there on the cold ground, holding his vacant corpse in my arms. I wailed and screamed like a wounded animal caught in an agonizing trap. I *was* a wounded animal. Grief has a way of pulling out the innate beast in us all, bringing forth the most severe of emotions, catching us in the whirlpool and drowning us in the depths of agony. Grief was tearing me apart from the inside out, ripping at my heart and leaving it in the same tatters as Kyle's ruined throat.

Hands gripped my shoulders, trying to pry me away from him, to take him from me when I needed him the most. "No!" I screeched, my voice sharp and echoing as I was heaved away from his body. "I won't leave him!" I clawed at the concrete, ripping my nails and leaving bloody trails as I fought to get back to Kyle.

"Cadence. He's not there anymore. I need you to let go of him. The Guard is here, and they need to try to find prints," the voice said, coming to me in ripples through the cresting waves of my psychological torture.

A sob echoed in my chest, rattling my vocal chords as I screamed and gripped his shirt with my bloodied hand. "He needs me! I can't leave him here by himself!"

"Cadence! He's gone! He's not there anymore. His soul is gone, Cady . . ."

The voice wasn't registering, the words just adding noise to my insistent shrieking. "No! I won't leave him alone!"

My hands slid over the hands on my shoulder as I dug my ruined nails into the flesh, trying to loosen the grip on me. They tightened further, the fingertips biting into my flesh. "Let *go* of me! He *needs* me!" My wailing was growing hoarse, my throat as ruined as Kyle's.

"Cadybug, please . . . Come here . . ."

That nickname. I recognized that nickname. I turned to look up into crystal blue eyes, rimmed red with his own emotional turmoil. The pain of his grip grounded me, yanking me from the maelstrom of misery that buffered my lost soul. A whimper escaped me. "Ezra."

He pulled me to him, encasing me in his arms as he practically lifted me off the ground and away from Kyle's desecrated body as The Guard swarmed him and started trying to collect any evidence possible. Ezra's arms were a shield, keeping me safe from the view as they worked over his empty vessel. I wondered if I'd become an empty shell, too, the grief hollowing me out and stealing any semblance of love and life I'd ever had.

Ezra's body shook and I looked up to find him sobbing with me, clutching me as though I was the only thing tethering him to sanity. "I'm so sorry it was him, but I'm so grateful it wasn't you," he choked out, his voice wobbling with the sheer volatility of the sadness and shock that trampled through him like a stampede. I understood how he felt; it mirrored my own vortex of emotional hell.

I gasped in horror when my eyes focused inside the car and saw the red amaryllis perched on the passenger seat.

CHAPTER 27

CADENCE

E zra and I stood like statues for ages, completely disregarded as The Guard scurried around to find evidence. Since there was no note with the amaryllis and Kyle's fingerprints were on it, they assumed that he was bringing the flower for me. Whoever the culprit was, they covered their scent with the pungent smell of ammonia that filled the air around us. I hadn't noticed it at first, but now I could smell nothing else. It cut through the metallic tang of Kyle's blood running over the pavement of the parking lot. My eyes never left his body, my view only being cut off by the guards prowling around the scene.

Unfortunately, they were out of their depth. Murder was a rare thing in this pack and was typically perpetrated by outsiders. Like the death of my grandfather the day Callum and my grandmother were taken. When I blinked, Kyle's body was replaced by that of my grandfather, lying on his kitchen floor with a purple arrow piercing his heart. Ezra quit attempting to divert my attention a while ago after realizing that it was fruitless.

"Cadence! Ezra!" A shout cut sharply through the images looping in my brain, pulling my gaze from the body for the first time. I saw Alex's blonde hair first, the streetlight glowing golden in the strands as she ran toward us. "I'd have been here sooner, but dad didn't want me to come. I had to run here because he took my keys." Glancing over her shoulder, her face paled before she turned back to me. Her eyes raked over my face, taking in my tearstained and agonized features. "Oh, Cadence . . ." she murmured, reaching out and brushing her fingers over my cheek.

The touch caused my fragile calm to fracture. I felt my face wrinkling as fresh tears spilled like lava over my cold cheeks. Four arms wrapped tightly around me, pulling me in and attempting to protect me from the agony digging its fierce claws into my heart and lungs. A pitiful keening escaped my already aching throat and the embrace tightened around me.

Another cry broke through the night, so anguished that I was certain my soul fractured at the sound. Alex pulled away, clearing my view and showing Kyle's father, Chuck, on his knees beside his son. His mother, Natalie, stood a few feet behind, her hands covering her mouth as tears leaked from wide eyes.

"Not my son," Chuck wailed, his nails scraping the asphalt as he tipped forward and bent his head down. His forehead pressed against Kyle's, and the image seared itself inside my skull. The anguish gripped me, pulling me forward until I stood beside Natalie. Her eyes, identical to Kyle's, shifted toward me unseeingly. When they focused on my face, she reached out and grabbed me, pulling me against her chest.

"I'm so sorry. He wouldn't have been here if it weren't for me." My voice cracked painfully in my ruined throat.

She gripped the back of my shirt as she held me against her like I could save her from floating away in the sea of grief we were both trapped in. "This isn't your fault, Cadence," she whispered, the words not easing any of the guilt that held me tightly in its grasp.

It *was* my fault. I didn't cut off contact from him and face the stalker on my own. I kept him in the path of danger, selfishly refusing to let him go and continue the life that he so deserved. I was to blame and I refused to believe anyone who told me that I wasn't. I pulled away from her embrace, walking backwards for a couple steps until her gaze shifted from me to her son once more.

Bernard Pierce, Alex's father, was standing there when I returned to my friends, his blue eyes examining me. "Are you okay?"

I thought about lying, deflecting, but saying that I was fine sounded like such an obvious lie. "No."

His lips pressed together and he nodded, looking over my clothing before flicking his eyes back up to my face. My own gaze dropped to my front, noting the dark staining that was drying my clothing into stiff wrinkles where I'd been holding Kyle.

"Do you know what happened?" he inquired, his hands tucked into his pockets. I'd always known he wasn't fond of me, but it was never more apparent than it was right now. His tone was cold, detached.

I shook my head, my eyes staying on my clothes like the stickiness of drying life soaked into the fabric had tacked my gaze to it.

He sighed heavily, pulling my vapid stare up to him as his face tilted up toward the sky. "This was done by an Ascended volsifi, which is the only reason you aren't a suspect. Go home, get cleaned up. We will reach out with further questions tomorrow."

Bernard walked away from me, allowing Alex and Ezra to approach. Ezra threw his coat over my shoulders, enveloping me in the comforting scent of teakwood and warm amber. I automatically inhaled deeply, pulling his scent into my lungs like a comforting blanket wrapping around my aching heart. His hand pressed against the small of my back, guiding me toward his car parked haphazardly just on the other side of the light. The door was still open, the engine running, abandoned in his haste to get to me.

When we were in the car, I stared out the windshield when something occurred to me. "How did you know?" I asked him, staring into the imposing darkness, even as his headlights tried to cut through it.

Alex spoke up. "I called him. He reached out to me when he was in the bathroom and told me what was happening with Kyle not showing up, so when dad got the call that there was something going on outside Axe Marks the Spot, I was worried he'd been assaulted. I never would have guessed he–"

Her voice cracked with emotion, causing my eyes to burn again. I dug my nails into my palms. My hope that the physical pain would alleviate some of the emotional duress was immediately dashed. Try as I might, the cavern in my heart wouldn't cease.

"Where is Jessica?" I asked, my voice sounding hollow and distant.

Ezra snorted. "I don't know, and don't really care. I kicked her out of the car when I saw her texting her friends, gloating about how Kyle didn't show up for you and making fun of you for it. I was already coming back for you when I got the call from Alex telling me that something was wrong."

"Did you see the amaryllis, too?" My voice cracked so harshly it hurt my throat.

My gaze drifted to him, catching the end of his nod. "I did," he whispered.

Alex sniffled in the backseat, the first fissure in her impenetrable armor I'd ever seen.

EZRA

As much as it pained me, I dropped Cadence off at her house with Alex before heading back to the estate. It seemed that the psycho wasn't going to hurt Cadence since he'd had plenty of chances to do so and didn't. Even if he tried, Alex was a formidable opponent, and I knew she was armed with her shuriken knives. Not even *I* wanted to go against her if she had her favored weapons on her. She could even take down Brody easily. As much as I detested him sometimes, I wasn't too proud to acknowledge that he was an excellent fighter.

I *was* curious about how much the stalker had tormented Kyle before his death, though I wasn't sure I could get an answer to that until the investigation was underway. As much as I trusted Cadence, I was certain that she hadn't told us everything she had experienced either. I'd never wanted to go through her phone before now, and despite wanting to, I knew I couldn't do that to her.

Deciding to go to Axe Marks the Spot to question The Guard about the investigation, I rerouted halfway home. As I pulled into the parking lot, my phone buzzed in the cupholder, loudly vibrating against the plastic. Looking at my texts, I expected something from Alex or Cadence and instead got a message from an unknown number.

Unknown

> I saw you holding her. Can't you take a hint? Was Wilkins' death not enough for you? Fine. Stay away or you're next.

A hint? This person thought murder was a *hint*?

Frowning, my gaze shifted around the outskirts of the lot, but there were too many shadows among the purposefully darkened homes in the area. The Deltas were keeping their heads down and out of the way of the Betas swarming their neighborhood. The Guard were taking their time, combing through every nook and cranny of the scene. I walked over to the Wilkins who were standing against the building, their faces drawn and tired looking with grief.

"Ezra. I didn't expect you to be back," Natalie commented, trying and failing to give me a smile in greeting.

I tried to think of something to say, shifting through one thousand different expressions. Everything felt too formal or not formal enough, and I rubbed my chin in frustration.

"You don't have to know the right thing to say all the time," she assured me, reaching out and gripping my upper arm. "I don't know what to say either."

Pressing my lips together, I tried to suppress the emotions swirling inside my chest. Before I could say anything further, my father appeared at my elbow. Hands behind his back, he looked every bit the unruffled leader that he was. It must be nice to not feel even a piece of the spectrum of human emotions.

"My deepest condolences," he stated, his tone stiff and formal. I knew he was lying, too familiar with his intonations to believe anything he ever said. "The Guard are about done collecting evidence and Dr. Barber will be cleaning the scene shortly. I thought I'd let you know in case you'd like to go home so as not to witness it."

Natalie nodded sadly, glancing at her nearly catatonic husband who took her arm in his. "Come on, Chuck. Let's go home," she whispered. Her hazel eyes glittered with unshed tears, her voice thick.

I watched them leave before turning to my father. He shifted his frosty gaze to me, appraising me and the smears of blood on my clothes. "She's lucky she hasn't Ascended yet, or I'd have her executed for this crime," he muttered so none of the bystanders could hear his words. "I've heard snippets of what was on his phone. If you think she's going to get any of my guardsmen watching over her to make sure she isn't hurt, you should reconsider that daft idea. I hope he does kill her. It would eliminate some of my *stress*," he sneered, adjusting his already straight tie. "Shame about the Wilkins boy, though. He'd have made an excellent Guard after graduating from PSG."

Rage flared within my chest, and I gritted my teeth to stop my mouth from saying something stupid.

His upper lip curled in response to my fury. Someone unfamiliar with his micromovements might think he was giving me a grim smile. "You will be sitting in on this investigation, unfortunately. Bernard seems to think it would be good for you to have some *experience* before you take my place. "

I could tell from his tone that he was less than pleased with the reminder that I'd soon be taking over for him. I briefly wondered if I could use his words against him once I'd taken the throne as King of the Volsifi in just a few short years. As a prince, I was going to be more than just the Alpha of the Scarlet Moon pack. It was a fact I tried to forget as often as possible.

"He also believes you might be some help in the investigation; that you might have some insight into the culprit of this . . . heinous act."

"Of course, father."

He did not look appeased by this. "You're dismissed. Go straight home. The last thing I need is for you to have any further interaction with that abomination tonight. I'm sure whispers are already circulating about why you showed up to comfort her and how you knew to do so."

I scowled at him before returning to my car. I ached to go to Cadence, to comfort her. I was also painfully aware that was an impossibility tonight.

In my car, I put both hands on the wheel and inhaled deeply, stopping as a metallic sharpness soaked into my sinuses. My forehead creased as I registered that I was smelling blood before turning toward the passenger seat.

In the darkness, I squinted at the long, frilly object before picking it up. I wrinkled my nose, the smell of iron overwhelming as the thing came closer to my face. Turning on the dome light, I felt my veins freeze as I looked down at the monkshood plant; the purple petals were stained a deep crimson with drying blood and I knew at once that it belonged to Kyle. Dropping the plant back into the passenger seat, I clicked off the light and glanced around for anyone watching. No one was paying me any mind.

My phone vibrated in my pocket, and I adjusted in my seat to pull it out. Blood smeared over the screen from my thumb, and I growled as it failed to recognize my thumb print. Reaching into the glove box, I pulled out a napkin and angrily wiped off my thumb and phone to unlock it. Immediately, a message popped up.

Unknown

> Just in case you didn't take my previous threat seriously.

Horrified, I dropped my phone into the cup holder beside me before peeling out of the parking lot to drive home.

CADENCE

I found myself standing on the edge of the cliff, staring down at the ravine below. It would be so easy to slide my feet off the edge. My toes were already over, clinging to the rock like a perching bird. Would I find Kyle if I did it? They say when you die in your dreams, you die in real life. Turns out your dream self also has no filter. It thinks all the selfish things your waking brain hides from yourself.

"Remember me?"

I lifted my face, looking up into the spitting clouds and closing my eyes. Unable to speak, I just nodded my head. I knew that if I opened my mouth, I'd just end up screaming. I no longer had words. Just hatred.

His hand found its way to my shoulder, his fingers gripping almost to the point of pain.

"Hathor. What has happened?" he asked, his voice commanding an answer.

I finally faced him. His eyes widened as he took in my appearance. Apparently, even my subconscious looked as appalling as I felt.

"What has happened?" he repeated, his tone gentling as his fingers brushed over my face. "You are crying."

"How can you even tell?" I asked, my voice cracking with the emotions that threatened to explode out of me.

He scowled. "Temperature. Answer the question."

I took a breath, but it shook. "I . . . lost someone."

His forehead creased. "Can I help you find them?"

My face crumpled as I shook my head. Understanding dawned on his handsome face, and that broke me further. I pressed my hands to my face as I started sobbing. His cloak found its way around my shoulders again, and I realized I was shivering from the cold of the storm that raged around us. Normally, it faded as the dream continued, but it was growing more intense as the time passed. Thunder and lightning flashed in the sky in a synchronicity I'd never seen. The ground rumbled beneath my bare feet. His arms wrapped around me, holding me tight and filling me with a warmth that made my shuddering sobs quake harder.

"I am sorry," he whispered, barely audible over the fury of the storm around us.

The rain was coming down in frozen sheets, stinging the cheek that wasn't pressed against the side of his neck.

"Let it out."

I shook my head, afraid to fall apart. If I fell apart, then it was real and Kyle would never return.

"You have to let it out."

My breath was coming in short gasps, moans filled the exhales in an uncomfortable display of grief.

"It won't stop hurting until you let it take you. Only after the swell will the storm calm."

Unable to hold everything back any further, I inhaled and screamed. He didn't let me go, clinging me to him so hard that his fingers made my frozen skin ache beneath them. The screaming went on for ages, my throat tearing itself apart with the effort of letting it go.

"There will be more swells, but it will get better," he assured me through the screams. I wasn't sure how I heard him. It was like he was in my head, assuring me from inside myself.

I felt other hands grabbing me, shaking me as I continued screaming.

"Don't forget me." His voice was in my head, though his mouth didn't move as the world started dissolving around me.

I thought of the words, projecting them into his head. 'Think of me, and I'll be here.'

He nodded; his expression solemn before he disappeared completely.

I gasped as I sat upright in bed. The coughing set in, ripping apart my damaged throat. I couldn't breathe as my world crashed down around me. Reality set in again. I looked around for the boy, but he wasn't there. Even if he had been, I don't think I would have recognized him. His face was already gone from my memory; any image I tried to conjure vanished from my thoughts.

Alex and Brody were there, staring at me with wide eyes as I hacked. Alex's hand was rubbing my back, soothing me.

"I'm sorry," I whispered, pushing my damp hair out of my face. My clothes were sticking to my skin. I must have been sweating. "It was just a dream."

Alex nodded, climbing out of my bed and wandering to my dresser.

"I'm going to go get you a drink. Water okay?" Brody asked. He left the room after I nodded.

Alex handed me a change of clothes and I hurriedly got out of my wet pajamas and put on the dry ones. We were halfway through changing the bedding when Brody reappeared with a glass of water.

Once we were settled back on the bed, I leaned back against the headboard and sipped the water. The iciness of it felt soothing against the stinging pain.

"Do you want to talk about it?" Alex asked, a wary expression on her face.

I shook my head, dropping my gaze to the glass of water. "No. Honestly, it's mostly gone anyway."

It was a lie, but I didn't want to explain years of history with a guy whose face I couldn't even remember.

Alex inhaled sharply and I glanced at her. She looked hurt, but I didn't know why she would be. So I set the glass down and disregarded the whole thing. I didn't have the emotional bandwidth to discuss anything.

I didn't have to say anything. Brody found his way to the floor and Alex laid down beside me so we could all pretend to sleep.

CHAPTER 28

EZRA

School was canceled for the next few days as the pack mourned its loss. The Wilkins were already at The Crest when I arrived the following morning. Chuck was part of the Guard, and Natalie sat against the wall, a thousand-mile stare boring into the floor. I sat down beside her, handing her a cup of coffee that she distractedly wrapped her hands around. I didn't bother to ask how she was doing. There was no point in forcing her to pretend she was holding up. She offered a dazed smile of gratitude before her hazel gaze shifted back to the white tiles on the floor in front of her.

I went into the calamity that had overtaken the usually tranquil Crest. It was the barracks and training area that hung out at the top of the mountain just above the Estate the Alpha family dwelled in. It overlooked the rest of the pack that spread out down the mountain with the Omegas being the farthest down. It was placed there so that if we were attacked from the other side of the mountain, they'd find our Guards first.

Guards ran around erratically, each one feeling the weight of their inadequacy. Scarlet Moon was so cut off from outside packs that there was no one to reach out to for assistance, and that was the fault of my father and grandfather. If the stalker wanted disorder and chaos, that was achieved. I was certain that was part of his aim. The total confusion and calamity had the entire pack on high alert and pointing fingers at each other.

I approached Bernard who was talking angrily on the phone. It only took a moment of eavesdropping for me to realize he was scolding Alex.

"We don't know who did this, so I need you to be home. This is not negotiable, Alexis."

I stared at his profile, waiting for him to finish his futile phone call. If he wanted Alex to cooperate, he just sealed his fate that she would not. She hated her full name and the use of it would only cause her to dig in her heels in obstinance.

"I don't care if you want to protect that *thing* you call a friend," he snarled, though he paused when he realized I was standing there. I wasn't sure what look was on my face, but he paled in response. "I'm sorry. I know you want to protect Cadence, but my first concern is my own daughter. She has her own parents to keep an eye on–"

He was interrupted. I could no longer hear Alex's shrill refusal, but he was still listening. That could only mean that she'd gone into her silent and deadly mode, and I pressed my lips together while waiting for the conversation to conclude.

"I want you back for dinner," he snapped before hanging up. I glanced at my watch and saw that it was only eight in the morning. He was giving her quite the leash to ignore.

I cleared my throat and glanced at the papers that were spread over his desk. It was printouts of text messages and my fingers itched to dig through them. "What have you found out?" I noted the bags under his eyes, evidence that he'd worked through the night.

Bernard sighed and rubbed his temples. "That something has been going on for months, both to Kyle and to . . . *Cadence*." I could tell him speaking her name nearly caused him physical pain and I shot him another glare before he dropped his gaze to the papers. "He'd been receiving threatening text messages since the end of January that slowly increased in frequency and intensity over the past couple months."

I sat down across the desk from him, clasping my fingers together in my lap to keep them from picking up and devouring the words on the pages. I saw some, though they were mostly Cadence's name and words of warning that made no sense without the rest of the messages.

"Who else was he texting?"

He frowned and picked up the stack before handing the entire bundle to me.

"Your father said you wanted on this case, and he'd agreed to it. Said you might have some insight into the students if it was one of them, and that's the only reason I'm telling you anything."

I didn't miss the displeasure he felt at admitting that I might be useful. I never once told my father that I wanted to be on the case but didn't have time to wonder why he wanted me involved before Bernard continued speaking.

"He also wants us to bring Cadence in for questioning. It was impossible that she did it, but she might have insight into who it is, especially since their texts together indicate that they were both under attack. He didn't text much of anyone else but her, other than refusing invitations anywhere she wouldn't be allowed to go–like Mooney's. It didn't appear there was much else happening in his world. We could speculate that he was trying to limit the collateral damage in case something happened to him, but it's just a guess based on his character."

I nodded. "Why didn't he shift to defend himself? Especially if this was a shifted volsifi that attacked?"

Bernard's blue eyes lifted to mine; his expression unreadable. "Because he was dosed with monkshood first."

My blood ran cold as I stared at him. "How was the attacker not poisoned when they bit him?"

"The monkshood was injected into his thigh via a dart that was found under the car. We tested it, and it was coated with the stuff. We assume that he shifted and went for the throat immediately, before the poison reached the throat. But it's all just educated guessing." Bernard's words were stilted; thoughts thrown out as they came to him. He looked frustrated as he flopped back in his seat and rubbed his eyes. "The whole thing is uncertain, and we aren't sure where to even look or who would have a grudge against Kyle of all people."

I had an idea, my mind flickering to Jason and Brody. Brody had seemed to forgive Kyle, though it could have all been an act. Jason, however, had definitely not forgiven him and made it known. Their friendship had ended shortly after Kyle started pretending to date Cadence.

The conversation lulled with Bernard. I leaned forward over the printouts of Kyle's texts and started reading through them. I started with the threats from the stalker, not wanting to impose on his relationship with Cadence quite yet.

All of them were relatively similar, threatening him to leave Cadence and claiming her as their property, essentially. I scowled, watching the texts get increasingly violent, some of them including myself.

Unknown

> If you think you're protecting Ezra from his fate, you're wrong. He's next. Right after you. Save yourself, leave the girl for her rightful mate.

Kyle never once responded, even when the stalker started prodding him.

> I saw you kissing her through the window of Sew What. What makes you think you deserve her when I'm her mate?

Are her lips as soft and delectable as they look? I dream of them often, biting them until they bleed so I can taste her life on my tongue.

Are you jealous that I've gotten to stand over her and watch her sleep while you're stuck fantasizing about being with her? All alone in your bed while I get to gaze upon her slumbering face?

That one included a picture of Cadence sleeping peacefully that made my blood curdle in my veins.

I kept going, reading more and more until my stomach clenched with guilt and I was overwhelmed with the horror of the situation. Kyle had been killed trying to protect Cadence and myself. He hadn't deserved to die, and I was pretty sure that he'd deserved Cady significantly more than I did. Pressing my lips together, I flipped to the texts between Kyle and Cadence.

What I found wasn't all that interesting. It seemed that if they had any in-depth conversations that they were mostly in person. Most of their texts were arranging plans, and he'd never once dropped any indication that he was going through anything outside of their relationship. She had divulged some information, including screenshots of some of the texts she'd received. I wondered if he'd ever told her anything about it at all. Knowing Kyle, I could only assume that he didn't. He'd never have wanted her to fret over his well-being.

Putting my head in my hands, I rubbed my eyes with the heels of my palms.

"You don't have any idea who this is either, do you?"

Shaking my head, I ran my fingers through my hair and looked down at the pile of papers in front of me.

"No, and the texts tell us literally nothing other than both of them were being stalked," I muttered, scowling in frustration.

"We don't have the manpower to follow her, so don't bother asking. Your father already made it clear he has no intention of protecting her."

A slow smirk quirked my lips upward as I examined him closely. "Don't worry. Alex and I will cover watching over her."

CHAPTER 29

CADENCE

I sat on my bed, staring at the comforter while Alex lay beside me. Her fingers gently brushed up and down my arm in a soothing manner, but I wasn't sure anything could soothe me ever again. When I closed my eyes, I saw him lying on the ground with his throat ripped open and exposed to the cosmos above. When I opened them, I saw him smiling down at me, felt his lips against mine and his hands on my skin. I was certain their imprint on my flesh was permanent, and it was both a painful and appreciated thing.

What I felt most was the overwhelming sense of regret. I'd never gotten to tell him that I loved him. I wasted too much time, spent it agonizing over his reaction instead of just finding it out. Would he have been happy? He'd told me he cared for me, but would that have changed when I exposed my soul to him? Cracked my ribs and showed him every vulnerable piece of me? Would his feelings have still been as strong when I told him that I was still in love with Ezra?

"There's no way to know the answers to any of those things, Cady." Alex's voice felt like it was drifting over me in an ocean of misery, a small boat gone adrift in the battering waves that desperately wanted to drag it into the depths of my wretchedness. I hadn't even realized I'd been speaking my thoughts aloud. I was completely unaware of my own body, numb and listless as I sat there in my bed.

I laid down on her waiting arm, using it to cradle the back of my aching skull. My eyes burned a moment before the hot trail of tears spilled out over my temples and soaked into my already dampened hair. The strands were sticking to my skin, but I didn't have the energy or will to move them away.

"I think that he would have loved you back, Cadence. I know he loved you immensely, and he'd have accepted your love even if it meant sharing your affections with Ezra," she said, brushing the wet trails from my temples and unsticking the hairs from my damp skin.

My face crinkled, my hands moving to cover my mouth as a choked sob escaped. "It's my fault he's dead. If I hadn't agreed to this stupid fake relationship, he'd still be alive. He could be happy, fall in love with someone who wouldn't have placed him on a silver platter for Kuorir."

Alex tutted, brushing her fingers through my damp and greasy hair. "You can't think like that. You have no idea whether or not he'd have been happy. He knew what he was doing and the choices he was making. He thought you were worth the danger and made that more than apparent every moment he spent with you in spite of being told not to."

I was openly sobbing now, my breaths coming in short bursts that rattled my body with the force of them. Feeling as though I were suffocating under the weight of my own grief, I sat up and gasped for air, wrapping my arms around myself as though I could seal the gaping wound in my aching heart.

"How could he do that? How could he risk his own life for someone like me? I wasn't worth that." I spit the words, an undeserved lash of anger splitting the sea of anguish and yanking me down the dry path toward my own destruction.

Alex sat up with me, her arms wrapping around my shoulders. "Because he loved you, Cadence. He saw what the rest of us have always seen. You are the sun, shining into our hell and casting out the wraiths as you go. You bring the monster in me to heel, reminding me of my humanity and that I crave it more than I crave the blood of your enemies."

My eyes widened. "Quit saying that shit, Alex. I'm not in the mood for your ridiculous pick-me-ups right now," I snapped, feeling even more guilty as she jerked away from me.

Uncaring, I wiped my draining nose on the bottom of my shirt. I didn't care about anything but dwelling in the ocean of agony. I was barely keeping afloat in it. There was a hole in the bottom, filling my safety with fear and pain. I deserved to wallow in it. Maybe if I was disgusting enough, the lunatic would leave me alone and find someone else. Alex should run and save herself in case he decided that I was worth it even if I acted like a troll under a bridge.

"I'm not lying to you, Cadence. I wouldn't lie about something like that. And I'd overheard him telling Brody something similar. I think it's why Brody backed off, even though he's enamored with you."

I tossed my head back, cackling. There was no humor to the sound, coming across bizarre and psychotic even to my own ears. Alex looked alarmed as I stood up, needing to expand my lungs as much as possible, as if my physical body was the reason my organs were collapsing.

"If this wacko knows what's good for him, he'll stay away from me. You should too. I know Ezra should, I've already gotten text messages about him. They started last night," I babbled, waving at her as if I could make her and her worried expression vanish by magic.

Alex appeared unimpressed, not bothering to hide it. I'd recognize that obstinate face of hers anywhere.

"I'm not going anywhere. You can be damn sure that Ezra isn't either. He'd be here now if he weren't embroiled in the case."

That caused me to pause, and I turned toward her.

"He's on the case?"

Alex nodded, pushing her messy curls off her face. I just noticed that her makeup was smudged, her usually pristine black liner dripping under her eyes, the dark tracks running rivulets down her cheeks. Immediately, the guilt returned. I realized that I'd been so absorbed in myself that I'd neglected her pain. We could have been suffering together, and instead I was soaking up all of her comfort while she was left out in the emotional storm alone, naked in the blizzard of grief.

I blinked, realizing that she had been speaking.

"I'm sorry. I know you're suffering too, Alex."

Her hazel eyes immediately brimmed with tears, causing the green to glitter in her irises. "I am."

Throwing my arms around her, she gripped me tightly as we both crumbled under the weight of the previous day. On top of the loss of Kyle, she was feuding with her father over me. I'd been half asleep while she was on the phone earlier, but I still heard the conversation inside my dream.

"I'm sorry about your dad. If you need to go home, I'll understand completely."

She pulled back and rubbed her arm over her damp cheek, smearing the black lines further.

"No. You're far more important than making my dad happy," she assured me, giving a watery smile. "I know we should eat something, but . . ."

"The idea of eating right now makes me want to vomit," I grumbled, finishing her open-ended sentence.

So instead of eating, we crawled back into bed and snuggled together. I suddenly remembered an earlier conversation.

"What did you say about Ezra being on the case?" I asked, looking up at the ceiling as she curled up against my side.

"He texted me earlier. Said that his father told mine that he wanted to be on the case, which seems weird to me. He said he'd talk to us later about it when he got here."

I made a face. "That's weird. Do you think Ezra wanted to be on the case?"

She shrugged, nudging my armpit as she did. "I have no idea. He hasn't been in contact much, barely enough to keep me in the loop."

I frowned, checking my inactive phone. "He never messaged me . . ."

"He knows how devastated you are. He didn't want to burden you."

Sighing heavily, I unlocked my phone and shuffled my standard playlist. "Hollow" by Lo Spirit started playing, and I tossed my phone onto the bed as if that extra bit of exertion would ease the ache in my soul.

It didn't.

CHAPTER 30

EZRA

Leaving The Crest, I flopped into my car as though my body weighed a ton. I knew I was exhausted. Mentally, I was completely empty. I'd watched the autopsy that confirmed it was an Ascended wolf that killed Kyle, monkshood injected into the thigh. We'd gone over all the evidence collected, though there wasn't much no matter how hard we looked.

It all pointed to a dead end.

I could speculate all I wanted, but there was no concrete evidence of anything at all. There wasn't even any saliva left behind in the wound, Kyle's throat wasn't even left at the scene.

Nothing, nothing, nothing.

Leaning forward, I put my forehead against the steering wheel and held back the sob that was aching inside my chest. I hadn't really had any time to process or grieve the loss of a good friend, one who had unnecessarily saved my ass and ended up dead for his efforts.

A buzzing interrupted my guilt, and I picked my head up to look at my phone. Jessica had texted forty-seven times and called almost as many, which made my rage flare. The messages teetered between anger that I'd literally shoved her out of my car with no explanation and begging me to take her back since I'd told her it was over. I didn't give her a reason, so I clearly didn't mean it. At least not according to her addled brain.

I'd never been surer of anything in my life as much as my love for Cadence. I was so in love with her that I knew I'd be okay with her dating someone else as long as she was happy. Throwing down my phone without responding to any of Jessica's messages, I drove to the only destination that ever mattered.

The next morning, we woke up like sardines in Cadence's bed. It felt so much like old times that I could almost ignore the storm clouds of grief that hung ominously over us. I turned off my alarm and stretched, turning around to hold Cady close.

When I next opened my eyes, I was looking up at David Nocetti who stared down at us with an uncertain look on his face.

"I'm home for the day. She can stay here with me if you and Alex want to return to school." He tucked his hands into the front pockets of his jeans.

I glanced over at Alex, who was looking between David and myself. Sighing, I carefully disentangled myself from Cadence and Alex did the same. "You're right. We should go in." I held out a hand to assist Alex out of bed so she wouldn't disturb Cady. "Morale and all that . . ."

David immediately sat at the end of the bed, leaning back against the wall and pulling out a book. *The Princess Bride* was emblazoned on the dust cover. "I'll be right here when she wakes. I don't think waking up alone would be good for her right now."

I nodded as Alex murmured, "I agree. This is the first time she's slept since . . ." Her voice cracked and my arm wrapped around her, pulling her to me as I planted a kiss on the top of her blonde head.

David nodded, giving us a sad smile. His eyes were rimmed with red, and I realized that he was hurting, too. This kind of thing impacts the entire community, no matter how well you know someone. I wondered how much David had come to know Kyle over the past couple months; how much he might have liked him and Cadence being together despite knowing about the deal.

Alex and I turned to leave, not caring that our clothes were worn and wrinkled. It seemed so inconsequential after what we'd been through.

The entire school seemed dimmed, the talk in the hallways less obnoxious and chaotic, like every student in the place was subdued by the trauma of a sudden death. We were all feeling the loss of Kyle, his light extinguished and no longer shining around us. Alex and I walked into the school arm in arm, a united front against whatever rumors might already be spreading. The two of us would be the face of the group until Cadence could show up herself.

We were barely halfway to Alex's locker when two of the people I wanted to see the least showed up in our path. Jessica was scowling at me, her angry glare mirrored on Jason's face. Alex and I stopped in our tracks, facing them head on.

"I called you over one hundred times, Ezra. Why wouldn't you call me back?" Jessica snapped, glaring at me and pointedly ignoring Alex's heavy leer.

I sighed, rubbing my eyes with my free hand before finally meeting her amber hues. "Because I had more important things to do, Jessica. I don't have time to deal with your petty behavior when we aren't together anymore."

She recoiled as if I'd slapped her, her mouth popping open in surprise. "Don't say things like that, Ezra!" Her eyes darted around the hall to make sure no one heard, but everyone around us had stopped to stare. "I know you didn't mean it when you said we were over."

Jason stepped forward, closing the gap between us as he glared at me. "You should be nicer to my sister, Ezra."

Alex threw back her head and laughed, but the sound was unhinged. When her head came forward again, she used the momentum in her body to shove Jason back a step. "You should mind your place, Jason," she snarled, her tone as sharp as a blade, all sense of the deranged humor absent.

"Come on, Ezra. Don't be like this," Jessica pleaded, tears beading along her lower lashes. I felt nothing but disgust. "You know you love me. You told me you did. I know you really want to be with me, stop being so stubborn."

I would have laughed if her words weren't so preposterous. "What? I don't want to be with you, Jessica. I *never* wanted to be with you. And as if I didn't already detest you enough, you lied to Cadence. You told her I had *sex* with you when I've never even *touched* you. Ever notice how you clung to me, and I never once reciprocated, Jessica? I wouldn't have had sex with you if my father held a silver stake to my eye with the threat of my death."

My patience snapped as she started loudly blubbering. I moved closer until my face was within spitting distance of hers. "You know why, Jessica? Do you *want* to know why? It's because you are nothing more than a pathetic girl scrabbling for power and good genetics. The thing is, the idea of breeding with you makes me want to castrate myself." My tone was cold, as ruthless as I felt. The words were meant to slice, cut her open as deeply as her lie had flayed Cadence's soul. "And that's all it would have been, Jessica. We will never be mates."

Her face was turning red, clashing with the orange of her hair as she stared at me with wide eyes.

"I only dated you because my father insisted. I was going to break up with you that night anyway after Cadence told me what you'd said. We are over, Jessica. I'm with Cadence now and forever. She was always the only one for me, it was *never* going to be you."

Jessica's mouth opened and closed a couple times, but no one had time to react before Jason did. His fist flew toward me, aiming for my face and I barely had time to deflect it before the other one followed. Without thought, I lost myself to my more animalistic side, shifting in seconds. Jason's eyes widened slightly as I lunged straight for his face. It took him a moment longer to shift, but then we were snapping jaws and ferocious growls that echoed off the metal lockers.

I saw a flash of red as Alex flipped Jessica onto the floor and pinned her down. I could smell the metallic scent of her blood in the air, hazarding a glance to see that Alex had one of her shurikens pressed into the hollow in Jessica's throat so she wouldn't fight back. Jessica had never trained and was completely unequipped to defend herself against a machine like Alex.

The distraction had cost me. I'd fallen into the defensive position, deflecting and backing up. But I was getting tired of defending and I stepped forward, getting a firm latch onto Jason's shoulder with my teeth and clenching my jaw. I wanted his death; I craved it as my sanity slowly slipped and bowed to the Alpha I was destined to become. My confidence that Jason was the one behind all of this only fueled my bloodlust, and Jason whimpering under the grip of my jaws did nothing to curb my desire.

Hands wrapped around my muzzle, fingers working their way between my clamped maw and yanking my bite apart until I released Jason. Growling, I turned to look up at Brody who was glancing between Jason and me as though we were the stupidest people he'd ever met.

"Knock it off before both of you get suspended. We have one month left of school, don't get yourselves thrown out now," he snarled, pushing me back another step from Jason.

Shifting back, I angrily wiped the blood from my lips and spit red onto the linoleum. Jason shifted back, sprawled naked and groaning on the floor. Brody handed me a pair of sweats from my backpack, and I pulled them on, continuing to glare at Jason.

He sat up, gripping his bloodied shoulder. "You hurt my sister, and I'd get thrown out of school if that meant you paid for what you did to her."

Brody looked at him and shook his head. "Are you angrier that he hurt your sister or that you no longer have a chance at entering the Alpha rank if they're not together?" he demanded, crossing his arms over his chest. "We just lost our *best friend*. You need to get your shit together."

Jason looked as though he might self-destruct. "Kyle stopped being my friend the moment he started dating Cadence," he retorted, completely ignoring the first question. He stood up, wavering slightly on his feet until he regained his balance.

A throat clearing had us all turning to find Mr. Rutger and Mr. Bowman staring at us in disappointment.

"Is there a problem here?" Mr. Rutger inquired icily, eyeing Alex where she still straddled Jessica's stomach, holding her hands to the floor above her head with one hand while her shuriken pressed into her throat.

"No, sir." Alex put her shuriken away and accepted my hand as I reached out to help her off the floor. Alex looked abashed, though I knew it was an act. I could tell by the way she glared daggers at Jessica who cowered like Alex was a wraith coming for her soul.

Mr. Rutger looked pointedly at Jessica, who reached for Jason but got no assistance.

"No, sir. No problems," Jessica muttered, trying to smooth her hair with shaking hands.

Nodding, Mr. Rutger looked over us all before waving a hand. The students in the hall snapped to attention, immediately evacuating the hall. I grabbed Alex and walked with her as everyone else dispersed. Glancing around, I met Jason's glare as he stared over Jessica's head. My eyes then caught Mr. Bowman, eyeing Brody as he stood beside him.

"He told Jessica off! Ezra actually told her that he would rather castrate himself than have sex with her." Alex laughed as she recounted the story to Cadence who sat on her bed looking rumpled and baffled.

"You didn't sleep with Jessica?" She looked at me with such hope that my heart shattered.

"Of course I didn't sleep with Jessica," I assured her, walking over and sitting beside her on the bed.

Cadence's eyes widened, tears causing the blue splash to glitter. "But you didn't deny it when I asked you about it," she rebutted, wiping at her eyes.

"You didn't really give me a chance. I should have. I was so angry that she would lie to you about it that I didn't even think to deny it. I didn't realize you actually believed her until you took off into the trees . . ."

She looked guilty and embarrassed. Her eyes flicked to Alex who nodded. "Ezra told me everything while he went to pick up Jessica. She insisted on going to Axe Marks the Spot, and he stupidly hoped that he'd get a chance to talk to you there. Even though I told him it was a terrible idea."

Cadence hiccupped a laugh then gave me the ghost of a smile. "That *was* a stupid idea," she muttered, brushing away the tears that had escaped and sped down her cheeks.

I nodded in agreement, reaching out and brushing a lock of hair that fell into her face. "It was an incredibly stupid idea, but I needed to talk to you. I was afraid that if I didn't get Jessica that she'd go hunting for me or alert my father and make things worse for you," I murmured, leaning forward and kissing her forehead when she didn't push me away.

She nodded. "That would have been horrible and made everything feel pointless. I'm sorry I didn't listen to you and that I believed that horrible bitch to begin with."

My eyes widened at the curse from Cadence. She was right, but it was still odd to hear her say it. Hugging her tightly and pressing a kiss to her lips, I allowed myself to truly start to relax for the first time in months.

CHAPTER 31

CADENCE

It didn't take much effort to talk my dad into letting Alex and Ezra stay at the house with me while he was gone. The three of us got ready for Kyle's funeral together, all of us dressed in scarlet, the standard color of mourning for our pack. The red of my dress reminded me of the blood that still remained soaked in the t-shirt and jeans I'd hidden in my closet. It was the last physical piece of Kyle I had left, and I wasn't ready to let go of it yet. I'd sobbed as I'd washed his life from my body, feeling guilty as it ran down the drain and away from me like he was nothing but filth on my skin.

I'd decided to skip makeup, knowing there was no way it would still be decent by the end of the day.

"Alex, you're going to look crazy by the time you can remove that stuff," I whispered, standing behind her as she lined her hazel eyes in thick black pencil like usual.

"I know," she whispered, avoiding eye contact in my mirror, "but I need some semblance of normalcy to survive this day."

Her words resonated with me, and I dropped onto the floor beside her to go through the motions of my own makeup routine. Ezra paced behind us, his eyes rimmed red from crying with us through the night. I glanced at him occasionally, seeing the droop in his usually proud shoulders, the way his gaze was unseeing.

"It's okay to keep feeling in the daytime," I told him, watching him pause and turn his blue eyes on me. "Just because you're in front of the pack today doesn't mean you have to hide the fact that you're also hurting. There is solidarity in tragedy, and you can feel the pain of that without fear. Emotions don't make you less of an Alpha."

Ezra blinked at me. Alex paused in the act of tinting her lips red.

"My father will judge or punish me for expressing weakness, especially in public."

His response made my already aching heart throb. "He's the monster here, Ezra. Don't let his fragile masculinity affect your ability to express yourself."

Ezra audibly swallowed as his armor cracked, exposing the bleeding wounds in his soul. Tears sprung to his eyes, the crystal blue sparkling with them. He suddenly dropped to the floor, pulling his knees to his chest. Arms wrapped around his legs, he dropped his forehead onto his knees as the dam that held back the grief, agony, anger, and fear burst. The feelings he'd been barely restraining, pushing against, and struggling to hide washed over us as Alex and I moved toward him.

It felt like we sat there like that for hours, a millennium of pain had passed, and I felt no less empty of it. If happiness could be as never ending as this suffering, then maybe there would be less hatred in this world.

We pulled ourselves together. Ezra stuffed his pockets with tissues since neither Alex nor I had anywhere to carry them. Stupid dresses. When we thought we could manage, that we'd poured out enough that we wouldn't overflow in public, we made our way outside. Ezra was the first out the door, but I slammed into his back when he stopped abruptly.

Peeking around him, I saw a vase full of amaryllis and monkshood sitting on the front porch. The red and purple looked almost luminescent in the glare of the spring sunlight. I'd been so looking forward to feeling the heated kiss of the sun on my skin, but now even that felt spoiled. Tainted.

Ezra was clearly at his wit's end for the day. With a savage growl that caused goosebumps to erupt over my flesh, he picked up the vase of flowers and stomped into the garage to dispose of the monstrosity. He looked crazed as he threw the vase into the large plastic bin with so much force that it shook, the glass shattering like an explosion. Some escaped the bin, cutting his hands as he glared at the offensive "gift".

Alex and I backed up as he stormed past and returned to the front door. It was already open, fortunately, or I'd have been worried he'd break the damn thing down in his haste. He stepped out onto the front porch and screamed, "Not today, you bastard! How *dare* you do this today!"

I ignored the vibrating of my purse as the three of us hurried to Ezra's car, but I couldn't ignore it anymore as we arrived at the Gardens of Ascension. I scowled at the text that was waiting for me.

Unknown

> It wasn't very nice of Ezra to destroy my gift like that. I thought you could use some beauty on such a dark day.

I resisted the urge to respond, hoping that maybe the stalker would catch on to the fact that I was never going to. Unfortunately, it didn't seem to matter if we responded or not, since the stalker had yet to be dissuaded from prodding us. If they wanted to incite rage, they'd succeeded. Ezra pulled out his phone and glanced at the screen as heat crept up his neck.

As angry as the expression on his face was, the grip of his fingers on mine was worse. He led me to where most of the pack was already congregated. There were children looking somber and some adults who were crying. Lucien looked sad, though the whole thing looked like a mask.

"Does he *feel* anything?" I asked aloud, getting the attention of Alex and Ezra.

Ezra scoffed beside me, appraising his father. "Sure. He feels boredom, disinterest, hate, and rage."

If I didn't believe those words with my entire heart, I might have laughed. Instead, I stared at Lucien as he made small talk and shook hands with those who approached him. When my eyes settled on the Wilkins, I thought my heart might collapse inside my chest.

While Natalie had appeared to be holding herself together as much as possible the night of Kyle's death, she was not doing so now. I could feel the wounds of his absence being sliced open again with each of her wracking sobs as we approached. Chuck stared forward without seeing, lost in the grief that seemed to consume him from the inside out.

When Natalie saw me approaching, she immediately threw her arms around me and held me like I was her salvation. "Cadence, I hope you're doing okay."

It struck me, how loving she could be in the face of such a loss. As we clung to each other, I felt touched that she still cared for me even as she stared down the death of her child. How large her heart must be, to be so loving in spite of so much hurt.

"I'm as okay as possible." I felt hot tears track down my chilled cheeks.

She nodded against my shoulder, pulling back to look at me. "I'm just happy he got to know love and affection from someone like you before he was pulled from this world," she murmured, brushing the tears from my cheeks.

I nodded, pressing my lips together to keep them from trembling. "I love him very much." My voice cracked with the emotions that filled my chest like a balloon about to burst. I was afraid that I'd die too if it did, and wondered if that was preferable to living this life without Kyle. "I miss him."

Natalie nodded, more tears streaking down her cheeks as she gazed at me with hazel eyes just like his. A strong hand gripped my shoulder and I glanced at Ezra, who looked so sad it felt as though I were looking in a mirror at my own anguish.

"Please don't be a stranger when you're home from school. It sometimes feels like you're the only piece of him that we have left in this life." She glanced at Chuck, still gazing transfixed at the ground.

I nodded, wiping the tears from my eyes with the tissue that Ezra supplied. "I will visit every time I come home," I promised, stepping away from them and into the crowd.

Ezra and Alex stayed glued to my side while my eyes wandered around the attendees. A few people glanced at us, but no one seemed to pay us much attention until I looked at Jason. His green eyes were openly glaring, his nostrils flaring as he stood beside Jessica with his arms across his chest.

"I think the creepiest thing about this day is knowing that the murderer is here, celebrating Kyle's murder and watching the mourners grieve the child he killed," I muttered as we all stared at Jason.

He didn't seem perturbed, watching us all in return until Lucien stood on the Ascension Pedestal to garner attention. Everyone found a seat and my two friends were so close I may as well have been sitting in their laps. Lucien's eyes scanned the crowd, his eyes lingering on the three of us for a long moment. When he noticed Ezra holding my hand, his jaw twitched, but there was no other indication that he noticed.

"Today we gather to memorialize the loss of one of our own. Kyle Wilkins, son of Natalie and Chuck Wilkins, was taken by a Luxnositel to meet Kuorir on the evening of April nineteenth. On this sad day, we will burn his earthly form to be spread among the trees so that he may be united with the Goddess in the land with the living once more. Does anyone have any words they would like to share?"

His blue eyes scanned the crowd as I sat there, outraged. The words he said were ones he'd say at any other funeral, but this one should be different. A child was *murdered* at the hands of a pack member who was still making threats against others, including his own *son*. And yet, Lucien stood there with his mask of sadness covering an uncaring interior while those of us with actual *souls* mourned the loss of one of our own. We lost a son, a mentor, a friend, a warrior, a *lover*, but he couldn't say anything genuine or kind to remember Kyle Wilkins with the decency he deserved.

Spurred on by the hate fire of my anger, fueled with my own mourning, I stood and walked to the dais without a trip, slip, or falter. I ignored the way Lucien's nostrils flared and gasps erupted from the crowd around and behind me as I made my way to stand directly at Lucien's side. He didn't try to hide the way he stepped apart from me, as though my touch might smite him on the spot. I wished it would. Even the Griffins would be a better fit than the child abusing Alpha we currently had.

"Good afternoon," I announced, my voice was clear and rang over the crowd without faltering. "Today we mourn the loss of one of our own, Kyle Wilkins. Kyle was taken from us cruelly and without thought. Kyle was stolen from our grasp by a coldhearted monster, leaving us to suffer with not just the death of a son, a classmate, a friend, a boyfriend, but also to suffer with our fear. This cruel act left the rest of us to hide in our homes with the curtains drawn and holding our babies to our chests in the hopes that we are not the next victims of their greed.

"We are left to fear for our lives while The Guard struggle to find retribution for his death. The Alpha has done *nothing* to find out who the murderer is. He lets us sit here, crying and mourning, while the very reason for that is hiding among us. Someone sitting in this crowd killed Kyle Wilkins, and Lucien has done nothing to aid in the hunt for them. After leaving the lower pack members to live in squalor and to survive with the scraps the Betas can spare, he doesn't even have the decency to attempt to solve the case. He cut us off from the rest of the world, leaving us here with no resources and no expertise.

"So, in spite of that, today we will celebrate the life of Kyle Wilkins. He was honest, caring, intuitive, and kind. He uplifted broken hearts and mended them the best he could. Kyle was funny and genuine, loving and thoughtful. He could make me laugh even as I thought my world was crumbling. He warmed my soul when I thought it might be frozen. Kyle was more to me than a boyfriend, he was a kindred spirit." I swallowed, losing some of my momentum as that balloon of emotions swelled to its breaking point.

"Today we mourn the loss of one of the greatest souls in this pack, taken from us to meet Kuorir much too soon. I hope he's enjoying his vacation from this realm in the Fields of Hope, because he did so much healing in this life, he deserves a break. I hope that when he's born again, I'll have the honor of meeting him once more. A life without Kyle is no life at all, and the rest of us will feel the truth of that every day until it's our turn to meet Kuorir ourselves."

There was a moment of silence as everyone let my words sink in. Natalie and Chuck looked touched and emboldened. Ezra and Alex looked proud. As my eyes happened upon Jason, my heart froze in my chest. His green eyes were so sharp I thought I might get sliced apart with them. Wrath seethed under the surface of his skin, flushing it red.

I refused to cower away from Lucian as he approached me. Fueled by my own rage, I tilted up my chin. I was waiting for him to dismiss me, but he didn't. Instead, he closed the gap between us with a cruel expression on his face. His hand pressed on my shoulder, wrapping his fingers around the back against my shoulder blade. I refused to wince as his nails extended into claws, digging their way into my flesh.

"You poor child. How sad it is to see you so blinded by grief that you can't see all we are doing to solve this case. We are doing all that we can, you just can't see it because it's behind the scenes. We have Guard members working tirelessly to bring the murderer to justice. All you need is a little *faith*."

His claws embedded themselves into my back, drawing blood. I could feel the wet ribbons running down along my spine and catching in the waistband of my panties. My nostrils flared, but I didn't move, didn't pull away. I would not allow him that power over me as I made direct eye contact with him.

Pupils widening, he stared down at me as he kept spewing platitudes, but I could no longer hear what he was saying. I felt a tug at my consciousness. My right foot slid backward a couple inches as my body tried to move without me controlling it. My eyes widened as I registered his gift, finally figuring out how he'd had the upper hand on Ezra even as Ezra grew into adulthood.

No!

The thought was screamed through my head, and my body quit pulling away from him. I forced a wall up in my mind, blocking him and his mental control out. His nostrils flared and his dead eyes flared with rage.

"You should have a seat with your friends," he said, a cruel smile carving his face into a terrifying mask of hatred. As I gazed up at him, I recognized the flicker of another emotion.

Fear.

Returning to school the following week felt weird and disorienting. The school, while subdued, seemed to have gone back to normal too quickly. I was worried that I'd fall apart in front of my peers. I still had many moments in the day that I had to hold my ribs together, so my heart didn't escape their grip.

The change in how I was treated was even more overwhelming. Students moved out of my way while smiling sadly at me. I was the girl whose boyfriend was murdered, the one who'd found him. I wasn't comfortable with it and wished they'd go back to whispering about why my family fell from grace instead of feeling sorry for me. All of us lost Kyle, not just me.

Ezra and Alex took turns walking me to class. I think they were afraid something would happen to me in the hallways if I wasn't guarded at all times. While I was also worried, it wasn't for myself. Clearly, this maniac wanted to steal my loved ones from me. I fretted about who they would go after next.

Ezra dropped me off outside of Species Cultures class before hurrying off to his own as the bell rang. Most of the teachers were unbothered by my entourage and them being late for classes. It seemed like they cared about me significantly more than The Guard. Perhaps it's because most of them were Deltas and considered less-than by the Alpha almost as much as the Omegas were.

Sitting down, I ignored Jessica's glare as Mrs. Walker stood at the front of the classroom.

"Today, we are going over the last species in our world." She gestured at the board behind her, the word luxnositel written in black against the whiteboard. "Who can tell me anything about this species?"

I glanced around the room as not a single hand raised. Mrs. Walker sighed and shook her head. "Anyone want to take a guess?" Her mossy green gaze shifted around the room. "Jessica?"

I was pleased to see a flash of panic flicker through her amber eyes as she looked around for help. No one saved her, so she sat up straighter. "Uhh . . . Lux-nose-it-all?" she attempted, saying each portion slowly and with no small amount of hesitation.

Mrs. Walker chuckled. "Nice try, Jessica. This word is luxnositel, luxe-naus-eh-tell. They are reapers who guide our souls to Kuorir, God of the Underworld, for judgment. They are also guardians to the most prestigious supernatural academy in the world, Potencia Sui Generis." She took a moment to write the name of the school under the name. "Potencia Sui, and that's pronounced sue, Generis is a school that is run by the most divine luxnositel to have ever lived, Ender. Ender has a direct connection to the Goddess, Levende, and it's said that they choose their students based on guidance from the Goddess."

My jaw dropped and I leaned forward on my desk. My father attended school at Potencia Sui Generis, though he'd always called it PSG. He'd always said that those years away from my mother were the hardest he'd ever faced, since she stayed here to work instead of going to school.

Jessica raised her hand, though she spoke without waiting to be called on. "They? Who are they?"

Mossy green eyes landed on Jessica, and Mrs. Walker looked displeased. "Why, Ender of course. They say to anyone who questions them that they are older than societal gender norms and refuse to choose a side of the binary." Her words were snippy and sharp, clearly offended that she had to answer such a question.

For once in her life, Jessica actually looked cowed. I was incredibly impressed by Ender, and I hadn't even met them.

Mrs. Walker moved on with the lesson, the distaste for Jessica vanishing as quickly as it had come. "Potencia Sui Generis, PSG for short by anyone who went there, translates to 'power of its own kind.' It uses the translation as its motto. It is quite a school to attend; it's the most prestigious school for supernaturals in the world. I've always wanted to return there since leaving." She said the last words dreamily, a wistful expression coming over her face for just a moment.

Snapping out of it, she looked over the class again. "Can anyone tell me what the other kind of reaper is?" She glanced at each of us before stopping at me. "Cadence?"

My eyes widened and I shook my head. "I'm sorry, Mrs. Walker. I don't know the answer," I rushed, blushing furiously with embarrassment.

Mrs. Walker nodded solemnly, having expected such an answer. "The other reapers are called wraiths. They are luxnositels that have forsaken their duties as reapers and instead consume the souls they are meant to collect. Lore says that luxnositels are turned into wraiths once they murder and consume the soul of a living being. Their wings change from black raven-like wings to the snowy white wings depicted by humans for their angels. It's said that this description was given by those who narrowly avoided their death by a wraith or witnessed another's death, and they thought that they were seeing heavenly angels." Mrs. Walker shook her head, her gray hair shifting around her shoulders with the motion. "Poor humans, they really have no idea what's happening on our side of existence," she said, the sympathy she felt apparent in her expression.

Exiting the classroom, I was surprised to find Brody waiting for me. Typically, I walked to my last class by myself, but it seemed that things had changed while Alex and Brody were in PE together.

"Alex asked if I could walk you to your next class since we share it."

I stared at him for a moment too long, apparently blocking the doorway since Jessica felt the need to shove me out of the way. Brody caught me before I fell to the floor, helping me regain my balance before immediately letting me go like I'd burned him. Scowling, Jessica scoffed and walked away, her skirt swinging around her hips. Brody made a rude gesture at her back and it took significant effort not to snort a laugh.

"Thanks," I muttered, sighing and walking toward my biology class. It was the one I was dreading the most since it was the only class I'd shared with Kyle other than lunch.

Brody caught up to me easily, his long legs allowing him to lope beside me at an easy gait despite my quick steps. The silence stretched on between us as I continuously glanced at his pensive expression.

I was just about to say something to fracture the silence when both of our phones vibrated. In perfect unison, we pulled them out to look at our newest text message.

Unknown

> Is Brody a threat now, too? Again? Cadence, my darling, you need to quit collecting all these obstacles for me to take out.

Brody sucked in a sharp breath. "They're contacting you now, aren't they?" I asked, my voice hushed as we glanced around the emptying hallway.

He nodded, showing me his phone. I read the messages, my forehead creasing.

Unknown

> When will you bastards learn that you can't have her? Leave her or you'll follow in Kyle's footsteps.

> I may even make it slower for you, just to let the lesson really sink in.

"Maybe you should go," I muttered, sliding my phone into my pocket and hurrying away from Brody. He caught up to me in a flash, his fingers gripping my arm and turning me toward him.

Suddenly, I found my back against the wall, Brody's form blocking me as he pressed me into the same alcove that Jessica had forced me into. I was just about to complain when his finger pushed against my lips. Silence descended over us as footsteps came down the hallway. Fear gripped my insides as I stared up into Brody's dark eyes as he examined my face.

The steps stopped behind Brody before a disgusted noise broke the silence. "Gross. Get a room," the voice chastised, and I immediately recognized it as Jason's. Then the footsteps continued on down the hall.

Brody and I stayed still until the steps faded away completely. Only then did he back away from me with an apology already on his lips.

"Don't. I'm not convinced that this whole thing isn't him," I grumbled, straightening out my shirt.

"A year ago, I never would have believed he'd stoop this low. Now, I'm not sure," Brody concurred, leading me toward the last class of the day.

Chapter 32

CADENCE

I was standing at my locker, my entourage circled around me with their own backpacks slung over their shoulders. The stress of life was weighing on me, and with shaking hands, I put my earbuds firmly in my ears. Safe and Sound by Point North and The Ghost Inside immediately started playing, soothing me with the heavy beat and strong lyrics. It was quite fitting for my current life, and it made me feel validated in my own chaos as the group of us headed for the door. My phone vibrated in my hand, causing me to panic as I lifted it to read the text.

Dad

> Hey, Cady. I have to work at the clinic for an emergency. Can you do my shift at the food bank?

Sighing with relief, I responded to the text with an affirmation and tucked it into my pocket. Without turning down the music, I looked to Ezra and said in what I hoped was a quiet voice, "Dad wants me to go to the food bank."

Judging by the way his eyes widened and a laughing smile crept over his lips, I had shouted the words much louder than I had intended. I glanced at Alex and Brody who were laughing as well. Pressing my lips together in embarrassment, I walked more quickly toward the car.

The four of us gathered in Ezra's car, Brody looking almost comical in the back with his long legs and large build. Glancing back, I couldn't stop the grin that crept over my lips. He mouthed something at me, but I shrugged in response and pointed to my earbuds before quickly turning around. I was just closing my eyes and settling into the music when "Changed by You" by Between the Trees started playing.

Keeping my eyes closed, I wrapped my arms around my chest as I was swept back to that night in Sew What. Kyle's hazel eyes filled my mind, that intelligent gaze hovering over me with such intensity that I was certain he could see into the very depth of my soul. As the memory played out, flickers of his eyes, dead and unseeing, broke through the happiness of that one beautiful moment. As his lips pressed to mine in memory once more, a ragged sob tore through my chest and a warm hand rested on my thigh and squeezed gently.

My eyes popped open and saw Ezra's hand on me, grounding me back into the present. I quickly changed the song to "Mess of Me" by Citizen Soldier, wiping the tears that had dampened my cheeks. "Sorry," I muttered, but Ezra shook his head in response.

I read his lips as he said, "Don't be."

Nodding, I stared out the window as we reached the tree line that divided the school from the Delta and Omega territories. Ezra pulled his hand away, giving me space. It felt good, being back around him. My soul ached for Kyle, missing him as crushingly as my mind and heart did. I knew I'd loved him before his passing, but after he was gone, I was more than certain of it. I'd overheard Jessica muttering about how I only said those things because I was looking at him through the rose-colored glasses of death, but I'd thought those things about him from the beginning.

Ezra parked the car across the street from the food bank, the little brick building standing among the surrounding houses with fenced-in yards. We all got out of the car and headed inside. Georgia immediately looked up as the bell rang, raising her brows as she took in the crowd that had entered the small waiting area of the place.

"Wow. I've never seen so many Betas in this little food bank before," she commented, smiling at us, though it didn't reach her eyes. "I take it they're protecting you?" Her voice was hushed as though she knew the murderer was listening.

Hell, I wasn't completely sure that he wasn't listening.

I nodded, stepping around the counter when Georgia reached for me. Her arms immediately went around me, pulling me against her in a spine crushing hug. "He was a wonderful young man," she whispered, putting her hand on my cheek when she pulled back.

I couldn't do anything but nod as I swallowed audibly, trying to push down the lump that painfully stretched my throat. She glanced around me at my three friends, who were hovering awkwardly in the waiting area, their eyes examining the bare white walls and empty boxes stacked against them for patrons to take. Turning her gaze back to me, she nodded. "They're a wonderful group, too. Thank you for coming in. I have to put the kiddos to bed since Angelo is working late. I don't know how they're still logging halfway through the night, but what do I know?"

I smiled sadly, standing back as she grabbed her things and went for the door. "Have a good night, everyone. Keep yourselves safe." She whispered the last sentence, her gaze flicking around the space as though looking for hidden microphones.

With the ringing of a bell, she was gone.

I sighed heavily, looking around the small space before examining my friends. Brody was leaning against the wall, his arms crossed over his chest as he peered at Alex, who stared back at him with a brow raised. Ezra was resting against the other side of the counter from me, looking at both of them curiously.

"Are you having a private conversation or something?" I butted in, leaning forward on the counter.

Alex grumbled and rolled her eyes. "Yes, but that's nothing new," she muttered, wandering over to the door and peeking outside. A glimmer in her hand brought my attention to the shurikens she had woven between her fingers, the tiny knives forming claws that protruded from between her knuckles.

I thought about asking her where she'd had those hidden, but quickly decided I didn't want to know and went back into the storage room. It occurred to me that I'd never felt safer when a sudden presence right behind me caused me to startle. Turning, I saw Brody hovering in the doorway with an unreadable expression.

"Goddess, could you *not* try to give me a heart attack?" I gasped, resisting the urge to put my hand on his chest and nudge him out of the small room. He was several feet away, but in this small space and with his hulking form, he felt way closer than he was.

He brushed his hand over his short hair, slouching against the doorframe as though he could read my thoughts and was trying not to seem so large. "I'm sorry. I was trying to be noisy."

I gaped at him as though he'd said he was Levende coming to visit me in person. "You were *trying* to be noisy? I don't even have headphones in."

Brody chuckled, rubbing the back of his neck and exposing a bulging bicep beneath his t-shirt. I'd never realized just how muscular the guy was. I had always known he was a large volsifi, but I'd never examined him so closely. Never had I noticed just how attractive he was; I was always distracted by how annoying I'd found him. His bronzed skin, black hair, and dark eyes had me swallowing and stepping farther away from him, my back pressed against the shelves behind me. I didn't understand these feelings, and it was easier to run than figure them out.

"Please don't be wary of me. I know I already apologized and that I need to prove these words to you, but I promise I never intended to hurt you. I had all these feelings that I didn't know what to do with and grew up thinking that all women liked forceful men. I saw it in movies and read it in books . . . it never occurred to me that I couldn't just aggressively show you my desires. I'm sorry. I won't overstep again," he pleaded, dropping his hand to his side and losing that edge of shyness he'd had previously.

I nodded, stepping away from the shelving, though not closing much distance between us. "I understand. I hope I didn't hurt you," I replied, fidgeting with the hem of my shirt. It felt nice to get a full, genuine apology from him, even if it was the second time.

He grinned at that, exposing the gap between his front teeth and the dimples in his cheeks. "You didn't. My gift is fire, though you did throw some real heat at me."

He held his hand in front of him, palm open and turned to the ceiling. A blossom of fire erupted from his hand, crackling happily in the space between us.

"Fire," I murmured, eyes wide as he dropped his hand from under the ball of flame. It was the size of a basketball and without thinking, I reached out and touched the side of it. "It's beautiful. Elemental magic is so rare among volsifi," I murmured, letting the warmth tickle over my fingers before pulling away.

Glancing up, I saw Brody eyeing me curiously, his thick, dark brows pulled together.

"What?"

Brody rubbed his chin, shaking his head. "That should have burned you. I wonder if you also have the gift of flame," he pondered aloud, reaching out and swirling his hand around the ball of flame and making it disappear with a pop.

I blinked, looking at my undamaged fingers. "Maybe. I feel hot frequently." I shrugged it off, disregarding the unease that twisted in my gut. Turning, I decided to check expiration dates in order to ease my anxiety.

Brody appeared beside me, examining the cans and looking for the dates. "I did too, for a month or so before I Ascended. Since my birthday is in October, I thought maybe it was just because it was unseasonably hot outside last year, but even ice baths couldn't cool me down."

"I don't think we've ever had a normal conversation before."

He gave me another grin, exposing that gap again and making me smile in response. It was such a perfect touch to his ruggedly handsome face. "I'm glad to share this first with you."

I laid in bed, staring at the ceiling. Everyone needed to go to their respective homes that night after Ezra dropped me off. It felt weird being alone, but maybe it was important. My chest felt bruised and broken as I watched Kyle in my mind's eye.

I'd found myself texting him about the conversation with Brody before I'd realized exactly what I was doing. My heart and lungs had immediately seized up, grief ripping the oxygen from my chest as I gasped fruitlessly for air. I'd read about grief in books before, but I didn't realize just how physically painful it would be to lose someone. Sure, Callum had disappeared, but I was a child, and grief was a word whispered in hallways, hushed declarations buried in tear-soaked pillows. My mother had started this way, wailing and raging through the house for months before she finally hid herself away.

My mind wandered to Callum, my twin who was a perpetual child in my mind. I let myself wonder if he was still alive, if he was thinking about me while I thought about him. Frowning, I angrily wiped at a tear as it slid down my temple and into my hair. Without thinking, I was putting my earbuds in again and putting on the song my mom played for me the first night I'd had the nightmare.

"Flying Dreams" by Katie Campbell was the song. I'd asked her once why she'd picked that one in particular.

"It was what I sang to you when you were babies. A lullaby that I couldn't get out of my head because of how many times I'd watched The Secret of NIMH *during the night. It always put you both immediately to sleep."*

The melody soothed my soul, even with the negative reminder of the nightmare I'd had so many times as a child. The nightmare of reliving the moment they were stolen from us by violent strangers. Humming quietly out of tune, I rolled onto my side and let myself drift off to sleep.

Callum was suddenly in front of me, his white-blond hair blowing around his head like he was caught in a fierce wind. His blue eyes, the right one with a splash of black like his pupil was bleeding, were staring at me with hardened hatred. I tried to walk toward him, but I ran into an invisible wall as he raised his hand toward me, palm out. My limbs suddenly felt heavy, and no matter how hard I tried to raise my arms and legs to run to him, I couldn't lift them from my sides or separate my feet from the ground. Legs growing too heavy, I couldn't stand any longer as I dropped onto my knees upon a stone floor with a heavy thud. My body weighed three tons and I was unable to move as I stared up at him.

"Callum, why won't you let me come to you?" My voice was pained, though his wicked expression didn't change as he gazed down at me from a much older face.

This Callum was my age, his white hair grown out and floating around his shoulders. "Because I don't want you to, Cadence."

I started crying, forcing my arms to drag from my sides and a couple inches into the air in front of me before breaking through whatever was holding them

down. Raising them over my head, I reached for him, begging him to come to me.
"Please, Callum. I need you."

"You don't need me, Cadence. You don't need me, and I don't want you. Stay
away from me," he ordered, his voice harsh and stinging me like a physical whip.

I was sobbing now as he turned and walked away, the black cloak he wore
swept the stone floor as he went. His footsteps faded and so did his silhouette as he
vanished from my sight.

I woke up to "Deep End" by I Prevail playing in my ears. Laying still, I was about ready to roll onto my back to stretch when I realized that something wasn't quite right. Darkness still filled the room for starters. Secondly, my heart was racing, and it took considerable effort to try to keep my breathing even. That was when I realized that there was a presence in my room, and it was hovering over me.

With a high-pitched shriek, I leapt out of the bed and started swinging at the person creeping up on me in the darkness. Music was still blaring in my ears, so I couldn't hear if they were saying anything as I kept throwing my arms around and screaming, "Get out of my room! Get away from me!"

The light turned on, blinding me and causing me to shield my eyes. My dad stood beside the switch, a hand on his heart as he stared at me with wide eyes.

Ripping my buds out of my ears, I screeched, "What the *hell*, dad!"

My dad, hand still on his chest and over his racing heart, looked at me incredulously. "I'm sorry, Cady. You were sobbing so loudly that it woke me up downstairs and I was coming to check on you." He pushed the hair out of his face that had started getting just a bit too long.

Reaching up, I wiped my cheeks with the backs of my hands and found that my fingers were wet with tears. "I'm sorry, dad. I'm just . . . on edge."

Nodding, he walked toward me, wrapping me in a bear hug that I never wanted out of. "I know, Cadybug. But you're so strong, even when things seem impossible. Everything will be okay."

Swallowing, I pulled out of his embrace and crawled back into my bed. He immediately tucked me under the covers and kissed my forehead like he did when I was young. "I love you, Cady. I'm so proud of you."

I blinked frantically, trying to keep more tears from spilling from my eyes. "I love you too, dad."

After he left and turned the light out, I quickly fell back asleep despite the aching in my knees.

CHAPTER 33

CADENCE

"I had a dream about Callum last night," I blurted out, dropping the bomb on my friends as we all sat at the lunch table.

Alex dropped her fork with a clatter and both of the boys stopped with their forks halfway to their mouths as they stared at me.

"It was really weird . . . I could have sworn it was real. I dreamed of him when I was younger once or twice, but he was always distant and didn't really talk to me back then," I continued, thinking of the bruises I'd had on my knees that morning.

I pushed the spaghetti around my plate, not feeling very hungry. The silence of my friends was uncomfortable, but I did my best to ignore it.

"Was he a kid still? Like, a five-year-old?" Brody asked, putting his fork down and giving me his complete attention.

I sighed and put my own fork gently down on my plate. "No, that's what is extra weird. He was our age . . . my age. He was my age when I dreamed of him before, too. I think we would have been ten or so," I answered, glancing between them.

"Did he say anything? Like where he's been for twelve years?" Ezra chimed in.

I scowled. "It was a dream, Ezra. He just told me he didn't want me. I told him I needed him, and he said I don't need him, and he doesn't want me," I grumbled, swallowing the lump growing in my throat. I'd cried plenty over this dream and was determined not to shed anymore tears over it.

Everyone looked surprised. Alex flinched, making a face. "That's rude." She picked up her milk and swirled it in the carton.

Shrugging, I twirled spaghetti around my fork despite having no interest in actually eating it. "It's probably just my subconscious. I was thinking about him before I fell asleep." I gave up on eating and picked up my tray as I stood.

My friends followed suit, not saying much of anything else as we dumped our trays.

ALEX

Ezra and I went to The Crest after school, leaving Cadence and Brody alone to continue making amends. It was an odd thing, feeling comfortable leaving Brody alone with Cady. I was very confident at this point that he wouldn't hurt her and would keep her from harm. Brody wasn't my biggest competition in battle training for no reason.

"There's still nothing new happening in the investigation into Kyle's murder," Ezra bit out, his fingers gripping the steering wheel as he drove us through Beta territory to the top of the mountain. "Lucien has continued to do nothing but bitch about Cadence calling out his incompetence at the funeral."

Even after all these years, it was odd hearing him call his father by his first name. Truth be told, I'd probably do the same if I had a megalomaniac for a father. My own wasn't a treat, but at least he didn't beat me. I was fairly certain he at least loved me. "I'm surprised that didn't spur him into action."

"It's probably because there's literally no evidence. *Nothing.* We might be able to figure something out from the phone number, but no one is putting too much effort into it. It's probably a burner number anyway," he muttered, his knuckles turning white while the steering wheel complained under his grip. "I just want to know who this bastard is so I can kill him."

I nodded, leaning back in the seat as he pulled into the lot for The Crest. "I want to slit their throat, both for stalking Cady and for murdering Kyle. He didn't deserve to die at all, and definitely not like that."

We walked into The Crest, heading for the locker rooms to dress for combat training. Not that there was much to dress in, since we were fighting as wolves today.

In a black robe, I walked into the gym to find someone already standing on the mat.

Jason, looking smug, stared at me as I entered the room and stopped. Ezra was right in front of me, his hands clenched at his sides. "What do you want, Jason?" he snarled, his aura enough to make *me* drop to my knees, and it wasn't even directed at me.

The smug look faltered slightly, though Jason kept his arms crossed over his chest. "I want you to get back with Jessica."

Ezra rolled his eyes as I stepped up to stand at his right side. I wasn't his General yet, but I would be in the future and would protect him from this threat now. Jason glanced at me warily, causing a small smirk to curve my mouth before I wiped it away.

"There's no way I'm going to get back with her, Jason. Now that we have that settled, how about you scoot on home to coddle her some more, eh?" he stated, his face still carefully blank. I could see the tension in his jaw that gave away his anger.

Jason laughed in a way that made goosebumps erupt over my arms. It was wicked. Evil. Unhinged. "Come on, Ezra. You dated her for a couple months; you can't just lead her on like that. It's not like Cadence needs *three*–oh wait, Kyle's dead now, so *two* guys panting after her like some wolves in heat. Leave her to Brody, and date Jessica." He took a step forward. "Then I'll only have to take out Brody to have her to myself."

Ezra's façade broke, his eyes glowing as his knuckles cracked with the tension he was putting into his fists. Jason's grin widened as he took another couple of steps forward until he was only six feet in front of us. "That's right, Ezra. I'm pining for your precious bitch. Have been for years, actually. I was hoping your dad would kill you off before we got to this point, but it turns out he has too much *restraint*. I thought maybe she had a thing for Alphas and that if you and my sister shacked up, she'd come for the next available Alpha." He pointed his thumbs at himself like a cocky child.

"Did you kill Kyle? Your own best friend?" I snapped at him, causing Jason to throw his head back and cackle.

"No, but I wish I did. Genius move to take him out, right? And by ripping out his throat? God, I'd have loved to do it." He slid his tongue over his teeth as they elongated.

Repulsed by his words, I pulled my shurikens from my pocket and laced the knives between my fingers, letting the rings on the handles collect in my palm. I was so angry and disgusted that I didn't even care that he was telling the truth. My power rang the bell of honesty in his words, but that didn't make what he was saying any better. "How *dare* you!" I snarled, moving before he could even defend himself and swinging my arm upward.

Nothing appeared on his face for a moment, and he looked at me like I was insane. "You didn't even get me," he muttered, aghast as he reached up and touched the wounds just as they started to drip. The crimson stained his pale skin as the micro slices finally started bubbling over with blood.

"I never miss," I promised, advancing toward him again and causing his eyes to widen with panic.

He backed up, tripping on the edge of the mat and falling onto his back with a crackling gasp as the wind fled his chest on impact.

"Alex!" Ezra shouted, but I was too focused on the kill. Even if Jason was telling the truth about Kyle, he signed his own death certificate with those hideous words. Cadence wasn't here to tame the beast inside me, and she was licking her lips, hungry for the blood of her enemy. Rage pooled inside of me as I licked my own lips in unison with the monster roaring to life inside of my soul. She was angry and vengeful, and I fed off the energy as I stood over Jason with my fist raised and ready for a fatal punch to the throat.

A hand dropped onto my shoulder, pulling me backward and spilling me unceremoniously onto the floor just outside of the mat. My tailbone crashed onto concrete, making a sharp inhalation cut through my teeth. Looking up, I saw the dark eyes of Mr. Rutger glaring at me with such intensity that I nearly cowed beneath him. However, my mind still roared with the thirst for blood, and I stood up and stared him down. I refused to bow to any man but Ezra, and even then, I'd have to think about it.

I glanced over at Ezra, confused as I realized he was not actually a human. His golden fur was curled over his body as he bared his teeth at Mr. Rutger and Jason. In a blink, Ezra was shifting back and glaring at our teacher.

"Is there a problem here?" Mr. Rutger inquired, his voice calm despite the storm in his eyes.

"No, sir," Ezra grunted, his eyes still pinning Jason to the mat.

I also stared at Jason, unsatisfied with his injuries even as blood dripped down his throat and stained the collar of his shirt crimson.

"Oh. Were you just leaving then?" Mr. Rutger looked steadily between the two of us.

"Yes, sir."

I nodded, turning on my heel and walking out of the gym.

"He said *what*?" Brody shouted, pacing around Cady's room. He seemed almost comically large in the small space, his quick circles spanning the entirety of the room.

"He wasn't lying either. I could tell. That doesn't mean he's not involved with the person who did," I muttered, sitting beside Cadence on the bed. She looked shellshocked, and I couldn't blame her.

Ezra sat in Cadence's desk chair, leaning forward with his elbows on his knees as he watched Brody storming around, likely wishing he could be doing the same. "You moved faster than I could. I wanted to kill him with my teeth, since I didn't get to last time," he said, sitting up straight and bracing his ankle on the opposite knee. "This is just insane. Did you know he wanted anything to do with Cadence, Brody?"

Brody stopped and shook his head. "No. He never once said anything about Cadence other than his regular insults." Cadence winced and Brody noticed. "I never agreed with the things he said. I may have been crude, but I never said anything negative about you or your appearance." His tone admitted his concern.

She nodded, looking down at her hands as they clasped together in her lap. While Brody may not have been so lucky with Ezra and me, I knew that Cadence would have forgiven him with time even if he had said mean spirited things about her. Cadence was forgiving to a fault, and that was one of the things I tried my very best to protect her from, getting hurt because of giving grace to losers who didn't deserve it.

Frowning, I glanced between the three of them, each lost in their own thoughts. Just then, my phone dinged and all four of us jumped. Glancing down, I saw a message from my father requesting that I return home to discuss the information he'd heard about the incident in the gym. I rolled my eyes and dropped it back into my lap without responding.

"Dad heard about the incident with Jason. Now he wants to talk about it." I glanced at Ezra.

Ezra was watching me closely, his pale blue eyes betraying the concern he felt for confronting his father later. "Lucien has been mysteriously quiet since Kyle's murder. I don't know what, but I think he's planning something."

"Planning something like what?" Brody asked, coming to a stop and crossing his arms over his chest.

Ezra shrugged, rubbing his face with his hands. "Who the hell knows? I'm certain that it's nothing good for anyone but him." He dropped his hands onto his thighs and stood.

Brody and Ezra switched places, allowing Ezra to start pacing the room. I turned my attention to Cadence who was staring down at the floor with tears sliding down her cheeks. Frequently I found myself wondering how much pain she was in and refusing to talk about. Reaching out, I took her hand in mine and squeezed her fingers, relieved when she squeezed mine in return. At least she was still present this time. Right after Kyle's murder, there were times she was so lost in her grief that she didn't respond to anything, not even physical touch. I had wondered briefly if her broken heart would kill her in the end.

Turning my attention back to the men, I saw them both watching Cadence. Their expressions were blends of concern and adoration. I felt a brief pang of jealousy that no one ever looked at me that way. I was more than happy that Cadence had attention and love, but I wanted that too. Hopefully my time would come.

CHAPTER 34

CADENCE

Now that Brody was fully in the rotation, I was very seldom alone. It had been a couple weeks of quiet other than random texts, and that was somehow worse than the constant onslaught. The lack of any happenings had me nervous that what was coming was going to be bigger, though I fiercely hoped I was incorrect. The four of us converged in the library after school nearly every day and during any free moments we had and quietly discussed updates and plans for rotations.

"I received some texts before, when I'd been showing an obvious interest in Cady, but they'd stopped shortly after the incident in the hallway when she threw me away from her. I assume it's because the stalker didn't think I was a threat any longer since I'd backed off," Brody said, looking down at his phone as though it might explode at any moment. All of us looked at our phones that way now. "I don't think any of us should ever be on our own."

"I'm surprised I've never received any texts from this person," Alex pointed out, gesturing to her own phone as it lay on the table.

I frowned. "Maybe it's because this person assumes that I'm straight?" I suggested, shrugging as everyone looked at me. "Maybe they don't perceive you as a threat because you're a woman and they figure I'm only interested in men."

Alex scowled. "If that's true, it's really annoying. Not that I want to be threatened but come on. I've been with women before."

I shrugged again, spinning my phone on the table to occupy the nervous energy in my hands. "I have no idea. It was just a suggestion. And just because *you're* not straight doesn't mean that I'm the same sexuality. They probably just assume I am because I was with Ezra, regardless of how archaic that is." I paused, fidgeting. "I don't even know what my sexuality is. I hear people talking about sexual attraction and I just . . . don't have it for anyone. Maybe I'm a dud."

Alex rubbed my back. "You are *not* a dud. I think you're just asexual."

"What does that even mean?" I asked, putting my face in my hands.

"Exactly what you said. Not finding people sexually appealing. You find people pleasing to look at, but it's more of looking at humans as a work of art than as sexual beings," Alex explained, easing my stress. It was a relief not to feel so abnormal.

I sighed heavily. "That's surprisingly accurate."

I peeked through my fingers to see Alex shrugging. "Sometimes I do my research."

"In any case," Brody interrupted, looking between us all, "I don't think any of us should be alone. Kyle was no Alex, but he wasn't a weakling either. It took someone with a tremendous amount of power to take him down. That's not something to take lightly."

Ezra's phone buzzed, a moment later Brody's followed suit. They both looked down and sighed wearily.

"More texts?" Alex questioned, though we both knew the answer.

Their nods were all the confirmation I needed. This had gotten out of hand long ago and I was on the verge of losing all semblance of my sanity.

"I take it The Guard is still refusing to intervene?" I looked between Alex and Ezra.

Ezra scowled. "They are. There's also been nothing new on the case. It's like the murder was committed by a ghost."

Before I could stop it, my brain took me back to that night, to the feel of Kyle's rapidly cooling body in my arms. His hazel eyes looking up at me, though they'd never examine me with that intensity of his ever again.

A hand on my shoulder brought me back to the present and I realized I'd been sobbing loudly. Wary eyes were looking at me from around the room and I immediately stood up. "Don't follow me. I need a minute to myself." I left no room for argument as I took off through the aisles.

None of them moved, taking my request seriously as I quickly escaped the library.

It was strange to walk the halls without my three constant companions. At least one of them had even been sleeping at my house every night, making sure I was okay and that no one was murdering me while they weren't there to stop it from happening. That thought made a shudder roll down my spine as I walked toward the closest restroom. I hoped that whoever the psycho was didn't occupy the school at that moment in time, or at least that they weren't following me.

Tears dripped from my chin, catching on the front of my t-shirt and dampening the gray cotton. I wiped my eyes, drying my fingers on my jeans. Feeling overheated, deeply saddened, and overwhelmed, I couldn't wait to hide in a stall from the rest of the world. Maybe if I could disappear into solitude, even for just a moment, I could reclaim my sanity and purge the grief that was threatening to overtake me again.

The bathroom was empty when I walked in, the tiles on the walls echoing my footsteps as I went to the farthest stall. I had just gotten settled on the toilet seat lid when the door opened again as someone entered. Not thinking anything of it, I took a moment to glance at my phone, swiping through social media as I took advantage of my rare alone time to ground myself.

I startled as someone hit the first stall, the door flying inward with a loud bang that made my brain rattle. Bracing my hands on the walls of the stall on either side of me, I willed my heart to still before abruptly standing up. The next door rattled the entire row as the stall door was thrown open and I swallowed the shriek of terror building in my throat. I knew in my soul that this was all for show, but that didn't make me feel any better as the stall door beside mine was whipped open. I clambered onto the toilet seat. Mine was next, and that made my pulse quicken with dread as silence rang through the room, pressing against my eardrums in the aftermath of all the noise.

Clamping my hand over my mouth to try and silence my panic, I crouched on the toilet seat and waited. The quiet felt like it was closing in on me, the monotonous lack of sound only broken by the person's breathing on the other side of the stall door. I felt like we were in a stalemate, and suddenly I was certain it would never end. My phone vibrated in my hand, the sound loud as it rattled against the wall I was using for balance.

I gasped in alarm and a low chuckle sounded from the other side of the door, exposing them as a male. The lunatic enjoyed my fear, inhaling it like a drug as he took a deep breath. I heard him lean his weight against the other side of the door, waiting to hear my reaction. I didn't feel I had much of a choice and glanced at the screen.

Unknown

> I can taste your fear. It's more intoxicating than any substance I've ever abused.

A small whimper escaped me and the male on the other side of the door groaned at the sound. I wanted to vomit, the snacks I'd eaten while we congregated in the library were revolting assertively in my stomach. Right then, I would take any punishment for any sins I'd ever committed if that meant this frightening person would leave me alone.

My phone vibrated again, and I started sobbing, the sound muffled by my hand. It was still pressed firmly over my mouth like it would save me from the wraith that was stalking me. He was so close I could practically sense his aura as it wafted through the thick plastic separating us. It made chills roll over my flesh like a physical caress. Not able to stop the keening wail that pushed itself from my body, I grieved life as I knew it. I checked the text that had come through and my sobs came freely. The floodgates opened. I cried like a child, the monster under my bed mere inches from my face.

Unknown

> I could easily get you right now. You're right there, mine for the taking.

> As much as I love the chase, I want you to come to me willingly.

> And you will, once Ezra and Brody are dead and burned. Just like Kyle.

Heavy footsteps walked away, relief and terror swirling in my veins. I wanted to reach for the hope that he was leaving like the Goddess' hand was extended toward me, but I didn't want to feel the crush of disappointment if he came back to continue his haunt.

I collapsed onto the toilet seat before melting to my knees on the floor as the door to the bathroom slammed shut behind him. Curling into the fetal position on the tiles, I barely even registered the filth as I pressed my hands to my face and let the tears continue to come. Holding them back was futile.

Time had become a thing of fairy tales as I laid there on the cold floor. I had no idea how much of it had passed, lost in grief. I knew that I'd never feel safe again, no matter where I was or who I was with. Every moment of every day for the rest of my life would be spent looking over my shoulder for a monster sent from the depths of the Plains of Purgatory where the wraiths reigned like wicked kings over the sinners of the earth. This stalker was my own personal hell, coming from the darkest pits to pull me down with him.

The door banged open and hurried footsteps entered as a scream tore from my throat before I could register its existence. Adrenaline hit me differently so soon after the terrifying encounter, and I whipped open the door with fists flying as I collided with a hard body. Arms came around me like a steel trap as I became a wild animal, clawing and biting my way to safety.

I barely registered the voices, continuing my assault on the faceless person holding me until a sharp slap caught me on the cheek and brought me back to reality. Ceasing my movements, I heard Alex's voice shouting my name as she grabbed my face in her hands and forced my dark eyes to meet her hazel ones. Her irises became my sole focus as I latched onto the familiar gaze holding mine. I knew in my soul that it wouldn't be permanent, but for this moment in time I was blissfully encased in serenity.

That night, I laid between Ezra and Brody, sardined in Ezra's bed this time. Alex had taken up residence on a futon we'd heaved in here from a spare bedroom. Lucien was occupied with meetings for the High Table of the Volsifi and would be out of town for the next several days. What they were discussing, none of us knew. Ezra said his father told him to butt out of it and it would be his business when he was the Alpha of the pack and King of the Volsifi. Typical.

Shadows hung across the ceiling like cobwebs, the only light coming from a nightlight in the bathroom. I found its gentle blue glow to be comforting as it made the dimness feel like some sort of portal to another world.

I wasn't sure any of us were sleeping, though none of us spoke. Each of us were lost in our own thoughts, the processes too incomplete to discuss yet.

"We need a plan to catch this guy," I said, breaking the silence that had gone on for far too long between us.

Brody shifted beside me, turning his deep brown gaze to examine the side of my face as he considered what I was saying. "Do you have one prepared for us?" he inquired, tucking his hands beneath his cheek. It was odd, to be looked at as the leader of our ragtag group.

Ezra and Alex said nothing, but I could feel them listening. "I need to be the bait," I whispered into the darkness, shrugging one shoulder like it was the most logical thing in the world.

"No," Ezra spoke beside me, his body tense with what I assumed was the idea of letting me use myself to draw in a predator. "That's not happening."

I sat up, peering at him, shifting to untwist my shirt from around my torso in frustration. "It makes the most sense," I rebutted, not flinching as he sat up suddenly and his face became too close to mine.

"I will not risk your life just to catch this guy," he snarled, his blue eyes cold as they bore into mine. It was the first time I saw any hint of his father in his gaze. I hated it. "We will figure something else out, but you will not be bait."

Refusing to back down even as his dominant aura flowed over me, I hardened my gaze and did not cower to him. "It's the only thing that will bring him out of the woodwork and you know it. He said it in black and white, he wants me to come to him willingly." I gestured to my phone where it sat on his nightstand.

Ezra's face was blank as he examined my face, like he was afraid if he looked away for even a moment that he might forget a feature of it. My own gaze never wavered. Alex sat on the futon, breaking the tie that hung between us like a physical object. The sledgehammer of her words came down on me and made anger flare in my soul.

"I agree with Ezra. I don't think that you should be the one to face him, and definitely not alone." Her voice was hushed, a gentle stream trickling between the two walls of obstinance that Ezra and I had evoked in our disagreement. If anyone could wear those walls away and create an agreement, it would be her.

Brody sat up and looked between Ezra and me. "I third that motion, if I'm given a vote. While I don't think you're incapable of defending yourself, you haven't been trained like the three of us have been."

"What do you propose we do, then?" I muttered, looking between the three of them.

"Bait and switch," Alex offered, looking at Ezra for his opinion. "We give him a place and he will find me there instead of her."

"He'll just leave," I rebuked, popping the bubble of her plan with ease. "If it's not me there waiting for him, he will either lash out and come for you, or he will run and then that advantage is lost forever. It has to be me."

"Again, I am telling you that that is not happening." Ezra put his metaphorical foot down.

The whole thing made me want to scream at him. We needed to do this, and he needed to quit being so stubborn about it.

"I didn't realize you were the sole decision maker in this quad," I snapped at him, my skin feeling too hot the more agitated I got. "This is my life. It's my decision." I could feel myself sweating, heat pouring out of me like I was a breathing furnace. "You may be the future Alpha of this pack, but I'll be *damned* if I let you govern my choices this way."

All of their eyes widened as they looked at me. Scowling, I looked between them before getting off the bed with a growl of frustration. It didn't matter what they were looking at, I didn't care. What I did care about was finishing this thing, and I knew the only way was for me to face the problem head on. I was tired of cowering away from my issues like a scared little mouse.

As I lifted my gaze to Ezra, I knew he did not agree with me in the slightest.

Chapter 35

EZRA

The next day was unpleasant, the four of us still felt off-kilter and I didn't like the discord. Alex, Cadence, and I had always been tight knit, fitting together like puzzle pieces. When Brody joined us, he clicked right into place like he had always been there.

I was certain Cadence felt betrayed by all of us for disagreeing with her plan. Also, I knew she felt like I was being overbearing and controlling by not letting her go through with her plan. If it had been anyone else, I might have considered it, and I knew that was grossly unfair. I didn't think that I could survive if anything happened to her. When I'd gotten that call from Alex the night of Kyle's murder, I was certain that a piece of me died until I'd seen her alive.

Lucien was returning home the next day and I was dreading his arrival. Preparations were being made for the upcoming holiday, Renovāminis. It was the spring holiday that our pack celebrated by planting new trees for those we'd chopped down through the year followed by a gala in the evening. It also happened to be the end-of-school celebration for the students. Sweetened bread was broken, and games were played at the gala. Fortunately, all pack members were invited, and it was held at the Gardens of Ascension.

More importantly, Cadence's birthday and Ascension was the next day, the fourteenth of May. She hadn't mentioned her own Ascension in months, but it had been weighing heavily on my mind. I could feel her power growing, though I couldn't tell what exactly it would be.

"It's not uncommon for powers to display before you Ascend," I said aloud.

"No, it isn't," Brody agreed beside me, jarring me out of my thoughts. I glanced over at him. His chin rested on his fist like his head was too heavy to hold up. "It's not uncommon at all. I did it myself, about one month before, though I never really got burned when I should have even as a child. I never burned from the sun either, but mom always said it's because I got her Hawaiian complexion."

I studied him, contemplating what he was saying. "You're right. Maybe I'm overthinking things," I muttered as Mrs. Walker stood up from the front of the class to give her lecture.

CADENCE

"Dad texted me and told me I needed to stop by the food bank before going home." I glanced up from my phone at my friends.

"Sure thing, Cadybug," Ezra replied, changing direction to head into Omega territory.

The drive was quiet, "She's Quiet" by The Home Team played softly on the radio as we all lost ourselves in thought. I pondered the possibility of going over Ezra's head and meeting with the stalker regardless of what my friends thought about it. It's not like the creep wasn't a text away. This insanity needed to end, and it wasn't going to if I didn't finish this. I wanted to Ascend in peace without worrying about someone attacking me after I'd grown into the volsifi I was destined to be.

Ezra pulled up to the food bank, parking the car alongside the curb. Humming to myself, I waited for my friends to catch up to me before we all entered the food bank. Blinking, I took in the sight before me before frowning in confusion.

"What's going on?" I examined all the faces occupying the small space. It was quite cramped, and my three friends crowded at my back.

Dad stepped forward, a bright grin on his face that had me smiling in return. I hadn't seen him this pleased in a long time, and it felt refreshing. I glanced behind him. Georgia was holding something behind her back with Molly's help. Alice, William, and various other Omegas stood around them, filling the space behind the counter and just in front of it.

"We appreciate everything you've done for us throughout your entire life, Cadence. You've been a bright spot in our dim lives since your birth." Dad took a moment to take a deep breath. "After your brother was taken from us, you've lived on proudly with your chin raised, never failing to put others before yourself. So, all of us scraped together the necessary funds to do something special for you in return for all of your unending kindness."

Dad took a step back, allowing Georgia and Molly to move forward. Georgia slowly unzipped a black garment bag, revealing something that glittered within it. My hands came up to cover my mouth as a golden dress was revealed, the skirt flowing out of the bag where the train brushed the floor.

"Is that the fabric you sent William to get that night I was here with . . ." A choked sob caught the words in my throat, making me unable to finish the sentence as Molly nodded.

"Yes, it's exactly that. We put together a gown fund for you and had Mrs. Walker contact the Shadowvale Coven in London for the fabric. It's made of upir magic and elvafe golden strands. It's as durable as chainmail and flows like liquid gold," Molly explained, nodding again as I hesitantly reached out to touch the dress.

It felt cool against my fingers, and while it maintained its foundation, it felt like I was dipping my hands into a chilled lake. Pulling my fingers away, I nearly expected them to be coated in gold, but they were still as pink as ever.

"Can I try it on?" I breathed, unable to take my eyes off the dress.

"Of course, you can. I insist that you do," she responded, pulling me into the back and gesturing for Alex to follow.

With the dress on, I felt like a goddess on earth. It twisted in the front between my breasts under a sweetheart neckline that extended around my upper arms in an off-the-shoulder style. It hit at my natural waist, making it look luxuriously tucked before flowing over my hips and to the floor. A slit ran up the right side, exposing my leg to the upper thigh as I stepped into the pair of strappy golden sandals they'd also gotten for me. Alex knelt in front of me, tying the golden ribbons around the middle of my calf into a delicate bow at the back.

When she tilted her face up to look at me, I tried my best not to cry.

"I feel like I'm bowing to a Goddess right now," she murmured, not even a glimmer of teasing in her voice. She meant those words, and it made me burst into tears.

Alex stood and took my hands in hers. "You should go and drop their jaws to the ground."

When I appeared, everyone was against the opposite wall so that they could see my entrance. As I rounded the counter, I noticed that Ezra and Brody were standing right in front. Ezra's mouth had fallen open, his eyes wide and glittering. Brody looked as stoic as ever, though I couldn't ignore the way his gaze swept over me with pleased appraisal before catching my eyes and holding them.

Embarrassed, I resisted the urge to disappear into the back. Instead, I lifted my chin as my father had praised me for doing. "Thank you all so much for this gorgeous gown. It's far more than I deserve. I imagine this cost a fortune, and I only get to wear it once . . ." My fingers wrapped in the skirt, the cool feeling sweeping over my fingertips.

"Once? You're wearing this for your Ascension as well." Dad stepped forward again and leaned down to kiss my forehead.

"We are supposed to wear white for our Ascension," I rebutted, frowning up at him.

Dad smiled proudly and shook his head. "Not you. You've always deserved to stand out from the crowd."

That night, I laid in bed. The room was mostly dark, the moon peeking in through the space between the slats of my blinds. Glancing to my closet door, I saw the dress glimmering in one of the stray rays of moonlight. Smiling to myself, I closed my eyes and drifted off to sleep.

The clearing appeared, sun dappling the distant mountains as it peeked through the light cloud cover. A mist fell from the sky, making my skin feel damp. I frowned and looked around the clearing before spotting the man standing just outside the clearing. His eyes were on me, eyeing me warily.

"Remember me?" I asked him, playing with the hem of my shirt.

"How could I forget the woman of my dreams?"

I pressed my lips together, dropping my gaze to my feet for a moment before looking up at him again. "How did you know how to help me last time?"

He rolled his jaw, averting his gaze from me. I waited, watching him consider what, or if, he was going to tell me. Sighing, he took a couple steps closer, as if he were afraid to get too close.

"My mother was murdered when I was twelve. I was forced to watch it happen."

My heart stuttered in my chest. I pressed a hand to my throat as the horror set in. "I'm sorry."

He didn't respond, gazing out at the ravine as he lost himself in his thoughts.

"Don't be. My father is a cruel man. She was not the first to die by his hands. She won't be the last." His voice was cold, clipped. The usual melody that it held was absent and I mourned the loss of it. "I wonder every day if I might be next. I think that's harder than losing her was. I'm not ready to follow her."

I nodded, glancing at the cliff's edge where I'd stood and contemplated my own death the last time I'd visited this place.

"I hope you don't follow her. The longer this goes on, the more certain I am that you're real. Maybe one day I'll meet you," I whispered, afraid to look at him as I wrapped my arms around myself.

He chuckled. "I am, unfortunately, real. How this connection forged or who you are, I don't know. I also hope to find out some day."

I shifted my weight from foot to foot. Contemplating. "Should we arrange it?"

Lifting my eyes to his, I watched him study me. "No. If it's meant to be, it will happen on its own."

He was right, but I still felt shunted. Ridiculous, since I had way too many men in my life to worry about at the moment.

"Do you forget my face when you wake, too?" I asked. Pursing my lips, I felt my face flush with embarrassment.

He nodded, sighing. "Yes. Try as I might to remember, it vanishes even as I wake. It's like my tortured existence needs more ammunition. I can't even remember the face of a beautiful woman when I'm not looking at it."

My face grew even hotter, flushing down my neck to my chest. His eyes examined me closely. "That blush looks good on you."

I half smiled, unsure how to respond. "Thank you."

He pressed his lips together. "I'm being woken," he said, his voice hushed.

I didn't want him to leave but nodded. "Don't forget me."

A tiny smile quirked one corner of his mouth. "Dream of me, and I'll be there."

Chapter 36

CADENCE

"Cady dear, can you hand me that sack of soil?"

As much as I'd wanted to wear my earbuds this morning, I'd refrained for this very reason. Straightening, I stretched my back before grabbing the burlap sack of soil that sat beside me and heaving it across the ground until I got to Brody.

"Goddess, you couldn't have come over for it yourself?" I snapped at him when he finally relieved me of the burden.

He grinned, exposing the gap in his two front teeth. "Of course. I definitely *could* have, but that wouldn't have been as much fun."

I glared at him, attempting to blow an errant strand of wavy hair from my face. It didn't work and Brody took it upon himself to tuck it behind my ear with a gloved finger. "Ahh, and now I've smeared your face with dirt. Perfection. I've always fancied myself an artist."

I curled my lip back in feigned annoyance. "And that's the only mark you'll ever leave on me, Brody Griffin."

He chuckled and raised one dark brow. "We shall see about that, Cadence Nocetti."

Scowling, I turned my back on him and returned to my tree, kneeling in the dirt and patting the soil around its roots. It was an oak sapling, one of many trees planted this year to replace all the ones we cut down to continue our trade for resources. Leaning down, I closed my eyes and whispered, "Dearest Mother of Nature, please accept this sapling in payment for all that you've provided us over the past year."

Standing, I turned to Alex who was leaning down to whisper to the sapling she'd just planted. Her unruly golden curls were piled on top of her head in a bun as chaotic as she was, and I smiled to myself as I watched her. As if sensing my gaze, her hazel eyes popped open and immediately met mine.

Taking off one of my gloves, I reached into the pocket of my leggings and pulled out a crocheted wreath. It wasn't going to last, I would have to replace it every year, but that was okay. I felt the eyes of my friends on me as I wandered into the tree line to find one worthy of my offering. My boots made only a slight crunching over the fallen needles that hadn't yet decayed and absorbed into the earth. It was challenging to find the perfect tree, because there were so many good options. I also didn't want someone to take it down before I could return and replace it. It was privacy that I craved; privacy for the alter I was creating in his memory.

The trees this close to the school weren't ever cut down. The ones we had been replacing were the nearest they would go, since logging was loud, and they didn't want to distract the students while also removing the shelter of trees.

I found one after several long moments; a beautiful eastern hemlock that was tall, but still relatively young. Kyle Wilkins was young, but just as wise and mature as this tree, which guarded everything in its sight. I could tell this tree was willing to accept my gift as I brushed my fingers over its trunk and the bark scraped against my fingertips. Reaching onto the tallest branch I could grasp, I hung the crocheted wreath in the fine, soft needles. The yarn was thin and eggplant purple, Kyle's favorite color, carefully woven into a dainty lace.

I whispered to the listening evergreen, "Please watch over this for me. I'm hoping that if this is kept safe, then Kyle will be happy until it's time for him to be reborn. It's all that I have to offer for him." I could feel the loving energy flowing beneath its bark.

My heart felt hollow, Kyle's imprint on my soul unable to be filled or forgotten. I knew that no matter how much time passed, that piece of my heart would ache with his absence. I just hoped that with enough time and love from others, it wouldn't ache with quite as much fervor as it did right then.

Touching my forehead to the trunk, I said another prayer to the tree and the gods as my fingers danced over the rough bark. Hemlocks held a spiritual significance, their elegant boughs giving the teaching to accept change gracefully. Pulling away, I tilted my head back to gaze up into the branches, the rich, green needles quivered with life. "Help me find you next summer, okay?"

I walked back into the clearing filled with fresh saplings. My friends were waiting for me in various positions of feigned relaxation. Ignoring their tension, I pulled my phone from my pocket and glanced at the time. "It's noon," I said, my voice more deadpan than I'd intended. Forcing my mouth into a smile to convey more emotion, I added, "It's time for lunch. Are we ready to go?"

A snort sounded behind me, and I turned to see Jessica, her flaming red hair in a plait over her shoulder. "Of course, you'd be excited for lunch. Or are you just excited to quit doing any actual physical activity?"

Shame stained my cheeks pink. The sun beating down from above did not help the heat growing in my face. Frowning, I turned my back on her only to nearly run into Alex, who was already heading toward Jessica.

"Why don't you go eat a horse tranquilizer, Jessica?" she shouted, fighting against me as I grabbed her arm to keep her from chasing the girl down. "You look so much like one, you might not even die from it. How unfortunate."

Brody grunted. "Don't offend horses like that, Alex."

"Let her go, Alex. She's not worth it. She's not worth *anything*." I spoke loud enough to reach Jessica, who levelled at me with a glare.

Her mouth popped open in a retort, and she took a step toward us before Jason appeared behind her and grabbed her shoulder. Leaning down, he whispered something in her ear, causing an evil smirk to appear on her face. "You're right." She giggled as she tucked her arm in his while they walked away from us.

"That was weird," Ezra muttered, leaning on his shovel and watching them leave.

Scoffing, I turned and picked up my tools to return to the bed of the truck they'd come from. "Whatever. I'm starving. Let's go eat and get ready for the gala."

EZRA

I adjusted my tie, golden to match Cady's dress, as I looked into the full-length mirror. It felt odd, but the four of us were gathered in Brody's house for once, still carefully avoiding the Pierce residence. Bernard had made it clear that he was disinterested in seeing Cadence as anything more than a nuisance.

"Don't you four look stunning," Stella Griffin complimented, appearing in the doorway of his large bedroom. Her bronzed skin and dark hair reminded me very much of Brody, her tall stature only adding to that vision. The black cocktail dress she wore hugged her lithe frame as she walked farther into the room.

Alex stood up from the couch against the wall, her own seafoam gown shifting with her movements, and walked over to hug Stella tightly. "Thank you."

"Alex, where is Ivan? Weren't you with him at the Novzima party?" Stella asked, glancing around as though Ivan might be hiding somewhere in the large room.

Alex flushed and shook her head. "No, we broke up in the beginning of March. I had too much going on to worry about appeasing someone else," she answered, causing Cadence to look up abruptly from where she sat on the edge of Brody's bed.

Guilt surrounded her, making me wonder if Alex had said anything to Cady about her decision to quit dating when everything started to truly hit the fan.

"I'm sure you'll find someone worth your efforts when the time is right." Stella offered a gracious smile. Then her dark eyes shifted to Cadence who fidgeted awkwardly as though she was hoping no one would notice her there. I watched Cady blanche at the attention.

Brody smiled and nodded at his mother before turning and looking at Cadence, who stood up. Her fingers twisted together, exposing her nerves as she smiled shyly at Stella.

"We've heard a lot about you, Cadence Nocetti. You have quite the legacy preceding you."

Giving Cadence no time to appropriately respond, Stella pulled her into a hug before pulling away and looking her over at arm's length. "You're a beautiful young woman. The Griffins have never truly aligned with Lucien on his decisions regarding your family. Your father has always been a selfless and humanitarian type who went above and beyond the call of duty as the pack's doctor. He was sorely missed when Lucien removed his title."

Cady was stunned, staring up at Stella with wide eyes. "Thank you, Mrs. Griffin."

"Stella, please. Just know that we will accept you. You have support from this family whether you're our future daughter or our Luna." She kissed her forehead before leaving the room.

Cadence looked shellshocked, glancing at Brody who grinned at her with a shrug. She turned around to hide her face from the rest of us, the gold of her dress rippling like liquid.

"On that note, I believe it's time for us to head out." Brody tucked his hands into the pockets of his slacks.

The gala was as gorgeous as always, taking place in the Gardens of Ascension. Some of the flowers had already bloomed along the hedgerows, speckling them in various shades of red, pink, and white. Small dots of light flickered among all the greenery, lighting all the paths in romantic dimness. Cadence's dress seemed to flow even more like molten gold, glowing in the yellow lights all around us. It was surreal, watching her move in a dress as magical as she was.

Music lilted through the air, a romantic blend of strings that encouraged intimate dancing. Brody and I followed Alex and Cadence as they wandered into the crowd that had arrived before us. The first couple of people to notice our entrance whispered to themselves behind their hands. Jessica was quick to realize where everyone's attention was going, and she turned just as I took Cady's arm in mine.

Her jaw dropped before she snapped it shut and clenched it. Her flaming hair and matching dress disappeared into the crowd, and I narrowed my eyes in suspicion before leading Cadence over to the tables that were practically sagging under the weight of food. The four of us gathered plates of various cheeses and pastries as well as some of the pineapple citrus punch before collecting at an empty table. A tall oak tree hung over us, the lowest branches just out of reach.

Cady's dark eyes lifted to the branches, taking in the twinkling lights that were twisted among them with a small smile. "The Renovāminis gala is always so stunning . . . It's so weird to think that this is the last time we will attend for the next four years," she mused, her voice wistful. "I wish Kyle could be here with us . . ."

Alex also looked up, admiring the tree as well. "I know. I miss him all the time."

There was a moment of silence as we all got lost in our thoughts. Kyle's face flashed into my mind as I gazed at Cadence and the misty look in her eyes.

Alex broke the tension. "This time next year, we will all be finishing our first year at Potencia Sui Generis, and that's really kind of amazing to think about. We are all out of school now and tomorrow night, we'll all finally be adults." She nudged Cadence who blushed.

"I don't want to think about Ascending," she muttered, shoving a large piece of cheese into her mouth to avoid any further comment.

Alex glanced around the table as we all fell into a conversation lull. Raising a brow, she looked between Brody and myself. "Well, boys, I'm going to take my darling friend onto the dance floor. Providing one of you two are her mate, she needs to enjoy her last night of freedom before being tied to one of you shits forever."

I rolled my eyes. "Even if she is one of our mates, we might not even know tomorrow," I countered, leaning forward with my elbows on the table and looking at Alex. "Maybe she'll be yours."

Alex flushed crimson, balking for a second before regaining her composure as Cadence looked between us. "Maybe. She'll be damn lucky if she is my mate," she rebutted, standing abruptly and yanking Cady behind her with such force that her chair was knocked onto its back.

Turning to Brody, I saw him watching the two of them jaunt away from us until they disappeared behind the bushes. "So, who do you think is going to end up being her mate?"

Brody pondered it for a moment, rubbing his chin in thought. "I'm not sure at all, to be frank. I do want to ensure that no matter which way it goes, this newfound friendship needs to remain intact. I'm disinterested in being in a feud with the Alpha over a girl, even one that incredible."

I nodded before extending my hand. He placed his in mine and we shook on it just as someone joined us at the table.

I saw our guest and my blood ran cold. Lucien was eyeing me with obvious distaste, an ugly frown gracing his face. Clearly, he didn't care if Brody knew his true feelings about me. That was mildly concerning for where this conversation was about to go. Inhaling deeply to sigh, I caught the scent of anise and scowled as my gaze dropped to the crystal tumbler filled with a poisonous looking green liquid.

"Do you really think that drinking Bismuth tonight is the best of ideas?" I gestured to his glass, my tone bored.

Lucien rolled his cold eyes, eyeing Brody with as much distaste as he usually regarded me with. "Griffin. Slumming it with my son, are you? And here, I thought you were actually a reasonable volsifi," he stated sardonically.

Brody's lips pressed together as he eyed Lucien. "I'd consider Ezra one of my closest friends. I suppose it would seem that I am not very sensible, no."

"What do you want, *father*?" I seethed, leaning back in my chair and crossing my arms over my chest. "Was I enjoying my time too much for you to tolerate? Had to come and impose your venomous presence?"

Lucien rolled his jaw as he leaned forward. "You were. You know how much I enjoy ruining everything you love." He leaned one elbow on the table. He meant it to be sarcastic, though I knew it was true. "Tonight happens to be the last night of peace before your abomination of a girlfriend Ascends. I'm making my last play to convince you that you're making a mistake and that Jessica Barber is more worth your time." He stopped and glanced at Brody. "Why don't you take her as your mate, Griffin? I've heard that you're pining after that harlot, too."

Brody stiffened before his eyes narrowed at Lucien until they were black slits on his face. The rage was visible for a split second before a good-natured smile split the expression in half. "We were actually considering sharing her. We can't choose or make her choose, so we figured a triad was our best bet. Threesomes every night, am I right?" He gave a lewd grin that I'd seen on his face often enough to feel ill at the sight of it, despite knowing it was all for show.

Lucien paled and glanced between the two of us, unsure if Brody was telling the truth. I couldn't blame him, Brody very seldom joked about much of anything.

"Well, that's appalling." Lucien leaned back and downed the rest of his drink with one swallow as if to chase down the repugnance he felt at Brody's words. "In any case, I promised Reginald Barber that Jason could have her earlier this evening when he asked me about it. Also, since you haven't been home and you've been apparently having threesomes with the abomination, the Council is here to investigate her for murdering Kyle Wilkins. Jason has come forward stating that she asked him to kill Kyle for her so that she didn't have to continue pretending to date him. Very tragic."

If I could burst into flames, I would have. "What did you just say?"

Lucien leaned forward again until he was inches from my face, the acrid smell of Bismuth infecting my sinuses. "I said," he slowed his words down as if talking to someone he deemed a complete moron, "Cadence approached Jason and asked him to remove Kyle from the picture because she was in over her head with their relationship." Lucien smiled wickedly as if this was his plan from the start. "He, obviously, refused, but felt the need to come forward and say something. He implied that maybe the mystery murderer is, in fact, known by her. Therefore, the Council arrived at the Estate this very morning for the trial of Cadence Marie Nocetti for solicitation of the murder of Kyle Wilkins."

He gave me a sinister baring of his teeth in lieu of a true smile. Glancing at Brody, I watched the blood drain from his face as the implication of what Lucien had said settled in.

"There's no way that's true. Why would you even believe that?" he snarled, slamming his fists on the table so hard our drinks were knocked over, orange liquid spilling across the glass surface of the table.

Lucien cocked a brow at him, tilting his head as he examined him. "It doesn't matter what I believe. We have a confession and must take it seriously."

I stood, knocking my seat over and Brody followed suit. "You will not get away with this, Lucien," I growled, feeling my inner animal snapping his jaws and foaming at the jowls with rage like I wished I could. Leaning over the table, I got into his face. Satisfaction stoked my fire as he pulled away from me. "Try it. Try to have her put to death for the murder of one of our friends, Lucien. He died protecting you and our family's secrets," I spat, growling the words.

Lucien's eyes widened infinitesimally before his expression hardened into his usual cool mask. "Be that as it may, I have to do my job and have her at least pulled in for questioning. I'm doing a favor by letting her Ascend as planned tomorrow."

I snorted, straightening and glancing at Brody. "Sure. When do you do favors when they don't benefit you?"

Lucien stared blankly at me, his pupils restricted and showing the full icy disc of his iris. "Never," he stated simply, causing me to narrow my eyes at him. "Even if we can't find enough evidence to pin her for the murder, she will still be incriminated when she Ascends. It's a win-win situation for me either way."

Unable to determine what that meant, I rolled my eyes and walked away from him. Glancing behind me, I saw that Brody was in hot pursuit. "Care for a sparring session? I need to get these nerves out," I snapped, still snarling viciously in my head at the urge to kill him where he sat.

He nodded in response. Silence descended upon us as we rushed toward the school. While most individuals would be at the Gala, there were always a few guardsmen at The Crest and neither of us cared to run into anyone else when we were brimming with violence.

Neither of us bothered to keep quiet as we made our way through the trees toward the school. I briefly pondered shifting and running there to make it faster, but I wasn't sure I could control my blood lust in wolf form. Brody must have had similar thoughts or was just following my lead since he didn't shift, nor did he suggest it.

I fortunately still had a key and I let us into a side door beside the gym. While I unlocked the girl's locker room so I could turn the lights on in the gym, Brody headed straight inside. Since no one would be at the school, I didn't bother locking the doors behind us. Truly, the only thing I could think about was blowing off steam.

Walking into the gymnasium, I saw that Brody was already down to his boxers. I stripped down, laying my tux on a bleacher beside his.

I had barely faced him when a fist flew past my head. Brody was taking offense, putting me immediately on defense. Snarling, I retaliated, throwing him on defense as I launched an attack at his face that he deflected to his shoulder. I was better with a sword than hand-to-hand combat, and Brody quickly had me back on the defense, infuriating me further and causing me to become more erratic in my movements until he laid me out on the mat.

Glaring at him, he put his hands on his knees and panted. "Let's go again, Alpha," he muttered, moving backwards and gesturing for me to come at him again.

CHAPTER 37

I was certain that I was going insane. It had been years that I'd been hiding in plain sight in this pack, waiting for her to notice me.

Standing beside the dance floor, I watched her laugh with Alex, her eyes glittering with happiness. I knew she was sad about Kyle, but I also knew she would come to realize that it was for the best. Kyle was a boat anchor, holding her back and keeping her from her potential.

Maybe my feelings on it were partly based on jealousy; watching them kiss in Sew What did burn up my insides with a rage that even *I* didn't think that I was capable of. His hands on her, those should have been my hands, my lips.

Pulling myself out of my memories, I jammed my shaking fists in my pockets and gripped until my knuckles cracked. It wasn't satisfying enough. I had watched Brody and Ezra come in with her, their ties matching the dress that made her look gilded, like they could claim her for themselves. It made me want to maim something, and maybe I would.

My gaze darted around the crowd, my sight shifting to check on auras, the colors overwhelming my brain for a moment before I looked deeper into them. Some speed runners, some low-level magic, nothing super interesting. I knew that the Alpha had an interesting power, and my gaze wandered until it landed on Reginald Barber. Now that was an interesting gift.

Inhaling deeply, the lighting distorted as my pupils dilated and I slowly siphoned some power from him. Taking powers from someone was a delicate thing; you couldn't take too much, or you could kill, or they'd notice how drained they felt and grow suspicious. Smirking, I reached over and brushed the person's arm next to me as I lifted my hand to casually brush against my chin. They didn't notice, but the result was immediate.

My thoughts were overwhelmed with theirs and I glanced beside me to see who it was. Jessica Barber was there, staring at Cadence with such vitriol that I could feel it even without being inside her thoughts.

What's so special about her anyway? She took Kyle from me. I loved him since kindergarten, and now Ezra and Brody won't speak to me or Jason. I hope this scheme of Jason's works because I want Ezra for myself. I deserve to have at least someone.

She visibly sighed.

He's so perfect. Those lips. I wish he'd kissed me just once. Goddess, he must be wonderful–

Turning away, I severed the connection to her before I heard anymore nauseatingly teenaged melodrama. I wandered through the crowd, tasting everyone's powers until I found ones that might be useful. It took a considerable amount of effort to ignore the beacon in the center of the dance floor. My mouth kept watering, thinking about how her aura was already glowing golden despite not having Ascended yet. Forcing my brain to move along the clusters of people, I finally spotted Lucien and pulled his power, tugging it and soaking it into my soul until I was done with it.

I considered stealing Alex's gift briefly before disregarding it. I didn't need the assistance of being a human lie detector yet. Once I was sufficiently pleased with the scope of my new abilities, I hunted for Ezra. Killing the son of the Alpha was a huge risk, but Cadence was worth it. If I was lucky, he and Brody would be together, and I could take them both out at once.

The crowd split briefly, exposing the two of them as they vanished into the tree line. Smirking, I quirked a brow and waited, biding my time until it wouldn't be suspicious for me to leave in a similar direction. I pondered how handy a tracking ability would be in this moment, but it'd been a long time since I'd had that particular gift. It wasn't one you stumbled across often.

Eyeing those around me, I decided that no one was watching and melted into the trees. Their scent was easy to follow, the smell of hot cinnamon and a bonfire mingled with teakwood and amber. Even as I inhaled their scents as I walked through the thick forest in the direction of the school, I couldn't help but wrinkle my nose. Why Cadence kept choosing to have them in her life when they reeked like that was beyond me. I wriggled my nose as I fought a sneeze. Pulling out my phone, I checked for texts from Cadence. There never were any. I knew there never would be, but that didn't stop me from checking constantly.

I approached the gym, hearing grunts and shouts as an angsty song filled the hallway as some kind of teenage-fueled rage transpired behind the doors. Rolling my eyes at their immaturity, I peeked into the gymnasium to see what kind of scene I would be dealing with when I saw both of them shirtless and doing combat routines in just their boxers. I couldn't stop the growl that escaped me as my upper lip curled back in an annoyed snarl. Of course, they'd fight it out like impudent children. How juvenile.

Stripping off my suit jacket, I didn't allow myself to hesitate before walking into the gym. It took several long moments for them to recognize me, but that allowed me to use the quick speed I took from someone at the party to run at them. I touched a bit of exposed flesh on both of them before returning to a safe distance while they looked around in confusion. I didn't need Brody turning that fire power on me just yet.

Both turned and stared at me blankly. I could hear the alarm of their inner voices as they wondered what had just happened. Chuckling, I made eye contact with both of them as they peered at me in shock, activating the power I'd borrowed from Lucien. How convenient.

Without giving them time to react, I made them both drop to the ground and immediately Ezra's mind flooded with panic and trauma memories of his lovely father.

"What do you think of the extra gift I borrowed from your father, Ezra?" I inquired, kneeling beside him and staring down at him. "I thought it would be especially impactful for you." I turned to Brody and grinned at him, too.

"It was *you* this whole time?" he bit out through clenched teeth, his anger exposed in his gaze though his expression remained stoic.

Grinning at him, I nodded. "It was me. In the flesh. I didn't *want* to kill Kyle, and I don't really want to kill you either, but alas, you wouldn't heed my warnings."

If looks could kill, I'd be just as dead as the Wilkins kid.

"Are you going to spew the typical victim inquiries? 'Why are you doing this?' 'How could you?' 'Please don't hurt us.'" I leaned back, waving my hands about my face in a mockery of the panic humans feel when facing their own mortality.

"I have to admit, I'd be disappointed if you did. Wilkins only panicked a little when he saw the needle coming. But he stood his ground, accepting his fate. I was quite proud of him, to be truthful." I looked between the two of them as I stood again and backed away. "Now . . . let's see how these cool powers work before I summon Cadence."

CADENCE

Dancing with Alex was exhilarating, but a piece of my brain wouldn't stop thinking about Kyle and how I wished he was there. It wasn't fair that he was stolen from us so ruthlessly, his ashes spread among the trees like that would pay enough penance for his short life that everyone could just move on with theirs. It was a drizzle of bitterness on the night that I couldn't ignore even if I wanted to.

Alex was not oblivious to the cloud of grief that hung over us, but we did our best to dance under it anyway. Kyle would not have wanted us to be sad on his behalf.

The music was good, though not as heavy or angsty as I preferred. Alex and I were moving to the beat, though she was much more graceful than I could ever hope to be. Feeling eyes on me, I turned and spotted Jason glaring with a gaze that weighed more than the earth. I faltered in my dance. Alex noticed and followed my gaze.

"Ignore him, Cadence. Tonight is the first night of the rest of our lives."

She gripped my shoulder and pulled me deeper into the crowd. Pausing again, I glanced around, looking above the heads of everyone else for any sign of Brody or Ezra.

"Didn't they say they'd join us?" I asked, leaning close to speak over the volume of the music.

She glanced around like she'd just realized they were absent. "I don't remember. Should we check the table and see if they're waiting for us?"

I frowned and pulled out my phone to see if I had any text messages from either of them. A couple messages had just come through from Brody, and I hurriedly unlocked my phone and checked it.

Brody

> I have both of your boys. If you want them back alive, come to the school gym without Alex. If I get even the slightest inkling that you're not alone, I will kill them with far less mercy than I bestowed upon Kyle.

> Make sure you turn off your phone so you can't be traced. I will know if you don't, my love.

My blood ran cold as I stared at my phone. Carefully, I schooled my face to appear far less disturbed than I felt. Lifting my eyes to Alex, I saw her staring pensively at her own phone. Putting mine away, her attention lifted to my face.

"I have to go to the bathroom. You'll stay here in the middle of the dance floor and wait for me, right?" she asked, glancing around as though looking for someone.

Feeling relieved that I didn't have to come up with an excuse, I nodded demurely. "Of course. I'll stay here," I replied, waiting anxiously for her to disappear so that I could as well.

When she vanished into the crowd, I immediately turned and fled into the forest in the direction of the school. The low hanging branches caught my hair as I hustled through them, ripping some of the strands out by the roots. I didn't care about carefully picking through the underbrush, storming through the foliage like a wild animal on a rampage. Fear and rage fueled me, pushing me forward even as the forest reached out with claws to slow me down. Talons from the trees and various underbrush scraped my skin, causing me to bleed as I stormed through on my way to my two lovers.

The only thing that stopped me was a fallen branch that I caught between two of my toes. Growling with fury, I yanked the thin branch from my sandals and whipped it into the trees with a scream before taking off again. Limping and gasping my way through the forest, I couldn't stop to think about Alex and how she'd feel when she realized I'd run off without her. I did wish several times during the sprint that I'd worked out more frequently as my lungs burned and a stitch relentlessly stabbed between the ribs in my right side.

Breaking out of the tree line, I didn't slow down to scope out the scene. I was on the gymnasium side of the school, but I couldn't enter that way. Snarling in frustration, I ran around the side of the school to find an entrance I could actually access. Prepared, the creep left a side door propped open, and I didn't even hesitate before running inside. In fact, it didn't even occur to me that it was a trap as I walked to the inside doors that opened into the gymnasium.

I didn't stop to think until my hand was on the door handle and I wondered briefly if I was too late, if they'd be dead on the other side. It was eerily quiet in the school, the only sound I could hear was my own panting and the racing of my heart.

It's not too late to turn around.

I hated myself for even thinking it; being a coward didn't suit me, despite me sometimes acting like one. I wasn't going to run screaming now. Not when Brody and Ezra needed me and could be gravely injured; I refused to think that they might be dead. I felt like my world was crumbling beneath my feet, a black hole of grief opening up beneath me all over again and preparing to swallow me whole.

Kyle's image flashed into my mind, his hollow throat and hazel eyes staring up at me without sight. He'd never see me again. What if Brody and Ezra were in there, gazing up at a ceiling that no longer truly existed for them? Panic gripped my insides, pulling my ribs inward and crushing my lungs beneath their weight until I was breathing in short gasps, black spots blooming in my vision.

Lost in my thoughts and the fear and anger creeping along my bones like a disease, I didn't even see the shadow looming over me until it was too late. I didn't have time to scream before a hand covered my mouth to muffle it, fingers pinching my nose hard. Suddenly, I couldn't breathe, and the panic shifted into survival as I wriggled violently in the arms that held me. My arms were pinned at my sides, sandwiched against my torso. My legs were free, however, so I kicked backwards like an angry mule as the person holding me grunted in my ear anytime I made purchase. For the first time that night, I wished I was wearing heels because the flimsy sandals were not causing enough damage.

The hands loosened just enough for me to gasp for air, the scent of Old Spice filling my nose, and worm my way out of them, hitting the floor hard and feeling the jarring up my spine as I landed flat on my ass. I moved to turn and look up at my attacker, but a fist tangled in the hair on the top of my head. A scream ripped free from my lungs as I was dragged toward the locker rooms right behind us. I thrashed on the floor in an attempt to loosen myself from his grip, but I quickly realized that there was no breaking free. Instead, I reached up and dug my nails into his wrist.

He growled in anger and turned around to sneer at me. I gasped as I registered silver eyes glaring at me like *I* was the monster. Mr. Bowman, my English teacher, squatted over me. His hands gripped both sides of my head before slamming the back of my skull against the floor hard enough that I saw stars and the edges of my vision flickered black. The fight was knocked out of me temporarily, and he took advantage of that moment by throwing me over his shoulder and carrying me into the locker room where there was only one exit. Hearing a key turning in a lock, I knew that my one and only escape was being blocked off. I panicked again, writhing in his arms in the hopes he would drop me.

"Knock it off," he snarled at me, pulling me off his shoulder and tossing me onto the floor like a doll.

I hit the tiled floor like a sack of sand, my skull screaming as the back of my head cracked against the floor for a second time. A groan pushed from my lungs along with all the oxygen they'd held. Blinking against the blackness creeping into my vision, I laid there, attempting to pull myself back together while he paced the floor in front of me. I watched him walk, trying to put the pieces together in my head.

Mr. Bowman finally turned to leer at me. His stare was both devoted and vengeful, and I wasn't sure which one frightened me more. Neither boded well for my probability of surviving this encounter. When he continued to stare at me without saying anything, I sat up slowly and moaned as the world sparked and swirled around me.

Closing my eyes, I put my head in my hands until the earth stilled again. I wanted to stand up and face him, but I knew that my legs would never hold me in my current state. As much as I didn't like the disadvantage of being trapped on the floor, I didn't see many other options. If I swayed on my feet, that would leave me even more vulnerable.

Breaking the silence between us, he chuckled low in his throat and the sound of it sent a chill down my spine. Its familiarity did little to ease my fraying nerves.

"Oh, Cadence. I can't tell you how happy I am to see you now that I know you're really mine."

I remained still, trying to assess my injuries so that I could plan an escape. Unfortunately, it included an added layer of stealing his keys and actually unlocking the door.

He waited a long moment before continuing, his pacing starting up again. The sound of his shoes squeaking on the tiles reached my ears through the clearing haze in my mind.

"You know, you really put me through an exorbitant amount of stress and pain this past year. You little minx, you really made me work for your affections," he enthused, finally saying something that prompted me to look at him. The

413

confusion must have been apparent in my features because he smiled at me unpleasantly.

"Making me take out Kyle; that was really something else. You were testing me, I'm certain of it. But that's okay because I passed with flying colors, especially now that I've immobilized Brody and Ezra," he went on, stepping toward me and causing me to skitter away from him. My head throbbed painfully, making my eyes water.

I didn't want him any closer to me, but he had the advantage of being on foot. He closed the distance as I reached the bank of lockers behind me, the cold against my back making me feel like a caged animal. His hand reached out to me, gently tucking a lock of hair behind my ear in a way that I think he meant to be endearing, but it only made me bristle. Slapping his hand away, I saw a flicker of rage in his silver eyes.

"Mr. Bowman," I started, but he immediately cut me off with a snarl as his hand fisted in my hair again. The injury to the back of my head screamed with the tugging on my scalp, but I could only groan in pain.

"My name is *Shane*. I'm your *mate*, not your teacher," he growled, face twisted in malice, and my eyes widened.

I stared at him in horror as he crouched before me, but he either didn't notice or didn't care as his face softened back to the easy smile that didn't reach his eyes. He was too close, his face took up the entirety of my vision, his scent slid into my sinuses and stained my memories. I'd never get it out of my head, that heavy original Old Spice smell that made my brain throb uncomfortably in my skull.

He never let me continue, instead going on to speak as his hand dropped back to his side.

"I had to have you. I've always had a knack for getting the things I want, and you are something that I *need*. Then I saw you with Ezra and I'd never been so *angry*." His voice quivered with an emotion I couldn't quite pinpoint, and his eyes were so empty that I thought they might swallow me whole. I imagined this was what a conversation with a wraith might feel like, getting lost in those hollow silver eyes. "I got a brief reprieve when he started dating Jessica, but then along came Kyle. That's when I was certain that you were testing me, putting obstacles in my way so I could fight my way to you and prove to you how much you mean to me."

He smiled again, wide and crazy in a way that made my heart thunder in my chest. The corners of his eyes crinkled. His eyes glittered in psychotic glee that made me certain my life would end soon by his hands. I'd never been so afraid of anything before in my entire life. I wasn't ready to die, not by a long shot.

I was trapped like a scared kitten, cornered and vulnerable and helpless. I think what made me the most upset about the entire situation was that I was about to become a statistic. I was another victim of a stalker. After this was over, I wasn't going to be Cadence Marie Nocetti anymore; I would be a victim. One of thousands, maybe millions, of women who were between the ages of fifteen and eighteen who were stalked, assaulted, tortured . . . even murdered. The glow of those metallic eyes told me that I was going to suffer endlessly at his hands. Suffer for ignoring him for so long, for testing him and his patience, for making him summon me like the wraith I was going to become.

I instinctively attempted to back away from him again as his fingertips grazed over my cheekbone and into my hair where he fisted it at the back of my neck like he couldn't let me go.

Shane stood, bringing me with him by my hair. I refused to cry out, to show him how much he was physically hurting me. I desperately tried to blank out my face, to show no emotion at all as I stared at him head on. I didn't want to give him the gratification of knowing he terrified me, of knowing that I was afraid.

"Such a scared little minx," he purred, using his free hand to press his fingers against my neck and feel my pulse thunder against them. Clearly, my mask was not good enough, and I made a mental note to practice it.

"Why?" I asked him, stalling for time. I didn't know how the hell I was going to get out of here, but I needed to formulate a plan. My mind went back to the keys that he had on him somewhere, the literal keys to my freedom through the door that stood waiting for me just ten feet behind him.

"Why?" he echoed, his voice sending goosebumps scattering over my flesh. "Because there's something about you." He paused, staring at me with those empty eyes as if he was trying to decide how much to tell me. "Your existence exhilarates me to the point that I can barely think about anything else. I can feel your presence like an ever-burning fireplace on a winter night. Even when I'm not near you, I can see your light like a beacon, calling the ship of my soul to safe harbor."

"How did you get into my house?" I asked him, still desperately trying to stall for time until I could get an escape plan. I didn't have any confidence that anyone was going to come save me this time.

He grinned manically at me, pride dancing on his features. "The window in your basement will pop open if you jiggle it enough with a knife. I found it the night you took dinner to your father at the clinic. That was the night you received the first amaryllis and ignored it. So, I broke into your house to take my gift back, and instead watched you dreaming in your bed."

He stared at me with a ferocity that made me want to scream. It was so unlike the intensity I was used to receiving from Kyle, Ezra, or Brody that it was alarming. "And then, after you told me I was beautiful that one day in class, I knew I'd never be able to give you up."

I tried to stamp down the panic and horror that swirled through my system, making my heart hammer painfully inside my chest. Blinking, I swallowed the fear and desperately formulated a plan. Fight didn't work. I needed to flee, but how could I possibly get the keys and escape when the door was behind him? The decision that playing into his fantasy might be the best option flitted into my aching skull, but the whole idea of pretending to fawn over him made my stomach twist.

"I wish I hadn't given back the gift of mind reading yet. I so want to know what's going on behind those eyes of yours," he murmured, his tone almost loving as he traced a fingertip down my temple before his thumb skimmed over my lower lip.

Summoning my inner Alex, I looked into his eyes for a moment before dropping my gaze to his lips and licking my own. His teeth sunk into his lower lip in response, and I ignored every instinct within me and pressed my body against his.

"That was truly genius. I knew that you could pass every test I threw at you," I purred, ignoring the way my body wanted to push him away from me. Revolted, I did everything I could to hide that reaction from my face as I flicked my eyes back to his and forced myself to pretend to get lost in their silver depths. "How long until you can mark me as yours?" I asked, feigning interest and fawning my way the hell out of this situation. I lifted my arm, skimming my fingertips over his short, dark hair.

A chuckle vibrated in his throat, the sound making fear lick over my skin. "I can't officially mark you as mine until your Ascension tomorrow, but I can certainly stake a claim with my scent. I could fill you with my seed and scent you as my mate until you have your ceremony. Then I'll make a mark on you the night of your birthday and you will be *mine*."

The mention of his *seed* made me want to vomit as nausea swept through me. Now that Shane's intentions had been laid out verbally, it confirmed what I already knew: that I had to get out of there, and fast. I needed to escape this before I truly became an assault victim. It didn't matter to him that mates were predestined. There was no choosing a mate. You either accepted your given bond, or you didn't.

My brain fritzed out in the worst way as he dipped his head and pressed his lips to my left collarbone, which was exposed over the top of my golden dress. It was one of the most sensitive places on my body, something I was grateful I'd discovered with Ezra and not with this monster. A disgusted groan left my lips as the sensation warped into something distinctly unpleasurable, but he interpreted it incorrectly as he pressed his entire body closer against mine until

I was pinned against the lockers. My skin felt alive with horror, and I'd never wanted to crawl out of my skin more than I did right then. I could survive as a skeleton, I was certain.

Pushing through my body's incessant need to lash out at him, I instead forced my hands to slide down his torso. Everything about his body made me want to die a little more inside, and I was sure a part of me did as his tongue slid up my neck to my earlobe. The sound of his heavy breathing filled my ear as he nibbled on me, and I gritted my teeth together to keep from screaming aloud as my fingers found their way to the front pockets of his slacks. Distracting him as my left hand found a key ring, I slid the other one behind his back and pulled him closer to me, digging my nails into his spine and eliciting another groan from him.

Fortunately, he was so distracted in his pursuit of my flesh that he didn't even feel me pull the wad of keys out of his pocket and into my closed fist to keep them from rattling. A shudder rolled over my body, making my knees quake with abhorrence as I steeled myself for my next act. I shifted slightly, barely finding the space to pull back my leg enough that I could bring my knee up into his groin as hard as I could.

His teeth scraped hard against my earlobe as he jerked forward in reaction to the agony that I was sure was spreading through his gut. I didn't care. I relished his pain as he backed away from me, tilting forward as his hands covered his groin. I seized the opportunity of his slow recovery and grabbed the back of his head, pulling it down as I brought my knee directly into his face. The sound of cartilage snapping echoed around me along with the scream he unleashed in his mixed surprise and pain.

Refusing to bathe in the glory of my success, I ran to the door as fast as my shaking legs would carry me while I sorted through the keyring. There were too many keys, all ten of them could have easily fit in the door and I knew my time was limited. Jamming the first into the lock, I twisted the key in panic as my fingers shook.

"Help! Anyone! Can anyone help me? Please!" I screamed, fumbling with the heavy ring of keys until I shoved the next one into the lock and turned it desperately only for my heart to sink as it failed.

A male voice called my name from outside in the hall and my heart leapt with hope as I recognized it. "Cadence!" Brody shouted, sounding as panicked as I felt.

"In here!" I screamed in response, shoving another key into the door and shouting in frustration as it, too, failed. "Help me!"

BRODY

I awoke with a groan, wincing at the brightness of the fluorescent lights hanging above me. My brain shuffled through the molasses of my muddled thoughts while I got my bearings. Sitting up, I held my head in my hands until the earth quit moving without me.

Glancing around, I saw Ezra lying beside me, his body covered in burns and soot.

Did I do that?

I wouldn't have done that. I'd have no reason to attack Ezra so viciously. But what *had* happened?

Thinking back, I frantically tried to get the cogs to turn in my brain as I stared at Ezra and watched for his chest to move. His breathing was shallow, but he was still alive as he lay beside me on his back.

Finally, it clicked into place. Shane Bowman came in while we were sparring so Ezra could burn off some steam. He touched us both faster than we could see and then trapped us when we'd made eye contact. Frowning, I winced as I recalled how I'd used my fire power against Ezra with no control over my own body while Ezra screamed until he'd fallen unconscious. Then Shane hit me in the head with a weight and knocked me out cold.

"Damn it," I muttered, getting up and stumbling to my clothes to check my pockets for my phone. Realizing it was missing, I growled and dug through Ezra's pockets, only to quickly realize his phone had also been taken. "Damn it!" I snarled, standing up and running toward the exit of the gym.

Just about to head down the hall toward the exit, I stopped when I heard a scream.

"Cadence!" I responded, hearing her begging for help.

My heart stuttered as she frantically shouted for someone to save her, but I could also hear a metallic jingling. Had he handcuffed her? I wouldn't be surprised.

Hearing the grating sound of a key being shoved into a lock, I realized she had *keys* of all things.

"Cadence, is Shane Bowman in there with you?" I called, banging on the heavy wooden door.

Without thinking, I put my hands against the surface of the door and used my gift to heat the wood. I would burn the whole school down if that's what it took to get to her.

"Brody, what are you doing?" she shouted through the door, the keys rattling as they fell to the floor on the other side of the door.

CADENCE

I jammed a third key into the lock as he hammered on the door from the other side and screamed my frustration as it was also the incorrect one. Then the whole door became so hot that the keys also heated up, startling me.

"Brody, what are you doing?" I snapped, my already shaking fingers dropping the keys to the floor when I'd started.

Shane snarled behind me, my skin itching as he closed the gap between us. "You're not going anywhere until I claim you."

His voice found its way under my skin and made me wish I could remove it and throw it at him if he wanted it so badly.

Brody banged on the door again as he tried to force his way in, but it was a door that swung out toward him. I knew it was useless for him to do that, but I didn't have time to say anything as Shane grabbed me from behind and heaved me off the floor.

Growling, I refused to go down easy and kicked off the door as hard as I could, effectively using my weight and momentum to knock Shane off balance and tilting us both over backwards. It was one of the few times I was happy I was overweight, since I could hear the impact, my body knocking the wind out of him with a squeak.

Scrambling, I fought with the golden skirt of my dress that had tangled around my legs, frantically leaning forward and shoving the keys under the door.

"Brody! The keys!" I shouted as Shane recovered and came at me like a freight train again.

Turning so he wouldn't be able to grab me from behind again, I pushed against the floor with my feet to shove my back up the door. He dug his fingers into the fabric of my dress at my waist and yanked me down toward him again, causing my knees to slam painfully against the floor. His hands grabbed either side of my face as he pressed his mouth hard against mine. The smell of Old Spice burned into my sinuses, burning against my brain and making my stomach roll.

Using his grip on my head to raise me with him, he stood us up and slammed me back against the door, my head taking its third hit of the night. Black spots flashed behind my closed eyes, my stomach tilting with nausea again. The kiss was all teeth and painful pressure against my lips. The bitter iron taste of his blood filled my mouth as it ran from his broken nose, making me wish for flight. I stopped moving, becoming the corpse I knew I'd become in his arms if I couldn't fend off this hellscape of a nightmare. I did nothing more but keep my legs straight enough to hold my own body upright, the rest of it limp in his grasp. My mouth stayed still; my teeth clenched together to keep his roaming tongue out of my mouth as he kissed me. It was then that I kind of wished a reaper would come and take me; relieve me from this never-ending horror. At least I could see Kyle again that way.

"Use your powers!"

Brody's voice broke through the haze of defeat in my brain, and he had a point, but I had no idea *how* to use my powers. I thought back to the last time I'd actively used them in a very similar situation to this one. I remembered how I'd felt, and it was angry. I was furious at being forced upon, at being assaulted. I didn't give up, praying for it to just end. I *made* it end.

The jingling of keys and metal on metal came from the other side of the door as he tried key after key in the stubborn lock. His voice cut through the door and my insecurities. "Get angry and just use it!" he snapped just before another key was jammed into the lock.

He was right, and I found it surprisingly easy to dip into my anger, like there was a bottomless well of it inside of me just waiting for me to use it. How dare this bastard come into *my* school and stake a claim on me like I was some kind of object to be owned and controlled? Who did he think he was? I saw the rage glimmering inside of me like a glow stick just waiting to be cracked open. I held it in my fist and shook it up to light that flame of fury even further.

I could feel my skin growing hot and a cry escaped Shane as he pulled away from me. His mouth looked angry and red, a couple blisters raising immediately where his skin had been pushing against mine.

"Do not touch me!" I ordered, allowing the anger to pour out of my veins like molten lava. My skin was golden and glittering as he took a step toward me.

I wanted him to feel afraid, but he looked awed instead, like I was his fever dream come true. I hated it with every ounce of my being. I wanted him to fear me like I'd been afraid of him for months. I wanted him to cower and pay penance for killing Kyle. Instead, he just took yet another step toward me and I snarled at him like a caged animal.

"So powerful," he breathed, his voice hushed as if raising it would cause an explosion. He was probably correct. "You haven't even Ascended yet."

My breathing was labored, my chest constricting as power and wrath built within me; the waves coming onto the beach of my patience and flooding it with outrage, though the tide never ebbed away. The problem was that I had no idea how to use it or just how much of it there was. If I was going to be completely honest, I was mildly afraid of myself. It was like I knew subconsciously that I was a ticking time bomb, set to detonate at some undetermined time.

"Don't touch me," I demanded again, and he stopped moving, his hand outstretched as it reached toward my face.

The sound of keys in the door was fading into the distance as I faced off with the person who'd made me feel unsafe in my own home, in my own pack. This was *my* pack, despite all its faults and shortcomings.

Shane did not heed my warning, and I snarled again as he approached me. Gnashing my teeth, I gave him one last sign of forewarning and he seemed to listen that time, stopping and staring at me with horror creeping into his face. Stepping back, he finally heeded what must have been shrieking alarms inside his skull before kneeling on the floor in front of me.

I felt powerful, like I actually might be the Luna Ezra was certain I'd become. And with that sense of power came control. Tamping down the magic that had built up inside of me, the glow receded, and so did my teetering stability.

I'd barely heard the door open behind me before strong arms wrapped around me. Brody breathed heavily against my hair as he held me close to him before I turned to wrap my own arms automatically around his shoulders. Gripping his bare back with my fingertips, I panted against him as he glared over my shoulder at Shane who was still crouched on the floor.

"Thank whatever god is listening that you're okay," he murmured, and in that moment of stillness, I could feel him trembling underneath my fingers.

He pulled back slightly, holding my face in his hands and looking over me as if he could sus out any damage I may have incurred. Unfortunately, all the injuries I'd received were internal, but there was no time to say anything before he dropped his head and pressed his lips to mine. There was no hunger in the kiss, just solace and compassion at the end of a shared nightmare.

We broke apart, blinking at each other in surprise before being interrupted by muttering behind us. Both of us glanced at Shane, his forehead pressed against the floor as he sobbed. My upper lip curled in disgust as he murmured something about beauty into the tile as he wept. Glancing into the dark eyes of Brody, we seemed to communicate without words as we both abandoned the locker room, shutting the door behind us. Brody twisted the key into the lock, bolting the door shut before we turned at the sound of footsteps approaching.

Alex appeared through the doors of the gym, toting Ezra along beside her. He looked worse for wear; his right eye nearly swollen shut, and blood oozed from his nose and his busted lip. His flesh seemed to have been burned and I glanced at Brody who gestured back into the locker room. Confused, I glanced between the two of them for another moment before he finally responded in words.

"Shane used gifts against us, making us fight each other while he watched."

Once Ezra saw me, he pulled away from Alex's arm and hurried toward me with a limp in his gait. Taking my face in his hands, he pressed his lips firmly against mine in a kiss that told me all of his emotions. It was eerily similar to the kiss I'd just shared with Brody, and both felt so natural and normal that it unsettled me for just a moment before Ezra pulled back to look at me as earnestly as Brody had just a moment before.

Kissing me again, he wrapped his arms around me. "You scared the hell out of us," he whispered in confirmation against my mouth before pulling away and resting his forehead against mine. He was out of breath, like he'd just run three miles to get there, and my vision grew blurry as the entire situation fully registered. I was overwhelmed and wanted to get out of there, but I knew that there would be many questions from The Guard when they finally arrested Shane Bowman.

CHAPTER 38

CADENCE

The questions seemed to go on forever, but all I had to do was tell them the truth. There was plenty of evidence on my phone, which I gladly handed over without any complaint. I couldn't help but wonder if this entire night could have been avoided if they'd questioned me the month prior when Kyle was murdered.

I was unable to stop myself from acting as cranky about the entire thing as I felt during my brutal interrogation. They'd also brought up some preposterous story about asking Jason if he would take out Kyle for me so that I didn't have to keep pretending to date him.

Balking at Bernard Pierce, I thought I might spontaneously combust while my cool vanished under the heat of my anger. "Why would I ask *Jason Barber* to kill Kyle for me? I wasn't *pretending* to date Kyle. I was happy with Kyle." My words came out in a snarl as I leaned toward him.

Bernard seemed unfazed, but I could hardly blame him when he had Alex for a daughter.

He shrugged. "Jason informed us earlier today that you had asked him to murder Kyle for you. He couldn't provide any solid evidence, but it was the first lead we've had. We were going to bring you in after you Ascended."

"Ahh, there it is. You wanted to make sure you could try me as an Ascended volsifi," I ground out, putting the puzzle pieces together aloud. "I was destroyed by Kyle's death. I never asked for or wanted it. Jason is lying. Is he going to have any repercussions for lying?"

Bernard regarded me with the kind of uncertainty I'd been doused with my entire existence.

Ezra appeared at my side, pulling rank while staring Bernard down. Bernard seemed just as unfazed by Ezra's presence as he was mine. "It's been hours. If you don't have all the answers you need by now, you can call her in at a later time."

My dad showed up just then, throwing the doors open and storming into the gym looking haggard. When his eyes found me, he immediately ran over and wrapped me in a hug so tight I was surprised none of my bones cracked with the pressure. "Are you okay?" he asked, the look on his face melting my heart with guilt.

I nodded, glancing over to Bernard again who eyed my dad with distaste. "Well then, I guess since *Ezra* deemed this interrogation completed, I must let you go." He turned his blue gaze to Ezra with obvious disdain. "If we don't have all the evidence we need, I'll hold you fully responsible to your father." Snapping his notebook closed, he turned and stormed away.

Brody was still in the corner where he answered questions, though his attention was firmly on me. His dark eyes were staring at me with a protective ferocity that pulled the air from my lungs with a gasp. Dad followed my gaze and frowned, barely suppressing a sigh. "Is there *another* person I have to worry about now?" He sounded as tired as I felt.

When I awoke, the sun was beaming happily against the back of my curtains, staining the room with dusty lavender light. Blinking, I took in my empty bedroom, my eyes automatically scanning for a splotch of red that had invaded my space so frequently it had become expected.

The previous night slammed back into my brain like a battering ram busting through my hippocampus. Gasping, I wrapped my arms around my ribs as all the thoughts and emotions that had been suppressed during my dreamless sleep washed over me. I couldn't escape the maelstrom of fear that gripped my heart and squeezed it firmly in its grasp.

I reached blindly for my earbuds on the nightstand, hyperventilating as my scrabbling fingers knocked the case onto the floor with a dull thud on the carpet. Diving toward them, I hit the floor on my forearms before doing an awkward roll as I jammed them into my ears and pressed play on whatever song happened to be waiting in the queue.

"HELLO LØNELINESS" by Ekoh and Lø Spirit blasted through my earbuds, the volume too loud from listening to music for over an hour the previous night. I shuddered, hurriedly clicking the button to turn the volume down until it was a still-too-loud-but-tolerable volume. Covering my ears with my hands, I dropped my forehead onto my knees, ignoring the discomfort of squishing my stomach in such an awkward position. After a moment, I couldn't push away the disgruntled pain and leaned my head back on my mattress, still holding the earbuds against my head as though they might melt out of my ears and leave me alone in the silence with my racing thoughts.

When the song ended, I heaved myself off the floor, my entire body sore from being thrown around the night before. I'd just put on shorts and an oversized tee when I turned around to find Alex, Ezra, and Brody standing in my doorway and staring at me. A shriek escaped me as I jumped practically onto the ceiling. Pulling my earbuds from my ears, I nearly shouted at them for startling me as anger tore through me. Taking a few deep breaths, I pressed a hand to my chest as though that might slow my rampaging heart.

"We came to check on you," Brody murmured, his broad shoulders nearly filling the doorframe as he leaned against it, his arms crossed over his chest in his typical stance that made his muscles bulge.

Ezra glanced at him before looking back at me. "It's an important day today," he said mildly, causing my face to crinkle before I pulled it back into an emotionless mask.

"I wish I could skip it."

Alex came forward and pulled me into a tight hug that I hadn't even known I'd needed. I gripped her shoulders, my fingers lacing into the holes of her crocheted navy cardigan. I only vaguely realized it was one of the ones I'd made for her. She pulled back, brushing hair from my face and tucking it behind my ears. "Don't wish that. It's the best day of your life so far. You get to become the woman you were always destined to be."

My chest shuddered as I shook my head. "I guess. I just feel like part of it was ruined because of Mr. Bowman. How can I recover from yesterday?"

Ezra stepped up beside me and placed his hand on my shoulder. Glancing at him, my eyes hovered over his body. His eye was still bruised a deep purple, but it was no longer swollen shut, and his split lip seemed mostly healed. "You're looking much better than you did yesterday," I commented, sighing heavily and glancing at Brody who looked incredibly guilty.

"I heal quickly," Ezra remarked, shrugging one shoulder before hooking his arm in mine. "Let's get food. It's almost noon."

The group of us went downstairs, rounding the corner into the dining room where we all stopped in our tracks. My mother was sitting at the dining room table. Her somber expression clashed with the cheery yellow walls, and she looked so out of place there that I almost thought someone had broken into our home again. The alarm that rang through my body at that thought made my breathing immediately become ragged until I came down from the height of my panic.

In her hand, she held a steaming cup of tea that permeated the air with its herbal scent. Swallowing the lump in my throat, I stood there and stared at her while she examined me closely before her eyes lifted to the group standing loyally at my back.

"We have to talk," she stated quietly, her crystal blue eyes gazing at me over the rim of her white teacup.

She blew across the surface of the liquid within it, and I continued to stare at her like I didn't know who she was. I could see the pained look on her face as she examined me, taking note of my expression as she set the teacup down on the saucer in front of her.

I didn't move, instead choosing to lean against the doorway of the room and cross my arms over my chest. I had no idea what she wanted to talk about, but I didn't think I could pretend that she wasn't a negligent mother and discuss things like we were chummy. She was such an absent parent that she didn't even realize the hell I'd already been through the previous day. Of course, she would choose this moment in time to want a heart to heart.

"Please sit, Cadence."

She gestured to the empty seat across the table from her. The pleading in her voice was what stirred me, and I moved to sit. Plopping heavily into the chair as my legs gave out halfway down, I ignored the look of distaste that graced her face for a brief moment. She continued to completely ignore the three other bodies that arced around my back, forming a wall of muscle and fierce protectiveness behind me.

Automatically, my hands wrapped around the hot cup that was sitting on the table in front of me. It was then that I realized I was shaking again . . . or maybe even still. This was such a foreign feeling, sitting at the dining room table with my mother like this was a normal thing we'd always done. It still hurt me that she seemed to forget she had another child after Callum was taken.

I continued to not say anything, the silence stretching on uncomfortably between us. It was like the table was actually a yawning cavern that kept us separated, the gap ever widening as the weight of her previous absence and current presence crushed me like a rock crumbling from the wall above and forcing me into the gaping hole in my heart that she left behind with Callum and my grandmother.

Her eyes reddened as I gazed at her, gaining a glassy appearance as I realized she was tearing up.

"Mom–" I shook my head to try to erase the image my mind had created for me.

"Cadence, I need to talk to you about what we are," she interrupted, saying the words quickly as if she'd change her mind if she didn't force them out as she thought them.

I waited for her to continue, lifting my tea to my lips and gazing at her over the rim of the white cup I held in both hands. The pauses and quiet moments between her words were driving me slowly insane. Talking to my mother wasn't something I desired to do to begin with, and her dragging out this conversation with dramatic lapses in conversation were putting me further on edge than I already was.

She finally continued on, and I could tell she was trying very hard not to rush through her story no matter how much I wished she would.

"My mother, your grandmother, was not a volsifi."

The words slammed into me like a physical punch to the gut and I nearly spit out my mouthful of tea. Instead, I choked on the liquid, coughing and sputtering as I fought to catch my breath.

Mating outside of your kind was strictly forbidden by the High Table, and I could hardly believe what I was hearing.

"Mother was an elvafe. She came from the Stargazer Kingdom in the Appalachian Mountains."

"Where the Dark Princes resides?" I asked, gasping as I set down my teacup with a loud clatter into the saucer.

Mother answered by nodding. "She met father when the elvafe sent her here to investigate the pack due to the rise of a new royal family. Lucien's father, Edward, was just coming into his place as the Alpha then, and they wanted to see if he was a threat to our very shaky peace treaty, as our pack was just claiming their spot at the High Table after the sudden death of Paul Wyland. He was the Alpha of the Silver Moon pack in Georgia and King of the Volsifi for over one hundred years. He mysteriously died before he'd decided to have an heir. He was too busy trying to fix things in our species to settle with his mate. That was when the Wolfe family became royalty as the oldest family."

I felt Ezra stiffen behind me, having never been told the history of how the Wolfes became the oldest volsifi family in the world. Since it was a conspiracy, it was no wonder it wasn't part of the curriculum for our school. Frowning into my teacup, I felt that my capacity for accepting any further information was at its limit. Unfortunately, my mother kept talking.

"While she was here, hiding among the pack, she met and fell in love with my father. They were forbidden, but they were promised peace as long as they did not bear children."

Mom closed her eyes then, taking a deep breath like this part of the story pained her deeply.

"When I was born, they pleaded with Alpha Edward Wolfe to allow them sanctuary as long as I did not have any elvafe magic of my own. I did not show any sign of the magic that the elvafe carry, nor did I have the mark of wings along my back."

My brows came together in confusion as I stared at her in stunned silence.

"When I mated with your father, it took me a long time to tell him about my lineage. When I did, he didn't speak to me for a week before coming back to me and deciding that he wasn't bothered enough by it to reject our bond. We agreed that we would not have children, but things rarely go according to plan. When I found out I was pregnant, I couldn't end it. I couldn't give up my baby, though we knew we were in severe trouble when we discovered that there were two of you."

I waited for her to continue. Instead, it seemed like she needed to prepare herself for the next part of the story as she stared into her cup like she wished she could dive into it and disappear. I felt the similar longing to vanish and forget this conversation. It was nice to get answers, but none of this story was what I had expected. While I knew where this was going, I refused to acknowledge it even to myself.

"I panicked and went to my parents to confess what we'd learned. My mother, Margaret, assured me that everything would be okay. We all knew what twins meant, but she gave me the backbone I needed to fight to keep you. Lucien was about to take his place as the Alpha and King, and he was informed by the pack doctor at the time about the presence of twins; this was while your father was apprenticing to take his place as pack doctor. As you know, twins are nearly unheard of and tend to be overwhelmingly powerful. They're a sign of change to come and make those who believe in superstitions fret about the potential for war. I knew when we went to the meeting at the High Table that things were not going to go in our favor. They demanded that the two of you be separated if either of you bore the mark of wings."

Brody gasped behind me, though I didn't acknowledge that he'd made any noise at all, completely lost in the web my mother was weaving for me.

"My pregnancy was long and hard, only compounded with the feeling of dread of losing one of you upon your birth. I could sense that there was magic within you both even before you were born, and I couldn't handle the ticking time bomb that was loudly counting down when one of you would be taken to the Stargazer Kingdom. I couldn't take back our word, no matter how much I knew it would kill me to lose either of you, especially to a ruthless king like Ramses Sayed. Meruem was already two, and mother had heard whispers of how he'd treated the boy, already training him to be a killing machine. I couldn't imagine a life like that for either of my babies."

I swallowed hard, momentarily forgetting that my tea even existed as I watched my mom across the table from me. My heart was hammering in my chest, and I felt my eyes prickling with unshed tears. My memory was going to catch up with this story, and I knew what was coming. That didn't make it any easier to hear it, and the gaping hole my brother left when he was taken was aching painfully in my chest.

"After you were born, the first thing your father and I looked at were your backs. We were so relieved when neither of you bore the mark of wings on your spines. I was hoping they wouldn't take either of you according to their agreement, but it appears that fear of change will cause people to go back on their promises. I was hoping that if either of you were to be taken, that it would be you because you were always so much stronger than Callum. You were a fighter, and he was sickly and needed you or he'd scream until he was with you again."

Her words felt like a slap in the face that burned down to my soul. While I vaguely understood her logic, that didn't make me feel any better about her wishing I'd have been the stolen twin. I stared at her; my mouth popped open in surprise as I furiously blinked away the tears that threatened to fall. I knew right then that a core memory was being created, this moment that I would never, ever forget or forgive as long as I lived. I wasn't sure that anyone could get over a betrayal like this.

"Yeah, well your being absent means that you lost both of your children," I retorted, the chair scraping loudly against the floor as I stood up. The sudden noise startled my mother, but I didn't think that was enough pain for her. I wanted to hurt her like her words deeply wounded me. "I cannot believe you just said that to me."

"Cadence, I would have died that day if you'd been taken too; the outcome would have been the same," she whimpered, standing up as well. I tried not to let the pleading tone in her voice anger me further. "I didn't want to lose either of you. You're my babies. My babies! I deserved to raise you both just like any other loving mother."

I laughed at her last sentence, throwing my head back and cackling as if she'd said the funniest thing I'd ever heard, but there was no humor in the sound, just pain.

"Clearly you only ever loved one of us," I bit out, leaning forward over the table.

My outrage was surprising, even to me, having never thought I'd say these things to my mother. My wrath was only compounded by the horrible trauma I'd already experienced.

"That was obvious from the day Callum was stolen from this family. You only loved one of your babies, and you died that day because the only person you ever loved other than yourself was stolen from you. If it had been me, you'd have mourned, but picked yourself up to take care of your precious *son*."

I spat the words at her, feeling my face grow hot with rage. My whole body was heated and glowing, power thrumming just under my skin as I glared across the wooden table at her, my dear mother. Her eyes widened as she stared at me, fear making her hands tremble and rattle the cup in its saucer as she gazed up at me. At last, I was getting a reaction I'd wanted, and it felt just as good as it did yesterday.

"I can tell that the elvafe blood is strong in you, and it will be in your brother as well. When you Ascend, we will discover if you even carry much volsifi blood in you. Everyone in the Alpha's close circle is waiting to see if you can be used against the elvafe in the brewing war spawned by your birth," she whispered, staring at me with horror written on her face. "I wouldn't be surprised if he already has the Council on grounds and waiting to ambush you."

Ezra gasped behind me, but I ignored him.

I scowled at her, standing up straight. "I will never be used as a weapon. I am not a pawn to be played against the other side, against my own twin brother."

I walked away from her as she audibly swallowed her fear. My skin was finally cooling down as the rage ebbed away, leaving me exhausted. My legs felt weak and shaky beneath me.

"I know, that's why I'm afraid for you." Her voice was barely over a whisper as I left the house, my friends following after me.

CHAPTER 39

CADENCE

After a tense breakfast where they tried to distract me, we congregated back in my bedroom. Alex's face was reflected in my mirror as she stood behind me to coerce my thick, dark hair into more cohesive curls than the tight waves it normally held. Her expression was drawn, the concern obvious on her pretty face. Frowning, I watched her work for a long moment, worrying my lip between my teeth.

"Do you think I should be afraid?" I asked, causing everyone in the room to stop what they were doing and look at me. I looked at the three of them in the reflection, noting the way Brody and Ezra glanced at each other.

Alex paled, pinning a curl to the back of my head with the kind of daintiness you use with a bomb. I didn't want to be a bomb, though I couldn't help feeling like I was a grenade with the pin pulled; time was ticking to the moment I'd stand on the pedestal and Ascend.

Ezra frowned as he sat on my bed, opening the book he was holding and staring at it as if he could distract himself with the text on the pages. "I'm sure everything will be fine," he murmured, gripping the book so hard his fingers were turning white, the binding crackling under the pressure.

Brody made no attempt to hide the fact that he was watching me closely, seemingly trying to calculate just how much of a risk I was. He leaned forward in my desk chair, putting his elbows on his knees and pressing his fisted hands against his chin. "We won't let anything happen to you. I would kill Lucien before he did anything to harm you."

"Killing him doesn't help. It will only put you in a terrible position." My words were short and sharp.

Ezra shrugged. "But if Lucien is dead, then I'm the Alpha and the King of the Volsifi." He raised his gaze to regard Brody with something like respect. "I would never hold you accountable. The bastard has it coming."

I pressed my lips together until my mouth was a slash in my face. "Neither of you are killing anyone. I'll be fine, no matter what happens to me." I returned to my own reflection, examining my pale face and the splash of blue in my left iris. Pursing my lips, I picked up my makeup and started applying nude shadow to my lids. Maybe if I made myself look like someone else, I could escape before I had to Ascend in front of everyone.

Nerves made it nearly impossible to apply my liner, the wing getting thicker and thicker until I had to wipe the whole thing off and start over. Alex sighed behind me, rubbing her hands against the legs of her jeans before spraying my hair with hairspray to hold it in place. My hair had grown over the past six months, brushing over my shoulder blades as I tried a second time to complete a simple eye look that I'd done almost every day for years.

When I'd botched the liner again, Alex gently took the applicator from me, and I automatically turned and closed my eyes. Within a moment, the black wing was perfect, and she took it upon herself to apply a bold red lip that emphasized the fullness of my mouth.

"Thank you," I whispered, leaning over to examine my face in the mirror. I'd never looked very confident before, but I couldn't help being surprised at the terrified expression on my face. The trauma of the past several months was apparent in the wide set of my eyes and wary look hidden in their depths.

Straightening, I turned and saw Brody holding up the golden dress I had worn the night before. I stared at it, trying very hard not to associate it with the horrific events that occurred while I'd been wearing it. Taking a deep breath, I shifted my mind back to the look on everyone's faces when they'd gifted me the dress, thought about how much money they had to have saved up to buy the enchanted fabric. It hung like a golden fountain, entirely untouched by dirt or grime and looking just as glorious as the moment it had appeared from inside the garment bag. They did tell me that the magic in the strands made it as strong as chainmail.

"I already looked it over," Brody said, his tone calm as he eased the frazzle of my fried nerves.

Nodding, I looked up at him, taking in his expression as he gave me a small grin.

"It breaks the rules, you know," I repeated, just as I had that day, looking between them as I pulled my shirt off to reveal just a slip so I could slide the dress on over my head.

Brody respectfully kept his eyes on my face, lifting the gown and dropping it over me and helping me get my arms through. I turned and he slid the zipper up my spine, his fingers grazing over my flesh and causing a shiver to raise goosebumps over my arms.

"Some rules are made to be broken," Ezra replied, coming up behind me and admiring my reflection in the mirror as I watched his face. His eyes glittered mischievously as he slid his hands down my arms until he laced his fingers with mine.

"You look breathtaking," he whispered in my ear, his breath skimming down my bare neck.

Alex appeared, pushing Ezra out of the way and linking her arm through mine. "Ready?"

No.

The word came unbidden, but it stalled on my tongue as I opened my mouth. I inhaled it, swallowing it down and burying it where it belonged. Summoning all the strength that Kyle had believed I had, I ruminated in his absence for just a moment before responding.

"Yes."

My Ascension dinner was the same as any other, tables laden heavily with food and punch bowls filled with various drinks. I stared at the food, the smell of it making my stomach roll in revulsion as I put a very small portion on my plate. Ultimately, the idea of shoving any of it down my gullet made me want to vomit. Maybe I'd feel better if I vomited.

Frowning, I decided not to do that. I'd managed to eat something for breakfast when Ezra drove me into Beta territory and the three of them treated me to food after the horrible conversation with my mother. The thought of her made my gaze impulsively lift to find her standing beside my father on the other side of the room. They were talking to Molly, though my dad's eyes kept flickering to me as if making sure I was still there and hadn't disappeared or been stolen from him.

I was fairly certain that he was just as traumatized from last night as the rest of us were.

A scoff interrupted my thoughts and I turned to find Jessica standing there. Jason was just behind her, his green eyes appraising me. I stared at both of them before snapping, "What do you want?"

Jessica rolled her amber eyes before raking her gaze over me as though I was the most disgusting thing she'd ever laid eyes on. "Man, I knew you were poor, but you could have at least worn a different dress. How tacky. Wearing the same hideously gaudy dress two nights in a row."

I rolled my eyes, turning my back on her as my friends approached.

"Oh, by the way," she called out, causing me to stop and glance at her over my shoulder. "I thought I'd let you know that I just got my acceptance to PSG. I'd been waitlisted, which I didn't really want anyone to know. However, I figured I'd tell you. I know Kyle got into PSG, but it turns out that after his death a spot opened up for me."

I turned to face her fully, horror gripping my limbs and making them shake.

"I really should thank him for that. It was really chill of him to die so I could go to there." She grinned, the expression something akin to pure evil. "How convenient for me, you know?" She laughed, the sound making my skin itch.

Something inside me snapped. The nightmare of everything that had happened to me had already been hanging off of my shoulders, building up into this mountainous mass of literal hell. Her red hair reminded me of the amaryllis that had plagued me for months, the threats, her taunts. A flash of Kyle's unseeing gaze made me swallow down the agony that clawed up my throat. Shoving all of the pain down, I tossed it into the bonfire of my fury and lashed out.

I let instinct take over and cocked my arm back before slamming my fist directly into her throat with all the rage that I didn't even realize was there. A loud squawking noise echoed off the stone walls as Jessica gripped her neck with both hands.

"Enough, Jessica. I've had *enough*. I cannot handle one more bad thing today, or I might just lose my entire mind with no hope of returning to sanity. Come near me again and I will do more than throw a single punch. I will end you."

I turned my back on her, my three friends were standing behind me. Alex was a step ahead of the two men, having clearly planned on coming to my defense before being stopped by the two hands on her shoulders. The room was silent as Jessica was pulled away from us by Jason, who glared at me over her head.

"I think I should feel bad, but I can't make myself feel anything at all," I mumbled, watching them leave for a moment before taking my plate and sitting down at our usual table.

Conversations slowly picked back up around the room, everyone letting the moment slide. Frowning, I wondered if I'd pay for that later, but couldn't bring myself to care about that either. Ezra and Brody sat on either side of me, Alex sitting across the table from us. I pushed food around my plate, wishing that ghosts existed. I understood humans gaining solace in feeling as though souls stayed behind to keep them company in their darkest moments. That wasn't the case, though it did ease my mind slightly that he was happily taking time off in the Fields of Hope.

After sufficient time had passed for everyone to finish eating, Lucien stood at the end of the room and gathered everyone's attention.

"Good evening," he said, all other noise immediately hushing around us. "Welcome to the Gardens of Ascension. As you all know, we are here to celebrate Cadence Nocetti's Ascension into an official member of the Scarlet Moon pack."

I stood as he said my name, smiling awkwardly as I twisted my hands in front of me, my fingernails digging into my palms as I tried to force myself to maintain reality. What I wouldn't give for a pair of earbuds right then. Instead, I played "The Blues" by Self Deception in my brain in a mild attempt to soothe my fraying nerves. Frowning, I glanced down for just a second as strong hands took each of mine and I noted Brody and Ezra staring at each other as they each held my hands in support. I had to admit that I didn't hate it as much as I probably should. I had no idea what would happen when one or neither of them were officially determined to be my mate.

Pushing that thought aside, I drew from each of their strengths as Lucien gave a speech about how he expected great things from me. I didn't miss the way his blue eyes sliced through me with a thinly veiled threat of compliance. It hit me like a sledgehammer right then that he was afraid of me.

My mouth popped open with that realization, and I hurried to shut my gaping trap before anyone noticed the startled expression on my face. A squeeze of both of my hands made me realize that neither of the men at my sides missed it. How astute they were.

"Now, if you'll join me in the Gardens, we will proceed with Cadence's Ascension," Lucien concluded as everyone stood.

With help from both men, I removed my gown so that I was standing in just the cream-colored slip I'd worn underneath. Ezra knelt behind me, untying the silk ribbons at my calves so I could remove my golden sandals. I relished the cool feeling of the stone flooring against the soles of my feet.

Ezra and Brody flanked me with Alex just behind them as we made our way into the Gardens behind Lucien. It felt like I had three bodyguards at my back, and I suddenly felt like I might actually need them to be exactly that once I Ascended.

Everyone remained hushed as I rounded the granite dais and walked up the steps to the top of it. The granite was even colder against my bare feet than the stone tiles had been. I moved to stand in the center of the red circle in the middle of the Ascension Pedestal, looking out at those around me. Lucien stood beside me, holding the white, sacred cape in his hands. He draped it over my shoulders, explaining the magic that allowed the ancient garment to shift with us during our Ascension while I fastened it at my throat. Turning, he abruptly left the Pedestal to join the crowd.

Like every volsifi before me, I took a moment to collect myself. Gazing at my three friends standing right at the edge of the dais, I tried to pull some of their strength into me while I attempted to steady the tremor shaking my fingers as I slowly lifted them up and out to the side. My head tilted back so I could look directly at the full moon as it hung above us, pregnant with the promise of a full life of magic and wonder. It was the most beautiful thing I'd ever seen in my life, like the Goddess herself smiled down upon me from the silver orb glowing above.

Taking a deep breath, I prepared myself for what was to come before saying the words we'd all learned.

"Mother Goddess Levende, most precious divine Luna, I stand before you as naked as the day you and Kuorir, most divine Alpha, gave me this life. I offer to you my body, my soul, my life on this night. Please grant me the gift of Ascension, so that I may shift into the glory of the wolf you have given me and so that I may join my pack as an equal."

I waited there for a long moment while nothing happened other than the weight of the cape pulling the clasp tighter and tighter against my neck. For a moment, I thought that maybe I wouldn't actually Ascend. My arms shook with the effort of holding them directly out from my body as whispers started in the crowd. It felt like my worst nightmare might be coming true. Then, just as I was about to give up hope that the Goddess would bless me at all, my back started to tingle in such a fierce way I wondered mildly if I was being electrocuted. It was like my flesh had been asleep my whole life and was suddenly waking up, the nerves sending off the pins and needles sensation to jar the comatose organ back to life.

"Dearest daughter, I've been waiting a long time for you to speak to me," an undeniably feminine voice spoke into my ear as though a woman was standing directly beside me. "You are being given a great gift, one meant to cause great change. There is a tremendous darkness coming and I created you to fight the impending shadows. I give you the gift of the sun," the voice whispered, dancing about my head as a breeze blew around me, sweeping the hood from my head and lifting my hair from my back and swirling it over my shoulders. "I look forward to speaking to you again in the near future," she murmured as the wind picked up.

The skirt of my slip and the cape swirled around me, rising away from my thighs as the wind picked up like a mini tornado that only I was caught in. Looking up at the moon, I could have sworn a woman's face smiled brightly at me from its surface and I reached toward her with my right hand as my feet were lifted from the cool granite dais. The wind spun me slowly, and I pointed the index finger of my raised hand toward the moon as it continued to promise me the glory of magic.

A burning sensation tore through my back, making me cry out in agony as the skin felt like my spine was being yanked from me, splitting my flesh open and leaving me deeply wounded. In my periphery, I could see a golden light glowing around me, bright enough to illuminate the night.

Hot, I was so incredibly hot as my spine continued to crackle until I was certain I had no remaining skin on my back. The cape was suddenly bursting into flames, the fabric melting and smoldering as something as bright and hot as the sun broke through. In just a few moments, the cape was gone, burned to ash that rained down on the dais in smoking embers.

The wind continued to spin me slowly, lifting me higher and higher until I was several feet above the glowing surface of the granite beneath me. That's when the shifting of my bones started. Excruciating pain seared my nerves as my skeleton shattered inside me so it could rearrange. I couldn't even make a noise as the cracking of my ribs forced the air from my lungs, making me feel like I was suffocating. I was familiar with this feeling, of my body collapsing in on itself with the loss of Kyle, but it was so much worse when it was physically happening.

EZRA

I watched anxiously with the rest of the crowd as Cadence stood there with her arms outstretched for what seemed like an agonizing amount of time. Glancing between Brody and Alex, we all had the same concerned look on our faces as the seconds stretched out into minutes. No one had ever needed to wait that long in my memory, and we'd seen quite a few Ascensions through the years.

Just when I was wondering if Cadence would actually Ascend at all, a wind blew around her, slow at first until it became a gale. It whipped the hood of the cape from her head, rustling her hair as we stood in the still, balmy evening air. The three of us stood rigid right at the edge of the dais as the wind lifted her skirt and the cape, causing them to blossom around her like an inverted halo before it wrapped the fabric around her legs as she slowly lifted from the surface of the dais. Cadence raised her right hand, one finger gracefully pointing at the moon as one knee bent into a gorgeous dance-like pose that outlined her voluptuous frame. As she spun in a slow circle, her back flashed to the crowd and I noticed with horror that the cape was smoking.

We all watched as a hush came over the gathered crowd, no one able to take their eyes off of her as she had the most unusual Ascension any of us had ever seen. The granite in front of us began to glow as a scream wrenched from her throat, startling me to my core. She sounded like she was in agony, and as her back turned to us again, I could see why. The cape was on fire now, though she was not burning with it. As the cape burned to ash, we could see two golden wings erupt from her fiery flesh. Flames licked along the edges as they unraveled from her, their glow remaining as they unfurled completely to display themselves to us. The light from them lit up the dark surroundings, easily outshining the full moon even as it hung low above us.

The design on the wings was something that took my breath away, the top wings coming to a point at their very apex and scalloping down to a full bottom. The bottom section of her wings split in half, coming to sharp points off to the sides like blades of pure sun fire. Inside the design of the wings themselves were swirls turning into blazing suns that stood out among the darker glimmering of the base of her wings.

Just when I thought the end had arrived and that we simply had an elvafe, we heard the sharp snapping of bones as she writhed in the air. Still hovering far above the dais, I watched with wide eyes as she clearly began the process of shifting into a wolf.

Fur as black as her hair sprouted from her skin, gasps erupting from those around me as even her fur began to glow. I could hear her gasping heavily as the shifting of her bones repeatedly knocked the wind from her lungs.

With a flash of light that blinded me, I heard her land deftly on her paws. When the light faded, I was gazing upon one of the most glorious beasts I had ever seen.

Her fur was jet black, wings still present on her back just behind her shoulder blades. However, half of her face, her paws, and the tip of her tail were glittering and sparkling with golden magic like she'd dipped parts of her body in pixie dust. As her eyes met mine, I saw the blue splash in her left iris glowing purple before she lifted her head to howl at the moon. However, unlike I'd ever seen, no one shifted to howl with her.

A brief moment of silence stretched on before chaos erupted all around us.

Epilogue

SHANE

My brain was completely occupied by Cadence Nocetti. The feel of her body against mine, her lips caressing my flesh. Kissing her had outweighed all of the fantasies I'd ever had, even as I stood over her sleeping body nearly every night for months. I was most angry that they'd confiscated my phone so I could no longer admire her visage digitally. Unfortunately, I would have to wait until I could escape the confines of this dungeon.

Looking around the dim cell, I tried to find any means to escape, though it appeared that The Guard of this pack were very thorough in their cleaning. I scowled, sitting down on the floor and staring at my knees as though they may turn into her if I gazed upon them long enough.

Thinking back on it, I considered that maybe I should have killed Brody and Ezra when I'd had the chance. It would have been so easy using Lucien's gift to make them kill each other and then wash my hands of the entire thing.

Instead, I'd gotten greedy. I couldn't wait a moment longer to summon the drug known as Cadence Nocetti.

If I closed my eyes and thought about it, I could draw her image into my mind. The sleek black of her hair as it fell in a thick, waving sheet against her back. Her eyes were what really drew me in. I first saw her when she entered her ninth year of school. I'd been walking around a corner and bumped into her, and she'd looked up at me with those large doe eyes. She was so innocent, something fragile I could break with my bare hands, but instead I wanted to treasure her forever. I wanted to keep her safe from insignificant and selfish teenagers. They didn't deserve her.

I curled my upper lip, snarling as I thought about the remaining two boys who thought they could stake some kind of claim on her. How could they think of such a thing when she clearly belonged to *me*?

Groping around the cell again, I was trying to find any tool to break so I could see her Ascend. I had tried to take her away so she could Ascend with me, but of course that didn't work out. I could sense the moon rising, I needed to see–

An explosion of power rocked my body like a supernova. If the sun had a solar flare, I was certain that I'd just been touched by it. My body quivered with the feeling of magic radiating over me, bringing me to my knees and leaning me forward until I was bowing in the direction of the Gardens of Ascension. The force of her Ascension hit me with such ferocity that I wept onto the stones beneath me.

After a few minutes, I recovered enough to sit up, wiping the tears from my cheeks with dirty hands as I started laughing. She had Ascended and it was just as glorious as I had expected. My blood sang in my veins as though I'd just taken the biggest hit an addict possibly could. My mouth watered with the delicious taste of her tremendous power even as I continued to laugh.

Cadence Marie Nocetti was every bit the goddess I knew she'd be.

ACKNOWLEDGEMENTS

Thank you to my husband for always pushing me to do better. Never let perfect stand in the way of better.

Thank you to my friends and family who read this many more times than I deserved.

Thank you to Mandi, Lexy, Beth, and my husband, Rob, for allowing me to discuss this with them nauseum with little to no complaining.

Thank you to Lexy Ray for line editing for me and making this book way smoother than it would have been without you.

Thank you to Sage Santiago for proofreading and polishing up my baby until it was the best that it could be.

I appreciate all of you and the work you did to make this project the masterpiece that it is.

ABOUT THE AUTHOR

Lacey Hall is your run-of-the-mill millennial with a deep seated love of fiction. She lives with her husband and two children in the strange world of Pennsylvania. Writing this series is her second full-time job, but she's hoping that eventually it will turn into her only job.

Lacey wrote her first short story when she was seven on a tiny notepad with a green Sharpie. When she reached twelve, she started writing online with other writers, honing her talent and expanding her creativity and the love of writing with others. In high school, she decided that she wanted to be a writer, but it was so unlikely that it was set on the backburner for over a decade. Now, with the support of her friends and family, she's striving to make that childhood dream a reality.

Lacey was inspired to write this book when she strived to make male love interests that weren't toxic. Once she started writing the story, it turned into so much more than a standalone novel with an asexual female protagonist with a golden retriever love interest. It turned into a whole new world and a several book series.

You can find links to all of her social media at:

https://laceyhallwrites.com

www.ingramcontent.com/pod-product-compliance
Lightning Source LLC
Chambersburg PA
CBHW051940020726
47501CB00001B/202